THE REVOLT

☆ ☆ ☆ ☆ ☆ ☆ ☆

THE REVOLT

★ ★ ★ ★ ★ ★ ★

BY
S. WISE BAUER

WORD PUBLISHING
Dallas•London•Vancouver•Melbourne

Library of Congress Cataloging-in-Publication Data:
Bauer, S. Wise.
    The revolt / by S. Wise Bauer.
        p. cm.
    ISBN 0-8499-3935-6
        I. Title.
PS3552.A83638R48   1996
813'.54—dc20   96-36042
                                                                                CIP

Printed in the United States of America

6 7 8 9 QKP 9 8 7 6 5 4 3 2 1

For my grandfather, James L. Wise, Sr.,
the anchor of four generations.

ACKNOWLEDGMENTS

☆ ☆ ☆ ☆ ☆ ☆ ☆

My thanks to:

Those members of the Virginia National Guard who were willing to stand around and speculate (on tape) about what they would do in case of a secession. None of them wanted to be mentioned by name; but thanks, guys, you know who you are.

Mel Diehr, for technical advice; Bob Staples, who kept my computer running; Brian Patteson, for information on the militia movement and exposure to the alternative media; Brooke Barrows, who kept me straight on details of colonial history.

Bill Edgar of Westminster Theological Seminary, for initial information and direction on researching the varieties of theonomy.

The reference staff of the Williamsburg Public Library, who put up with my removing huge stacks of books from the reference shelves and leaving them all over the tables.

My father, James L. Wise, M.D., for proofreading, initial editing, and information on murder, sudden death, and various kinds of gunshot wounds.

I owe great gratitude to Nelson Keener at Word, who has been enthusiastic about this book from the beginning. Thanks for the encouragement, the newspaper articles, and the bread-and-butter work.

Jessie Wise kept me sane, fixed dinner when I forgot, and played countless games of Little Lamb with the boys. Thanks, Mom.

Finally, I've called on my husband, Peter, for duties ranging from editing, fact-checking and error-hunting, to diaper-changing and grocery shopping. I love you more than I can say; thanks for making my work as important as your own.

Servant of God has chance of greater sin
And sorrow, than the man who serves a king.
For those who serve the greater cause
may make the cause serve them,
Still doing right: and striving with political men
May make that cause political, not by what they do
But by what they are.

—T. S. Eliot
Murder in the Cathedral, I

PART I

☆

SECESSION

CHAPTER 1

Monday, March 18, 12:30 A.M.

ALEXANDER WADE, secretary of defense for the United States of America, was asleep when Virginia threatened to leave the Union for the second time.

On the third ring of the telephone, Wade hauled himself out of the deep swimming darkness and swung his legs over the edge of the bed, wearily, and heaved himself up. He was an oblivious sleeper, and the phone that connected him to the White House was in the next room, with a speaker run through the wall near the head of the bed. This was his method of making sure he was awake when he answered.

He shuffled through the door, around the corner, and picked up the receiver.

"Yes?" He peered blearily at the watch he wore even while sleeping. Not yet one A.M.; the president probably hadn't gone to bed at all.

A well-known voice said, "Mr. Secretary, the president would like to see you at once."

"Oh . . ." Wade restrained the impulse to swear. George Lewis, the chief of staff, was puritanical about such things. He said instead, "What for?"

"The agent in your kitchen has instructions."

"Are we being bombed?"

"That might be simpler," George's voice remarked.

"Oh? What's going on?"

"I'll see you here, Mr. Secretary."

"Thanks very much, George," Wade said sourly.

But George Lewis had hung up. Wade replaced the receiver and drove his knuckles into his eyes wearily. The president's chief of staff was ten years younger than Alexander Wade. Lewis was an efficient administrator and a keen political mind, but he had never been personally close to either the president or his secretary of defense, who had been friends and allies since the beginning of their political careers thirty years ago. But Lewis did have the apparent virtue of eternal wakefulness.

WADE HAULED UP THE SWEATS he slept in and headed for the staircase. The Beltway townhouse had three bedrooms upstairs, a sitting room and dining room and kitchen downstairs. He was alone tonight; his daughter, Deborah, was on spring break from William and Mary, and she hated Washington, so his wife had gone to the Maryland farmhouse to be with her. He had planned to take two days off in the middle of the week and drive out to Maryland on Tuesday.

"Bet I won't now," he mumbled. The light was on in the kitchen and the close-fitting shades were drawn. The Secret Service agent, a slim woman in her thirties, was wearing a gray wig and a baggy sweater and skirt. She was lacing up a pair of clunky running shoes. Alexander Wade rubbed the back of his neck, peevishly.

"Well now," he said, "I'd guess we're walking."

"Yes, Mr. Secretary. Just to the corner of Chalfonte and Elmore. Your car will pick you up there. If you'd wear a hat, sir, and a long coat and exercise shoes?"

"Have we got a dog?"

The agent said solemnly, "Yes, Mr. Secretary."

"And they say the United States government is inefficient. Okay; give me five minutes." The agent had given him the standard media-avoidance procedure, so whatever crisis awaited him at the White House was important enough to bring reporters out to his home.

In the bedroom, he peered cautiously around the corner of the shade.

Cameron Mills Road was silent. Two dark cars were parked across the street. He saw a sudden transient gleam behind the black glass of a windshield. Someone was lighting a cigarette. At the end of the road, another car drew quietly up against the curb and cut off its lights. The vultures were circling.

He dressed quickly, put on running shoes and a trench coat, and jammed his old-man's hat down over his prematurely silver hair. Downstairs, the agent was waiting by the cellar door. Wade followed her silently down into the basement, through another door, into a passage that took them through the secured basements of the two adjoining houses. At the end of the second basement, a white wood door led into a brick-walled staircase that smelled of earth and weeds. They emerged, heads first, up into an expansive suburban backyard surrounded by a split-rail fence. A toy poodle was tied to the nearest fencepost.

"I ought to rate at least a Great Dane," Alexander Wade mumbled.

"People look at Great Danes," the agent said, practically. She looped the poodle's leash around her right hand. She was left-handed, and wore her nine millimeter within easy reach of her left arm over the baggy sweater, underneath the old-lady plastic raincoat.

They were on Chalfonte now, a block down from his pickup point, two elderly people with insomnia walking a dog while the media waited outside the house of the secretary of defense.

THE PRESIDENT WAS IN THE FAMILY QUARTERS, in the TV room, standing in front of the dark window with his hands behind his back. He looked over his shoulder.

"Alex," he said. "Thanks, George. You can go."

George Lewis said stiffly, "Yes, sir," and stepped back. Alexander Wade drew the door closed behind him, shutting out Lewis's stone-solemn face. For decades, the chief of staff had been the second most powerful man in the country. George Lewis had attained the coveted position to find that the president's trusted secretary of defense occupied the real seat of influence.

"Did anyone see you?" the president asked, still with his back turned.

"No. We took the Treasury Annex tunnel. It was cold and wet. Got any coffee?"

"On the sideboard," the president said.

Wade had walked briskly, but he was a fit man and the exercise had barely boosted his heart rate. His head ached with sleep and his skin was clammy with cold and night fog. The president turned around. He was still fully dressed, an elegant man in his fifties with aristocratic bones and a face like an ascetic nobleman. He had broken into a long line of common-man chief executives and taken the electorate by storm, running as an independent—the first president since George Washington to swear allegiance to no political party.

Wade turned to pour himself a cup of coffee. "Lynda awake?"

The president shook his head. The first lady, a shrewd woman, had profited by her predecessor's example; she spent her time working against domestic violence, never dipped a finger into public policy, and was beloved by all. Wade shrugged off his trench coat and sat down in one of the armchairs that faced the TV, cup in hand. CNN was on, the sound turned down. He had half-expected to find the president surrounded by aides and press liaisons and policy experts. The fact that he was alone meant the crisis was petty, or else so inflammatory that the chief executive had sealed it off from his staff, giving himself time to think.

"Well?" he said at last. "Why the cloak-and-dagger stuff?"

"Were you asleep?"

"Of course I was. I'm not George."

"Where's Perri?"

"In the country. Deborah came home Sunday afternoon." Wade shifted and propped his feet up on the small table that sat in front of him, avoiding a plain manila folder that lay on its glossy surface.

"Good."

"Good what?"

"Good that Debbie's out of Virginia."

"Why?"

"I've lost Virginia."

"What?"

"Just a guess at tomorrow morning's *Post* headline." The president sat down across from Wade, abruptly. He said, "The governor of Virginia called a news conference at midnight and threatened to secede from the United States unless I meet ten demands in forty-eight hours. Three of those have to do with the Supreme Court. I can't meet any of them within forty-eight hours, no matter what I do. So I may as well take the moral high ground and tell him no. We have until midnight on Tuesday."

"*Secede?*"

"That's what I said."

"Why would he want to do *that?*"

The president rolled an eye at him. "Multiple reasons," he said tartly. "This is the governor of Virginia. Charles Merriman, remember? He hates everybody north of the Potomac."

"Charles Merriman," Wade said slowly. He folded his hands around the coffee cup, feeling the heat on his skin. So this was no petty crisis. The president was riding high after a series of successful foreign policy decisions. He had never cast himself as a domestic politician, which had actually boosted his reputation with an America still dumbfounded by the inept foreign policy of the previous administration. But the loss of a state, even for a brief period of time, would give pause even to the most cosmopolitan of voters.

"Is it the tobacco legislation?" he asked. The president had gained huge popular support for his push to fund healthcare and cancer research through a dollar-per-pack tax on cigarettes. That single issue had defined him as a man who had the country's good in mind, a man free from the corrupting influence of the huge tobacco corporations. In forty-seven states, anyway; the tobacco-growing states—North Carolina, Kentucky, and Virginia—had bombarded Washington with protests.

"Nothing's been said about tobacco," the president said. "Or the shipyard either; but neither Newport News nor Richmond is likely to be pleased with me, just now."

"Have you consulted with the attorney general?"

"I haven't consulted with anyone but you. I just saw the news conference myself. I've got a hundred people who want to see me."

"This is Ramsey's pigeon, not mine." The attorney general, Ramsey Grant, was a brilliant man, and certainly the threatened secession posed immediate legal questions.

"This is *our* pigeon," the president said. "Ramsey's a good man, but I need you for this. This could bring me down, Alex. I know it's unorthodox to involve you. Domestic conflicts don't exactly fall under the aegis of the Pentagon. But I don't care. I need you to help steer me through this."

Wade knew the president well enough to hear the threat behind this request: *If I go down, you will too.* Alexander Wade grimaced and pinched at his nose, thoughtfully.

"Well," he said, "we need to ask Ramsey what the legal status of such an act is."

"Ramsey's in California."

"Then he can fly back. Can Charles Merriman *do* this?"

"Theoretically," the president said, "he can do anything he wants if he has enough people on his side. This isn't a constitutional revolt, Alex. It's a plain old revolution. If you're determined to cut loose and start over, none of the rules of the parent country apply."

"What did he say?"

"I've got the videotape of his press conference," the president said. He came forward, dropped his weight into the overstuffed chair beside Wade, and touched a button on the remote control that lay on its arm. The television came to life. Charles Merriman stood in Capitol Park, narrowing his photogenic eyes against the glare of TV cameras filming at midnight. Ten feet behind him, the light caught the tall white columns of the Virginia Capitol, rising up out of the dark. He was picturesquely disheveled and his collar was open.

"I like that," Alexander Wade remarked. "The Thomas-Jefferson-I've-been-up-all-night-writing-the-Declaration-of-Independence look."

"Shut up and listen," the president said irritably.

"Thank you for coming," Charles Merriman said. His voice had a very faint trace of that Southern accent which evokes Windsor Castle rather than Raleigh. "All of you should now have a copy of Virginia's ten demands to the United States—"

"Are they demands or threats, Governor?" a reporter shouted from the crowd.

Merriman narrowed his eyes, peering into the lights. The glare made hollows under his handsome cheekbones and silvered his dark hair.

"These are not threats," he said mildly. "These are responsibilities which Washington must fulfill on behalf of Virginia's citizens. My hope, naturally, is that Washington will do what I've asked. Here's the threat: If I get no response, I am fully prepared to declare Virginia independent from the United States on Wednesday morning." Amid a chorus of yells, he raised his right hand. "Now I know you have plenty of questions about that, but let me reassure you that it is both possible and probable. Let me also assure you that if this lamentable event does become necessary, it will be achieved without bloodshed. The law known as *posse comitatis*, as you may be aware, bars the president from deploying the armed forces of the United States on domestic soil against United States citizens."

Wade turned his eyes away from the screen and protested, "How can it be both *possible* and *probable*? If it were, Montana would've been gone long ago."

The president threw Wade an annoyed glance.

"This isn't a statement of strategy," he said. "This is shameless pandering to Virginia's voters. Sheer campaigning."

On the screen, another reporter was calling out, "Do you really think the citizens of Virginia will support you in this?"

"I think the citizens of Virginia are weary to death of high taxes, over-legislation, and rising crime," Charles Merriman answered.

"But the radical right-wing religious conservatism behind this decision is bound to disturb many Virginians," the reporter objected.

The governor leaned forward into the cameras. His dark blue eyes glinted in the light. The magnetism of his personality was powerfully evident.

"I'm going to say something shocking," he said. "I—and dozens of elected officials all throughout Virginia—have come to the conclusion that the Constitution of the United States is fatally flawed. It was written in a good-faith attempt to govern men. But it is based on ideas of the Enlightenment. It assumes that humanity is, at the core, logical, reasonable, and good. If that were true, the Constitution would work. It gives principles, you see, and assumes that the people governed will be able to take the principles and apply them properly in individual situations. That sounds abstract, I know. Let me give you one specific example."

Merriman paused. The camera moved away from him toward the rapt crowd of reporters.

"Look at that," the president snapped. "He's got them eating out of his hand already. That man's dangerous. Every time I hear Charles Merriman speak, I wonder what would happen if he told the whole Virginia legislature to drink poisoned Kool-Aid."

Wade said nothing. He had a sudden premonition of what was coming. He kept his eyes on Charles Merriman, standing straight and appealing against the shining white stone.

"Two years ago," Virginia's governor began, "a national guardsman named Matthew Franklin was murdered in Oregon Hill. Some of you may remember the case."

"Very likely," Wade mumbled. Matthew Franklin's murder and the ill-fated investigation that followed had drawn a firestorm of criticism down on the Richmond police. Merriman, newly elected, had protected the detectives involved, insisting that they had done nothing wrong. He had been excoriated in the national press as a foe of due process, even becoming the subject of a searing "20/20" exposé. Virginians had rallied behind their governor, and eventually the furor had died down. But Merriman nursed a lasting grudge over the whole incident.

Charles Merriman went on, "Sergeant Franklin was a career guardsman who had spent fifteen years serving the Commonwealth. He was in Richmond's Oregon Hill district, early in the morning, on some errand of his own. His wife was with him. The two of them were walking along the sidewalk when Sergeant Franklin was shot and killed. Eyewitnesses placed a man named Jerry Tindell on the spot. Three days later, a policeman saw Tindell with Franklin's wallet. The policeman reported back to the detective in charge of the case, and they obtained a search warrant for Jerry Tindell's person and house."

"And then they screwed up," the president said, his voice bored. This was an old story.

"The Richmond police searched Tindell's belongings," Charles Merriman continued, "and found Matthew Franklin's keys and his watch, and the gun used in the murder itself. But these items were found not in Jerry Tindell's house, but in his girlfriend's suitcase, which was sitting out on the front sidewalk when one of the policemen opened it. That suitcase wasn't covered by the warrant. And so Jerry Tindell was never even tried. Understand what I'm saying. The police know who the killer is. They even found the murder weapon, and the dead man's wallet, taken from his body while he lay in agony on the street. But they can't arrest the killer because the evidence was found in the wrong place." Merriman shook his head, his voice was full of disbelief. "The Constitution says that the people of the United States shall be secure against unreasonable searches and seizures, and no warrants shall be issued but upon probable cause, describing the place to be searched and the persons or things to be seized. That's the Fourth Amendment. Now, if we were a truly good and reasonable race, that clause would work exactly as it was intended to work. It would protect the innocent without giving shelter to the guilty. But two hundred years of legal rulings concerning the Fourth Amendment have produced the opposite effect. The guilty are protected, and the innocent suffer. Why is that?"

Merriman threw his arm out toward the crowd of attentive reporters.

"Because we're *not* good and reasonable," Merriman said, "and the Constitution has the reason of man as its basis for justice. It assumes that we can take the principle of the Fourth Amendment—or any other stipulation of the Constitution—and use it in a reasonable way. But human reason isn't reliable. It's changeable and flawed. When we try to base justice on the character of man, we end up with a changeable and flawed system. That's what we have now. That's why I am proposing that Virginia return to an older law code—a code of justice based not on the character of unreasonable man, but on the unchanging character of God."

"And what difference would that make in the particular case you've described?" a voice asked.

"This man would be tried," Charles Merriman said, "by a jury of his peers, based on all the evidence against him. Period. And if found guilty, he would be punished."

"How?"

"To quote God Himself," Merriman said, "if anyone sheds the blood of man, his blood will be shed in return. Which sounds archaic, but is merely a Hebrew phrase for capital punishment, which has been legal in Virginia since 1975."

An aide stepped up beside Merriman, whispering in his ear. The governor glanced at his watch.

"I'll leave you with this thought," he said. "At present, Virginia is ruled by a government which—even though it is incapable of punishing the guilty and rewarding the innocent—still demands up to twenty-five percent of the average worker's income. Whereas God Himself, in all His justice and power, only asked for ten percent. Washington thinks it is divine. Here in Virginia, we can't swallow that pretension any more."

The same reporter who had begun the questioning shouted out, "And you expect Virginians to follow you in this, Governor?"

"We'll see," Merriman said. The elegant Southern voice had no hint of fear in it. "We'll see."

The screen went dark. The president put down the remote control. He lifted the folder from the coffee table and handed it to his friend.

"These are the demands," he said. "They came by private messenger, half-an-hour ago."

Wade opened the folder. Inside lay a thick piece of plain cream paper, with a single arrogant signature scrawled at the bottom: *Charles Aaron Merriman.*

"No stationery," Wade said. "No title. No sign of his office as governor." He ran his eye down the paper; it contained a long paragraph at the top, followed by a list.

> Unless the president of the United States responds to these demands within forty-eight hours, I will declare the Commonwealth of Virginia to be separate and independent from the United States of America, and I will use all resources of the Commonwealth to defend Virginia's citizens from any further oppression. In so doing I am upholding Virginia's heart and soul as expressed in our state motto. *Sic semper tyrannis: Thus always to tyrants.*

> • A constitutional amendment to balance the federal budget.

- Restoration to the original owners of all land claimed for conservation purposes in the last twenty years.

- Participation in the Social Security program of the United States of America to be entirely voluntary on the parts of the citizens of the Commonwealth of Virginia.

- Reversal of mandatory state funding for all Medicaid abortions.

- Reversal of legalized organ harvesting from anencephalic babies.

- Revocation of assisted suicide rights for terminal patients.

"At least he doesn't want you to disband the United Nations concentration camps in Montana," Wade said, in carefully horrified tones.

"Read," the president ordered, "and sit on your peculiar sense of humor until the forty-eight hours are up."

- Full repayment of the United States of America's national debt within forty-nine years (Lev. 25:8-17).

"What's Lev?" Wade demanded.

"Leviticus," the president explained. "In the Old Testament. George looked it up for me. Every fifty years, all debts are supposed to be cleared."

"A pleasant idea," Wade said, "but impractical." He went back to reading.

- Revocation of equal-rights protection in housing and employment for self-admitted homosexuals.

- Lifting of the restrictions on teaching religion and religious principles during public education.

- Reduction of federal income tax to a 9 percent flat rate.

"Nine percent," he said out loud. "And this came by private messenger?"

"Yes."

"He's being careful. If he'd used the U.S. Postal Service, we might have been able to dredge up a federal charge of some kind."

The president snapped, "I want Charles Merriman on a plate! He's always been a rogue and a misfit."

"This goes far beyond discontent with the Supreme Court. Or the tobacco issue either. He wouldn't do this if he didn't have other Virginia
officials ready to support him."

"Yes. Yes, I know."

Alexander Wade brooded over the paper. Presently he observed, "He
said *respond* to his demands, not meet them. You can fulfill his conditions if
you simply address these concerns in a public speech."

"And say what? These are good suggestions, Governor Merriman, but
the Supreme Court has a great deal more power than I do, and the U.S.
tax rate will just have to remain at three times what you suggest?"

Wade conceded the problem. "Can we charge him with treason?"

"Not unless he picks up arms. Article Three, Section Three: 'Treason
against the United States shall consist only in levying war against them or
in adhering to their enemies, giving them aid and comfort.' He's doing
neither. He's just making demands."

"Ten demands," Wade said slowly, "and a reference to the Old Testament. What else have you got on Merriman?"

"Right now? Only what George has been able to dig up in a hurry. A
file on Merriman's inauguration, texts of his State of the Commonwealth
speeches."

"Let me see."

"Next to the coffee," the president said, not moving from his chair.

Wade pushed himself up and walked to the sideboard, where a thick
folder lay beside the coffeepot.

"Ten demands," he said under his breath, "and a nine-percent tax
and a reference to the Old Testament. Is this what I think it is?"

"You'll find out in a minute," the president remarked. But Alexander
Wade had already riffled through the sheets of newsprint and copy paper.
He yanked a press cutting from the folder and flattened it onto the sideboard.

"Kenneth Balder," he said, looking down at the grainy newspaper
photograph. "I might have known it. Kenneth Balder's behind all this."

The press cutting was an article from the *Richmond Times-Dispatch* on
Merriman's inauguration, with a photograph of Merriman looking directly into the camera. Behind his shoulder, a tall blond man was just

visible, his head turned away from the lens. The caption read: *Kenneth Balder, ex-convict and founder of the California Institute for Theonomic Law, at the inauguration of Virginia's new governor.*

The president said mildly, "Now you know why I want you involved, Alex."

"They're going to try it," Wade said, hardly believing his own words. "They're going to put all of Kenneth Balder's crackpot ideas into practice. That's why Merriman sent ten demands. These are supposed to be the Ten Commandments of a new country. Merriman and Balder are going to try to make God's laws into Virginia's law." He could hear his voice shake. Behind him, the president gave an incredulous chuckle.

"You still loathe him as much as ever, don't you?" he said.

"He humiliated me in my first public case. It was months before the public prosecutor let me speak in a courtroom again."

"That was twenty-five years ago. What an amazing capacity for hatred you must have, Alex."

Wade folded the newspaper clipping over, slowly. Finally, he turned around.

"Well," he said, "if I do, you're going to benefit from it, aren't you? You want me in on this because I'd like nothing better than to bring Kenneth Balder down."

"And Merriman with him," the president said, nodding. "It's almost two-thirty A.M. We have forty-four hours left before Merriman's deadline. I'm addressing the nation at nine this morning. We'll start by giving the American people all the facts. Bring me all the details of Kenneth Balder's conviction, and we'll work it into whatever the speechwriters are cooking up for me."

"Yes, Mr. President."

"If we clear this up before Monday, Debbie can go back to William and Mary."

"She'll be much relieved," Alexander Wade said dryly. "She's got a date for the Beaux Arts Ball. I'll have to talk to the attorney general right away."

"Call him, then," the president said, standing up to see him out the door. "I've already spoken to him, so he'll be awake. Alex . . ." he was choosing his words carefully, "don't place too much trust in Ramsey's . . . recommendations."

"Ramsey's a good man, Mr. President."

"He's a Democrat," the president said, economically. "If I'd been able to fill my cabinet with independents instead of all these party stalwarts, I'd be happier now." He opened the door and George Lewis, hovering in the hallway, darted in.

THE SECRET SERVICE AGENT, minus the wig and raincoat, was waiting for him at the foot of the staircase.

"My office," Wade said.

"Your car's waiting, Mr. Secretary."

"The Annex tunnel again?"

"Yes, sir," the agent said, apologetically. The tunnel was still cold and damp, and he emerged from the door at the back of the Treasury Annex into dark night. For some reason, he had expected dawn. He had only been with the president for fifty minutes.

The car waiting for him was the plain dark limo again, not the secretary of defense's car with the red light on the top. He slouched in the backseat, watching the streetlights blur past him. The limo swung onto the bridge that would carry him into the Commonwealth of Virginia. The familiar blue sign was just ahead, the red cardinal and white dogwood painted on the state's outline.

WELCOME TO VIRGINIA

Just beyond it another sign warned, BUCKLE UP, VIRGINIA. IT'S A LAW WE CAN LIVE WITH. A third notice declared: RADAR DETECTORS ILLEGAL. He passed in and out of Virginia half a dozen times a day. The state's border had never imprinted itself on his thoughts before.

The third floor of the Pentagon was still quiet. A contrast, Wade noted, to the last crisis, when the discovery of a nuclear warhead in a small, unstable Eastern country had flooded the hallways with anxious officials. He turned on the lights in his own office and sat down behind the massive oak desk, staring for a long moment at the papers in front of him. Finally, he pushed them aside and picked up the telephone.

"This is Wade," he said to the switchboard. "Get me Ramsey Grant. And when you've done that, get Allen in here."

"Yes, Mr. Secretary."

The ringer burred and was instantly replaced by a crisp and wide-awake voice that said, strongly, "And high time too."

"Ramsey? It's Wade."

"Alex? Why are you calling?"

"Better sell that Blue Ridge ski lodge."

"Where's HM?" The president's nickname, a tribute to his minor-royalty profile, irritated the chief executive and was never used to his face.

"He's with George and the press people, preparing a speech for nine this morning. Ramsey, I need you here. We've got work to do."

"I'm already on the legal aspect. I'll be east as soon as the red-eye flight can bring me."

"I'm not talking about the legal aspect."

There was a faint pause. Ramsey Grant's voice asked, thoughtfully, "What's your part in this?"

"Looking out for the president's interests," Wade said, stating the obvious.

He could hear a slight annoyed intake of breath. The attorney general said, "Are you calling out the National Guard, Alex?"

"Not yet."

"You'll have trouble justifying it. Not unless you've got civil disturbances, or proof that Merriman's running a drug ring from the mansion. I'm afraid nicotine doesn't count."

"Proof's not my job."

"Don't ask too much of me, Alex."

Wade would have liked to say, *The FBI's had an agent in Merriman's mansion for a year, and you knew about it from the beginning.* But he wasn't supposed to know that, and the sentence would reveal that someone high in the Federal Bureau of Investigations had talked too much. Instead he said, "I'd like to see you as soon as you get in."

"Well," Grant said dryly, "it'll be hard to avoid you, won't it? Good morning, Alex."

He hung up. Alexander Wade replaced his own receiver and leaned back in his chair. Soon Allen Preszkoleski, the assistant secretary who served as his right hand, would arrive with a phalanx of aides. They could dig out all the details of Kenneth Balder's unsavory past, and tell America who was helping Charles Merriman reform Virginia's laws. But he had a creeping feeling that this revolt would not be so easily smothered.

This is only the beginning, he thought.

Wade had inadvertently carried the picture of Merriman and Balder out of the president's sitting room. He unclenched his left hand and smoothed the newsprint out in front of him and stared at Kenneth Balder, impressive and broad-shouldered in his impeccable suit. Balder had put on weight in the years since his trial. He had been thin then, but tall enough to look down his nose at the young assistant prosecutor; fair-haired and immensely attractive, a handsome boy with a heart of ice.

"Not this time," he said to Kenneth Balder's black-and-white face. "Once was enough. You won't humiliate me twice." It was a line that called for applause, but the only response was a muted stirring in the hallway.

CHAPTER 2

Monday, March 18, 6:00 A.M.

MARGARET FRANKLIN WAS DREAMING of her husband's murder. The street lay empty and eerily lit with the light that comes before the sun. In the dream, she always saw Matthew from the back, walking down the black street with the vacant doorways gaping on either side. His shoulders were broad under the dark, heavy coat. A cup of coffee steamed up from his right hand. Far down the narrow street, the green-and-red glow of the convenience store flickered drearily in the slick puddles. Suddenly his head lifted and turned, as though he'd heard a voice. But the dream was always silent and the collapse itself was noiseless, his hand flinging the coffee away from him and the drops catching the distant store lights as he crumpled. She turned her head too slowly, and caught only the flicker of movement in a dark doorway as an unknown figure slipped away. She could feel her feet on the wet blacktop. *This time*, she thought, *I'll reach him soon enough.* But Matthew turned his face against the street, and his clenched hand relaxed into death.

Margaret Franklin woke up gasping in horror. Still half in sleep, she told herself, *It was just a dream*, and turned to the empty side of the bed. And then came the sickening moment when she recognized the intersection of dream and reality. Matthew was gone. It had happened a hundred times in the last two years.

She got up, her bare feet striking the cold boards of the farmhouse floor with a shock, and groped for the jeans and sweatshirt beside the bed.

The downstairs kitchen was still dark; the sky outside the wide windows was black, paling imperceptibly toward gray. She cut on the radio, automatically, and made her way toward the coffeepot. Her only son had moved into a Sandston apartment, six months earlier. Without his company, ghosts seemed to haunt every dim corner of the lofty old rooms.

The coffee started to run noisily into the pot, and she sat down at the wide board table. The familiar voice from the radio chattered on. The disorienting haze of grief began to fade away.

". . . simply dramatics. The next two days will be Virginia's last before the court order goes into effect. Now Governor Merriman has the eyes of the whole nation on him for forty-eight hours. We can expect demonstrations in front of this huge audience. . . ."

The faint red glow of the power switch under the coffeepot was the only light in the room. A second voice interrupted from the radio, sharper and aggrieved.

"The reason we're at this pass now is the constant dismissal of all complaints by people like you, Tom. You've assumed for years now that any protest from the states is toothless and powerless. But when protest after protest brings no response from Washington, action becomes more and more inevitable."

"If this were Montana, John, maybe I'd believe in the crisis. But we're talking about Virginia. Virginia, the first capital of the United States, the place where independence was finally won. The northern counties have such strong economic ties with Washington, D.C.—"

"Virginia," the second voice snapped, "has a history and a tradition that far predates the United States. Virginia has already left the Union once. And this last Supreme Court decision struck at the heart of Virginia's present freedoms. You've got to remember that the northern counties—Loudoun, Fairfax, Prince William, Arlington—are completely different in character from the rest of the state. It's the other ninety-one counties that should concern us. And if you want to talk about economic ties, remember that Virginia is a tobacco state, and the pending dollar-per-pack sales tax on cigarettes is likely to put hundreds of tobacco growers and thousands of tobacco workers out of business. And don't forget that national defense is big business in Virginia. This administration has made drastic cuts in defense spending, and that's hit Virginia workers especially hard."

"I don't deny that," the first voice retorted. "But what do you think Charles Merriman is going to do about it? Turn out the National Guard and defend Interstate 95 against the United States Army?"

"I certainly hope it doesn't come to that. But I think the popular support for Charles Merriman is going to surprise a lot of onlookers. The Virginia legislature's got a Republican majority for the first time in decades. The voters have already shown themselves to be on Merriman's side. And you may remember that highly publicized buy-out of the *Richmond Times-Dispatch*, late last year. The new editor is a religious conservative —"

The telephone rang. Margaret sat where she was, fascinated by the radio. A breath of cold air drifted along the pine-board floor and curled around her ankles. The scent of the dried herbs that hung in the rafters above her floated down and mingled with the dark scent of fresh-brewed coffee. The sky outside was lightening and a spike of black pines showed against the horizon. The calm voice from the counter said, "This is 'Morning Edition,' from National Public Radio. Support for NPR comes from the Anheuser Busch company, stopping underage drinking before it starts."

The ringing went on. Margaret thought, *I turned off the answering machine.* She dragged herself up from the table and toward the telephone.

"The time," said the radio, "is six-ten. Weather for this Monday, March eighteenth, in the Richmond area: Sunny today, with a high of fifty-nine—"

Margaret groped for the phone in the darkness. Only her son would call at this time in the morning. The thought gave her a hard, cold jolt, just below her diaphragm. She had begged Garrett not to join the Virginia Guard, but he had insisted.

"Hello?"

Someone at the other end took a breath.

"Hello? Garrett?"

"Margaret Franklin?" a male voice said at last.

"Yes?" Margaret said, puzzled.

"Maggie. . . ."

"Who is this?" Margaret said. The words were involuntary, even as memory brought his face back to her mind.

"This is Kenneth," the deep voice said. Something twisted inside her. She put her hand blindly against the door frame. Out in the hall, the dawn was beginning to seep through the glass panes of the front door. Gray light touched against the old cherrywood table and glinted faintly from the glass of the picture hanging above it.

"Ken," she said, gathering herself. "Ken. Well . . . you never *did* do anything conventionally."

His voice sounded momentarily amused. "You mean calling at six in the morning, after all this time?" Behind him she could hear excited chattering, a ringing telephone, the slam of a door; he seemed to be calling from a room full of people.

"Yes," she said. "I was awake."

"You were always an early riser," he said lightly. The immediate reference to a shared past was disarming. He added, before she could draw a breath, "Maggie, I know about Matthew. I'm sorry."

"Oh," Margaret said, awkwardly. She had imagined this scene more times than she could square with her conscience. Her daydreams had always put her in the position of strength. Encountering him by unlikely chance, discovering him still in love with her, telling him gracefully of Matthew's murder and watching him grope for the proper response. She said, stumbling for an answer, "How long . . . when did you find out?"

He hesitated on the other end of the line, while she stared at the gleam of sunrise inching across the hallway floor.

"I knew when it happened," he said, finally.

She could feel her heart beating uncomfortably against her chest. It seemed impossible that his voice could still draw her toward him, after all this time; after twenty-five years spent trying to forget him, trying to convince herself that Matthew was the dearest object of her heart. She had not spoken to Kenneth Balder since his conviction, the conviction that she had helped to bring about with that simple admission to the jury.

Miss Keil, were you ever afraid of Kenneth Balder?

Yes. Yes, sometimes I was.

"Maggie," Ken said, "I don't have much time to talk. I'm coming east. Will you see me?"

"To Virginia?"

"Yes. Will you see me?"

Margaret glanced out the front window. She could see her own figure reflected indistinctly in the windowpane, a slim woman in jeans and a dark sweatshirt, shoulder-length hair caught hastily back. After a moment she said, slowly, "Yes, if you like."

"In a public place?" His voice was carefully neutral.

"Do you know where I live?"

"Yes," he said. Someone was talking to him in the background, in a low hurried voice. She had the feeling that his attention had suddenly shifted away from her.

"Where are you?" she asked suddenly.

"California. I live here."

"Isn't it three A.M. there?"

"Unfortunately."

"Why are there so many people awake?"

"We've got work to do. Haven't you been listening to the news?"

"Er—just for a minute."

"Turn it back on. I'll call you when I get into town. Maggie. . . make me some coffee." His voice changed slightly.

"Ken—"

He had hung up. Margaret stood with the telephone in her hand. She could see outside now; the farm, the neat rows of bedding plants, and the three greenhouses under the sober light of early morning.

"Still paranoid," she said, out loud. *As though anyone would bother to tap Kenneth Balder's phone line.*

Ken had always possessed an enemy. In college it had been the military establishment, a lost war, and a corrupt government. The old code brought it all back. *Make me a cup of coffee:* there's a listener outside the door, a follower in the hall. They had published an anti-war newspaper, she and Ken and Matthew and poor dead Mary Miranda, and distributed it late at night, creeping through the dark campus after Ken's energetic, rangy form. He'd blacked his face once. She and Matthew had laughed at him. And the last time she had seen him, he had been standing in the hallway of the Berkeley courthouse, a prison guard on either side. She had emerged from the courtroom, still clutching Matthew's hand; and Kenneth Balder had seen them both, and turned completely around so that his back was to his friends and his face to the doors that led to jail.

The radio was still chattering. She replaced the receiver, took a stride to the counter, and turned up the volume. Her daily NPR fix had become suddenly more important.

"In news headlines this morning, Governor Charles Merriman of Virginia has threatened to secede from the United States. The governor made this announcement at midnight on Sunday, at the state Capitol. Bob Alexander reports from Richmond."

The reporter began, "Washington was rocked this morning by the announcement that Governor Charles Merriman intends to declare Virginia separate from the United States unless the White House meets ten demands. Independent polls show that a majority of Virginians support the policies reflected in the demands. At his office this morning, Governor Merriman elaborated on his original announcement."

Charles Merriman's familiar voice came on, clear and forceful.

"Today is not a day to argue complicated theories of government, to rant about the intentions of the founding fathers, or to drag out the empty names of amendments or the Constitution and wave them as banners to rally the ignorant. Today I ask only that the United States of America respond to our just complaint. And if there is no response, democracy is indeed dead."

"I need a cup of coffee," Margaret said, out loud. She reached for the pot and poured the steaming dark liquid into Matthew's old pottery mug.

If just complaint brings no effect, democracy is dead. The words niggled at her mind. A familiar phrase in the wrong place. She walked across the kitchen and opened the door into the next room. The muffled radio droned on.

MARGARET TURNED ON THE LAMP that hung over her desk and set the coffee mug down on the wood surface.

The long, narrow room had once been a screened porch overlooking the backyard of the old farm. Matthew had turned it into an office, with a large window overlooking the little back garden. They had begun this nursery together, coming out from California with high ideas about making a living from the land. Two years later, when it actually seemed possible to turn a profit from the plants, Matthew had abruptly joined the Virginia National Guard. He signed the papers before he told her what he was doing, and by the time she discovered his intentions he was fully enrolled. She was furious, angry enough to think of leaving him, bewildered over the sudden change. Matthew had been as anti-military as the rest of them.

Only then had she begun to understand how much of Matthew's life had been spent in Kenneth Balder's shadow. Matthew was finally breaking free from the mesmerizing personality of his oldest friend. And so she found herself bound to him by pity, and sympathy, and a loyalty which prevented her from walking away. Garrett was born a year later. She threw herself into the work of raising her son and turning Franklin's Plants into a thriving business. By the time Matthew died, the income from the nursery almost equaled his guard salary.

She pulled out her chair and sat down. The window was in front of her desk. Behind her, on what had once been the outside wall of the old New Kent farmhouse, a huge plastic-surfaced calendar held the year's planting schedule. The corkboard on the short end wall was covered with notes, chores, and reminders. Neatly stacked in-boxes held orders, checks, and tax papers. She leaned her head into her hands, breathing in the smell of coffee, refusing to turn her head toward the right wall. She knew every word of every article pinned up there, every bureaucratic sentence of the police report thumb-tacked across the top, every line and dot in the photograph at the center of the wall. The pursuit of Matthew's murderer had absorbed her for two years. She was willing to believe that Jerry Tindell had pulled the trigger, but she was convinced that something darker and more complex than a mere robbery had led to Matthew's death. He had come home from his shift, asked her to go with him to Oregon Hill, and then he had died. She had spent the months since his death trying to unravel the chain of events that had brought them to one of Richmond's worst districts so early in the morning.

She had discovered that another man from Matthew's National Guard unit lived in Oregon Hill. But police shrugged this away as a coincidence. After all, the man had a solid alibi. She'd told them of Matthew's half-dropped hints over trouble in the unit. When police refused to investigate the guard, she started inviting the men from the unit over to dinner, along with their wives and families. At first they had come. But now they made excuses, their voices full of irritation, veiled faintly over with pity.

It was March. She'd posted nothing on the board for almost four months. The trail was grave-cold.

In sheer frustration, she had started making weekly trips to the office of the Richmond chief of police. The receptionist politely gave her coffee. She could imagine the word going from mouth to mouth each time she approached the glass doors. *There's Mrs. Franklin again. Who's going to listen this time?*

Chief Caprio had no time for elaborate conspiracy theories. And, entirely against her will, she had infected Garrett with her own doubts. He had left Virginia Tech before his senior year and joined the guard, rejecting her protests, determined to find the reason for his father's death.

Matthew's murder was her public obsession. In the bottom drawer of her desk, under a stack of recent seed catalogues, lay her private one. She opened the drawer and slid the bulging folder from its hiding place. The top newspaper cuttings were yellowed and disintegrating. A huge headline, *Student Protester Convicted in Coed's Death*, topped a blurred photograph of herself and Matthew, both impossibly young in California sun, leaving the courthouse. The headlines dwindled in size as time went on. Years later, *Kenneth Balder Paroled* had been a tiny item in the local California paper.

She spread the articles out, searching for the profile of Kenneth Balder that had appeared two years ago in a San Diego weekly. She had found it in a surreptitious search of the Williamsburg Public Library's newspaper database. She ran her finger down the columns of text until she found the paragraph she remembered.

> Although Balder insists that the California Institute for Theonomic Law is apolitical, in the last year Balder himself has been present at the inauguration of two new Republican governors, Paul Sorenson of Minnesota and Charles Merriman of Virginia. And Balder's gone on record with his praise of Merriman, defending Virginia's new governor against opponents who have called Merriman a gadfly and an intolerant rabble-rouser. "He's a true representative of the people," Balder says. "He was elected by an overwhelming majority because Virginians know he's a just and courageous man. Of course, he spends his time protesting injustice. If just complaint brings no effect, then democracy is dead."

She let the folder rest on the desk. Damp spring air moved gently through the screened window. Across the stretch of green earth, she could hear the sounds of the neighboring farm; chickens restless for breakfast, a cow clanking its horns against the metal gate; a mockingbird scolding from the high branches of the maple that brushed the roof of the old porch.

She gazed out the nearby window; light lay in streaks and patches across the grass. Ken's words were in Charles Merriman's mouth. Ken was coming to Virginia. And behind Kenneth Balder waited a vast shadowy network of unlikely warriors, ready to fight for a righteous cause.

She began to shuffle the papers back into the folder. Her hands moved quickly, while her thoughts washed around and around like driftwood in a churning tide.

CHAPTER 3

Monday, March 18, 5 P.M.

ICHMOND INTERNATIONAL AIRPORT was slightly more crowded than usual. Kenneth Balder walked through the hurrying passengers around him, his jacket slung over his shoulder and the leather case in his hand. It had stayed on his lap through the entire journey, including changes at Denver and Atlanta. In Atlanta someone had recognized him. But for the most part, he had traveled unnoticed. This was difficult for a man of his height, but nine years in prison had taught him useful techniques for avoiding the spotlight. He had not made eye contact once in his journey east.

He stepped onto the escalators and sank downward toward the airport's first floor. Directly in front of him, workmen were removing a banner that had hung on the wall across from the escalators. It was half down already, but he could guess at the first words:

RICHMOND WELCOMES THE VIRGINIA DELEGATES OF THE ACLU.

So it had already begun, even thirty hours before Merriman's deadline.

Balder collected his suitcase at the baggage belts and picked up the keys to the rental car. The faces of the two men behind him in line were vaguely familiar. *Journalists*, he thought, without bothering to recall names or affiliations. The next two weeks would see a flood of the curious. Balder thought he heard his name as he left the lobby, but he let the glass doors close behind him without turning.

He drove straight out of Airport Drive, toward I-64. The expected car was not behind him, but in front of him, driven by a dark-haired man whose form was almost entirely hidden by the raised headrest of his seat. *Easy enough*, Balder thought. *Where else would I be heading but the Executive Mansion?* On a sudden whim he pulled off the nearest exit, swerved into the parking lot of a 7–Eleven, and got out. The brown car was nowhere in sight. He bought a candy bar and a newspaper and pulled the rental car back out of the convenience-store parking lot, circling around toward the interstate on-ramp. The brown car reappeared, just ahead, traveling toward the center of Richmond.

Balder shrugged to himself and leaned forward to search for the evening news on the unfamiliar car radio. At the sound of a well-known voice, he paused with his hand on the seek button.

". . . An equally effective protest on behalf of states' rights could have been mounted without such divisive threats. But this is on a par with Charles Merriman's entire policy of government. His commitment to the Republican Party comes a poor second to his own rigid religious convictions. Governor Merriman has displayed great, a very great disloyalty to the party that elected him."

"Are you saying, Senator, that Virginia Republican leaders knew nothing of this?"

"Certainly not." The senior senator from Virginia sounded even more irate than usual. "The Republican Party is dedicated to fiscal responsibility—but we have broadened our ideological base over the past years, as you well know. In direct contrast, Charles Merriman has become more and more involved with the radical Christian right."

Kenneth Balder said to the radio, "You're in trouble with your own party, Senator, and you know it."

"But the Republican Party in Virginia has a reputation for preferring a narrow ideological base," the reporter persisted. "It's supported Oliver North, Mike Farris —"

"*I* supported neither candidate," snapped the senator, "and I represent the mainstream of the Republican party, whereas Charles Merriman has consistently identified himself with the fringe. It is a sad day for the Republican Party when we finally capture the legislative majority in Virginia, and immediately use our new status to humor the radical religious right. Do you know who contributed to Merriman's election campaign? The Christian Crusaders, Americans for Decency—"

"Don't say it," muttered Kenneth Balder.

"—the California Institute for Theonomic Law, which happens to be headed by Kenneth Balder. Balder himself gave heavily—"

"And legally," Ken interjected.

"—to Merriman's campaign."

"And to twenty other state and local campaigns."

"This sort of alliance puts Charles Merriman at the very edge of the Republic tent, practically standing outside it—"

Kenneth Balder cut the radio off with a grimace. At the institute, "All Things Considered" was known (and not affectionately) as SPIT, an acronym for "Some Points Ignored Totally." Charles Merriman had wide and loyal support in Virginia. The voters who had put him in office were no fringe, and supporters of Merriman's revolution were already salted throughout Virginia's county and city governments. The next two days would come as an unpleasant eye-opener for National Public Radio.

He was well into the city now, passing by the Richmond Coliseum on his left. Traffic flowed around him, heavy and unchanging. He slowed down, unfamiliar with the old Richmond streets; Richmond, with its cemeteries filled with the bones of men who had died saving Virginia from the Union. The thought gave him an uncomfortable prickle along his spine.

CHARLES MERRIMAN WAS WAITING for him in the polished front hall of the Executive Mansion.

The brown car had peeled off and disappeared as Balder pulled up to the iron railings that protected Capitol Park. A crowd scattered in front of his car. Behind the bumper, three Richmond policemen closed in to prevent the spectators from surging in through the gates. The iron bars closed behind him, and a fourth officer bent down to the window.

"Kenneth Balder?"

"Yes."

"Do you have identification?"

He fumbled through his pockets and produced his California driver's license. The trooper examined it and waved him on. He pulled around the circular road that encircled the Capitol and got out in front of the Executive Mansion's lawn. As he approached the little guard shack set into the cream-colored wall, two grim state troopers descended on him. He submitted to a brief search, holding out the briefcase. The troopers stepped back to let him through, and he walked across the pavement and climbed up the front steps. The Executive Mansion was the oldest occupied governor's mansion in the United States: elegant, flawless, meticulously restored.

Charles Merriman opened the door before he could raise his hand. The governor was wearing tattered khaki pants, an old West Point sweatshirt, and socks. The casual dress was alien to his familiar, polished, network-news image. But energy still radiated from every controlled movement.

"Dr. Balder," he said.

"Governor."

"Did they search you?"

"Thoroughly."

"Those two at the front gate think I've gone mad, but they're still determined to keep anyone from killing me before I can be impeached. Did you bring it?"

"Yes, but I haven't had time to iron out—"

"Good man. Come this way. We're all in the den upstairs."

Kenneth Balder followed Charles Merriman past two formal sitting rooms, under an arch, and up a staircase that wound through a landing and opened onto a wide carpeted hallway. On this floor, the polished antiquity gave way to informal clutter. Merriman was unmarried, and the business of governing had overflowed into his private quarters. The den at the far end of the mansion was untidy and full of people. Newspapers sat in piles on the floor. On the opposite side of the room, a small knot of people had their heads together around a VCR. A tape of Merriman's interview with NBC was running, the sound low and almost drowned by the buzz of voices. Another aide was making telephone calls in a corner, and several more were scurrying in and out of doors. Wide windows provided a view of the garden below—a large holly tree surrounded by clipped miniature boxwood, and pansies gold and white under the setting sun.

"My partners in crime," Charles Merriman said, gesturing at two men huddled over the table in the center of the room. "James Macleod, the new editor of the *Richmond Times-Dispatch*. He'll serve as press secretary."

Macleod was stocky and red-haired, older than Merriman. He extended his hand without standing up and said, "I've read all your books, Dr. Balder. Your work's had a great influence on me."

"It's mutual; I have a file of your editorials," Kenneth Balder said.

"You follow Richmond news, then?" asked James Macleod.

"I have, since I met Charles."

Merriman said, "And Joseph Fletcher, the Virginia adjutant general. He'll serve as secretary of defense. If we're forced to use the National Guard, Joe will handle the details."

"General," Balder said.

"Joe's fine," the adjutant general said, shaking hands. He was Merriman's height but much thinner, brown-eyed and balding.

"Now then," Charles Merriman said, rubbing his hands together. "Dr. Balder's brought the blueprint for—"

"Governor," Kenneth Balder said. Merriman paused, looking at him expectantly. Balder set the briefcase down. He was suddenly aware of the fact that he'd been awake for almost twenty-four hours. His neck hurt and his eyes were gritty. He said, carefully, "We need to discuss the timing of your announcement. I've told you before—"

Merriman held up his hand.

"Let's all sit down," he said. "Have you eaten, Dr. Balder?"

"On the plane."

"Coffee, then?"

"Yes. Thank you."

The governor went off through the door. In his sudden absence, Kenneth

Balder sat down on the other side of the cluttered table, conscious that James Macleod's blue eyes were evaluating him with concealed amusement. Joseph Fletcher was gazing at the door, waiting for the governor's return. Balder knew that Merriman's staff was fanatically devoted to him, in part because the governor had a habit of wandering off to run his own errands himself instead of lifting a finger to an aide.

Merriman reappeared with a green Chesapeake Bay mug and handed the coffee over, straddling the chair on Balder's right.

"Go ahead," he said.

Balder cleared his throat. He was suddenly aware that he had lost the advantage of height, and that the ultimatum he was about to lay down would only have a fraction of its original power. He turned his head and looked squarely at Merriman. Against the growing dark outside, the wide windows reflected their images—Merriman's dark, magnetic, and charming; his own broad-shouldered reflection, the blond hair that had darkened only slightly with age, bright against the glass.

"I will not be manipulated," he said.

Merriman looked straight back at him. After a long pause he lifted one shoulder slightly.

"Go on," he said. "Feel free to stand up, if you'd rather."

Balder set the coffee down.

"Listen to me," he said. "You're less than two days away from an act of tremendous magnitude. And danger. But I already have a network of sympathizers with this cause, and the organization to rally them behind you. You'll have enough popular support to pull this revolution off. But you've got to follow my advice. You told me you wanted me as chief of staff. That means you need to take my counsel seriously."

"Of course," Merriman said smoothly.

"You're not doing it," Balder snapped. "I advised you to wait until two days before April fifteenth, so you could make taxes the rallying point. You promised you would. Next thing I know, you're on the evening news making threats."

"This was the proper moment," Merriman said decisively. James Macleod nodded in approval. "Public sentiment was—"

"Public sentiment is not a legitimate basis for government," Balder replied sharply. "That's what's gotten us into this mess. Poll-watching instead of listening to the truth. You told me you wanted to follow the laws of God, not the opinions of men."

"Yes," Merriman said, "but I have a whole legislature full of men who think their opinions matter. I have a majority, true, but I decided it would be safer to declare independence while the House and Senate were out of session."

"They'd still have been out of session on April thirteenth."

Merriman said pacifically, "It's done now, Dr. Balder. Let's move on to action. We can fuel our revolt on the just indignation of Virginians everywhere—"

"I'm not a voter. Save your rhetoric for the press."

Merriman rubbed his top lip, taken aback. He said at last, making one further effort at reconciliation, "I do take your advice seriously, Dr. Balder. I intend to give you wide discretionary powers. Frankly, I need your followers to swear on to this revolt if it's going to work. But this decision was mine."

Balder stood up. The three men at the table had to crane their necks up at his height. He said, "Listen to me. We're starting a war. No one's taking us seriously now, but at midnight on Tuesday everyone north of the Potomac will start shouting for our heads. If we've miscalculated—if the president ignores the public relations nightmare and the implications of *posse comitatis* and sends in troops—you could both lose your heads in an unpleasant and literal way."

"He won't," the adjutant general said with certainty.

"You can't be sure of that."

"And how about you, Dr. Balder?" inquired James Macleod. "What are you risking in this second Civil War?"

"My life's work. Let's understand each other, gentlemen. You want to form a country whose law is based on God's laws for His people. I've studied God's laws for fifteen years. I took a doctoral degree in comparative religions at Harvard and spent the following decade studying and writing about the Old Testament. I have a blueprint for such a country in this briefcase." He nudged the case with his foot. "Three years ago you, Governor Merriman, contacted me to tell me that a grassroots revolution was underway in Virginia. In three years, you said, over half the county and city offices would be occupied by people who believed God's law to be the only legitimate basis for government. Come and see what's happening in the East. So I came. I was impressed. More than impressed. I was overwhelmed. So, in answer to the governor's request, I sent copies of all my writings to your office. This morning I heard my words quoted without my permission."

"We had no agreement of secrecy," Merriman snapped back.

"But if it was understood—" James Macleod began.

"It's done," Merriman observed. His voice was curt. "I have Virginia solidly behind me. I have North Carolina watching in fascination. The governor called me this morning. MacDonald Forbes. A sincere boy. He's interested in joining us."

Balder said, "You know, don't you, that the press thinks the revolution has to do with the tobacco tax? If North Carolina joins us, they'll be certain of it."

"Let them. This has nothing to do with tobacco."

Kenneth Balder glanced over at Joseph Fletcher, who was nodding. Merriman had chosen his adjutant general well; Fletcher would support him in whatever actions he took. James Macleod had developed a worried crease in his freckled forehead, and Balder turned toward him.

"I'll tell you what I'm risking in this second Civil War," Kenneth Balder said. "Twenty-five years ago I was convicted of manslaughter. If I become a visible part of this revolt, in two days every single detail from my trial will be known to every housewife and ten-year-old child in this country. Not only that, I guarantee you that Washington will make hay with it. I was followed here, you know. The FBI has probably already amassed a roomful of files on me, in the last twelve hours. This, after I've spent two decades living my conviction down. If it's to be resurrected now, it'll have to be for good reason. I'll be your chief of staff, Governor, but if you ever again quote from my writings at the wrong time and the wrong place and against my advice, I'll take my papers and my constitution and my network and my years of work back to California, and issue a strong condemnation of this revolt."

There was silence in the room. James Macleod's mouth twitched momentarily into a smile. Balder hoisted the briefcase onto the chair beside him, opened it, and took out three documents bound in gray covers.

"Here," he said, "is the proposed constitution of the Reformed American States. It is based on God's law, as revealed to Moses in the Pentateuch. It's still imperfect and it needs more work, but I didn't think this time would come so soon."

He held the bound documents out to the two men sitting across from him. For a moment no one moved. Balder could hear his own heartbeat pounding in his ears. These were the men who owned the possibility of a country run by God's rules, and he wanted to see that country leap into existence so badly that it tasted like metal in his mouth.

He knew a great deal about these men. James Macleod, his red hair turning white at the temples, had his hands folded comfortably across his belly, waiting for Merriman to move first. One of the *Times-Dispatch* reporters was a loyal supporter of the California Institute for Theonomic Law. She had returned his phone call within an hour.

"He calls himself a zookeeper, Dr. Balder. A brilliant editor, but to him readers are only the dumb creatures in the zoo. He feeds them with words and opinions, and they swallow it whole. He's passionate for truth, but people . . . well, as far as he's concerned, they're clumsy creatures that hear truth and distort it into whatever patterns suit them. When he bought the *Times-Dispatch*, two-thirds of the reporters resigned in protest."

"Does he know who I am, or will I have to explain myself?"

She had laughed. "He's got a row of your books on his office shelf. But he thinks you're too compassionate."

Kenneth Balder thanked her and hung up. It was not a criticism he'd ever heard before.

He turned his gaze towards Joseph Fletcher, middle-aged and competent. Fletcher had happily attended the Episcopal church since childhood. He was a Christian who never thought about doctrine, a man who followed Charles Merriman out of personal loyalty rather than theological conviction. Merriman had nominated him for his post, and seen him confirmed by the Republican majority; Fletcher owed his career to his governor.

Kenneth Balder looked back at the chief executive of Virginia. Charles Merriman had begun his term as governor promising change and a return to prosperity and safety. After three years in office, he had seen the glowing promise of reform turn flat and gray; he had a legislative majority, but the minority blocked him at every possible turning, and he had a Democrat for second in command. The lieutenant governor, Bob Watkins, had just announced his intentions to seek the governor's office on a platform of increased governmental intervention in the lives of poor and disadvantaged Virginians. Merriman, incensed, had given his third State of the Commonwealth Address on television instead of before the representatives. He had declared that he would never again seek office, as he would never again be fooled into thinking that elected office gave any man the power to represent the people to Washington. The white-tentacled monster, he had called it. The phrase had already passed into the language. But Virginia's constitution barred her governors from serving consecutive terms, and the new country would provide Charles Merriman with his only remaining chance at power. Merriman was a zealot for justice, apparently unconcerned with his own political future. But he was proving an unpredictable and difficult ally, and Balder wondered how many more layers were hidden underneath that photogenic surface.

Charles Merriman stretched back and clasped his hands behind his head.

"Put your papers down, Dr. Balder," he said. "You were in the air at nine this morning, weren't you?"

Balder blinked at him.

"Er," he said, "yes."

"Well then," Merriman said, "sit down for a minute and catch up on the day's news. Come on over here."

Balder followed him to the middle of the room. Merriman cut off the videotape of his own news conference, and the watching aides scattered as he waved his hand at them. He took a second tape from the top of the monitor and inserted it. The blue screen flashed on and was instantly replaced by the draperies and seal of the White House Conference Room.

"We'll just go past Tom Brokaw's breathless commentary," the governor murmured. "The president kept them waiting a long time. . . . good theater . . . ah, here it is."

The rapidly changing picture slowed. The president of the United States strode to the podium. Balder was aware of the sound level in the room, dropping away to a murmur as men and women all around him turned to watch.

"Good morning," the president said. There were weary lines in his face, and he looked more than ever like benevolent royalty. It was an immensely popular persona.

"I have come this morning," the president said, "to respond to the demands made by Virginia Governor Charles Merriman. Governor Merriman has threatened to separate the Commonwealth from the United States of America. He claims to be acting on behalf of the people of Virginia. But he refuses to discuss the Constitution of the United States. This is because the Constitution and the Bill of Rights furnish the American people with all the protection from tyranny that is needed. Governor Merriman is not acting to protect his constituency. Governor Merriman is tapping into the frustrations created by a small and vocal group of religious fanatics in order to increase his own personal power. I speak now directly to the people of the United States: Join with me in condemning this divisive and inflammatory act. And I speak also to the United States citizens who live in the Commonwealth of Virginia: Do not let this power-hungry and intolerant man lead you away from the traditions of your great state. Virginia has always stood as a landmark of freedom. And now Charles Merriman wants to take that freedom away."

He paused, apparently overcome with emotion. Macleod gave a loud snort.

"Be quiet, Jim," Merriman snapped.

The president, having conquered his surging passions, raised his head.

"We are in danger," he said solemnly, "of losing the cradle of freedom to a narrow and bigoted religious intolerance. Charles Merriman's list of

demands may not sound religious to you. But they are the Ten Commandments of a new era. It is a matter of public record that Charles Merriman
is deeply involved with the radical California Institute for Theonomic Law—
a far-right think tank that wants to put the laws of Israel into force here in
the United States. Members of the press, these people are called
theonomists. That means they want the United States run as a religious dictatorship. We're talking about outlawing divorce and stoning homosexuals."

Kenneth Balder said indignantly, "He's talking about John Cline in
Santa Fe. Not about CITL."

"Oh," Merriman said, "he knows who you are."

"Charles Merriman," the president announced, "is known to be close
friends with CITL founder Kenneth Balder. Between them, they have
orchestrated a campaign to stack local offices full of men and women who
share Balder's peculiar convictions. Make no mistake. Charles Merriman
is a tool. If this secession takes place, Virginia will be under the direction
of a man who spent years in prison on a conviction of manslaughter."

There was a rustle in the throng of press. It was repeated throughout
the room, as Merriman's staff turned to look at Kenneth Balder. Balder
put his hands in his pockets. The casual move took every ounce of self-
control in his big body; he could feel nervous energy thrumming through
him, like vibrations along a tight-stretched cord. He thought, suddenly:
Margaret heard this speech hours ago.

"Kenneth Balder was convicted of manslaughter while still in college,"
the president repeated. "He smothered a fellow student during a late-night
antiwar protest. Prosecutors suggested that Kenneth Balder killed this girl,
Mary Miranda Carpenter, because she was endangering the success of his
mission. At the time, the team of prosecutors—including my own secretary
of defense, Alexander Wade, who is working closely with me during this
crisis—portrayed Balder as a cold-blooded and calculating man, willing to
do anything, shed any amount of blood, in order to advance his own personal causes."

They had dug up an old picture of Mary Miranda. Balder stared at it.
His tongue had gone dry in his mouth. Merriman paused the VCR on the
picture and Mary Miranda Carpenter hung there, straight fine blonde hair

framing her young face, achieving a brief and substanceless life on the screen. He had expected the president to rant that the Executive Mansion was captive to the tobacco industry. This attack, a hundred times more dangerous, showed that the White House comprehended the purpose of the revolution. It was a revolution of morality. And so the United States had decided to destroy his character.

"I was only convicted of involuntary manslaughter," Kenneth Balder managed, at last. "The prosecutors never convinced the jury of any of that."

"Yes," Merriman said, lazily. "Well, the president didn't exactly say so, did he? All he said was that the prosecutors tried to prove it. He told the truth."

"I've changed," Kenneth Balder said, with all the conviction of that spectacular conversion in his voice.

"I don't think the president believes in redemption," Merriman remarked. He blanked out Mary Miranda's face. Balder tore his eyes away from the screen. Behind him, the chatter of the room swelled up again; a telephone rang, and someone answered it. Merriman turned around from the television. The muscles of his face and body had changed minutely. He was no longer an opponent, but a charming petitioner with an undeniable request.

"You're not going to be real popular out there in the United States, Dr. Balder," he said. "But we believe in your work here, no matter what the rest of the country thinks. We need your expertise. You've done more work in criminal justice than any other theonomist; and swift and sure justice will attract more people to Virginia even than economic reform. Maybe God is sending you a signal, Dr. Balder, confirming that you need to throw your lot in with Virginia. Now—" He came forward a step, holding out his hand. "—could I look at the proposed constitution?"

Kenneth Balder fumbled mechanically for the books. There had been something else. He collected himself with an immense effort; in his ears, his voice sounded cool and composed.

"One final piece of advice, Governor. The words *civil war* have been spoken for the last time. This is no Civil War. It's a second Revolution; and let's hope that the rhetoric of just rebellion makes the possibility of bloodshed palatable to all of your indignant Virginians."

Merriman smiled at him.

"Certainly," he said. "We'll do just as you say. Let's have a look at this. And then we can get right to work on a second Declaration of Independence."

He bent his handsome head over the bound document, walking absently away. Joe Fletcher followed him. Kenneth Balder was aware of James Macleod's covert stare, surveying him from behind the gray cover of his proposed constitution. He turned his eyes toward the dark garden beyond the wide windows.

"That wasn't the end of the tape, you know," Macleod said suddenly, too softly for Charles Merriman's ears. "There was more to the press conference."

"Oh?"

"The president didn't end with you," Macleod said. "He ended by announcing that the attorney general of the United States was preparing charges against Charles Merriman."

"Charges? What charges?"

"Left unspoken," Macleod said, succinctly.

"Are they going to arrest him?"

"That," observed James Macleod, "depends on if they get the charges together before or after Charles declares Virginia independent. Should make for an interesting day tomorrow." He buried his nose back into his book.

Outside the dark glass, tiny lights were coming on all over the garden below. They transformed the dim mass beyond the windows into a delicate tracing of walls and branches. A chime clock somewhere in the depths of the house struck ten sweet notes.

Maggie, Kenneth Balder thought again. He had hoped that the great gap of time had dulled the horror of that trial. . . . He could see no prospect of leaving Richmond soon. The deadline was only twenty-six hours away.

CHAPTER 4

Monday, March 18, 9 P.M.

G ARRETT FRANKLIN—most junior member of the Security Police Squadron, Seventy-eighth Fighter Unit, Virginia Air National Guard—was dozing on his feet when his sergeant's voice woke him up.

"Franklin!"

He jerked himself out of his comfortably hazy twilight and blinked at Clint Larsen, leaning back in his chair in front of the security screens.

"Saw a shadow out there," Larsen ordered. "Go check it out, would you?"

Garrett straightened himself, crossly. He'd already answered one false call. Unseasonable lightning, cracking in the distance, had set off the alarm to the arms vault just as his shift began. He seriously doubted that Clint Larsen had actually seen a shadow behind one of the F-16s that sat silent on the concrete yard outside the windows of the security office. Larsen, stocky and blond, was generally easy to get along with; but when he was bored or on edge he became a bully.

He heaved his M-16 up and took himself out the door, down the hall and the steps that led out to the planes. The March night was windy, and bits of rain spat into his face. The shadows beneath the planes were empty of any menace.

When he came back in, Clint Larsen was still sprawled in the chair in front of the security screens. Davidson Smith, tall and thin, was leaning against the window that looked out to the planes. Both men were grinning.

"Don't wander out there like it's a blowing door, boy," Larsen said. "Put the gun on your shoulder."

"Sorry," Garrett mumbled.

"You young guys get sloppy. One day you'll leave the M-16 in the truck and haul your butt in there and find some nut-case peace activist under the plane with a homemade bomb."

Garrett Franklin tried to look suitably impressed. But this was Sandston, a scattering of family grocery stores and brick bungalows, far more rural than the nearby Richmond suburbs; and the planes were Priority C, only one step above a mere secured area. The air national guard base sat just on the other side of Richmond International Airport, known locally as RIC, around the corner from the Richmond Army Guard headquarters. RIC's main terminal squatted on the other side of the airfield. In the year he'd been part of the security force that baby-sat the air national guard planes, the most exciting moment had been caused by a squirrel shorting out the front-gate alarms.

Clint Larsen yawned and stretched. He said, "Any coffee left?"

"Not much," Garrett said.

"Man, I'm bored. We got to get this TV fixed." The little TV that whiled away the hours for the security detail had blown out two nights ago, and Larsen had complained steadily about it.

"Captain's coming," Davidson Smith said, craning his neck around to see out the side window of the second-story room. "Walkin' like a man with a mission. He's got something on his mind."

Garrett wandered out of the second-story operations office into the little anteroom. He had come on duty two hours ago, fresh from watching the evening news, strung up, waiting for war to break out. But he'd found the Seventy-eighth Fighter Unit in its usual Monday night condition—quiet and half-deserted. He tried to talk about the threats of revolution, but Larsen shut him up with a single piercing glance. Later, Garrett had managed to corner Davidson Smith in the hallway outside, but the older guardsman had merely shrugged.

"Politicians," he said, shortly. "Doesn't mean anything."

"Larsen's all edgy—"

"Larsen's *always* edgy. If he knows something, he hasn't told me about it."

The unchanged security routines had gradually lulled him back into peace. He picked up the coffeepot and swirled the sludge at the bottom, wondering whether the pleasure of fresh coffee was worth the effort of making more. Behind him, the alarm to the arms vault went off again. Larsen slapped at it and swore.

"We got to get that wiring looked at," he complained. "Franklin—"

"Okay," Garrett said, resigned. "I'm on my way." He had his hand on the doorknob when his commanding officer opened it from the hallway outside. John Ames, captain USAF, was one of twelve squadron commanders at the base. He had commanded Matthew Franklin at this same post.

Garrett said, "Evening, sir—"

"Come in here," Ames said curtly, "and shut that door." He stalked past Garrett, into the security office. Clint Larsen said, "Sir, I was sending Franklin to check an alarm."

Ames reached out and flicked a switch. Immediately the screen showing the area in front of the arms vault blanked out.

"Never mind that alarm," he said. "The three of you listen to me." He leaned against the bank of screens, folding his arms. Ames, square-chested and solemn, was career guard, in his early thirties, with several years at Pentagon headquarters under his belt.

"You men have seen the news?" he demanded.

"Sure," Larsen said.

"You know what's going on?"

"We been called out?" Davidson Smith demanded.

"Not yet," Ames said. "But I've heard from the office of the Virginia adjutant general. One of his aides called. They say that Merriman's promised to use all resources of the Commonwealth to defend Virginia's citizens from any further oppression from the United States, and that means us." He cleared his throat. "Listen," he said, "I want you guys to be prepared. The president might call us out before the governor does. But the adjutant general's office told me what the United States is planning to do in the future. I guess they're calling commanding officers all over the state. They say there's going to be even more defense cuts in the next two years. Apparently the Pentagon's talking about eliminating seven Virginia National Guard bases and reducing personnel at six others. We might be unlucky."

"Again," Davidson Smith added. He was career air force, sent into the guard by cuts. Ames nodded.

"The adjutant general's office also says that the secretary of defense has recommended two base closures in Virginia," he said. "Fort Lee in Petersburg and Fort Story in Virginia Beach." He gazed out the window at the planes, sitting idle on the concrete outside. After a moment, he added, "The last thing they said to me was, 'Prompt and decisive action at the highest levels is required to prevent irreparable damage to the future defenses of the Commonwealth of Virginia.'"

The security office telephone rang. Garrett snatched it up before Larsen could answer.

"Virginia Air Guard Security Police," he said.

"This is Jim Redfield's assistant, from Channel Twelve. We've got a report that the governor has called out the army guard. Has the air guard been mobilized?"

Garrett put his hand over the receiver and mouthed *Press* at Ames. Ames grabbed for the telephone.

"We have no information at this time," he said, and hung up. Garrett looked at his captain uncertainly. Clint Larsen and Davidson Smith had fallen silent. Ames folded his arms across his square chest. He said after a moment, "Well, I'll head on over to Communications. I've got work to do. Franklin, you're just going off duty, aren't you?"

"No, sir. Not 'til three."

"You can go a little early today."

"I thought I might—"

"Go home, Franklin," Ames said. He turned around and walked out of the security office. Clint Larsen puckered his lips into a soundless whistle, his eyes on the ceiling. Davidson Smith had suddenly become absorbed by a frayed spot on the strap of his M-16. Garrett cleared his throat.

"Er," he said, "okay."

He checked his weapon and hung his badge on the board inside the door of the arms room, just off the security office. When he came back out, Larsen was alone.

"See you later," Garrett said tentatively.

"Yeah," Clint Larsen said, his voice sounding perfectly normal.

Weird, Garrett thought, letting himself out of the big dingy building and trudging toward his rattletrap VW Rabbit. If Governor Merriman were leaving the United States with his state, wouldn't he want all the guard alert and on duty? Instead Captain Ames seemed to be clearing the base of all but the bare bones; and on a Monday night like this, with no drill or flying scheduled, the base could chug along with ten or twelve men. Only the security police, one squadron of the base's support group, was on duty. Logistics, maintenance, communication, and the fighter squadron had all gone home.

Garrett blew on his fingers and started the motor. The heat in the old car had quit working around Christmas, but he didn't have the money to fix it, and he'd rejected the option of asking his mother to help out. He pulled slowly out of the parking lot, around the curve leading toward the security checkpoint. The guard on duty waved him briskly through and disappeared back into the guard hut. Tonight, no one wanted to talk.

Garrett accelerated past the fighter planes that stood at the base entrance, caught in permanent mid-flight on their concrete pillars. He drove out Falcon Road, past the continually burned-out building that sat grimly at the front of the Richmond Fire Training Academy, past the alternate entrance to the base, past the rows of identical brick bungalows, and turned right onto East Williamsburg Road. He had rented a basement apartment in one of these endless houses—two small rooms and a bathroom with cobwebby, rectangular windows cut high in the walls.

He braked gently to a stop in front of the driveway and sat for a moment, thinking. *Why would Ames send me home early?* He was the newest member of the security squadron, the youngest . . . maybe the least trustworthy. *But what could the security squadron possibly be up to?* It was a very small segment of the base's total force. *What could Ames do with two men?*

He got out of the car and slammed the door, and instantly the memory of the false alarms rose up in front of him; Ames shutting the arms vault alarm off and leaning against the security screen, obscuring it from sight.

Arms. That's what the security squadron controlled. Access to the base weapons.

He shook his head impatiently, walking toward the basement staircase. The air guard was fully capable of carrying out any function of the regular air force. But although the guard had plenty of weapons, its ammunition was controlled by the regular services. The nearest stockpile would be . . . where? Fort Eustis, squatting on the banks of the James? Fort Lee, just down the road at Petersburg? Surely Governor Merriman wouldn't call out the guard, if he knew they'd have guns without bullets and planes without missiles. Merriman had been a guardsman himself, back before entering politics.

Garrett let himself quietly into his kitchen. It was a tiny room with a rickety table, closet, and a square cube of a refrigerator. A microwave and toaster occupied a minuscule counter next to the sink. He opened a can of soup, shoved it into the microwave, and made his way into his bedroom with the bowl. His bed, the only piece of real furniture in his tiny bedroom, was an unmade tangle of blankets. A small black-and-white TV perched on a milk crate against the far wall. He flicked it on and sat on the end of the bed, eating soup absently and watching the news. The local stations had pre-empted their regular programs to run clips of Merriman's latest speech. The governor was standing on the lawn of the Executive Mansion, and his voice sounded forceful and convincing.

"The men who first settled this land knew that power corrupts. They knew that any governing body with the ability to run a country also, inevitably, gains the power to oppress that same country. They recognized the potential for evil. And so they wrote that duly elected representatives of the people—such as myself and those who stand with me—are the true, local, lawful government. We are the protectors of the people. We have the moral right to interpose ourselves between the people of our Commonwealth, and a higher level of government which has turned tyrannous. This is called *interposition.* And it is an integral stone in the political foundation of our Commonwealth."

The TV station cut away from Merriman, and flashed new pictures across the screen. Tobacco employees setting off fireworks. A surging demonstration in Merriman's support at Red Hill, Patrick Henry's estate out west in Charlotte County.

Garrett finished his soup and put the bowl down. He sat for a moment, thinking hard, and was suddenly struck by the realization that he'd left his knapsack with its change of clothes and paperback book under the microwave stand, back at the security office. He could go back and get it. He could find out what was going on. At the thought, the whole cautious side of his nature rose up shouting warnings at him. *Stay put. Don't cross them. Leave them alone. Do as you're told.*

He hunched his shoulders, scowling at the moving figures on the TV screen. He'd joined the Virginia National Guard because of a single conversation with his father the week before Matthew Franklin died, a conversation that gave color and life to all his mother's theories of a guard conspiracy. They'd been down in the patch of woods behind the house, where his father had wanted to build a pond as a surprise for his mother. They worked most of the warm morning. When they'd finished, they sat with their feet in the water, sweating gently, a cooler of soda between them. Matthew Franklin grinned at his son with affection, swigged down the last drops of Coke in his can, and offered Garrett a secret.

"I've got to do a dirty job," he said.

"What, Dad?"

"At work."

"What is it?"

"A flagrant violation of the rules," Matthew Franklin said, "and I've discovered it and have to turn in the offenders."

"You don't want to do it?"

"No. But I ought to. They'll both be booted out, and I think they could be charged with a crime." He spun his Coke can on his forefinger, concentrating on the red and white stripes. "I haven't told anyone else about this yet. I'm still . . . thinking. About the best way to handle it."

"I won't say anything," Garrett promised. The confidence had swelled him up with pride. Two weeks after his father's funeral, he had walked into the local guard recruiting office and announced, "I want to join my father's unit."

"We can't guarantee you'll be posted at the airport," the recruiter said cautiously.

"Can you try?"

"You can request it."

"What are the odds?"

"Pretty good," the recruiter said, "but I wouldn't want you to join for that reason."

"No. I want to join."

It had been a quixotic reason to join; a few vague words from a preoccupied man. But the suspicion had leaped into his mind that first wretched morning, and had never been dislodged. A policeman had brought his mother home at dawn. The sun had just come over the grass; he'd been sleeping, awakened by his mother's horrible sobbing on the front porch. Two intolerable hours later he thought: *Matthew Franklin was about to get someone kicked out of the guard. Matthew Franklin was planning to charge someone in the guard with a criminal act. Matthew Franklin conveniently died.*

He arrived at the Sandston base to find himself in constant company with the two guardsman who had worked with his father—Clint Larsen, a stocky powerful man who swung from sullen quiet to talkative aggression within the space of minutes, and Davidson Smith, tall and competent and bitter. He was disappointed to discover that both men had alibis for his father's death. Davidson Smith had been publicly and loudly in the security office when Matthew Franklin died miles away in Oregon Hill. Clint Larsen was actually living in Oregon Hill at the time. But although he and Matthew Franklin had gone off duty together, Larsen had arrived home to find his seven-year-old in the throes of an asthma attack. He had taken the child to the Medical College of Virginia and spent the night in the emergency room.

If either man had played any part in Matthew Franklin's death, it had been indirect. But Garrett was irrationally certain that the connection existed. And so he trailed along behind them, ate with them at the mess hall, allowed himself to be fleeced in poker games, all the while playing a wistful wide-eyed part and waiting to find the knot behind the tapestry.

He got up in sudden decision, switched off the TV, and let himself quietly out of the basement door. He had the uneasy creeping sensation that some massive force was tunneling along underneath him and would come exploding out of the ground when he least expected it. He had joined the air national guard to find his father's murderer. He had never intended to fight, in any war, at any time.

THE SECURITY CHECKPOINT was locked, and the guard came out at once. He bent down to the window, his enormous shoulders filling the glass.

"Back already?" asked Jerald Williams. Williams was the son of an African Methodist Episcopal pastor; he was efficient, amiable, a crack shot.

"I left my knapsack in the security office."

"Yeah? Can't you get it in the morning?"

So something *was* happening. He'd come back here before at odd times and in odd ways, and invariably the guard on duty had waved him cheerfully through.

"I left a present for my mother in it. See," Garrett said, embarking on his carefully polished story, "tomorrow's the day she and my dad got engaged, and she's always kind of down, so I bought her something, and I left it in my bag. I meant to take it home and wrap it so she could have it first thing in the morning. Otherwise she cries at breakfast."

This was an unbreakable tale; it explained why he wanted the knapsack immediately, and it circumvented the remote possibility that someone who had served for years with Matthew Franklin might remember Margaret's birthday, or the date of her wedding anniversary. They might think it unlikely that his intelligent and self-possessed mother cried at breakfast, but the only real awkwardness would be if Clint Larsen or Davidson Smith insisted on seeing into his knapsack, which held only sweats and a paperback book. In that case he would have to explain that his current science-fiction novel, *World War III: In the Balance*, was meant to satisfy his mother's little-known passion for stories of alien invasion.

Jerald Williams said dubiously, "I'd better check with Larsen. Hang on a minute." He went back into the guard shack, shutting the door behind him. After a few moments of inaudible conversation behind the glass, he came back out.

"Okay," he said, "go on up. Make it quick, would ya? This gate's supposed to be secure, this time of night."

"Yeah. Thanks." He put the car back into gear and headed for the parking lot. The base looked perfectly normal, avionics and the propulsion section all sound asleep under the lights.

He ran lightly up the stairs. The hallways were quiet; he tapped at the wooden door of the security office and waited for an answer. Larsen opened it after a moment, knapsack in hand.

"This what you want?" he said. His body was solid in the doorway. Over his shoulder Garrett could only see the top of Davidson Smith's head, silhouetted against the board of lights and monitor screens.

"Yes. Thanks. I might have left my badge—"

"I'll find it for you."

"Oh," Garrett said. "Yeah. Okay, then." He took the bag, shifting his eyes away from Clint's direct stare. In the control room, a light began suddenly to blink. Smith didn't move.

"Night," Clint Larsen said.

Garrett said stubbornly, "The vault alarm's going off."

"Yeah. We've had more lightning." His blue eyes dared Garrett to contradict this.

"Want any help?"

"You're off duty," Clint Larsen said. "Better go home. I'll walk you to your car."

And we won't go anywhere near the arms vault, Garrett thought. He walked beside Clint Larsen, listening to the older man talk.

"You handled that phone call pretty good, Franklin, handing it over to the captain like that. Jim Redfield—he's persistent. Worth his weight in gold to Channel Twelve. He called here when your dad was on duty, as soon as Desert Shield went public. Wednesday night, that was. A flying night. Bernard Shaw was describing the tracers going down in the desert on CNN, and Redfield called to ask if our planes were headed over because he could see 'em in the sky. Like we could get over there without refueling twice in midair."

Garrett sneaked a look at the older man's profile: light hair, strong nose, tight worried lines around his mouth contradicting the lighthearted chatter. He followed Larsen through the outside door into the parking lot and climbed into the Rabbit, aware of Larsen's eyes watching him steadily as he pulled away. Jerald Williams, waving him brusquely past, locked the gates behind him.

Past the Fire Training Academy building, he came softly to a halt and strained his eyes down the access road that led around to the base. It looked closed. He rolled down his window, and heard the soft sound of distant motors. A red tail-light blinked and disappeared. There was a small fleet of army trucks out there, where no one had any business to be.

Fort Lee and Fort Story, bound for extinction, were shifting ammunition stores. The air guard was armed.

Garrett thought, *Now we can fight,* and felt fear swell up unwelcome into his throat and mouth.

CHAPTER 5

Tuesday, March 19, 7 A.M.

THE ROOSEVELT ROOM had a fire in the hearth, which meant the president had already been through it once this morning. He liked fires. Alexander Wade considered the flames drearily, then closed his strained eyes. It was Tuesday morning. They had seventeen hours left. At the moment, he wanted nothing more than an hour alone with Charles Merriman, and he would happily have shot that smooth-tongued, fair-headed Norse god of an ex-convict. Perri had just called to inquire, with unshielded exasperation, whether he intended to spend any time at all with his daughter in the last spring break of her college career.

"If I don't stay here," he had told her, "Deborah won't have a college to go back to."

"Huh," Perri snapped. "That's as likely as Fidel Castro inviting Ross Perot to come help establish capitalism in Cuba."

"Stranger things have happened," he said; but Perri was unimpressed.

Wade opened his eyes and considered the attorney general of the United States, who was less attractive than the leaping fire.

"There was a red sunrise this morning," he said, thoughtfully. "Storm's coming."

The attorney general snorted. They were propped on one of the sofas, underneath a portrait of Theodore. The president disliked coming into the

Oval Office to find his guests already seated. Even senior cabinet officials waited in the Roosevelt Room, just a few steps from the Oval Office door, until the chief executive was behind his desk. This morning the president was late, buried in yet another press conference.

Wade shifted impatiently on the gilt upholstery. He had already thrashed the matter out with Ramsey Grant the day before. Grant had flown into Washington early on Monday afternoon, red-eyed and rumpled. Wade had taken the precaution of entering the Department of Justice by a back door, an hour before Grant's arrival, and had stood at a third-floor window to watch Grant's limo drive up Constitution Avenue. A horde of press swirled behind it. He was waiting at the door to the attorney general's office when Grant came into the hallway, trailing his aide and deputy behind him.

Grant had greeted the secretary of defense by snarling at him. He was a tall, thin man with rattling quick speech, and he'd had no lunch.

"I've been summoned to see HM first thing in the morning," he snapped, "and there's nothing we have to talk about between now and then."

"There is," Wade had said, calmly.

Ramsey mumbled under his breath, a sentence of which Alexander Wade caught punctuated with several creative obscenities. He said, "The Cult Infiltration Act may be law, but it's still a touchy matter in this country, Ramsey."

Grant surveyed him for a moment, and then lifted one angular shoulder. "Get me some lunch," he said to his aide. "Chinese is fine. Bill, wait a minute, would you?"

The deputy attorney general shrugged. Ramsey Grant stepped into his office, with the secretary of defense behind him.

"What does that mean?" Grant demanded, as soon as the door swung closed.

"It means I'm not going into a meeting with you and the president unarmed."

"Odd adjective for the secretary of defense to use."

"Come on, Ramsey. Do you want to bring this to a quick end, or do you want secession and a spectacular trial of Charles Merriman with yourself playing a leading role?"

Ramsey Grant grinned suddenly.

"I'll give you both," Wade said. "We'll save the presidency and you'll still get your trial."

"How?"

"We'll arrest Merriman at two minutes after midnight."

"We can't arrest him at all. Ever heard of the Fourteenth Amendment? Sit down over there," Ramsey Grant said, pointing at a chair and tossing his overcoat over a nearby table, "and I'll fill you in the legal aspects. Go away." This was directed at the deputy attorney general, who had ventured to tap on the other side of the door. Grant strode to his desk and punched the intercom button.

"Ellen," he said, "I'm not to be disturbed."

"Yes, sir," answered the voice of the executive secretary. Grant sprawled into the chair behind his desk and started to unbutton his cuffs.

"Arresting the governor of Virginia doesn't fall under the authority of the federal government," he said. "Let me introduce you to the Constitution of the Commonwealth of Virginia. It does, in fact, provide for sudden fits of paranoia in the executive branch. The governor can be voted unfit for office by a majority of the General Assembly. Unfortunately it doesn't happen to be in session. I'm not sure this particular legislature would boot him out in any case."

"There must be another way."

"Of course there is. The governor may also be declared unfit to hold office by the united efforts of the Virginia attorney general, the president pro tempore of the Virginia Senate, and the Speaker of the Virginia House of Delegates. If they all sign a statement agreeing that the governor is unable to carry out his duties, the Virginia legislature can convene and vote the lieutenant governor in. I need not tell you that to have Bob Watkins in the governor's seat would solve all of our present problems."

"And?"

"The attorney general of the Commonwealth is on a photo safari in Alaska. I've got the Alaska park police out looking for him. Alaska's a big state, and it appears that he is maintaining radio silence for the good of his soul. The attorney general," Ramsey Grant said, leaning back and clasping his long thin hands behind his head, "has been treated for stress-related ailments, and the fishing trip was a personal gift from the governor for the attorney general's birthday. To help him recover."

Alexander Wade digested this in silence. Ramsey Grant fixed him with an ironic eye.

"Here's the kicker," he said. "In odd-numbered years like this one, the Virginia legislature convenes on the second Wednesday in January, runs for thirty days, adjourns, and then reconvenes on the sixth Wednesday after adjournment to consider any bills returned by the governor. Tomorrow is Tuesday," Grant said, unnecessarily. "The sixth Wednesday happens to be the day after tomorrow. I'm assuming that Merriman's forty-eight hours began at midnight Sunday and end at midnight Tuesday. So he's going to declare independence one minute before the legislature can legally reconvene and impeach him. Naturally, the first thing he'll do is dismiss the legislature and form a new governing body. He's planned this carefully, the cocky—"

"What about federal law?"

"Charles Merriman," the attorney general said, "has not set foot on federal property since this whole thing began. Furthermore, he hasn't communicated with any elected officials in local county and city seats. Until he actually tells the U.S.A. to shove off, we can't arrest him. I'm sure you see the difficulty. Until midnight, he's the governor of Virginia and it's the sole job of the Virginia legislature to remove him. Unfortunately, they can't. After midnight, they can; but by then he'll have announced that the legislature no longer has any power. And if he has enough followers, it won't."

"*Does* he have enough followers?"

"I've spent an entire morning catching up on Charles Merriman," Ramsey Grant said. "He's never taken any risk that wasn't iron-clad. If he moves on with the declaration of independence, it means he knows he has the popular support to pull it off. He's been setting this up for a long time. And speaking of popular support, he may not be talking about tobacco, but you can bet hundreds of tobacco buyers and wholesalers and machinery manufacturers and warehouses and retail outlets are thinking about it awful hard. And you ought to know that the Newport News shipyard has been griping for three years because so many contracts have gone to Philadelphia. If Merriman goes out and hustles up some foreign business for the thrice-cursed shipyard, Newport News'll fall down at his feet and worship him."

"Ramsey . . . how do we know he hasn't talked to other elected officials?"

"Huh," Ramsey Grant said, sounding amused. Alexander Wade chewed on the inside of his lip. He needed to know who that FBI agent was, and what information he'd gathered; and Ramsey Grant had little incentive to tell him. He decided, with regret, to sacrifice his highly valuable contact within the FBI—the associate deputy director of investigations, who fed him useful information, for a price. He'd spent the last twelve hours trying to think of another way to twist Grant's arm.

He said, "I don't think the American people would be thrilled to discover that you issued orders for the infiltration of both a peaceful religious group and a state government."

Ramsey Grant sat up suddenly. Wade could see the possibilities tick through his mind, with an almost visible click as he settled on the obvious name. *The FBI*, he thought, *will be getting a new associate deputy director of investigations.*

The attorney general leaned back again, with a wide slow grin. "I see," the attorney general said. "I give you what we've discovered, and you don't tell the voting public that I authorized the infiltration of the California Institute for Theonomic Law? A legal act, by the way."

"Yes. But intrusive and highly unpopular. And I'm not sure that putting an agent in Merriman's Capitol is even legal. I would have to check," Wade said, thoughtfully. "It might be a highly public endeavor."

"Huh," Grant said again. "And what do *I* get out of this?"

"Ah," Wade said. Allen Preszkoleski had come up with the outline of a plan, and his aides were filling in the details at this very moment. He held up a finger. "First, you tell us where Merriman's planning to declare independence. Second, you send four agents down to arrest him. Instead of arranging to delay him until after midnight so that the legislature can assemble and impeach him, we'll let him declare independence and arrest him two minutes afterward. A two-minute independence won't hurt the presidency—"

"What do I get?" Grant repeated.

"You get your federal trial. You can play the guy in the white hat on national TV for weeks and weeks."

Grant thought this over. He said, at last, "It's a risk, Alex. If we use the FBI instead of letting the Virginia legislature handle this, we'll be making a tacit admission that—if just for those two minutes—the constitution of Virginia is no longer in effect. You'll be recognizing Virginia as an independent state."

"For two minutes, I'll take the gamble," Wade said. "The philosophers can fight that one out after we've got Charles Merriman in custody. What's the agent's code name, Grant?"

Ramsey Grant balanced his options for a moment, and then nodded. "Patrick," he said.

"As in Henry?"

"Yeah."

"Very funny," Wade said, sourly. "Now, let me see the file."

FIFTEEN HOURS AFTER that clandestine agreement, the attorney general and the secretary of defense sat in the Roosevelt Room, waiting to see the president. George Lewis put his head through the door, and both men rose immediately.

"He's ready," George said. "Please don't mention the *Post*. He read it first thing this morning and I've just gotten him calmed down."

The *Washington Post* headline had read, *The Second President to Lose a State*. Wade nodded, walking solemn-faced into the yellow room behind Ramsey Grant's thin height. The president himself was looking drawn. His pale skin stretched over his high cheekbones, and lines had carved themselves into his forehead, under the elegant silver shock of hair. A fire burned in the Oval Office grate.

"Good morning, gentlemen," he said. "I don't like the sound of the news reports. They're all digging up various abuses of states' rights and wondering why no one's tried this before. And the Balder issue's not playing. Merriman's too well liked, and his supporters know that nobody can control him. Can't we find something else?"

"We may not need to," Wade said. "We have a plan."

"Yes?"

Wade looked over at Grant.

"Sir," said the attorney general, "we have an FBI agent working as one of Charles Merriman's aides."

"Excuse me?"

"The Cult Infiltration Act gives the FBI the authority to investigate any religious or cultic group which we think may pose a danger—"

"Yes, I've heard of it. Why wasn't I informed?"

"We didn't think the information worth your attention, sir," Grant said, gritting his teeth. The truth was that the president didn't like to hear details that might influence domestic policy until they were confirmed, double-checked, and ready for concrete and immediate action. So far, the procedure had worked. He had conducted his foreign affairs with dazzling success; he knew every ridge and wrinkle in the bumpy affairs of the former Eastern Bloc countries. In the past, Alexander Wade and Ramsey Grant had worked with George Lewis to produce domestic policies, and presented their boss with conclusions, not questions.

The president asked, "You had an FBI agent sitting on top of a secession, and didn't think it worth mentioning?"

"Sir, there was absolutely no warning—"

"Apart from Merriman's personal relationship with Kenneth Balder?"

"Yes, sir. But there was no hint that it would turn into this—"

"But you were concerned enough about the California Institute of Theonomic Law to keep track of Kenneth Balder's contacts?" The president's voice was rising upward.

Ramsey Grant cleared his throat. He said, "Sir, we got interested in CITL by accident. Two years ago a man who once belonged to the Living Sacrifices moved to California and started to work for the institute. We followed him out because we suspected him of involvement in two abortion-clinic bombings. I've brought you his file, Mr. President—"

Wade had read this file the night before. It detailed the activities of one Larry Hamilton, a member of the radical anti-abortion group, Living Sacrifices. The Living Sacrifices had been one of the first groups investigated by the FBI under the Cult Authorization Act; the group picketed the homes of abortion providers and one of their members had been implicated and finally arrested in the deaths of two doctors in Nevada. Larry Hamilton, a Norfolk member, had written several pamphlets in support of what the group called "justified homicide," and had twice been arrested for distributing those leaflets too close to the White House. When Hamilton had departed from Virginia to apply for a job at CITL, the FBI had followed him. Hamilton had a low-level job as a data processor at the California Institute, and CITL was apparently unaware of his militant background. At this moment, he was still peacefully typing update letters in the institute's San Diego office building.

But the FBI, keeping tabs on Larry Hamilton, had gradually grown interested in CITL itself and its radical theories of government. The bureau director had authorized an infiltration of the institute, and an agent began work as a travel coordinator in Kenneth Balder's personal office. When Balder first flew east to visit Charles Merriman two years ago, a second agent—a thin blond veteran from a Baptist family who looked fifteen years younger than his real age of forty-three—had been sent to the mansion, on the suggestion of Ramsey Grant himself. The president tossed the file down.

"Your Richmond agent is bloody useless," he said coldly.

"Merriman planned this secession entirely on his own time," Ramsey Grant said. "Our agent is one of his aides. He'd heard nothing. Sir, even the Cult Infiltration Act doesn't authorize us to investigate the personal life of a governor."

"Investigating the legislature is bad enough," snapped the president. "If this news gets out, do you know how it'll sound? All the sympathy Merriman's garnering is because of the public sentiment towards states' rights. If Virginians find out that the federal government had a spy in their own Capitol, to keep an eye on their elected governor—" He relapsed into silence.

"Sir," Alexander Wade said, "the point is, Merriman's out in the open now. Patrick—Grant's agent—has told us where the declaration of independence will take place."

"Where?"

"On one of the Civil War battlefields—Richmond Battlefield Park, at midnight." Wade briefly outlined the plan to arrest Merriman. The president listened, his chin sunk on his chest.

"Who are we using?" he said at last.

Ramsey Grant said, "The FBI will send four agents for the arrest."

"Well," said the president, sourly, "thanks very much for your cooperation." He shifted his weight slightly so that he faced Wade directly.

"You'll go," he said. "I need someone I can trust."

"Sir," Ramsey Grant began, "the secretary of defense is not the correct—"

"We'll make him correct. The Pentagon's in Virginia, isn't it? This is a matter of national defense."

Wade shook his head. "If anyone sees me," he said, "it'll make things ten times worse. We can send an assistant secretary."

"You," the president said, unreasonably. "You're a civilian. There's no legal problem. We'll use a Maryland National Guard helicopter and set you down at Richmond International Airport, Alex. And as for you—" This was directed to Ramsey Grant: "If I go down because of this, I promise I'll take you with me."

Ramsey Grant said nothing. Wade, watching his lean face, heard the flicker of thought behind his eyes as clearly as a shout. *I'm not losing my career over Charles Merriman's temper tantrums.* He sympathized with the sentiment. Grant caught Wade's stare and turned his face toward the window. The bare limbs of the trees outside the Oval Office were white in the weak spring sunshine.

"Gentlemen," the president said, "let's get to work."

CHAPTER 6

Tuesday, March 19, 11 A.M.

B
Y ELEVEN IN THE MORNING, Margaret Franklin had put in almost a full day of work. She straightened up, feeling the ache of six hours' bending in her back and shoulders. The arched greenhouses were full of the dark scent of earth; one long wire table held budding pansies, but every other surface was covered with dirt-filled flats, potting soil speckled by tiny upthrusting blades of green.

She had been up since well before sunrise. The last few hours of the night had been broken and restless. Every time she drifted into sleep, she found herself back in the California courtroom. Sometimes she was merely watching, as Ken saw his character dissected in front of his eyes; sometimes she sat on the stand and helped. The dreams were crowded with noise and nonsense. For some reason, Matthew was sitting on the front row of the spectator seats in his guard dress uniform.

Finally she rolled groggily out of bed, padded into the kitchen, made coffee, and went out onto the front porch. The March air was dark and cold, but she could smell spring rising up from the ground. She sat down on the porch swing and folded her hands around the warm cup and composed her thoughts. This was her ritual, the time when she emptied out her mind and inspected its contents and put it back into order. During her hour of morning introspection, she could examine her life and judge how it was lining up with her own personal creed, a faith assembled from bits and pieces of all the world religions she'd considered and rejected. She had never believed in a God who interfered in human affairs; to her, that was a cop-out, an excuse for people to indulge in weakness and wait to be bailed out. She believed in an order, rules established by some divine spirit or force. Inexorable laws that everyone had to live by, or pay the price.

She stilled herself, and brought the first law of her personal creed to the front of her mind.

Unsparing honesty with myself.

Be honest, she told herself sternly. *You feel like something monumental is about to happen because Kenneth Balder is coming to Virginia. It has nothing to do with Charles Merriman and his fights with Washington.*

Compassionate honesty with other people.

I never felt anything more for Matthew than respect, and gratitude, and friendship. But I married him, and found myself bound to him by loyalty and guilt—so strongly that I could never leave him or tell him the whole truth.

Integrity in all my actions.

And I still owe Matthew the truth about his death. I have to uncover the reasons for his murder. I owe it to him, and to Garrett. It's the least I can do for a man who loved me without question and without reservation for twenty-three years. I can't let Ken distract me. Not until I'm finished.

Margaret fixed her eyes on the horizon, where darkness was giving way to a faint gray light. Every action had a consequence. If you followed the rules, the future unfolded in front of you without wrinkles. If you broke them, a wrinkle was likely to run unevenly through the rest of your existence. Her own life proved it. She had broken the rules over two decades ago. She had lied because she felt betrayed, and she'd married a man she didn't love. She'd spent more than two decades trying to smooth out the wrinkle. She'd been loyal to Matthew, and loyal to her son. Even when Kenneth Balder was released, she had refused to contact him.

She had first seen Ken across a crowded college cafeteria, tall and conspicuous, big hands and feet promising even greater size and his blond hair pulled into a defiant ponytail. Even then, twenty-five years ago, she had thought, *He has the eyes and mouth of a prophet.* Not a crusader, with a sword and shield and an army behind him, but an empty-handed man shouting truth to a deaf crowd. For two tempestuous years he had been the core of her life, the center of every thought and desire. Even now, the syllables of his name still brought back a sickening flood of grief and love and fear, the smell of his skin and the sound of his voice. The months after Mary Miranda's death had been punctuated by her hasty marriage to Matthew one shining day in a gray horrible sea of weeks. She and Matthew had left California and come east as far as they could, and Ken had gone to jail.

Now he was coming to Virginia; and Virginia was full of rumors of war.

THE HANDS OF HER WATCH were moving toward noon, and the day's work was almost done. She stripped off her gloves and headed back toward the front of the greenhouse. She had a slateful of commercial deliveries to make, but they could wait until tomorrow. On Tuesdays, she visited the chief of police.

In the house, she changed her clothes and inspected herself carefully in the mirror. In college, she had lived in denim and flowered T-shirts, and she still spent most of her working days in sweatshirts and jeans. But when the nursery began to flourish, she had gone out and bought two extremely expensive suits at one of Richmond's haughtiest dress shops. This one was a deep soft blue, and the jacket and skirt lay against her figure with quiet elegance. *It ought to,* she thought, gathering her light brown hair up into a knot at the nape of her neck. She still felt faintly guilty when she considered the price. But the business owners she dealt with didn't argue or haggle when she wore that particular suit. Oddly, Matthew hadn't liked it. Maybe it hadn't fit into his picture of her—the round-faced, devastated teenager he had rescued.

INTERSTATE 64 bore its usual moderate load, a thin stream of late-morning traffic heading into Richmond. The city's towers crawled into view with reassuring normality. Margaret loosened her fingers on the steering wheel, and some of the uncomfortable apprehension began to seep away. Virginia might be on the verge of a new era, but its lawyers and bank tellers were heading to work as usual. She put her foot on the accelerator and the old nursery truck roared around the curve that would bring her face-to-face with the city's skyline.

The tall executive buildings rose into sight, and she slammed on her brakes in amazement. Traffic stretched out in elongated lines in every direction. Straight ahead, on the road that led past the Coliseum into Richmond's heart, cars idled as far as she could see.

She inched into the city with painful slowness. When the signal lights of a parked car began to blink just ahead of her, she slowed and waited for the spot to empty. The city was crawling with police officers; two cruised by while she maneuvered the unwieldy truck over onto the side of Fifth Street.

She fed the meter and started toward the headquarters of the Richmond chief of police on foot, cutting across the Coliseum parking lot. The March morning was clear and windy, the sidewalks crowded with excited Richmonders. She made her way through the mass of people toward the well-known dingy office building, climbed up the stairs, and pushed open the glass doors. The familiar bureaucratic smell of wax and mediocre coffee floated to meet her.

"Mrs. Franklin!"

The receptionist was actually standing up. Margaret looked at her with surprise. Every Tuesday afternoon, she climbed these steps with the sure knowledge that she would sit in the waiting room for several hours, exposed to the pitying eyes of passing workers, until some underling could spare the time to sit with her and tell her, yet again, that the Richmond city police had uncovered no trace of a conspiracy; that the stress of Jerry Tindell's continued freedom was undoubtedly affecting the clarity of her thought and no, the case hadn't been closed. Detective Stott probably kept the file on Matthew Franklin's death right on the top of his desk. . . .

She said warily, "Morning, Sandy."

"You're early today. Coffee?"

"Er . . . sure. Shall I wait?"

"The chief will be free in just a minute. Why don't you sit right there?"

Margaret sat down, taken completely off guard. The room was filled with a tight, suppressed excitement. In the corridors beyond the front desk, she could hear hurried feet and low voices. Sandy, trim and middle-aged, had barely returned with coffee before another secretary appeared with a murmured message.

"The chief asked to see you as soon as you came in," Sandy explained, handing the coffee over. "He's ready now. If you'll go with Marie . . ."

Margaret found herself following the blonde Marie into the depths of the building. In another moment she was in Daniel Caprio's office, awkwardly shifting the coffee so that she could shake the hand he held out to her. The Richmond chief of police was a tall, round-faced man nearing sixty—practical, short-tempered, his voice graveled with constant overuse. She hadn't seen him for over a year.

"Mrs. Franklin," he said. "I may have good news for you. Sit down."

Margaret sat down. She was aware that her face was set in cold unresponsive lines. It was disconcerting to spend months fighting city hall, only to have it leap up and greet you just as the struggle seemed hopeless. She knew Daniel Caprio was a good and decent man, a Presbyterian elder and a tough cop. He was an even tougher administrator, and he had declined to spend any more time on Matthew's hopeless death.

"I'm sorry I haven't seen you for several months," the chief began.

"Yes," Margaret said, "your schedule doesn't allow much time for lost causes, does it?" She could hear the plain bitterness in the question.

Caprio narrowed his eyes at her, visibly deciding to do away with pleasantries. He said bluntly, "Mrs. Franklin, if I'd had *my* way, the man who murdered your husband would already be locked away. Detective Stott did his best to get an arrest. You know that as well as I do."

"None of you listened to anything I had to say," Margaret countered. "Other than that, I'm sure you all did your best."

"Let's not waste time trading blame," Caprio snapped. "We followed every solid lead—"

"You've never paid any attention to how odd it was that Matthew should come straight home from duty and ask me to go to Oregon Hill with him at five in the morning."

"You went without asking him why," the chief countered.

Margaret said doggedly, "It was one of our promises, that we'd do whatever the other asked, without asking for explanations." She'd been through this before. She was determined to go through it again, as many times as proved necessary.

"And because you didn't ask for an explanation, that whole line of questioning winds up in a dead end."

"It isn't a dead end. You never investigated Clint Larsen. He lived in Oregon Hill."

"On a different street."

"He lived on Oak. We were on Elm. Matthew might have made a mistake."

Chief Caprio slammed his hand down on the desk. "Mrs. Franklin," he growled, "we've been through this a dozen times. When your husband was killed, Sergeant Larsen was at the MCV emergency room with his daughter, who was suffering from a severe asthma attack. *He had nothing to do with Matthew Franklin's murder.* If you insist on going around and around in this circle, nothing I'm going to say will help you." He leaned forward. "Get your eyes off this conspiracy thing and look at what's happening around you. Governor Merriman's set to reform the court system, top to bottom. We're finally going to get some justice in this city."

"You mean . . . you think he can pull this off?"

"Yes, I do. The governor's got support from local governments and police departments all across the state. As soon as he declares Virginia's independence, I'm going to recommend to him that we re-open the whole issue of Jerry Tindell's guilt. The case was on his mind, you know. When it hit all the national news broadcasts, I met with him. I never saw a man so furious. He wasn't mad at the detective who opened Tindell's girlfriend's suitcase without a proper warrant. He was mad at the system. He said, 'Justice is the highest calling we have as human beings. How can such a miscarriage happen in a state that was founded only three hundred years ago on the laws of God?' I told him how. And now we're going to see some reform."

"A new investigation?" Margaret asked. "Or just a witch-hunt for Jerry Tindell?"

"Witch-hunt? There's no doubt that Tindell pulled the trigger." Caprio flipped open a folder that lay on his desk. "I've pulled all the reports out again. You saw movement in the dark when your husband fell." He jabbed his finger against the top paper in the file. "You go running to a nearby convenience store for help. In the meantime, your husband's body is robbed. The day afterward we pick up a drug dealer who says he saw Tindell at the scene. Three days later, Stott sees Tindell with Franklin's distinctive wallet. What more do you want?"

"My husband told my son—"

"Yes, Mrs. Franklin. We've been over that. Hearsay from the deceased, and *vague* hearsay at that."

"Tindell's motive was completely unconvincing—"

"Jerry Tindell's brother had just been killed in a confrontation with Richmond police. Tindell was high, and your husband was in uniform and looked like a cop, in the dark."

Margaret set her cold, untasted coffee on the edge of Chief Caprio's desk. She knew the evidence was convincing. But Tindell, interrogated by police, had insisted that he'd stumbled across the body and robbed it. It was a sordid and disreputable story, but the police version of events didn't explain Matthew Jefferson's presence in Oregon Hill at five in the morning.

Chief Caprio cleared his throat.

"Mrs. Franklin," he said, "look at it this way. If we re-open the case, the whole series of events will be examined again. If there's a conspiracy, we'll find it. Our hands won't be tied by procedural details. We can discover the truth. You don't trust the system, do you, Mrs. Franklin?"

"I haven't trusted the system for twenty-five years," Margaret said bleakly.

"You wait," Caprio said. "You wait, and watch, and testify when we call you. The system's going to change. This time, it's going to work."

When she left police headquarters, Margaret stood on the sidewalk for a long moment, ignoring the pedestrians who pushed past her. She felt slightly dazed. Daniel Caprio's last words had been a promise. If

Charles Merriman won his fight with Washington, Matthew's murder would be fully investigated. She had to convince the new investigation to go after the guard connection, before Jerry Tindell was convicted and Matthew's case was closed for the second time. The discovery of the truth about Matthew's murder was her chance for atonement, her only opportunity to make up for her lack of love.

A cold March wind gusted into her face. Capitol Square was just a few blocks ahead. Driven by curiosity, she crossed at the signal and walked hastily toward the center of Virginia's government. The white walls of the Capitol loomed up ahead of her, with the Executive Mansion tucked in behind it.

Capitol Park was closed, and the sidewalk in front of the locked iron gates was heaving with people. Police surrounded the common, their faces set grimly outward toward the crowd. She wriggled her way into the excited, sign-waving mass. Just ahead of her a tall, dark-haired man in his forties was arguing with a policeman. The officer's shoulders were pressed back against the iron rods of the gate.

"I've got to see Charles right away—"

"Governor Merriman is only seeing appointments today, sir. He'll reopen Capitol Park after the deadline passes at midnight tonight."

"Don't you know who I am? I've been an elected member of the Virginia legislature for ten years, and now the Assembly building is locked and I can't get into my office—"

"Sir, the Virginia legislature is not currently in session."

"But you're keeping me out of public property!"

"Sir, the governor has declared this building temporarily closed to the public, by virtue of the emergency powers given him by the Code of Virginia, Section 44, Paragraph 146.16."

The representative paused, thrown off balance. Margaret stared over his shoulder at the white pillars of the Capitol. The portico was empty, but she could see lights in the windows. Ken might already be here in Virginia, after twenty-five years of absence. She might at this moment be standing mere yards away from him, separated by a single wall.

She wrested her thoughts away from the possibility. She had spent more than twenty years trying to live out the loyalty she had promised Matthew; and that task wouldn't be finished until she performed this last duty for her husband. Instead she tried to picture a Virginia without ties to the rest of the country. Her imagination immediately produced a montage of scenes from late-night TV movies: armed civilians lying behind barns, storm troops in the streets, cities burning on the network news.

BACK AT THE NEW KENT FARMHOUSE, she carefully hung up the blue suit, took off the silver earrings and bracelet, and sat down on her bed in her slip. The sun was creeping down toward the western horizon. Garrett would be on duty. She reached for the telephone that sat on her bedside table and dialed, impulsively. Almost immediately a crisp voice said, as always, "Good afternoon, Virginia Air Guard."

Margaret hung up. This was absurd. The air national guard was carrying on in happy ignorance of Charles Merriman's plots. The governor's threat of secession was undoubtedly a publicity ploy, just as the network commentators had suggested. And Garrett wasn't a child; he was twenty-two, and his mother had no business checking to see whether or not he was at work.

But if Merriman doesn't secede, Matthew's murder will stay unsolved. I'll have to keep fighting.

Suddenly, such thoughts were unbearable. For the first time in two years, she found herself completely weary of the struggle for justice. She was appalled at herself. She pulled her jeans on, struggling to recover the passion of bitterness that had burned inside her since Matthew crumpled to the street with a bullet in his chest.

CHAPTER 7

Tuesday, March 19, just before midnight

THIRTY-SEVEN MINUTES before Charles Merriman's declaration of independence, Alexander Wade was in a helicopter over Virginia in a screaming March storm. Rain was bucketing down all around them. In the swirling blackness he could barely see the runway lights, flashing below as the chopper headed for the helipad on the far side of the airport. The helicopter lurched sideways in a violent gust of wind, and Wade clutched at the sides of his seat. His fingers were stiff with cold, and his stomach was twisting ominously. This storm had broken at seven; it was howling down the eastern coast from Maryland all the way to South Carolina.

The pilot brought the chopper into a vertical descent. As it touched onto the pad, Wade was unbuckling his seatbelt, reaching for the door. He couldn't see beyond the blowing silver sheet of rain. It beat into his face as he crouched beneath the whirling blades, making blindly for the wall of light cast up into the rain by the spots at the edge of the helo pad. A hand gripped his arm.

"This way, Mr. Secretary." The agent was yelling through the storm. Wade stumbled through the pouring water, across the lights, until his hands hit the smooth surface of the car. He fumbled for the handle and slid into the welcome dry silence. An agent shut the door behind him. The other two climbed into the front.

Wade huddled in the backseat, shaking with cold and airsickness. The car, a plain blue Chevy Caprice, had been provided by the bureau office on Greencourt Road; it was equipped with a powerful engine and unmarked plates, and it lurched beneath him, gathering speed as it headed from the airport. Grant had proposed using the Virginia National Guard for this arrest, but Alexander Wade had vetoed that idea.

"That's all we need," he said, "to draw out a confrontation between the president and the governor as to who has ultimate authority over the state guard."

"The president does," Grant said.

"I guarantee you eight out of ten national guardsmen wouldn't agree. We'll just treat this as though Merriman's acting entirely on his own, out in left field without any company. It'll make it much easier for everyone to settle back into their places after the arrest and pretend they never thought much of the idea in the first place."

So the FBI was the only agency involved in this arrest. The Bureau of Alcohol, Tobacco, and Firearms, which had more experience with antigovernment forces than any other agency, had bowed out, pointing out that there was absolutely no proof of any firearms violations anywhere in this entire situation, that tobacco had never actually been mentioned by the revolutionaries, and that Charles Merriman was a well-known teetotaler. ATF had become wary and short-tempered after the Waco firestorm.

They were winding down Route 60 now, going through the old warehouse district of Richmond toward Battlefield Park. The narrow streets were black with rain. The agent at the wheel slid carefully through the red lights that blocked them.

Wade lifted the padded sleeve of his parka away and peered at his watch. Eleven twenty. They were scheduled to be at the park well before Merriman's speech began. With any luck, his network would already be in place.

At seven-thirty that evening, Alexander Wade had finally extricated himself from the White House on the plea of snatching three hours of sleep in his office. He had spent those three hours with Allen Preszkoleski and two of Allen's most trusted staff members, watching them make telephone calls behind locked doors. Exhaustion dragged at his eyes and hands. But before ten P.M. the aides had contacted and convinced a quorum of the Virginia legislature—the Democrats and moderate Republicans who loathed Charles Merriman and all his white-knight reforms. They were assembling now in Fredericksburg, waiting for the stroke of midnight to begin the process of declaring Charles Merriman unfit to govern. He had no intention of allowing the governor his two minutes of independence. In his mind, the risk of giving Virginia that brief span of independence was far greater than he had let on to Ramsey Grant.

With the rump legislature in place, Wade dispatched three truckloads of off-duty MPs down the long green stretch of I-95. They had orders to arrange themselves around the edges of the crowd at Battlefield Park, armed with blanks and smoke-bombs. The legislature couldn't possibly run through the procedural maze of voting Merriman out of office in under half-an-hour, so it would be twelve-thirty before Charles Merriman was powerless. At midnight, as Merriman began to speak, the carefully engineered riot would begin. Wade was counting on the reflexes of a trained bodyguard; when shots were heard, Merriman would be removed by his security detail, and it would take at least thirty minutes for order to be restored.

And by twelve-thirty, the legislature would have acted under the authorization of the constitution of the Commonwealth. Charles Merriman would no longer be the sitting governor of Virginia. He would be, temporarily, a private citizen, and the immunity from civil arrest promised by Virginia law would no longer apply. A quick check assured Wade that the governor had not bothered to apply for a crowd permit. And although Wade could not get through to the Richmond city police, the Park Service could arrest Merriman for illegal assembly, since the crowd would be swarming over a historic site. By one A.M., the revolution would be over, Charles Merriman locked safely away in a holding cell for the night. Ramsey Grant would have to live with the disappointment of losing his televised trial. As far as Wade was concerned, the four agents he had with him were solely a backup force, a second option. But if he'd told Grant that, the attorney general would never have agreed to supply the men.

The blue car swung right, around the curve that led to the great green expanse of the battlefield. Wade had told the Park Service to pick up Kenneth

Balder as well. He had not yet found a charge on which Balder could be held, but he felt a sour tightness in his throat whenever he pictured the man boarding a plane back to California.

He sat up, peering into the blackness. There was the vast empty space of the park ahead of him, and the points of light dancing against the hillside, created by the television cameras and journalists. The driver slowed. In ones and twos, and then in larger knots, walkers blocked the road in front of them. The sedan's headlights illuminated the grass verge, crowded with parked cars. So Merriman had a big turnout for his speech. Wade noted that at least three of the trucks they passed had no license plates.

"Here," he said curtly.

"Sir?"

"We'll walk."

"Yes, sir."

The agent maneuvered the big sedan into a spot on the muddy grass. Wade scrambled out. The cold rain hit him in the face, and he slipped in the trampled earth. Headlights behind him illuminated the blacktop road, with his shadow stretching away ahead of him. More cars were pulling onto the verge. A constant stream of people on foot poured toward the battlefield. He caught a wide-eyed stare from a passing woman, and pulled his parka's hood over his head. They trudged through the rain toward the lights. The mass of people around them was growing thicker. Up ahead, to the right, ribbons separated the parked cars from a huge grassy clearing. They followed the flow of the crowd around the barrier, into a huge milling pond of watchers on the battlefield itself. All around them, voices were raised. Against the trees, at the far edge of the battlefield, batteries of bright lights illuminated the dripping dark green leaves. White TV trucks glinted on the access road beyond. Striped umbrellas bloomed over the heads of reporters like parasols at a garden party. A CNN camera crew went scurrying past, heading toward a low wooden platform that had been built at the far end of the field, just under the trees. It stood illuminated and empty.

"Okay," Wade said quietly. "Around to the right. Let's get closer." It was eleven forty-nine. Merriman should be in view any moment, and the riot would begin in eleven minutes. They inched through the press of raincoats and plastic boots, drawing closer to the front of the crowd.

Around the platform, sudden activity erupted. Reporters were scurrying suddenly back to their cameras. The front of the crowd began to sway and heave.

"Sir!"

The youngest agent had grabbed him by the elbow and was shaking it, frantically. "Sir!"

"What?"

"Sir, he's not here!"

"Not here yet, you mean?"

"Sir—"

Behind the youngest agent, a thin blond man in a gray suit said briefly, "Patrick, sir. He's gone. This was a diversion." His voice was matter-of-fact and cold.

Wade swore, efficiently.

"You're Patrick?"

"Yes, sir."

"He sent you here?"

"All his aides are here. We understood that the governor and his bodyguard would be coming in by helicopter ten minutes before midnight—"

"Where is he?"

"Sir, no one knows. All the TV stations and newspapers were given this location. All his staff. I sent out a hundred personal invitations from the governor myself. He must have guessed that we'd try to arrest him—"

"He's got to declare independence now," Wade said. "While he's still governor. And it's got to be public."

Rain was in his eyes. Wade scrubbed at his face, resisting the impulse to swear again. Eleven fifty-nine. Suddenly a shot went off, just to his right. Smoke billowed up from the back of the mass. The crowd heaved up against him and he stumbled, clutching at Patrick to keep his footing. The man was wearing a nine-millimeter under his gray suit jacket. The shouts were so loud now that Wade couldn't hear the words the agent at his side was bellowing at him. He'd started a riot on Park Service land, and his watch read 12:00:00.

He pushed Patrick away and looked wildly around him. Nearby, a dark young reporter was shouting into a microphone, in front of a truck with a satellite dish on top. He strode to the truck, past the reporter, and yanked the door open. A startled technician in earphones looked up.

"Hey, buddy, we're broadcasting here—"

Wade climbed in and slammed the door behind him, shutting out the astonished face of the young reporter, the five puzzled FBI agents, and the roar of the crowd.

"You've got reception?" he demanded.

"What do you think you're doing?" the technician asked indignantly. He was a short stocky man, and the inside of the cramped van reeked with cigarette smoke.

"Turn the local news on."

"We *are* the local news," the technician snapped. "That's Jim Redfield of Channel Twelve, out there."

"Not Richmond. Get one of the eastern cities. Who's got a station in Norfolk?"

"Listen, you—"

"I'm the secretary of defense for the United States of America—"

"I'm Elvis. This is just my night job."

Wade yanked the door open. The reporter, gamely carrying on with the broadcast in the middle of a rising riot, turned involuntarily toward the movement and his mouth and eyes widened.

"That's Alexander Wade!" he blurted. "Mr. Secretary, could I get a comment from you? Were you expecting this? What's Defense's role in this? Here, Mike, get that camera over here—"

Wade slammed the door in Jim Redfield's face. "Now," he said to the technician, "get me a Norfolk station."

The technician shrugged. "Channel Three," he said. "They're on the other side of Williamsburg. Here." He swiveled to his switchboard, and in a moment the monitor against the back wall flicked away from Jim Redfield's indignant face, to lines and then a clear color picture.

"Bless my soul," the technician said, astonished.

"Williamsburg," Wade said grimly. "The first capital of the United States."

Charles Merriman was standing in Colonial Williamsburg, in front of the old Capitol, in the cul-de-sac at the end of Duke of Gloucester Street. There was a small crowd in front of him, and a single camera. A portable spotlight cast a bright halo around him and illuminated the deep red brick rising behind him. Above the wall, a lantern lit the top spire of the Capitol building. Rain fell gently through the light.

"— fellow Virginians," he was saying. "I call you this because it is an identity that comes before any other. I speak of the rights of states, but also of history. Fellow Virginians, we stand on the first English settlement in America. In 1606, Virginia was settled for the purpose of spreading the Christian religion. We stand on the site of the first representative legislature in America. Here, rule by the people was first tested and pronounced to be a success. And here also, a faraway government of tyrants removed right after right, and enforced wrong after wrong, until another governor of Virginia rose and said to his people: 'Is life so dear or peace so sweet as to be purchased at the price of chains and slavery? Forbid it, Almighty God!'"

Alexander Wade clutched at his head. The technician remarked, "Not a good day for you, eh?" and grinned.

Charles Merriman said, "These are the words of Virginia Governor Patrick Henry, speaking out against the chains of unjust taxation; and rejecting the slavery of a central government that regulated the commerce, the policies, the bearing of arms, and even the beliefs of those who supported it through those very taxes. A Virginia statesman, Richard Henry Lee, asked the Continental Congress for a Declaration of Independence. And I now quote from that Declaration." He bent his head, slightly.

I'll skin that agent while he screams, Alexander Wade thought. *Does he think he was put in the governor's office to fetch tea for Charles Merriman?*

The old words came clearly from Merriman's mouth. "'Prudence, indeed, will dictate that governments long established should not be changed for light and transient causes; and accordingly all experience hath shown, that mankind are more disposed to suffer, while evils are sufferable, than to right themselves by abolishing the forms to which they are accustomed. But when a long train of abuses and usurpations, pursuing invariably the same object evinces a design to reduce them under absolute despotism, it is their right, it is their duty, to throw off such government.'"

Wade leaned forward. At the edge of the TV picture, he could just see the back of a tall man in a dark raincoat. His blond head was bent toward the ground, his profile invisible. His shoulders were broader than memory painted them, his height greater; but Wade would have recognized Kenneth Balder anywhere.

"Today we declare that it has become necessary for the citizens of Virginia to throw off such government. Therefore, as the elected governor of the Commonwealth, I do solemnly declare that the Commonwealth is, and of right ought to be, a free and independent state; that it is absolved from all allegiance to the United States of America, and that all political connection between it and the United States is and ought to be totally dissolved; and that as a free and independent state, it has full power to levy war, conclude peace, contract alliances, establish commerce, and to do all other acts and things which independent states may of right do."

TV lights were shining into Merriman's face. He shielded his eyes slightly with his hand.

"Virginia now flies the banner of the Reformed American States," he said. "This is not the time to read our entire constitution. It will be publicly distributed in the next few days. I will summarize. The Puritans who founded America knew that government based on any standard but God's revealed will would eventually founder to relativity and self-interest. We have seen it happen here. And so the Reformed American States will restrict itself to the proper, threefold role of government: To protect human life, as is written in chapter nine of the Book of Genesis; to defend the law-abiding from the lawbreaker, according to the thirteenth chapter of Romans; and to maintain a peaceful and orderly society, as laid out in chapter two of the Book of First Timothy. All other functions will be privatized. And in order to carry out these tasks, the state may not require from its people more than God Himself asks in the tithe. The tax in the Reformed American States will be nine percent. A flat tax. No sales tax, no property tax, no tolls. That figure will not rise until God Himself raises His rates."

His voice had gone suddenly dry. Wade heard a rising murmur from the listeners in front of him. It grew into applause, then cheers; and then Charles Merriman was surrounded by a waving, grinning, back-slapping crowd.

"Turn that thing off," Wade said harshly.

"Are you kidding?" said the technician. "Greatest show since the Charles and Di divorce—"

Alexander Wade slammed the heel of his hand against the control and jerked open the door. The agents were pressed against the side of the truck in an attempt to escape the stampeding crowd.

"Come on," he said curtly. "We're finished here."

"Sir, the riot!"

"Let the park police handle it." The off-duty MPs had been ordered to shoot off the blanks and then remove themselves from the crowd. They would be heading back to the plain gray trucks that had carried them down to Richmond. Wade had no one with him but these five agents, and although they were armed, the sight of a Bureau weapon would do nothing but rocket the panic upward.

"There," he said. "The access road." He started through the trees toward the glimmer of streetlights on pavement. The agents stumbled along behind him. Branches slapped against him, soaking him with rain. The toothless legislature would be meeting now in Fredericksburg, unaware that Charles Merriman's two minutes of independence had stretched into infinity. Arrest now would mean a much greater use of force; and Merriman was surrounded with supporters. What if a single Virginian were injured. . . . or killed? He could see the pictures now, broadcast coast to coast; he could almost hear the rhetoric that would follow. *Did you think America was a free country? Just don't try to leave it!*

He said, out loud to the wet woods, "That was the shot heard 'round the world."

And to himself he added, *He's beaten us in the first round, Mr. President.*

CHAPTER 8

Wednesday, March 20, just after midnight

KENNETH BALDER STOOD IN THE RAIN with his breath rasping in his own ears and his hands shaking with adrenaline. He was barely aware of the water dripping into his eyes. When he turned to look down Duke of Gloucester Street, he could see the gathering growing by the moment, people running down the middle of the dim street to join the crowd in the cul-de-sac. Merriman's helicopter was sitting on the grassy field between the Williamsburg Capitol and Francis Street; the blades had begun to whirl. He felt the governor's grip on his shoulder.

"Come on!" Merriman shouted. "You and I should be out of this."

Hands were tugging at his clothes and arms. He freed himself from the press, half-running beside Merriman through the crowd sifting toward them. They ducked under the strong wind of the chopper's blades and scrambled in. As his foot left the ground, Balder felt the seat rise beneath him. The Capitol with its single lantern (*one if by land*, said some forgotten voice in his mind, *two if by sea*) and the growing crowd faded into the wet darkness beneath him.

"Well done," Merriman said, clapping him on the shoulder. "Well done. Not a sign of Washington! It was a brilliant idea, Ken. Brilliant! We've done it, haven't we?" He let loose a sudden whoop of sheer delight. His dark hair shone with rain and sweat. "We've done it! I'm the governor of the Reformed American States, for however long God grants us. How did you know there would be a spy in the mansion?"

"Because you called *me* in," Kenneth Balder said. He had to raise his voice above comfortable levels, to be heard over the chopper's churning blades. The helicopter lurched sideways in a sudden gust of wind, and Balder felt his stomach lurch in response. "They follow me around. I've had an agent at CITL for two years."

"Oh?" Merriman's voice changed, fractionally. "How did you know?"

"Instinct," Balder said. He had been twenty-one when he entered the California state prison system, a privileged adolescent who had never been treated roughly in his life. Prison had almost broken him, but he'd developed a weirdly accurate sense for being watched.

"I had no idea the FBI took such an interest in you," Merriman said. Ahead of them, the chopper pilot had his hand to his radio earpiece.

"Sir!" he said.

"Yes?"

"Message for you, sir, from the adjutant general."

Merriman took the earpiece, awkwardly. "What is it, Joe?" he asked, and listened to the nearly inaudible answer. "Yes," he said at last. "Of course. Let 'em try to deny us that. You get the order out and I'll sign the papers in twenty minutes." Another pause. "They did? We didn't think of that. . . . Never mind. It ended well."

He shook the headset away and handed it back to the pilot.

"They're rioting in Battlefield Park," he said. "You were quite right. The FBI did try to stage an arrest. We did well to set up a false location. I'm mobilizing the guard."

"So soon?"

"We'd planned it for Thursday anyway," Merriman said reasonably, "and our weakest point was the possibility that the troops would be federalized before we could bring them out. Providence is working for us. We can legally mobilize the Virginia Guard in answer to a riot."

Kenneth Balder said slowly, "Did you arrange the riot?"

"Of course not," Merriman said indignantly.

Balder gazed at him thoughtfully. Engineered riots and manipulation of the public sentiment were things of the past; in a theonomic government, one did not resort to such tactics. He wondered whether Charles

Merriman had fully grasped this fact. Merriman said, raising his voice above the chopper, "Joe says the legislature tried to meet in Fredericksburg to remove me from office. We declared independence first. That's one in the eye for them." Merriman chuckled and added, "We'll have our first cabinet meeting in the morning. I'd like to appoint you my chief of staff. We've got to get that constitution ready for publication. And Governor Forbes from North Carolina has asked us for an update. I think I can convince him to come along with us."

"Governor—"

"Yes?"

"I've got personal business to take care of, first thing in the morning. I can't—"

"*Personal?*" Merriman repeated. His dark eyes were curious.

"It won't take me long, Governor, but it's very important. If we could meet at noon instead—"

"Certainly," Charles Merriman said. "Certainly. We can do without you until then. Anything I can help you with?"

Kenneth Balder shook his head.

"Well," Merriman said, after a fractional pause, "can I offer you a car?"

"I've got my own."

"You'll be sleeping at the mansion again?"

"Yes. Thank you, Governor."

"Certainly, Ken."

The chopper swung again, and a ball of ice pinged against the windscreen.

"Miserable weather," Merriman said. He was silent, the window beyond him reflecting his clean profile and the sweep of his dark hair. Balder looked away, out his own window. The ground below him was one massive slab of blackness. Rain and clouds obscured the lights of the Richmond suburbs. It was all dark down there.

HE SLEPT THAT NIGHT in the mansion's guest cottage, a two-story house with an iron-railed balcony overlooking its own walled garden, and

an open fireplace in the brick-floored kitchen. He woke before dawn to the
sound of logs being chunked into the fire. Merriman had provided him
with a housekeeper for his stay.

Balder dressed softly and let himself out into the garden, walking gingerly across the bricks to the door at the far end. He laid his hand on the
knob and found it locked. The wall was higher than his head. He stood for
awhile in the early morning dark, picturing himself climbing to freedom,
only to be caught, halfway over the wall, by the flashlight of a security
guard. Eventually he turned around and went back into the cottage.

"Good morning," Balder said carelessly, passing the kitchen.

The housekeeper, a slim young man in his thirties, said politely, "Good
morning, Dr. Balder. Will you be eating breakfast here?"

"Later. I'm going out for a walk."

"Yes, sir."

Balder strolled out the front door. A stocky security guard stood
squarely in the middle of the walkway that led from the guest cottage to
the side door of the mansion. The front lawn lay empty to his left. The
storm had cleared, and the air was cool and dry.

"I'm going for a walk," he said. Merriman had already replaced his
state police detail with guards from a private force called Westminster
Security. This guard wore the new badge, bearing the symbol of the
Reformed American States—a mountain wreathed with a stylized cloud
of smoke—and the motto of the new country. *Defend and execute.* Those were
the sole functions of the ideal government.

"Yes, Mr. Secretary. Officer Woodson will go with you." He gestured
toward the house, and another security guard appeared from the shadows.

"Not necessary." Balder could see a gleam of pink at the horizon now.

"Governor's orders, sir."

"Not this morning."

The guard paused, nonplused. His instructions had apparently not
included dealing with obstinacy on the part of the R.A.S.'s second-highest
official. Balder gave him a curt nod and walked past, reaching into his
pocket for the keys of the rental car, parked over behind the Capitol. He
could hear footsteps behind him. He let the keys settle back into his pocket

and redirected his steps, across the mansion lawn and out the side entrance to Capitol Park. The gates were unlocked this morning, and the trooper standing in the breach gave him a curt nod as he passed.

Balder came out on Broad Street and ambled along, breathing deeply. Ahead of him was a small pastry shop with newspaper boxes outside. He stopped, bought two papers, and went in. The shop was half-full, and although he earned a few curious glances from the well-dressed businessmen crowding the counter, no one spoke to him. He ordered coffee and an apple tart and settled himself at a small table in the corner. The *Washington Post's* headline read *Breaking Away: Virginia Dizzy With Freedom*, and the story featured an interview with an enthusiastic member of the Ashland Patriot's Militia and an unflattering photograph of Merriman. The *Times-Dispatch*, under James Macleod's direction, had chosen to run a front-page story about the virtues of a flat tax. Around him, conversation ebbed and flowed.

". . . nine-percent tax, I could fund that expansion—"

"Yes, but who'll you sell to?"

"Washington can't block exports from Virginia. I'm sure Merriman's thought of that already—"

Balder peered over the top of his paper. A thin man in a navy blue sweatshirt wandered through the door, cast a casual eye around the seats, and ordered coffee. He leaned against the counter waiting for his cup, positioned directly across from the door, his eyes fixed absently on the entrance. Outside the plate-glass window, a businessman with a briefcase waited for a bus which seemed to be a long time in coming.

"Reilly, Ace of Spies," Kenneth Balder muttered, under his breath. He fought down an insane desire to giggle, bounced twice on his seat in obvious discomfort, and retired to the men's room, leaving the newspapers open at his table and his fork still in the apple tart. He had intended to scramble out the window, but it proved to be a tiny rectangle high in the wall. Fortunately the bathroom itself had an exit door, prominently marked. A red alarm panel blocked the push-handle. He pulled out the pocketknife that hung on his key ring, carefully severed the yellow and blue wires that connected the alarm to the latch, and pushed the door soundlessly open. He was in an alley that led out between tall blank brick walls.

The alley decanted him onto Eleventh Street. He walked briskly along the sidewalk until he could flag a passing taxi. The driver peered at him suspiciously, but slowed to a stop.

Balder climbed into the backseat, and looked behind him as the taxi pulled away. The sidewalk was placidly empty of pursuers.

"Is there a car rental agency nearby?" he said.

"Havin' trouble?"

"More than you can imagine."

"Airport's only place open this time of morning. There's a car place there."

"Fine," Balder said.

"It's a pretty good ways, but you could get on the interstate real easy."

"Great. Take me to the airport."

He only half-listened as the driver chattered away about Merriman's declaration of independence and the prospects for lower taxes. When the taxi ride ended, he added a huge tip to the substantial fare.

"There you go," Balder said, seeing the man's astonished face. "And you only have to pay nine percent on that, so make sure you report it."

ON HIS SECOND RENTAL CAR OF THE REVOLUTION, Kenneth Balder emerged from Airport Drive and followed the blue markers to the interstate. The sun was rising directly ahead. He felt an unfamiliar surge of exhilaration and freedom. The next five hours were his alone, and there was no agent on his tail; the eyes of the United States and Charles Merriman alike had overlooked him. He took a right at the Providence Forge exit and found himself in the middle of silent green.

Franklin's Plants lay just beyond the exit. He had never been to the old farm, and he wondered for a moment if it would have been more appropriate to call first and ask Maggie for directions.

But the farm's exact address had been known to him for eighteen years. In prison, he'd pinned a map to the wall above his bunk, with the locations of everyone who'd betrayed him marked on it with colored pins. His cellmates—all but the last—had laughed at him.

Gonna go kill them when you get out, college boy?
No. I've never killed anyone.
Put you in here for no good reason, did they? Me too. All of us innocent as the day.
It was an accident.
So why the map?
Because it's all I have left.

The map had been burnt years ago. Part of beginning a new life and burying the old. But he hadn't been able to erase the New Kent farm from his memory as easily. As soon as he heard Maggie's voice the address rose irresistibly from the depths of his mind. *I-64 west from Richmond; take the Providence Forge exit to Route 155 south, then left on Route 118 for three miles.* The words had stayed with him; they meant Matthew, once closer than a blood brother, and Maggie, as lost to him as though she were dead.

The sign on the road, green and painted with a delicate tracery of white-and-red blossoms, read FRANKLIN'S PLANTS: FLOWERS AND SHRUBS FOR PRIVATE AND PUBLIC NEEDS. The pseudo-archaic wording harmonized nicely with Matthew's name. He turned into the long country lane. The gracious old house lay in front of him, a cluster of low greenhouses to the right and a small plantation of saplings to the left. It was old red brick, with a low wall enclosing the front yard. Flagstones led from the driveway up to a white-painted porch.

Kenneth Balder parked the rental car under a bare-limbed maple tree and let himself through the small gate in the wall. The yard was planted with mint and something else that smelled sweet under his feet. Nothing stirred inside the house. The sun sent long morning shadows across the clipped grass. Tiny blue crocus blossoms lay in clusters along the edge of the grass. He put his foot on the bottom step just as the door opened so that he looked her straight in the face, and saw the old flash of joy for a moment before her expression changed into something less welcoming.

"Kenneth," she said.

He went up the stairs the rest of the way.

"Hello, Maggie."

The hall behind her displayed polished wood, rag rugs, and a small beautiful Williamsburg table under a primitive landscape. She had twisted her ash-brown hair into a knot at the back of her head. There were only a few light streaks in it made by sun, rather than age. He'd never seen her hair pulled away from her face. He remembered a wide-eyed, round-faced, idealistic girl who refused to swat flies because of the violence involved. The lovely gray eyes were unchanged, but her face was thinner than he remembered and her cheekbones higher. Her shoulders were stiff in the doorway.

"I should have called," he said awkwardly.

Past her came a warm, welcoming smell. Margaret's eyes were steady and noncommittal. When she spoke, he felt his heart thump uncomfortably against his chest. Her face had changed, but her voice was unaltered. He had always loved her voice.

"I thought you might come this morning," she said. "I made you a cup of coffee."

But she made no move to let him past. With sudden wryness he put out his right hand.

"Shake?" he offered. "We can pretend the truce is temporary, if you like."

He saw her mouth twitch with sudden amusement, and by impulse he climbed the last step and took both her hands in his. What could he say to the woman he had loved and lost, when years of silence and a prison sentence and the death of a rival husband stood in the way? She was wearing a green William and Mary sweatshirt and jeans with a smudge of dirt at the knees, as though she'd been in the greenhouse just before his arrival, and a piece of her hair had curled down from the knot onto her neck. Her hands were strong and slender; and for a moment he could feel nothing but an intense longing that was only partly physical. The rest had to do not with her person, but with the air of calm normality she carried with her.

He cleared his throat.

"Maggie," he began. A dish clattered behind her. The sound from the invisible kitchen registered on his thoughts only gradually. He released her hands at once.

"I'm sorry," he said, fumbling for the words. "You have company?"

"Company, no. Come in and meet my son. He's here for the day." She moved away from him as she spoke, not meeting his eyes.

So you called in a bodyguard, Kenneth Balder thought. He followed her through the hallway, into a lofty wood-floored kitchen with exposed beams and wide, bright windows. Breakfast dishes and an unfolded *Post* lay on the table. A tall boy turned from the sink, rubbing his hands against his jeans. Margaret said, "Garrett, this is Kenneth Balder."

The boy came forward, politely, and held out his hand. Matthew had been only two inches taller than Maggie herself, but Garrett towered over his mother. His face was Matthew's, as it had been before age and frustration marked any of them. The brown hair and rock-steady dark eyes, the straight firm mouth and low forehead, were all Matthew's. Balder shook the hand, which was larger than he had expected.

"Garrett," he said.

"Sir," Garrett said. "I saw you on TV. What do they call you now?"

"Chief of staff," Kenneth Balder said, feeling incredibly silly. Garrett was obviously impressed. He took another swipe at the counter with his dishcloth, lingering.

"Want some coffee?" Garrett suggested.

"Sure. Thanks."

Balder accepted the steaming cup, and sipped at the burning liquid. His words seemed to be transfixed, fast in his mouth. He couldn't speak frankly to Margaret with Garrett's calm eyes on him. He felt exactly as though he were trying to seduce Matthew's wife while Matthew watched; and all he wanted to do was talk theology, so the sensation was highly unfair. It wouldn't go away. Maggie had developed a suspicious wrinkle at the corner of her mouth.

"Like to walk through the greenhouses?" she suggested.

"Er . . . yes."

"Come on, then."

"I'll just stay here and finish the dishes," Garrett said, in a slow, ironic drawl. Ken felt his ears going red, as he followed Maggie through the back door of the farmhouse; and Garrett chuckled behind him before the clatter of pottery started up again.

They walked through the immaculate yard behind the house, where Bradford pear and dogwood reached bare limbs up toward the blue sky.

She opened the door of the first greenhouse for him. Purple and gold pansies clustered in pots, all along the dirt floors.

"They're beautiful," he said.

"I like this work," Margaret said. "It seems worthwhile, somehow. The next greenhouse is mostly herbs. I supply fresh herbs to a number of local restaurants, and some of the bed-and-breakfasts. I play around with remedies, but I've never had the time to do it properly. My commercial accounts take up most of my time."

"Does Garrett live here?"

"Not any more. He came back last night late. He's in the air national guard. Security Police Squadron, Seventy-eighth Fighter Unit, right down in Sandston."

"He hasn't been mobilized?" Balder said, incautiously.

"So it's true? Some of the units *have* been called out?"

Kenneth Balder found himself at the end of the greenhouse, and turned around. She was right behind him, which he found disconcerting.

He said, awkwardly, "That's really not my authority, Maggie. Merriman's appointed the adjutant general to be secretary of defense." She was wearing a faint perfume that smelled like flowers beside a stream. It was a familiar scent, and he was thrown suddenly back twenty-five years, watching her dress in front of the mirror. He discovered that his hand had moved slightly toward her hair.

"Go on out that door," Margaret said. Her face had flushed slightly. He pushed, and found himself standing on the edge of a wide field just beginning to mist over with green.

"Early wheat," Margaret said. "My neighbors farm it."

"How long has Garrett been in the guard?"

"He joined after Matthew died. He's in his father's unit." Her voice was matter-of-fact.

The morning air on his face was cold and liberating, after this whirling and confused week. He felt suddenly that the twenty-five-year gap barely existed, and he said unwarily, "Maggie, what about Matthew's death? How did it happen?"

Her shoulders stiffened at once.

"God hated us, I think," she said, "and the rest is all public record, Ken. You can find it if you want."

"I'm sorry. I—"

"Why did you call me after so long?"

"Because I was tired of wishing for you," he said, risking it all on one toss.

"And because Matthew was dead?"

"I'd hardly have called if he were alive."

"He missed you, Ken."

"He knew where I was," Kenneth Balder said, hearing the betrayal of the last two-and-a-half decades like acid in his voice. "He joined the guard as soon as you came east. He went as far away as he could and chose a job with the men I said were the enemy, and he convinced you I was dangerous and married you. What did you want me to do? Send a bottle of champagne?" He caught at the words, but they were already out.

Margaret's voice had turned flat and cold. She said, "Matthew never told me you were dangerous."

"Why did you say you were afraid of me, then?" Kenneth Balder demanded. He hadn't intended to ask the question so soon. Margaret turned away from him and walked along the edge of the field. She said, without looking back, "Tell me what you're doing here, with Charles Merriman. Did you write his speech, Sunday night?"

Balder collected himself. He was falling back too easily into patterns he had given up long ago. He said, "No. No, I didn't write it. I didn't know he was going to give it."

"They were your words, though."

"Yes. We've been acquainted for years."

"Why did Charles Merriman use your words?"

"Because he doesn't want to boost state's rights. He wants to start over." She was still ahead of him. He said to her shoulderblades, "Maggie, do you really want to talk about politics?"

She said calmly, without turning around, "I haven't seen you for twenty-five years, Ken. I'd like to know what you believe now, since everything I thought you once stood for proved to be false."

He took a deep breath.

"Well, then," he said. "This has nothing to do with state's rights. There's no way a state can revolt and hope to justify itself by the Constitution; the Constitution was written for the express purpose of subjecting the states to the federal government. We're breaking away from a whole system of government that was always doomed to fail. Charles Merriman wants a second Revolution. He's going back to the original founding of Virginia as a Commonwealth in its own right."

"And what do you have to do with that?"

"If he doesn't use the Constitution, he needs a whole new framework for government. I have that. I have a vast network of people who believe it and support it. Maggie, love, please don't walk away from me—"

Margaret turned around. He saw with horror that she was near tears. She said, "How do you do it, Ken? Cause a whirlwind wherever you go? Gather so many people around you, who are so convinced that you're right?"

"I hope that it doesn't have anything to do with me," Kenneth Balder said "I hope that people gather around the truth of what I say."

"People gather around *you*, Ken. We both joined you, Matthew and I. And he was older than you. You were boys together and you'd followed him all your life. And when you both grew up, you still convinced him to become the disciple while you turned into the leader."

"Well," Ken said, "he broke away in time."

"Only because he remembered that he'd once been the boss. If you'd happened to be older, he'd have followed you straight into jail. And now you've had a spectacular conversion, so you're leading people into Christianity. It's just the next cause on your list."

"I've always been looking for God. The causes I found before were only substitutes."

"Always so sure of yourself."

"I doubt myself every day."

"*You?* You *doubt* yourself? You've changed, then."

"Yes, I have."

"That highly public conversion?"

"It is real," Balder said. She had always listened willingly to all he had to say. Now the wide, beautiful eyes were like gray stone. He said, digging desperately for the right words, "Listen, Maggie. Back in California I used to do this on paper. Create a government based on God's law. Build it up, stone by glorious stone. And it would disappear as soon as I looked up. And now here I am, in one of the oldest seats of government in the United States, surrounded by men who hold the fragile power of that government in their hands. How could I not doubt myself? All my life I've trailed disciples behind me. I know that. I don't even know why they followed, most of the time. And now I'm asking a million people to walk into war. They might actually do it. Maggie, in jail I had a copy of Brother Lawrence's writings. I read it so often that I can still tell you exactly where the coffee stains are, and what they're shaped like. I memorized almost all of the Second Conversation: 'I desire only that I might not offend God; for when I fail in my duty, I am used to do so; thus will I always do, whenever You leave me to myself.' And if God isn't in this, it will fail."

"It'll destroy you if it does."

"Yes," Kenneth Balder said, voicing a truth he had not yet admitted to himself. "Yes, it will. But if it doesn't fail, we'll see true justice, here on earth. Maggie, my heart, don't walk away from me a second time."

Margaret pushed her hands into the pockets of her jeans and studied the horizon intently. He could see her blink, but the tears were back under control.

"Come back to the house and give Garrett some advice," she said at last.

"Maggie—"

She turned back toward the farmhouse without answering.

In the kitchen, Garrett was sitting at the table, eating toast and jelly. His mother said blackly, "You've had one breakfast already."

"Hours ago," Garrett said cheerfully.

"Margaret says you're in the guard?" Balder asked. It was almost a physical effort to redirect his attention from Margaret Franklin to her son. He'd half-expected a show of resentment from the boy, but Garrett was either unaware of or unconcerned by the past. He said, "Yes, sir. I came home last night because I go back on duty tonight, and I didn't . . . well . . ." He crumbled his toast without looking at Balder's face.

"You don't want to end up in the middle of a war," Balder said dryly.

"No," Garrett said immediately. "I don't want to fight."

"I can't guarantee it," Kenneth Balder said, "but I seriously doubt there will be any fighting. This is the age of paper revolutions, Garrett. We'll have a harder time with the U.S. Treasury than with the U.S. Army. I can guarantee you'll be called out, probably tomorrow morning, but that'll be purely for show. I don't think you need to worry. You're going to have a more immediate concern than that. It may happen that the president and the governor will both issue orders to the guard, and you're going to have to decide whom to obey."

"The governor's our commander-in-chief," Garrett said at once.

"Yes. Well, the balance has shifted over the past years. You swear allegiance to both, and the question of a conflict is never addressed."

"Well . . . what should I do?"

"You do as your conscience demands," Kenneth Balder said. Maggie was leaning against the window, and the sun behind her illuminated her hair and turned her outline into gold. "But speaking as Merriman's chief of staff, I can tell you that you will not get into any legal trouble by obeying the governor rather than the president. He's the shield between you and the power of the federal government."

"What if the unit splits?" Garrett demanded. This prospect seemed to concern him more than the wrath of Washington. Balder said, "Do you think it will?"

"I don't know. I don't want to leave my unit." There was an unusual passion in his voice for someone who didn't want to fight. Balder looked at him curiously. He said, "Stay with your commander and do as the governor says, and I promise you'll find yourself safe."

He glanced up at Maggie. With the light behind her, he couldn't read her face. He noticed suddenly that the shadows had shortened alarmingly. The hands on the kitchen clock were rising toward eleven.

"I'm due back in Richmond," he said.

"I'm due there myself, Friday," Margaret remarked, without moving.

"You are? For what?"

"I'm meeting with the chief of police about re-opening Matthew's case."

Balder thought rapidly. Merriman had planned out the following days for various administrative and civil groups in Richmond to meet with the new government, but he hadn't yet delivered the schedule to his cabinet members. He wondered whether he was also due to meet with the chief of police.

"Will you walk with me to my car?" he asked, standing up. "Garrett—"

"Nice to meet you," Garrett said, his mouth full of toast.

Margaret walked beside him, down the steps and across the grass to where his car stood under the trees that fringed the road. When they were out of earshot, he said, "Maggie, don't tell Charles Merriman about . . . the past."

"Why not?"

"I don't want him to know about—"

"Us?" Maggie said, dryly. He had refrained from the pronoun. Her use of it sent his heart bounding upward.

"Yes."

"Why not?"

He put his hand on the door handle and searched for the words that would match the uneasiness wisping about his mind.

"I'm being followed," he said. "I don't know whether by the United States or by Merriman's people. Maggie, Charles Merriman's a hard man to read. Sometimes I think he's simply using any means possible to bring this new country about. Sometimes I think he's dancing everyone around him like puppets on strings. I don't want you on a string."

Margaret turned her head to look down the road. She said, "I'm not on anybody's string, Ken. I've spent the last two years trying to get justice for Matthew. That's all I care about right now. I have no problems with a government based on the Old Testament. I've read some of the Old Testament. There are good rules in it. I believe in rules. If the Old Testament works, I can accept its usefulness."

"We're not following the Old Testament because it's useful. We're following it because it's true."

"Yes. Well, your truth seems to change, Ken. You never used to believe in God. You believed in peace, and even that proved to be an illusion."

Kenneth Balder said slowly, "Do you believe in forgiveness, Maggie?"

He saw, with some satisfaction, that the question had rattled her.

"Ken," she said at last, "if I thought you were all through playing God, I might not be afraid of you."

He looked at her for a long moment, and then picked up her hand and turned it over and kissed her palm. She slowly turned red.

"I'll have to prove it to you, won't I?" he said.

He released her hand. Garrett was looking out the window, his dark head a blot against the bright glass.

"Good-bye," he said. When he looked in the rearview mirror, at the end of the long lane, she was still standing on the immaculate grass, the bare branches of the maple trees casting lace shadows over her.

He watched both before and behind him, all the way back to Richmond, but the cars around him changed constantly. No spy was following. The uneasiness remained, like a faint sound that disappears when the listener strains to hear it.

CHAPTER 9

Wednesday, March 20, 1 P.M.

MARGARET STOOD IN THE YARD, watching the dark blue car turn slowly onto the highway. His voice on the telephone had not been greatly changed, but she did not recognize the impulsive blond giant of twenty-five years ago in that tall and elegant man. Even so early in the day, he had worn a beautifully cut charcoal suit. He was distinguished and reserved; and although his words were blunt, his blue eyes had remained shielded.

The telephone was ringing faintly in the kitchen. She heard the indistinct sound of Garrett's voice answering. She could still feel Ken's lips against her palm. His presence turned twenty-three years of marriage into a mere parenthesis. He was as spellbinding now as he had been then, so long ago.

"Mom?"

She turned around. Garrett had come out onto the porch. He said uncertainly, "It's someone for you."

"Who?"

"He says he's from the Defense Department."

The horizon seemed suddenly to rush in at her with blinding speed. She turned around and walked carefully back to the house. Garrett had laid the telephone gingerly on the counter. She picked it up. Outside, a mockingbird was singing loudly in the maple tree.

"Mrs. Margaret Franklin?" a voice said on the other end. A warm voice, slightly uncertain, relatively young.

"Yes?"

"Your maiden name was Margaret Keil?"

"Who are you?"

"I'm an assistant to the secretary of defense for the United States, Mrs. Franklin. My name's Allen Preszkoleski. I'm calling from the Pentagon."

Garrett was standing in the doorway. She shrugged at him, and mouthed, *I don't know.*

"What do you want?"

"Mrs. Franklin, you may not remember, but my boss—Alexander Wade—was part of the team that prosecuted Kenneth Balder for the death of Mary Miranda Carpenter."

At once, she felt every sense within her sharpen.

"Yes?" she said, guardedly.

"You don't remember?"

"I don't think about those days, Mr.—"

"You can call me Allen," the voice suggested kindly. His voice was reassuring.

"All right. I don't remember your boss." She had never again recognized anyone from those dreadful weeks; certainly the cabinet of the president of the United States contained no familiar face.

"He spoke to you in the hallway, after the trial. He showed you two letters."

Memory poured back. She said, "Alexander Wade! I remember. He conducted part of Ken's cross-examination. . . . The whole courtroom was laughing at him."

Allen Preszkoleski cleared his throat and said rapidly, "I don't mean to resurrect your own ordeal again, Mrs. Franklin. We know that you and Matthew Franklin were never implicated in the death, and as far as we're concerned justice has already been served for both of you."

"Matthew's dead," Margaret said.

"Yes, I know. I'm very sorry."

"How did you know?" It was odd, this warp in time. The same players—she and Ken and Alexander Wade and the United States government and even Matthew, by proxy—back in the game again. Old attitudes echoed back from the past; all the skepticism and bristling suspicion of adolescence.

"In light of present developments, it's hardly surprising that we're keeping ourselves informed about all the players. You and Mr. Balder were involved at one time, and we'd like to make sure that you don't get hurt in this revolution."

"And what is that supposed to mean?"

Allen Preszkoleski's voice grew more soothing, as though it sensed the misstep.

"Mrs. Franklin, the United States could move into Virginia and quell this revolt at any time. But we want to avoid any use of force. It would inevitably result in some injury, maybe even loss of life, and we certainly want to try every peaceful means to bring Virginia back into compliance with federal laws. Your son is in the guard, isn't he?"

Margaret looked across the room at Garrett. This was becoming like one of those unreasonable nightmares where something was stalking her, knowing every step before she made it. Garrett had peeled open a package of crackers and was sitting on the table, stuffing them down with his eyes eagerly on her. The sight restored some normality to her kitchen. She scowled at him and drew her finger across her throat.

"Sorry," Garrett whispered, looking down at the empty wrapper.

"Mrs. Franklin?" the voice said, insistently.

"Why did you call me?"

"We'd like you to come up to Washington and give us some help. We can fly you up, or if you'd rather—"

"What kind of help?"

"We can go into that once you're here—"

"I'll come if I know why I'm coming. Otherwise, I've got a business to run."

"Well," the voice said apologetically, "I understand your point of view, entirely. We're very concerned about Kenneth Balder's involvement in this revolt. He came across state lines to help Charles Merriman, you know, which gives the FBI an interest in the case, and we've had him under investigation for some time. . . ."

"What for?"

"I'm afraid I can't give you any details about ongoing investigations, Mrs. Franklin. Let me give you a few facts from the past, if I could. Mr.

Balder has spent eleven years running the California Institute for Theonomic Law. Did you know that contributions to the institute for the last five years have run well over two million dollars per year?"

"Great heavens," Margaret said, involuntarily.

"Yes. It's a lot of money. And the publicity from this revolt will probably bring in even more money for the institute, and for Kenneth Balder personally."

"Are you sure that he profits—"

The voice persisted, "Are you aware that, two years ago, Kenneth Balder testified as an expert witness in the Richmond trial of a man accused of bombing an abortion provider? Unfortunately a janitor was killed. A single woman supporting three children, I believe. The bomber pleaded theological conviction as a basis for his actions."

"What's the point of this?"

"We think Mr. Balder could be made to see that his part in this whole situation could lead him into a great deal of trouble."

"So you'd like to use me to convince him to take himself out of play?"

"That's a rather vague summary of our purposes, Mrs. Franklin. If you'd be willing to come up to Washington—"

"I don't want to leave my farm unattended," Margaret said decisively.

"This is a matter of national security. I'm sure that we could help you out, put someone there to take care of the farm while you're away. Margaret—" his voice was friendly—"I understand that the Richmond police department hasn't been able to bring your husband's murderer into court. I'm sure we could request some FBI assistance on the case. They'd be very grateful for your help, you see. And the Virginia Guard isn't a good place for your son right now. We'll see that he gets out of the guard and well-launched on a second career. Or we can help him get back into college, if he'd prefer to finish his degree."

There was a silence.

"That's very generous," Margaret said at last.

"Can we arrange a time, then?"

"Why don't you just arrest Mr. Balder?"

"Well, as we've said, we're anxious to avoid any show of force. The American people deserve a peaceful resolution to this situation."

"And so you want me to come out and slander Mr. Balder to the press?"

"Certainly not," the voice said. "We can work out the details once you're here."

Margaret nervously fingered the phone cord. Those accusations against Kenneth Balder had a savage sound. Defending a bombing that killed a bystander? That was like him, like the pitiless forceful boy she had known, standing up for an abstract principle while bodies fell around him. But she was being asked to betray Ken a second time.

"Mrs. Franklin?"

"No," she said suddenly. "No. I won't do it." Her eye fell on Garrett, listening eagerly, and she amended her words. "Not now. Call me back— call me again tomorrow. Tomorrow night. I have to think."

"Margaret—"

She hung up the telephone. Garrett demanded, "Was that really the Defense Department?"

"I think so," she said slowly.

"What did they want?"

"They wanted . . . Garrett, this is complicated. I should explain something. Your father and I never told you much about how we met, or got married. Kenneth Balder was an old friend of ours. Mine and your father's."

"Yes?"

"Well . . . when we were all in college, he was convicted of manslaughter."

"I saw it on the news. He spent eight years in prison. He doesn't look it," Garrett said, naively.

"Yes, but your father and I were there. A friend of ours was killed accidentally. We were all trespassing on military property, but Kenneth was more or less leading the group." *More or less;* what a weak phrase for Ken's all-enveloping presence. "Her parents wouldn't let it rest, and eventually he was charged with involuntary manslaughter during the commission of a crime. It's a class-five felony. One to ten years of prison. Your father and I were charged with trespassing and had to pay a fine. We didn't have anything to do with the death, but we were there."

"If you already paid the fine, what does the Defense Department want?"

"They want me to help them bring it all up again. This revolution will only be successful if it's popular, Garrett. If they can smear Kenneth Balder enough, it might swing public opinion back away from Charles Merriman. And Ken's got enormous support from people who follow his foundation. The government doesn't want all those people on Charles Merriman's side."

Garrett stared at her thoughtfully. It was Matthew's stare, calm and weighing the options; and at last he said, "I like him."

"You do?"

"Yes. He's real. He knows what he's talking about."

They looked at each other across the empty kitchen.

"I've got to get to work, Mom—"

"Garrett, if you don't want to be involved in this, we can go up to Washington. You won't even have to report for duty tonight. You won't have to fight."

"There won't be any fighting."

"We don't know that, darling."

"I can't leave the unit, Mom. I know the men too well. I'm getting close to the truth about Dad's death. I just know it."

"Garrett, it won't comfort me to find out the truth if you get yourself killed."

"I won't get killed," Garrett said, with complete assurance. "I can't leave the unit now. And it's getting close to my shift. Mom, I've got to go back by my apartment and change. Mom . . do *you* want to go to Washington?"

Margaret shook her head. "Not until I see your father's case closed," she said, admitting the truth.

"Well, I feel the same way. This is important to me."

"I'm certainly not leaving Virginia without you."

"Then we'll both stay," Garrett said. "Mom, it's okay. Nothing's going to happen."

"I remember thinking that," Margaret said dryly, "a long time ago."

But he had already run up the stairs. She could hear the weight of his tread overhead. He would be stuffing his clothes into that tattered old duffel bag, ready to head back into the middle of the fray. She went out into her office and sat down at her quiet desk, and put her thudding head into her hands. She could still hear the echo of her own voice; and the details of twenty-five years came flooding back to fill the emptiness between the bare phrases. *Manslaughter, not murder. It's a class-five felony. One to ten years of prison.*

FOR KEN, it had been the maximum sentence of ten years, shortened only by his parole for good behavior. She couldn't picture him in that cell; she and Matthew had never visited, never even written. To this day she turned the television off when the camera moved to a prisoner in a cell.

Ken had been fortunate. The prosecutor had pressed for second-degree murder, claiming that nineteen-year-old Mary Miranda Carpenter had been intentionally suffocated by Kenneth Balder, age twenty-one, because her hysterical screaming would have revealed the accused in the act of committing a felony. He had failed with the jury, but the theory had lingered in the mind of the sentencing judge. It was odd. She remembered the fine fair hair and the high eager voice, but she couldn't summon Mary Miranda's face to her mind any more. She would have been forty-four this year. Mary Miranda's elderly parents were dead, and there was no one left to mourn twenty-five years of missed life.

On the stand herself, she had drawn all her strength from Matthew's intent dark eyes. She wasn't even able to look at Ken, defiant behind the dark oak table. During the second day of questioning the thought flashed into her mind, *He'll be safe. I can trust Matthew.*

"Miss Keil, what is the explanation for your presence on military property?"
"We were going to paint on the concrete. . . ."
"Paint, Miss Keil?"
"Protests. Paint protests on the concrete."

The public prosecutor had been stocky and middle-aged, with a cool Boston accent. A younger lawyer at the prosecutor's table made notes constantly on a yellow legal pad. He was short and brown-haired and intense—Alexander Wade at thirty-one, busy making his mark in the world.

The prosecutor inquired, "And you were not aware that Mr. Balder was carrying explosives?"

"No. No. We had no idea. It was supposed to be a peaceful protest."

"Were you aware that you were committing a felony?"

"No. A misdemeanor. Only carrying paint. We were ready to risk that."

"So the four of you trespassed on federal property—"

Ken's expensive lawyer shot to his feet, and the prosecutor withdrew the word.

"The four of you," he amended, "were present on federal property for the sole purpose of splashing paint on concrete?"

"Yes," Margaret said stubbornly. The prosecutor's lifted eyebrow was a miracle of unspoken skepticism. He turned back to his table and consulted his papers, and Alexander Wade leaned forward and whispered to him.

"What happened next, Miss Keil?"

"Mary Miranda started screaming."

"Why?"

"Objection!"

The prosecutor sighed. "Tell the court in detail what you saw," he said, with the immense patience of someone dealing with unreasonable children.

"A spotlight came on. We were lying in the grass. I thought it would go overtop of us. Someone—a guard, I guess—started shouting, and then Mary Miranda jumped up in front of me and screamed."

"And then what happened?"

"She came back down on the grass."

"Excuse me?"

"She was standing up screaming, and then she went back down on her stomach and was quiet."

"Mr. Balder pulled her down?"

"Object—"

"I couldn't see Ken," Margaret said. It was true. It had been dark. She didn't know why Mary Miranda had succumbed to hysterics; the only explanation was the impulse of the hunted to face the hunter, the same irrational surge of energy that made a quail break from cover and fly up into range. Maybe she had suddenly seen that Ken carried more than paint. Maybe the searchlight and shouting male voice had alone tipped her into panic.

"Miss Keil, what is your relationship to Mr. Balder?"

"Objection!"

"The two of you shared a residence for some months?" the prosecutor amended.

"Well, not formally—"

"Miss Keil, were you ever afraid of Kenneth Balder?"

Ken's eyes were steady on her, but she refused to look at him.

"Yes," she said, barely hearing her own voice. "Yes, sometimes I was."

It was a revelation that startled her. She didn't truly think Ken would ever lay a hand on her. But she was afraid of that iron streak in him, the willingness to subdue everything to his purpose in life. Mary Miranda had threatened his purpose, that warm night. She hadn't seen him pull Mary Miranda back down; he had been wearing dark clothes and a black bandanna over his light hair. She didn't want to hear him tell the story.

But Matthew drew her into the seat beside him, his hand strong on her arm. Mary Miranda's elderly parents sat in front of them, the mother weeping silently, the father quiet; his wrinkled hands were folded in his lap, and his stare never left Ken's bright head.

Kenneth Balder, on the stand, had developed deep lines from his nose to the corners of his young mouth. His blue-eyed gaze was steady and his voice was firm. Somehow, this assurance conveyed not truthfulness but arrogance. And when Alexander Wade rose to conduct the cross-examination, Ken was unable to resist mimicking him. Wade was a competent young lawyer, but he had an unfortunate habit of twisting his head to the left as he asked his questions. Ken turned the questions neatly back on the questioner, and as he did so he copied the motion so faithfully that the jury began to giggle. Alexander Wade grew flustered, and asked three unallowable questions in a row before the prosecutor stood impatiently up to take his place.

"What were your actions, Mr. Balder, when Miss Carpenter began to scream?"

Ken, catching the eye of his lawyer, answered the question without elaboration.

"I grabbed her ankle and pulled her back down on the grass."

"Did she stop screaming?""

"No."

"What did you do then?""

"I put my hand over her mouth."

"Why, Mr. Balder?"

"So she would be quiet," Ken said. For a moment, his voice imitated the unnatural patience of the prosecutor's tone. In the back of the courtroom someone laughed. The judge frowned.

"And why was it important that she be quiet?"

"So that we wouldn't be discovered."

"In other words, so that you would not be discovered on military property with explosives—an act which you knew to be a felony, not the misdemeanor charge which covers mere trespass."

Ken's lawyer remarked, without bothering to stand, "Perhaps my colleague would be so kind as to save his closing argument for the end of the trial?"

"Mr. Meyer," the judge said, "please confine yourself to questioning the witness."

"Yes, Your Honor. You were carrying explosives, Mr. Balder?"

"I think that's already been said," Ken snapped. His lawyer covered a yawn, delicately, and Ken settled back into the chair and looked away. He said, rapidly, "I was afraid that Mary Miranda would be injured by someone firing in her direction, if the guards knew that we were near the hangar. She was hysterical and I was trying to keep her from harm."

This explanation, which would have been unthinkably thin before Kent State, carried weight with a jury still shocked by the deaths of four protesting students. Kenneth Balder had attempted to protect Mary Miranda Carpenter from a military that was now universally distrusted. She had died of accidental suffocation during a panic attack. He had been acquitted of second-degree murder, convicted of manslaughter, and given the maximum sentence. Margaret Keil and Matthew Franklin had been fined and given suspended sentences for trespassing; and they had gotten married at a registrar's office and moved east. Ken had been fire and tempest; Matthew was a rock, unmoving and certain. Matthew would never have killed in an attempt to do good.

She turned on npr's "All Things Considered" while she fixed dinner for one. After listening for an hour, she had gained no clearer picture of the struggle. Everyone interviewed contradicted whoever came before.

There's no constitutional provision for this; that's why we fought the Civil War.

My esteemed colleague hasn't grasped the very basic principle that this has nothing to do with the Constitution, since Merriman's rejected it and returned to Virginia's Cavalier roots.

At income tax time, the IRS will start seizing property.

No, they won't; Charles Merriman has returned to the federal government all moneys paid into the state system since January.

Charles Merriman is guaranteeing that the interstates will be maintained at Virginia's expense, with a small fee collected at the state borders.

Immense protest from the Washington, D.C. suburbs, commuters shouting about the huge traffic jams that tolls at the borders would cause. An irate banker, snapping, "This is all a pipe dream. There won't be any tolls. There won't be a separate state. The whole thing will fall apart in twenty-four hours." Pause. "Maybe forty-eight, tops."

At the top of the hour, the voice of the local news anchor was hurried and excited. "This just in," he said. "We have an unsubstantiated report that the Virginia National Guard has been called out. Guard headquarters in Richmond, Charlottesville, and Fredericksburg have all refused to confirm this action. The governor's office is unavailable for comment. Again, according to information received by us, the Virginia National Guard has been called out. This has not yet been verified. Stay tuned to 88.9 FM for further updates."

Margaret dried her hands, slowly. *Garrett's in no immediate danger,* she told herself. The guard was a peacekeeping force. Virginia was bound to be unsettled, in times like these. She walked over to the small black-and-white TV that perched above the sideboard, and cut it on.

Alexander Wade appeared, interviewed while getting into his car, the familiar self-assured gray-headed figure she had seen, without really noticing his features, in *Time* and *Newsweek* photos. She had never connected that distinguished face with the young man behind the table, solemnly writing Ken's words on yellow paper. But she suddenly recognized the microscopic tilt of his head to the left, as he spoke to the reporters surrounding him.

"The Department of Defense recognizes the full responsibility of the Department of Justice to handle this affair," Alexander Wade was saying. "The attorney general of the United States has the situation under control. Defense has no part in this. This is not a matter of national security; it is purely a matter of internal politics run wild, and the Department of Defense has nothing to do with its resolution. As you know, the United States protects the rights of its citizens by barring troops from deployment on domestic soil."

Someone yelled, "What about the rumor that you were seen in Richmond, just before Charles Merriman declared independence?"

"There's absolutely no truth in that. Now go pester the attorney general."

She muted the TV, waiting for another news flash about the guard. In his years in the guard, Matthew had been called out twice; but he had been at home both times. She didn't know whether Garrett would be allowed to telephone his home. The familiar Channel 12 anchor appeared shortly.

"We have received a report that the Virginia National Guard has been called out. Guard headquarters have refused to comment. The governor's office is unavailable."

The telephone was silent. She thought once of calling Ken, but he had left no number, and she shied away from dialing up the Executive Mansion and asking for him.

She scooped up the still-unread newspapers and took them up to bed with her. *The Richmond Times-Dispatch* was blatantly victorious; the *Washington Post* implied that everyone in Virginia had suddenly gone mad.

Just before sleep, she had the horrifying fear that she might dream of Matthew's death again, with Garrett in her husband's place; and the idea kept her awake a few more minutes. But when she finally slept it was deep, black, and soundless.

CHAPTER 10

Wednesday, March 20, 6 p.m.

GARRETT FRANKLIN had barely gotten his badge on when an alarm went off in the security office. The base was noisy and swarming with guard personnel. On Wednesdays, the fighter group flew, and the Security Police Squadron had a full complement.

Clint Larsen, on duty at the desk, shut off the noise and swiveled around in his chair. Outside the glass window, the planes were surrounded by people; maintenance and security, the pilots in full gear. Clint was busy tonight, and in a good mood for a change.

"Vault again," he said. Behind him, the black-and-white monitor for the front-gate camera scanned the cluster of press and TV cameras gathering at the chain-link fence. Garrett nodded, slinging his M-16 across his shoulder.

"Good form," Larsen said, as an afterthought, "in case someone's taping you for the evening news."

Garrett grinned and went out the red-labeled door, down the corridor and toward the vault. In obedience to Clint Larsen's instructions, he put the M-16 on his shoulder and checked out the disturbance. He was annoyed to find his heart beating hard against his breastbone. It was an odd night at the base, with all the usual bustle and organized disorder of a flying night, the planes soaring up above the clustered lights of Richmond International Airport's main terminal, just across the runways from them.

But the security officers were tight-mouthed and nervous. He'd actually caught Clint Larsen with his hand on the nine-millimeter Beretta issued to the security squadron, watching the front-gate monitor with a deep crease between his eyebrows. Captain Ames had been practically invisible, in his office with the door closed. He'd heard the indistinct sound of a one-sided conversation; the captain was on the telephone. The door cracked slightly as a staff sergeant slipped through.

"No, sir. The Air National Guard provides a hundred percent of intercept capabilities for the air force, so we're equipped to defend our own air space." The voice paused. "Well, sir, it would weaken our national ability to intercept incoming hostiles if you were talking about the entire air guard. But we're only one state—"

The door swung closed again. He went softly past the captain's door, out into the cool March evening.

The alarm was a false one. He checked the vault and straightened. From there he could hear the subdued chatter of the press at the front gates. Three army guard units had been activated the night before to deal with that riot in Battlefield Park; and the press was certain that this signaled the beginning of war. He scratched the back of his neck, looking around. A plane roared overhead, momentarily drowning out the voices. When it had passed, the murmuring sound had changed. It was rising in pitch. He could hear a faint grating sound and a clink. The front gates were closing. Above him, the clamor of engines climbed upward again. He lifted his eyes and squinted into the darkening sky.

The planes were coming in.

He slung the M-16 over his shoulder and sprinted back toward the gazebo, charging through the ground-floor door and up the three flights of stairs. Captain Ames was already at the security office doorway. He skidded to a halt. Ames looked over his shoulder and said, "Get a grip, Franklin."

"Yes, sir—"

"We're in business, men," Ames said. His voice was matter-of-fact. "We've been mobilized by Governor Merriman. First Squad will secure this base, Second and Third Squads under Sergeants Smith and Larsen will secure Richmond International Airport. I'll send you as many men as I can spare, Larsen. We're getting a couple of military police units from the army guard to help you guys out."

Davidson Smith came around the corner from the arms room, already in battle gear. Garrett rubbed his hands on his thighs. He could feel sweat starting along his hairline and at the back of his neck.

"Any questions?" Ames inquired. "Good."

"Sir," Garrett said, "are we under a state of emergency?"

Ames looked him over, his light eyes preoccupied and his sharp-featured face blank.

"Not exactly, " he said. "Come with me, Smith. Franklin and the rest of you, report to your fire team leaders."

His square shoulders disappeared down the hallway, Davidson Smith behind him. Garrett swallowed, trying to remember the procedures. He'd been through all this in training, and again on drill weekends. . . . but a faint gray haze seemed to be covering his memory. He stared blindly through the glass window at the running figures below. At this time of evening, the base was still crowded with daytime personnel, overlapping with the newly arrived night shift. His own day stretched from five in the evening until the early hours of the morning. On his duty days, he drove back to his Sandston apartment in the still dark that comes before sunrise. It was his favorite time of day. Often he would wander around his block before crawling into bed, sharply conscious of being alert while the rest of the world slept. Sometimes he wondered if his father had felt that same heady exhilaration, taking that last walk of his life at two in the morning in Oregon Hill.

"Franklin!" Clint Larsen snapped.

He jerked himself into motion. Clint Larsen was the head of the Third Squad, commanding three fire teams. Garrett himself handled the M-60 for his three-man team and reported to C-Fire Team Leader Kevin Camp. He hauled his Kevlar vest out of the arms room and took himself down to the assemble point to find Camp.

The vault was open and Smith was inside, handing the weapons out. Clint Larsen arrived on the scene a moment later and said curtly, "White, Chevlos—you two go clear the press away from the front gate. Fire teams for Third Squad, let's go. Now!"

Garrett fell in behind Kevin Camp, between Noonan and Georges, the other two members of the fire team. The M-60 plus ammo and tripod were heavy in his hands; the gun alone weighed twenty-four pounds. Clint Larsen stood at the head of the Third Squad, his strong-featured face alight with excitement.

"Third Squad, listen up," Larsen said loudly. "The governor has deployed the Virginia National Guard in all border counties to watch the interstates and prevent any military invasion. As of right now, our position is solely to protect the Commonwealth of Virginia against unjust aggression on the part of the United States government. Right now, we have one of the most important jobs in the state—to guard the airport. Richmond International will be one of the prime spearheads of any invasion. The Third Squad will be deployed inside the terminal itself, while the Second Squad will monitor the runways. The State Police are already posted at Airport Drive. The remaining forces will remain on alert within the base itself. We're going to let the United States know that Virginia won't roll over and play dead. Let's go!"

Garrett followed the man ahead of him. He was waiting for someone to say, "Is this legal?" The words never came. He kept his eyes on Larsen, at the front of the column. Both the master sergeants—Davidson Smith, tall and dark, and heavy light-haired Clint Larsen—had served with Matthew Franklin. Clint was in his early thirties, Smith closer to forty. Both were career soldiers. They had been friendly in an offhand way when he first arrived at the base, giving him the benefit of the doubt as the son of a well-liked master sergeant who had met with a tragic end.

He had gone through those first days in a haze of uncertainty. The decision to join the guard had been quick and impulsive. After the usual battery of tests, he'd been enlisted and sent to training camp. He sweated through the training and the memorization of books of rules, gritting his teeth and thinking, *Dad did this first.* There was nothing of the warrior in Garrett, and he loathed pointless activity and rote memory work.

He could feel suppressed excitement radiating from the men around him: Kevin Camp was humming under his breath. The squad moved in formation, through the door and out into the cold March night. The stars on the horizon had disappeared into Richmond's artificial glow, but over-head scattered points of light shone down. He scrambled into the truck, feeling his fingers stiff with cold and the floorboards rough under the soles of his polished boots. The trucks swayed away from the base, past the Henrico Fire Department training facility, out to East Williamsburg Road and turned left. He crouched between his team members, clutching the M-60 and repeating to himself like a mantra, *Dad did this. He was called out for the big hurricane, for the riot at the shipyard, and he did his duty. Dad did this first. . . .*

The trucks ground to a stop in front of the terminal. The guardsmen leaped out, just as they had practiced in a dozen drills. It seemed slightly ridiculous to be doing it here, scattering businessmen with dress bags in all directions. The Second Squad trucks continued around them, heading for the runways. They would post themselves on the airstrips themselves, to make sure that no one managed to leave the airport without passing through the terminal with its x-rays and metal detectors.

The Third Security Squad hustled into the lobby, past the check-in lines and a crowd of wide-eyed passengers, and halted in front of the new car display which stood between the baggage carrels and the entrance doors.

"Listen up," Clint Larsen ordered. "Fire Team C—" he gestured at Garrett, standing with Camp and Noonan and Phillips—"post yourselves at the top of the escalators, on this side of the metal detectors. I'll stay with you. We're going to create a security bottleneck there. We've got to route all arriving passengers through one detector before we let them out. We'll use the other detectors for the routine pre-boarding checks for outgoing passengers. Offer any needed assistance to the RIC security guards. If they want you to help open suitcases, do it. Fire Teams A and B, spread out through the terminal. Watch for suspicious passengers. Anyone who rings a bell that says 'military' with you, ask for an ID. Go!"

The groups disappeared into the depths of the airport, past the espresso bar and the bustling first-floor restaurant. Garrett trotted after Clint Larsen toward the escalators. They came to a temporary halt on the bottom step. He caught sight of himself in the darkened window glass and grinned. The sight of five fully armed national guardsmen standing in a fierce group on an escalator, waiting patiently to be lifted upward, suddenly tickled him.

They stepped off at the top and strode stiffly across to the security gates. RIC routed all passengers through two metal detectors on the right side of the bottleneck at the top of the escalators, while outbound passengers walked through the open space at the left.

"Okay," Clint said briskly. "Spread out across here. Franklin, Noonan, Camp, cover this open area. We'll leave a passageway on your right, Camp, right next to this metal detector. Franklin, route them through next to the window, and they can circle around through the detector and then come out on your right, Camp. Phillips, take the top of the escalators. Make sure no one gets by you without circling back around through the security check."

"Can't we get the escalators turned off?" Brady asked.

"Noonan, go check on it."

"Yes, sir." Noonan hurried off.

"We're on duty now," Clint said, satisfied, to the middle-aged woman at the metal detector. She lifted a sardonic eyebrow at him.

"Honey," she said, "can't tell you how much safer I feel," and went back to rummaging through the purse of a thin blonde woman who was looking apprehensively over her shoulder at the armed men.

Garrett set himself in guard posture, feeling like one of the guards at Buckingham Palace; stock-still and not allowed to flinch, even when tourists tickled their noses. Traffic at RIC seemed slightly heavier than normal. A steady flow of curious passengers came pouring out of the terminals, through the narrow passage on his left, directed by Phillips back around through the left-hand metal detector, doing a final loop and emerging from security between Camp and the wall of the detector. Outbound passengers, sent through the single detector on the right, began to pool into a discontented crowd. Eventually Noonan came puffing back, and shortly afterward the escalator ground to a stop, to a chorus of complaints from the passengers. The exiting slowed until a mass of incoming passengers waited impatiently beyond the guard cordon. The security guards worked efficiently through the crowd, their jaws moving rhythmically on their chewing gum and their eyes never leaving their screens.

Clint Larsen, pacing up and down, halted close to Garrett and looked out over the crowd.

"Sheep," he said contemptuously.

Garrett sneaked a sideways look at him. He could feel curious eyes from the crowd, examining his full battle dress, thrilled to see physical evidence of a rebellion.

"Who?" he said tentatively, out of the corner of his mouth.

"All these people," Clint said, watching them file past. "Waiting for someone to tell them they're free, and then waiting to see what happens."

"Aren't you glad about this?"

"Of course I am," Clint Larsen said. "It's twenty years overdue. I'm thrilled." He leaned slightly closer, and added, "*You* don't seem so happy, Franklin."

Garrett paused.

"It's pretty tame, isn't it?" he said, wistfully. This was the product of careful practice in front of a mirror, and it rang incredibly false in his own ears, like something out of an old Hardy Boys book. Just then the detector rang out, and Clint pulled himself away and strode over to consult with the security guard. A slim man in a gray overcoat backed out, drawing Clint and one of the security personnel after him toward the far side of the hallway. Clint jerked his head at Garrett, who unstuck his feet from position and followed. Noonan and Camp moved slightly together, filling the gap between them.

"Raise your hands, please," the security guard ordered, in a bored tone of voice.

The slim man put his hand inside his coat and produced a palm-sized black leather folder. He flipped it open, and Garrett saw the shield with the eagle and blindfolded figure of Justice, made familiar by dozens of TV shows.

"Federal Bureau of Investigations," he said, in a low voice. "I'm based in Richmond, and I'm rejoining my office."

"Great," Clint said. "Go right ahead. Leave the gun here."

"But I'm authorized—"

Clint said, pointing, "I have orders to keep all weapons on *that* side of the metal detector. Hand it over."

The agent looked from Clint to Garrett, and then beyond them at the other three guardsmen. Clint said, "There's another squad on the runways, buddy, and the state police at the gates. Hand over the gun."

The slim man reached slowly under his coat, produced a nine-millimeter, and relinquished it to the security guard. He said, "You know you folks are breaking federal law, here. The FBI is independent of state and local jurisdiction."

"Well now," Clint said, "that's only true in the United States of America, isn't it? Back through the detectors."

The agent cleared his throat, but another look at Clint Larsen's face seemed to change his course of action. He shoved his hands into the pockets of his gray overcoat and trudged back toward the detectors. This time the metal framework around him remained silent.

"That was so easy," Garrett said, astonished.

"That was a try-on, not a serious attempt. Just you wait. This is only the beginning. They won't let us go without a struggle."

"Washington—"

"Not Washington. The World Parliament."

Something inside Garrett rose up in triumph. So there *was* something here that didn't show on the surface. He hadn't wasted two years in careful cultivation of the man.

"What's that?" he said, wide-eyed.

"There's a World Constitution slowly being ratified," Larsen said, in a voice almost lost under the buzz of the crowd, "and it's up before Congress now. If the U.S.A. doesn't ratify it, we'll lose our chance to participate in the world economy. And the UN is pressuring Washington into acceptance. They'll do it, Franklin. They don't care for freedom or independence in Congress, not so long as they get paid. The whole U.S.A. is going to crash and burn, and the governor pulled Virginia out of the wagon just in time."

Garrett watched the FBI agent walk past Phillips and head for the silent escalators. He had the feeling that a great deal rode on his next words, and he wished his thoughts moved more quickly. Over to his left a passenger began to protest loudly.

Garrett offered, "We've got to be careful to guard our freedom, then. I mean, won't the—er—World Parliament send in soldiers, or something?" He worked to get more indignation in his voice and added, "We can't let some World Parliament take Virginia away from us!"

Clint said scornfully, "The guard can't fight the UN. Not enough men."

"What'll we do, then?"

"We'll have to cooperate with other patriots."

"But how will we find them?"

Clint grinned faintly. "Want to meet them?"

"Yes! Yes, of course."

"You wait, then. You will. I'll take you."

"Who are they? When—"

"Hush up, boy," Clint said. "Get back in line."

Garrett took a firmer grip on his gun. He said, "I do want to meet them."

Clint Larsen smiled, faintly, walking away from him.

He took himself back to the cordon and stood, watching the restless crowd sift by. He swallowed, feeling excitement rising up in the back of his throat. He had been right. Clint Larsen may have had an alibi for Matthew Franklin's death, but his surface normality concealed something else, something more sinister. And all he had to do to get a closer look was wait.

Outside the glassed-in walls, dark coated the runways. Another plane dropped down onto the concrete. Garrett could only see the lights, flicking rapidly away over the black surface.

CHAPTER 11

☆ ☆ ☆ ☆ ☆ ☆ ☆

Thursday, March 21, noon

D ON'T DO IT," Alexander Wade repeated, for the fifth time. "Mr. President, you don't want this kind of confrontation. Not now. Let's pretend they aren't there."

"And just how do we do that? There's guard on every square foot of Virginia. All I want to do is call them back to our side."

Wade looked wearily across the table at the president. The chief executive had no talent for waiting games. He was a man of swift and decisive movement; he tended to act, in fact, like the Lord of the Manor his aristocratic face suggested. The president put both his elbows on the table. He said, "I have ultimate power over the guard, Mr. Secretary."

"Look here," Wade said, getting to his feet. The cabinet was in the military situation room in the Old Executive Office Building. Clustered at the end of the thirty-foot table along with Wade and the president were the treasurer of the United States, a short man with indigestion; the national security adviser, looking as though he thought Virginia was very small potatoes after Iraq and Palestine; the director of the CIA, who wasn't particularly interested in the Old Dominion as such, but wanted Camp Peary back; the secretary of transportation, nursing a cold; the secretary of commerce, who was married to the brother of the national security adviser; the director of the FBI, a heavy and formidable man whose name opened doors anywhere in the city; and the attorney general. Ramsey Grant was slouched in the seat beside the director, his long legs stretched out in front of him.

Wade let his glance pass over Grant and rest on the director. The last
few days had revealed that Ramsey Grant had a surprising influence
within the FBI; and in response, Alexander Wade had done a great deal
of hard and quiet digging. The night before, he'd finally discovered a fact
which had certainly never been made public. Ramsey Grant had served
as an FBI agent, and for several years had worked in the behavioral science
services unit. He had spent his entire working career profiling criminals,
laying out their probable characteristics, keeping records on every twitch
and mannerism of convicted psychopaths. This information had not appeared in the background check the FBI had supplied to the president, at
the time when Grant's appointment as attorney general had first been
considered.

Wade turned his back on Ramsey Grant and the rest of the cabinet
and jabbed his finger against the map of Virginia. They'd chosen this
room because the president didn't want the full cabinet to watch him
thrash around like a gaffed flounder, and also because the military situation room had a map screen. The little huddle of administration
officials took up less than a quarter of the chairs.

"Look here, Mr. President," he said again. "He's put the National
Guard at the airports. We sent a guy out to RIC in a private plane
and told him to go through the terminal with his gun and badge,
and he lost the weapon on the way out. The guard's not letting anyone bearing arms through any airport. Not just Richmond, but
Petersburg too, and all the little airports. West Point, Farmville,
Lynchburg—we've checked them all. Even the private airports are
guarded. He's got guard at all the ports, from just north of Knotts
Island all the way up to the mouth of the Potomac." His finger
skimmed along the southern border of Virginia. "There are guard
checking licenses and doing truck searches at every road into North
Carolina—17, 32, 95, 85, all the way up to Cumberland Gap. Guard
all along the Kentucky and West Virginia borders, all the way north
and then back east until Clarke County. He's even got guard on the
Shenandoah. Ramsey here sent a guy down it with a canoe and a
fishing pole and a Maryland driver's license, and two guard boats came

sailing after him and told him to go fish in his own state. Now look. No guard here." He pointed to the blue line of Interstate 95, where it crossed from the District of Columbia into Arlington. "Not a sign of a rifle on 495 anywhere. No guard at Leesburg or Herndon. Nothing at Dulles."

He looked over his shoulder. They were all watching. Ramsey Grant was pinching his lower lip thoughtfully.

"I'll tell you where those guard are," Wade said, scooping up the red pencil that lay on the lectern, just below the map screen. "They're on Route 17, where it runs into Clarke County from Loudoun. They're blocking 66 where it crosses from Fauquier into Warren. They're sitting on 95, just outside of Fredericksburg. And that tells us that Merriman's going to dump these counties."

He put the tip of the pencil on Fairview Beach and ran it along the line of the Rappahanock River, up to Chester Gap, and then through Manassas Gap all the way to the Maryland border, excising an irregular square from Virginia's hump.

"The suburban counties," Ramsey Grant said. "Loudoun, Fairfax, Prince William, Stafford, Fauquier, Arlington."

"Exactly."

"Why those?" asked the national security adviser, sounding bored.

"Because Fairfax is full of United States federal buildings and employees, including Langley; Arlington has the Pentagon, among other things; Prince William and Stafford contain Quantico and the U.S. Marine Corps Reservation; Fauquier has the Vint Hill Farm Military Reservation, and Loudoun, of course, has Dulles. He's not stupid. He knows he can't secede with the Pentagon and an international airport."

"He's seceded with the Farm," the director of the CIA muttered. At the same time, the treasurer objected, "Those six counties have the highest per capita income in the state. Not to mention a huge amount of commercial tax revenue. Doesn't he want the money?"

"No," Wade said. "To start with, there's no commercial tax revenue in Merriman's new system. The nine-percent tax applies only to personal income. There's no corporate tax and no sales tax. Sure, the personal tax from all those triple-figure Washington salaries would be useful. But he'd have to take over responsibility for medical treatment in those five counties, and they happen to have the highest Medicaid demands in Virginia, because the HIV infection rate in northern Virginia is about triple that in the rest of the state. Furthermore, maintenance of the road system up here would take a huge bite out of that nine-percent tax. So he'll dump the AIDS victims and the road maintenance along with the potential income. And, don't forget, he'll keep all the economic infrastructure created by the tobacco industry, which otherwise would be lost. In the end, he won't come out so badly."

"Not so badly?" the treasurer asked, incredulously. "I ran the figures this morning. He'll have to cut the state budget in thirds. On a personal income tax of nine percent, he can collect a little under six billion, if he's lucky; and Virginia's budget last year was over fifteen billion. He'll create financial chaos. Look here." He produced a sheaf of papers and handed them around the table. Wade came silently away from the screen and reached for his own copy. Rows of figures lined up under a neat heading: THE COMMONWEALTH OF VIRGINIA.

"Virginia's budget for last year," the treasurer announced. "I'll round this off, for simplicity's sake. The state's total revenue was fifteen billion dollars. Okay? Let's start with the taxes. Virginia collected three-and-a-half billion dollars in individual income taxes, a bit under three billion in sales tax, almost three hundred million in corporate income tax. Various other taxes: six hundred million in gasoline tax, sixteen million in tobacco tax, eighty-five million in alcohol tax—"

Alexander Wade, sitting with his head propped in his hands and his copy of Virginia's budget in front of him, felt drowsiness creeping up around him like a warm bath. Since Monday he'd had only broken hours of sleep, mostly on a cot in his office. Whenever he allowed himself a moment's stillness, exhaustion washed over him with seductive force. Now, listening to the treasurer's drone, he wanted to shout out, *This revolution has nothing to do with Virginia's budget, and no accounting will show you the minds of two men who think they understand the purposes of God.*

He blinked, watching the columns of figures reel in front of his eyes.

The treasurer droned on, "Two-and-a-half billion from the federal government. He'll lose that, of course. On the next page—"

The cabinet turned to the next page, obediently.

"—we have a little under four hundred million in license fees, fifteen million in property tax—"

At this rate, Wade thought, *it will take a very long time to reach fifteen billion.* He said, "Mr. President, this isn't really the point, right now. If Merriman cuts the state budget by too much, he may grow unpopular; but we won't see the effects of that for months. We have to decide what to do now. Today. And my advice remains the same. Let's take up a defensive posture. Make no military threat. Let's take every civil remedy we can. Let's send the IRS in, when Virginians all fail to pay income tax. And Elizabeth has suggested economic sanctions."

The secretary of commerce said, "It won't do tobacco interests much good to manufacture cigarettes, Mr. President, if they can't export them to the other forty-nine states. Merriman's probably counting on having people from all over the United States making tobacco runs into Virginia so they can stock up on tax-free cigarettes."

The president leaned back in his chair.

"So we wait?" he said. "That's all you've offered me since Sunday."

"Not just waiting, sir. The IRS—"

The president said impatiently. "That won't work; and I'll show you why." He leaned forward and held a clear sheet out to Wade. "I received this document by private messenger, early this morning, and copied it onto a transparency."

That explained a bit of information Wade had filed away; that the president had been seen padding down the staircase in his bedroom slippers, headed for the first floor offices with a paper in his hand.

"You'll excuse my not handing out copies," the president added, with a glance at Ramsey Grant, "but I'm sure you'll understand that this information must remain inside this room."

Grant inclined his head. The treasurer folded his budget back up, stiffly. Alexander Wade took the transparency from the president's outstretched hand and laid it on the overhead projector.

The Reformed American States
The Executive Mansion
Richmond, Virginia
R.A.S.

The President of the United States
The White House
Pennsylvania Avenue
Washington, D.C.
U.S.A.

Mr. President:

Due to the long-standing relationship between the Commonwealth of Virginia and the United States of America, and because of our shared history and the purposes we at one time held in common, the cabinet of the Reformed American States has resolved to extend unusual tolerance toward the United States during this time of transition. We propose the following arrangements between our two countries:

1) Transportation between the two countries will not require passport presentation for the space of one (1) year. The R.A.S. reserves the right to search all persons and vehicles passing through her borders.

2) The R.A.S. will maintain all former interstate highways at her own expense, and will allow citizens of the United States to utilize them for a nominal fee to be paid at the borders.

3) The R.A.S. recognizes the ownership of certain properties by the United States government, and will consider them as foreign soil. While we will not exercise any of the rights of government over the sites listed below, the R.A.S. reserves the privilege of treating the boundaries of each site as a foreign border, and will demand identification and perform searches on any persons leaving or entering these sites:

Arlington National Cemetery, Arlington

The Pentagon, Arlington
Dulles International Airport, Fairfax
The Vint Hill Military Reservation, Fauquier
Quantico, Prince William
The United States Marine Corps Reservation, Stafford
All federal sites, Langley

Here the first page of the overhead ended. Alexander Wade reached silently to change the transparency. Merriman had not, in fact, posted guard at those particular sites, which supported his theory that the governor was prepared to lose the six northern counties. But if he relinquished the southern military bases as well, half the United States' iron justification for reacting with force to the secession would be gone.

He replaced the overhead with the next sheet of the letter. The list continued:

Fort A.P. Hill, Caroline
Camp Peary, James City
Fort Eustis, York
Camp Pendleton, Virginia Beach
Oceana Naval Air Station, Virginia Beach
Naval Weapons Station, Williamsburg
Norfolk Naval Station
Little Creek Amphibious Naval Station

The R.A.S. recognizes that the defenses of the United States of America are highly dependent upon these sites. We do not wish to deprive the U.S.A. of her defenses; we ask only for a peaceful settlement of the differences between our two countries. However, as the United States will not be able to make full use of defensive weapons located in another country, we request an immediate meeting with the secretary of defense to discuss a reasonable timeline for the relocation of these defenses. When U.S.A. forces have been returned to their own country, the R.A.S. is willing to purchase the buildings and facilities at a reasonable price.

4) The moneys paid into the United States Treasury by the people

of Virginia will be considered fair exchange for the federal funds invested back into the Commonwealth. Thus, we now stand on equal footing. In a gesture of goodwill, the governor has also ordered all citizens of the R.A.S. to file tax returns for the previous year, to pay all taxes owed, and to pay all estimated taxes for the first quarter of the present year. But we hereby serve notice that Virginia is free and independent of any debts incurred by the United States of America after midnight on Tuesday, March 19; and owes no duties to the United States of America after that date. Any efforts of the United States to collect funds from the people of Virginia after this date will be considered unjust foreign aggression.

In return, we request that the United States of America honor all holdings of Reformed American States citizens which may fall outside the boundaries of our country, treating them as foreign-owned sites and extending to them the rights and protections due any foreign-owned properties.

As of midnight, March 19, the Commonwealth of Virginia—under the protection of the Reformed American States—assumes ownership, protection, and responsibility for all national forests, parks, and wildlife areas within her borders.

The R.A.S. will be pleased to send an ambassador to Washington, D.C. to discuss a time and place for meetings to work out the proposals contained herein.

By the authority of the people of Virginia,
Charles Aaron Merriman
Governor of Virginia
Acting Chairman, Reformed American States

Alexander Wade waited for the cabinet to finish reading this astonishing document. He could see it in their eyes when they reached the final paragraphs; a mixture of incredulity, disbelief, and the dawning knowledge that Charles Merriman had stopped the lion's mouths.

The treasurer spoke first. He said, "But if he holds to this, the Internal Revenue Service won't be able to take legal action until the next quarterly filing date. September. That's over three months. Mr. President, by September they'll have the rest of the world believing Virginia's a separate country. This thing will gather too much momentum to be stopped."

Someone asked, "So it isn't true that Merriman returned all federal money paid into the state system since January? I heard that on CBS."

"No," the treasurer snapped, "of course it isn't. He may have put the rumor out. But that money's long spent. No; what he's doing here is far more subtle. He's postponing the legal confrontation until months after Virginia becomes *de facto* a separate country."

The president raised his head. He said, "Anyone else have something to offer me? Phil?"

The secretary of transportation said dubiously, "If he keeps the interstates and ports open, Mr. President, and doesn't restrict air space, I don't see what protests I can make." He blew his nose, miserably.

"Dan?"

The director of the CIA said, "I can't train my people on a compound that belongs to another country. Either we get the state back, now, or move the Farm somewhere else. Quickly, Mr. President. You know that the foreign situation—"

"Yes," the president said. "Jack?"

The national security adviser observed, "I have one thing to say, Mr. President. Chechnya. Do you happen to remember how the world reacted to Gorbachev when he wouldn't allow the republic to break away? Do you know how it will look to the rest of the world if we use any sort of force to get Virginia back? The guardian of freedom, lassoing people yelling for freedom and tying them down."

The president dropped his chin onto his chest. After a very long moment he said, "Alex, anything to add?"

"Just this," Alexander Wade said. "We're walking on a line half-an-inch wide. If we deploy the army, the navy, the air force, the marines, then we're either breaking the law, or else we're admitting that the law against deploying the military against U.S. citizens no longer applies because Virginia is, indeed, a separate country. We must avoid that at all costs. And Mr. President, speaking as the secretary of defense, I can tell you that our national defenses are not weakened as long as I still have full jurisdiction over the bases Merriman has listed. Temporarily, anyway. It wouldn't work in the long run. But for right now—"

"We wait?" the president snapped. "That's all you've offered me since Sunday night."

"Mr. President, in a few weeks those two men are going to start issuing laws based on the Book of Deuteronomy. Have you ever *looked* at Deuteronomy? How popular is Charles Merriman going to be when he starts stoning gays and forcing people to go to church on Sunday morning?"

The president sniffed. "Ramsey?" he inquired.

The attorney general let a few seconds of silence go by. At last he said, "I'm with Wade on this one, Mr. President. I think we wait. And in the meantime, we take the step Elizabeth suggested to me just before this meeting started. Economic sanctions. We've discovered—" he gestured to the silent director of the FBI beside him, "that Merriman's sent for another Christian reconstructionist—John Cline, the renegade economist from Santa Fe. Elizabeth's seen his work."

Elizabeth Archer, the secretary of commerce, said, "He believes all interest payments are unbiblical. He'll tell them to stop all welfare, all Medicaid, all food stamps. If we wait, people will come running out of Virginia. We can begin the process by cutting off trade. When some of the big corporations with Virginia plants—Nabisco, Anheuser Busch, and the paper companies in Hopewell, and the James River Corporation—discover that they can't export to the other forty-nine states, the revolution is going to grind to a halt. And Mr. President, if I might suggest it . . . the first thing we ought to do is stop the postal service. I agree with the secretary of defense. When these people get a taste of what they call freedom, they'll discover that it's only another word for inconvenience and poverty."

The president held out his hand for the overhead. Alexander Wade snapped off the light and pulled the transparency from the screen. The room was suddenly darker.

"Very well," the president said. "I seem to be forced onto the path of prudence. We will re-evaluate the situation the day after the first justice codes are published. I will meet with the postmaster general at once. Elizabeth, I want an immediate plan of action for the economic sanctions. Let's get this into Congress as soon as possible. And Sam—" this was directed to the treasurer, "I want a careful eye kept on income tax returns filed by Virginia taxpayers. I'm not impressed by Merriman's nobility. Virginians are going to use this to try to squirm out of every tax dollar they owe, and I'll bet half of next year's votes that Charles Merriman isn't going to crack down on the offenders."

"Yes, Mr. President."

"And I'm calling out the Maryland and North Carolina Guard," the president added. "This is not negotiable. I refuse to pretend that there is no threat here. We can't tell the rest of America that we're not doing anything in particular to counter this. Bringing out the guard on either side of Virginia will make it clear that we're not going to tolerate literal revolution in this country."

The cabinet, duly warned, rose silently and fumbled together their papers and briefcases. Someone's Virginia budget fluttered to the floor. Wade lingered, as the other administration officials filed out the door.

The president snapped, "I've got an appointment with the speechwriters. I know you're dying to tell me I shouldn't call out the guard, Alex, but make it short."

Alexander Wade thought sourly that he might as well save his breath. When the chief executive got that look of obstinate righteousness on his face, God Himself couldn't shift him from his path.

"You shouldn't do it," he said doggedly. "It's a hostile act. And it may backfire."

"Noted," the president said. He strode away, aides scurrying in his wake.

TWENTY-FOUR HOURS LATER they were huddled in the Oval Office, incredulous. The president had issued the order to turn out the National Guard; and the Maryland Guard had duly reported in loyal defense of the Union. At the moment, over 55 percent of the North Carolina Guard had failed to respond to the executive order.

Alexander Wade lifted his head at last from the figures.

"Mr. President," he said, "it's *spreading*."

PART II

★

INDEPENDENCE

CHAPTER 12

Friday, March 22, early afternoon

T HE CROWD AROUND Richmond's Capitol Green had changed. The protesting, pushing mass had given way to sightseers, pointing and taking pictures. National Guard in dress uniforms replaced Merriman's private security force, and the security cordon had moved back toward the Executive Mansion, re-opening the green to the public. Hardly anyone had taken advantage of this fact.

A new flag flew over Thomas Jefferson's white pillars. Margaret, squinting up at it against the shining sky, could see the unfamiliar symbol: a mountain wreathed by smoke, against a white background. Black letters, too distant to read, circled the mountain. Virginia's familiar blue flag flapped beneath the white pennant: Justice, with her foot on the neck of Tyranny.

She followed the chief of police up the curving asphalt, toward the Roman front of the Capitol. She'd met Daniel Caprio at his office earlier. She had understood that he would update her on Charles Merriman's interest in Matthew's case; and she had been surprised when he rose and said, "The governor has asked us to come over to his office."

At the front steps of the Capitol, a polite guard sergeant at the front steps checked their names against a list and motioned them on. They climbed up toward the wide double doors, where a young secretary stood waiting.

"Welcome to the Capitol," she said. "If you'll follow me, I'll show you to the governor's office."

They marched through the rotunda, past the life-sized statue of George Washington, and turned left. Emptiness echoed under their feet. Several doors, half-open from the hallway, showed offices with computer screens dark and padded chairs unoccupied.

"Quiet here today," Margaret ventured.

"Most state employees have been given a temporary paid leave," the secretary explained. She led them up narrow marbled stairs that turned four times. Margaret could hear Caprio puffing behind her. They came out, unexpectedly, onto the banistered gallery that gave a clear view of the first floor below and the colored dome of the rotunda overhead. Ahead of them, gold letters over a doorway read: *The Governor's Office.*

"The governor usually works in his private southeast office," the secretary said, "but he's chosen to use this office today." She led them along the banisters, through the door. A receptionist sat in front of another copy of Virginia's seal.

"Morning, Chief Caprio," the receptionist said cheerfully. He reached for the telephone on his desk and said, "Governor, the chief is here with Mrs. Franklin." At the inaudible answer, he nodded and put the receiver down.

"Go on in," he said.

Daniel Caprio led her past the desk and seal, through another door, and she found herself shaking hands with Charles Merriman. He was taller than she had expected; the thick straight dark hair fell over his blue eyes, and there was a faint smell about him of something spicy, like oranges.

"Please sit down, Mrs. Franklin," he said, releasing her hand. "Morning, Dan; how's crime?"

"Down, at the moment," Chief Caprio said cheerfully. "All the perps are waiting to see what happens next."

Merriman smiled and turned back to his desk, revealing the far side of the room, sunny southern windows, and leather chairs. Kenneth Balder rose from one of the chairs. His tall body was dark against the window. Margaret stared at him, startled, and then remembered his words. *Maggie, don't tell*

Charles Merriman about the past. I don't want you on his string. He met her eyes with polite blankness, but she had seen a moment of surprise in his face.

A stout red-haired man stood up on his right. Merriman said, "I've taken the liberty of asking two members of my new cabinet to join me in my meetings today. Would either of you like coffee? Or a Coke, maybe?"

"No, thank you," Margaret said. Caprio shook his head. Ken was now gazing at his feet. Merriman said, reseating himself, "My chief of staff, Kenneth Balder. This is Margaret Franklin. And the chief of police, Daniel Caprio. You haven't yet had a chance to meet him."

"Mrs. Franklin," Ken said, courteously. "Chief Caprio."

She shook his hand, and a thrill went up her arm. *You fool,* she chided herself, *coming out in goosebumps like a high-school girl with a crush.* She sat down hastily on one of the chairs facing Merriman's desk. When she saw Ken, the memory of his voice, his hands, his body, still came to her with overwhelming clarity. It was a good reason not to look him in the eye, in the presence of three other people. If she didn't look at him at all, she wouldn't be distracted from the task at hand.

"And James Macleod, my press secretary," Merriman went on. The stout red-haired man inclined his head. "The adjutant general has been appointed secretary of defense for the Reformed American States, but he's busy elsewhere today. We're still in the process of appointing a fifth member of the cabinet, who will act as our treasurer. Please, everyone, sit down."

Ken lowered himself back into his chair. Caprio sat down beside Margaret, blocking Ken's profile from view. She fixed her eyes on Charles Merriman.

"Well then," Merriman began, "let's move on to business. Mrs. Franklin, we'll be publishing the new constitution of the Reformed American States in tomorrow's *Times-Dispatch.* I'll give you an advance copy before you leave. I think you'll find it self-explanatory. These next two weeks we'll be working out a new code; that is, specific laws to cover criminal and civil matters, tax rates and collections, and so forth."

Margaret nodded.

"Chief Caprio, of course, has been involved in the formulation of the criminal codes. But I want to be sure that those who will be affected understand the theoretical foundations for what we're doing, Mrs.

Franklin . . . and so I've committed Ken here to explaining theonomy twenty times per day for the entire weekend." He gave Kenneth Balder a grin.

"How will I be affected?" Margaret asked.

"I haven't had time to discuss this with Dr. Balder," Merriman said, "but I'd like to re-open your husband's case as the first trial under the new system." He swiveled his chair to face Kenneth Balder.

"I'll hand this over to you, Ken," he said. "Dr. Balder, in case you're unfamiliar with his work—"

"I don't think anyone's unfamiliar with Kenneth Balder, after the last week of television and newspaper stories," Chief Caprio said dryly.

"My unpleasant past has been thoroughly aired," Ken agreed.

Caprio added, "It's kind of ironic, isn't it, Dr. Balder? Wouldn't you have been executed, under the system you propose?"

The chief's voice was curious, not hostile; but Margaret felt her stomach twist. She sensed Charles Merriman's sharp blue eyes on her face, and schooled her features into disinterested attentiveness. She had no idea whether this was successful. Merriman, after a moment, removed his gaze from her and settled it back on his chief of staff.

"In point of fact," Ken said calmly, "my own situation would be covered by the Old Testament cities of refuge clause. It was an accidental death. You'll find that the Old Testament death penalty is only imposed in cases of brutal and premeditated murder."

I imagine he's used to talking about it, Margaret thought, incredulously, *and now he can do it with no emotion in his voice.*

"Which means," Ken added, "that under our new laws, I would have gone to a designated location and remained there, voluntarily, for a prescribed period of time. So certainly I would have forfeited my liberty for quite a while. But in the meantime I could have continued to work, support myself, and contribute to society, instead of becoming the drain on the taxpayer purse that I actually was. Prison offers no opportunity for penance, or recompense either; only for corruption. I was twenty-two when I went into the California prison system. I came out at thirty-one. If it had not been for my conversion to Christianity, I would have emerged a much more accomplished criminal."

He looked directly at Margaret and added, "How much do you know about what we're trying to do here, Mrs. Franklin?"

"You intend to use the Old Testament laws as your guide for criminal justice?"

"That's right."

She steeled her voice. Until she was able to bring the whole matter of Matthew's death to a close, she refused to be overwhelmed by Ken. It had nothing to do with forgiveness; this was a simple matter of loyalty.

"Why the Old Testament?" she inquired.

Ken said, "Because it contains the law of God. The press calls us Christian reconstructionists, but we prefer the term *theonomists*. Take that word apart, and you'll find it means, simply, 'the law of God.' We do want to reconstruct society, but only by God's guidelines. And the Bible tells us that God is immutable. He does not change. So the rules for living in the Old Testament aren't outdated. If they were, we'd be dealing with a changeable God."

He got up from his chair and started to pace up and down on the small strip of carpet between his chair and Charles Merriman's desk. He said, "We believe this: God created humanity, and mankind can only function if we follow God's rules in every sphere of life. Especially in politics. All law is based on man's views of himself and his moral responsibility to God. . . . so all legislation is a profoundly religious enterprise. And whenever we start to use our own reason to govern, we begin to go wrong."

He paused.

"I understand that," Margaret said.

"God doesn't leave us to stumble around and find His rules for living on our own. He's a God of the Word, and so He wrote them down for us, in the Bible. Once there was a nation that had a blueprint for living—the Israelites. God gave them just laws that are still valid today."

"All of them?" Margaret asked.

"All but the ceremonial rituals," Kenneth Balder said. Any society which doesn't run on God's laws is bound to self-destruct eventually. Look at all the nations that have come and gone. Even the Israelites were taken into captivity when they refused to obey God's law. And the United States government never had all that much to do with God's law. The Declaration of Independence starts off with the laws of nature; nature's God runs a poor second. America was founded on the Enlightenment. Man's mind, not God's. So American society only lasted as long as the informal influence of God's law remained strong. Through about 1950, in fact. Now the society is collapsing. We can only save ourselves from the wreckage by cutting loose from it, and boarding another ship."

"By declaring independence?"

"Exactly."

"And turning us into a Christian version of Iran?"

"That's the easy response," Ken said. "It only proves you've been reading *Time.*" The retort held a faint sting. He looked as though he had not expected her to criticize. "We're not talking about a society of repression, Mrs. Franklin. We're not going to sent the police to check on whether you're mixing milk and meat. From our point of view, the need for laws about diet and sacrifice have passed. We're interested in the laws for running society—a just society, where law-abiding people live in peace and lawbreakers are justly punished."

"Would I be forced to attend a Christian church?"

"No. God's law was never meant to regulate belief; that's an internal matter, between God and your own soul. The law was meant to bring justice in the civil sphere, between man and man."

Margaret objected, "Don't the Ten Commandments order you to keep the Sabbath?" "How can you enforce that without interposing the government between God and my soul?"

"Have you ever read John Cotton's abstract of the laws of New England?" Ken asked.

"No, of course not."

"The early Puritans wrestled with the same problem. You'll find that their laws—many of which we'll put back into effect in the new code—make no effort to regulate the heart. There are penalties for cursing God in public, for open practice of Satanism, for making an actual idol and setting it up for worship. All those are public and outward actions. Charles tells me you run a nursery, Mrs. Franklin." The blue eyes were innocent, and very faintly amused.

"Er," Margaret said, "yes. In New Kent."

"Under the civil laws, then, you'll be required to close your nursery on Sunday. That's a business regulation enforced in the civil sphere, related to the Fourth Commandment. But no one will force you to use that free Sunday to worship God. Your worship is no business of the law. Unless, that is, you begin to publicly teach that God is imaginary."

"So no freedom of expression?" Margaret persisted.

"Freedom of expression has never been an absolute good," Ken said. "Even under the Constitution of the United States, you can't threaten someone's body. How much more important is the soul? Those who teach God's nonexistence are tempting others away into eternal darkness."

He paused for a moment. "And lest I begin to sound like a religious fanatic, Mrs. Franklin, let me point out that if you want a law-abiding society, you can't let people teach that there is no God. Otherwise morality becomes only a matter of opinion, and law becomes a matter of argument rather than enforcement. If you wonder what I mean, look around you." He waved his hand at the window and, presumably, the rest of the United States that lay outside it. "For that reason, the laws of New England tolerated private heresy—to a degree—but made public teaching of heresy a capital crime."

"So you would execute people for public heresy?"

"That brings us to the criminal codes," Ken said. "The Mosaic solution for a violent society is: Murder earns capital punishment. Any killing apart from accident, warfare, or self-defense is punished by execution. That's written into the fabric of the legislation of Moses. Capital punishment for heresy, though, that's another question. You have to take into account the difference between Israelite society and the present-day society. Some theonomists don't, of course. John Cline, the notorious Santa Fe theonomist, insists that the Old Testament be followed in every single detail, even when those details are culturally invalid. But the Puritans considered that while actual killing was a crime against humanity—I'm putting this into modern terms, of course—and could only be satisfied by execution, heresy was a crime against the community of faith and could be satisfied by banishment. From a practical point of view, I'm bound to say that sending blasphemers across the Potomac will result in much less public furor than stoning them on Capitol Green." He paused for effect and when his comment elicited no response, he added, "That was a joke. Stoning's not an essential part of the criminal justice code."

"What are the penalties? Imprisonment?"

"No," Ken said bluntly. "Prison doesn't work. Our modern prison system is a legacy of the Quakers who fondly imagined that if a criminal were given a chance to learn and meditate, his inner light would reveal the error of his ways and he would come out of confinement a moral man. The products of our prison system have tended to discredit this theory. Restitution of the victim by the offender is the most common punishment for non-capital crimes."

Merriman moved in his chair. Margaret tore her eyes away from Ken to look at the governor. She'd almost forgotten his presence, and that of James Macleod, listening peacefully from his own chair. It had been years since she'd seen Ken's charisma in full operation, and she had forgotten the full force of personality he could bring to bear in an argument. Here, in his presence, she could barely remember Matthew's face.

Charles Merriman said, "Let's discuss your own situation, Mrs. Franklin. Do you know the case, Ken?"

"No," Kenneth Balder said, after a long moment.

"Her husband was murdered here in Richmond, and the killer remains at large due to a technicality."

Ken's blue eyes shifted to her face. She fixed her eyes on a point beyond his left shoulder.

"I think the case could stand a fresh investigation," she said. "I'm not at all convinced that the man in question had a good motive for shooting my husband. There are other possibilities. He was suspicious about his National Guard unit, and one of the sergeants lived in Oregon Hill—"

Daniel Caprio said hastily, "We can go over this later. Let me ask you this, Dr. Balder. Aren't you concerned about the fact that this particular offense took place before your new laws came into operation?"

A silence stretched out between the leather chairs. Merriman said, "Ken, are you with us?"

"Yes. Yes, of course. There's no statute of limitations on murder. It doesn't become any less wrong as time goes by. Naturally, anyone who has already been tried would be beyond the reach of a newly-instituted system—"

"Margaret's case never went to trial," Caprio said promptly. "Jerry Tindell, that's the man's name. Never even arrested."

"I see," Ken said.

Merriman said insistently, "So we could offer Mrs. Franklin, for example, a trial for her husband's killer?"

"Yes," Ken said, "if there were sufficient evidence." His voice was puzzled, and there was a crease between his eyebrows.

Margaret began, "The evidence of Matthew's own suspicions about the guard has never been—"

"As I mentioned to you earlier," Merriman said, overrunning her, "this would be an excellent first case for us. It would be a perfect illustration of the difference between the old administration and the new."

"I could look into it," Ken suggested.

"Looking into it won't do any good unless you consider all the facts," Margaret said sharply. She was aware of Merriman opening his mouth again and she said, "Please. Mr.—Dr. Balder. If you re-open Matthew's death and simply go over the same ground, all that will happen is you'll bring up all that agony again. . . . for all of us . . . without justice coming from it. I thought that's what you wanted here. Justice. That's all I'm asking for."

She halted, ashamed of the bare pleading in her voice. Ken's expression had become suddenly unfamiliar. After a moment, she recognized the new emotion. It was compassion, something she'd never seen in him before. He promised, "When we reopen the case, we can see that all avenues of investigation are fully pursued. I understand."

She cleared her throat and looked away. She'd almost lost herself there; abandoned herself to that unfamiliar gentleness, without even knowing it. She took a deep breath and tried to summon Matthew's face to her mind.

Merriman rubbed his hands together. "Very good," he said. "Do you have any other questions, Mrs. Franklin?"

Margaret steeled herself. She thought, *All I'm doing is showing him that my interest is only in Matthew's case. . . . not in him. And I have to know the truth.*

"You're trying to bring peace and order back to Virginia?" she asked.

"Yes, of course," Merriman said, with slight impatience.

"Is it true that Dr. Balder testified in a case against an abortion clinic bomber where he attempted to have the man's actions excused on the grounds of theological conviction?"

"*What?*" Ken said. She kept her gaze on Charles Merriman's dark face. His eyes had changed, very slightly. He said, "Of course not."

"It isn't?"

"No. The infamous Southside Bomber; I'm surprised no one else has dug that up. Where did you hear about it, by the way?"

"From an acquaintance."

"Dr. Balder did in fact testify—"

"I was called by the prosecution," Ken said sharply.

"The prosecution?"

"The bomber claimed the defense of justifiable homicide. I was asked whether justifiable homicide was in fact part of a biblical response to abortion. As an expert in biblical law, I said no. Your acquaintance didn't tell you that?"

"Is it true that all the publicity about you and your institute in California will help you make money?"

"Certainly not. CITL is a nonprofit organization, and I take no salary. They pay my airfares, that's all. If the institute does benefit from the secession, the money will go straight into the operating budget. I won't see a penny of it."

Charles Merriman said hastily. "Is there anything else?"

"I would like to be sure I have answered all of Mrs. Franklin's accusations," Ken said stiffly.

"Er . . . Mrs. Franklin?"

Margaret shook her head, wretchedly. She rose from the chair and Ken put his hand out. His fingers were cold.

"Good afternoon," he said.

STANDING ON THE BROAD FRONT PORCH of the Capitol, she became aware of Caprio's brown eyes, fixed on her face. He said at last, "You dislike the new chief of staff, Mrs. Franklin?"

"No," she said, "not exactly." She shifted the newspaper that Merriman had handed her, clasping it under her arm.

"What, then? You had your knife in that man."

"I like to know people's motivations," Margaret said, stubbornly. Her resolution seemed to have given way to a gaping empty pit.

"That's all well and good," Caprio said, "but I wouldn't annoy him, if I were you. He's the energy behind the reforms that are going to bring you justice." He started down the Capitol steps ahead of her, and then added. "After fifteen years of watching crimes go unpunished, I've got no illusions left about the American system. Virginia's the only place where you're going to find justice, Mrs. Franklin. You'd better be careful."

MARGARET HALTED AT THE ROADSIDE MAILBOX on her way in to her house, but to her annoyance the mail had not yet arrived.

The old truck bounced uncomfortably up the rutted lane. She needed new shocks, and the road could use a load of gravel. If she didn't have to shell out that hefty quarterly income tax payment in the fall, she'd be able to improve it and maybe hire some afternoon help. She was barely keeping up with orders as things stood.

The house was quiet, but the red light on the answering machine was blinking. Her first thought was *Ken!*, and she hit the button with a surge of anxiety. The beep was followed by Garrett's uncertain voice.

"Mom? I'm okay. Just wanted to tell you. I'm not supposed to say what we're doing, but it doesn't involve any fighting. Looks like I might be away from home for a while, but please don't worry. Everything's going to be all right. I'm not in any danger." There was a little silence. She waited for him to go on, but the silence was followed by a slight click.

"Mrs. Franklin, this is Allen Preszkoleski calling from the Pentagon—"

She punched the *Reset* button hastily, and watched the blinking light change back to steady red.

"That's the last time I listen to you, Mr. Defense Department," she muttered. She pulled out the coffeepot and dumped fresh grounds into the paper filter. Her head had begun to hurt again, and her jaw ached with tension. She leaned against the counter and shook open tomorrow's *Times-Dispatch* as the coffee began to drip into the pot.

CONSTITUTION OF THE REFORMED AMERICA STATES

Under the law of Almighty God, we, the people of the Reformed American States, do establish this constitution to provide for the just and peaceful administration of the Reformed American States.

Article I: The Executive Department

Section 1. *Executive power.* Executive power shall be vested in an executive council, which shall consist of the duly elected governors of all member states of the Reformed American States. The chairman shall hold his office for two years, and may not serve two terms in succession.

Section 2. *Chairman.* The chairman of the executive council shall be appointed from among the member governors of the council, by unanimous agreement of the remaining member governors.

Section 3. *Term.* The term of the chairman shall be two years. No chairman shall serve for more than one term in succession.

There was a great deal more, all in tiny newsprint, running down to the bottom of the page, where the last section read:

Article X. Entrance of Member States into the Reformed American States

She tossed the paper onto the table and stared at it. Garrett was lying. She hadn't raised him for twenty years without knowing the innocent blank sound of a lie in his voice. And yet all the news, print and radio, continued to insist that the guard was in no danger; they had been posted merely as a warning, and the reporters had been much more interested in the vagaries of the North Carolina turnout. *So,* she thought, *any threat to Garrett must have to do with his investigation of Matthew's death.*

She took her coffee out to the greenhouses with her, pulling on the earth-stained gloves she kept by the side door. She had a huge order of vinca to fill, and the tiny seedlings were crowding themselves out of the huge flat pans they had been sowed in. She moved them into the damp black soil of the plastic planters, six to a flat, grape and white and the tiny white ones with the red star in the middle. It was all very peaceful, except that her mind was full of worry for her son.

She let anxiety occupy all her thoughts. As long as worry consumed her, she could push away the memory of that stunned, betrayed look on Ken's face.

CHAPTER 13

☆ ☆ ☆ ☆ ☆ ☆ ☆

Friday, March 22, 5 P.M.

I THOUGHT you were bringing in a number of victims of crime, so we could hear their stories," Kenneth Balder said. He could hear the strain of anger in his voice. Merriman said, pacifically, "We had intended for you to meet several others—"

"You never told me you wanted her case to be re-opened right away."

"I'm sure I mentioned it to you yesterday."

"You most certainly did not."

"Don't you want her case re-opened?" The question sounded innocent. Balder veered away from the subject, overtaken by sudden caution. He snapped, "And who's been spreading rumors about the Southside Bomber?"

The governor's telephone began to ring, insistently. The governor put his hand on it and said, "Ken, I really have no idea."

"Mrs. Franklin implied that the National Guard unit should have been investigated. Why wasn't that done?

"Investigating the guard is pointless," Merriman said sharply. "Especially now. The guard is too important for Virginia's defense to risk any negative publicity—" The ringing went on. Merriman picked the receiver up with an apologetic grimace.

"Yes?" he said curtly. At the same moment, a tap came on the door. Balder strode over and wrenched it irritably open. Behind him, Charles

Merriman came halfway to his feet and then settled back resignedly into his chair.

"Give me a minute," he said to the telephone, and covered the mouthpiece. "Afternoon, John. You know Kenneth Balder, I think? Ken—John Cline, recently of Santa Fe, New Mexico."

Behind the young secretary, a tall gray-haired man with a Roman nose extended his hand.

"We've met," John Cline said.

Kenneth Balder held himself perfectly still. He could feel the beginnings of rage roiling up inside him. He eliminated every trace of anger from his voice and said, carefully, "Have you come to see what we're doing?"

"I've been invited to be your treasurer," John Cline said. His slow deep voice almost drowned out the sound of Merriman's staccato answers to the invisible caller. He grinned at the younger man. "Well," he said, "we've got work to do, haven't we? I trust I'm early enough to keep you from turning the Law of Moses into complete milk-and-water?"

Balder walked past him. Alone, in the hallway, he let anger take over his limbs. He threw himself out the door, across the green, and past the onlookers, ignoring the sudden rise in babbling voices as he passed. He strode down Broad Street, past the huge stone buildings that housed Virginia's government. He barely could see around him for the red film of rage washing up to cover his eyes. People were pointing and calling. Only three days ago, he had eaten breakfast on this street without anyone recognizing him. Three days of Jim Macleod's newspaper articles and national TV crews following him from meeting to meeting had forever shattered his anonymity. His knees were trembling with fury. It was the red demon which had haunted him all his life, the sin over which he spent hours in agonized prayer; and in all the years he had struggled with rage, he hadn't felt such a rush of anger since Mary Miranda had screamed and screamed, putting that whole mission—the culmination of months of planning—at the edge of disaster. He could still feel his hand coming down across her open mouth. He had been lying half on top of her, smothering that devastating noise, when he felt her breathing stop beneath him. God only knew, even now, whether the force he had put behind that palm had been to keep her safe, or had been born of the burning blind desire to have her simply extinguished.

A car drove up behind him. He turned his head. It was Charles Merriman's plain black car, with the National Guard driver impassive in the front seat. Merriman rolled the window down. His face had gone white.

"Ken," he said, "get in."

Kenneth Balder spat out, "Do you have any other surprises for me? A two-year-old murder case, orders not to investigate the guard, Southside Bomber rumors floating around, John Cline as treasurer—"

"Ken, get in. I need you. We've got trouble. There's been an armed attack on the North Carolina border. Mac Forbes just called me. If we leave now, we can get there before the media cameras. Ken, we've just lost the postal service, and there's a bill suggesting economic sanctions in the House right this minute. If we don't get control of this now, we've lost the whole war."

Kenneth Balder, standing on the sidewalk, saw two roads in front of him. A return to California: Maggie left with her suspicions of him and her unsolved murder case and her unending absorption with the past; and God only knew what legal battles he would face with the United States government, after his part in all this. Or this ongoing revolution with Charles Merriman, walking in the dark behind a man with complex and clouded motives. And a cabinet position in tandem with John Cline. He detested Cline's style and distrusted his scholarship. But at least at the end of that road he could see a kingdom where the lion lay down with the lamb; and at the end of the other road was a desert.

He reached for the handle of the door and slid in next to Merriman, ducking his tall head under the limousine's doorframe.

"I've got my helicopter standing by," Merriman began. His voice was relieved.

"Listen to me," Kenneth Balder said, coldly. "One more surprise, and I'm leaving this revolution. One more. You tell me *what* you're doing, *why* you're doing it, and *how* you're doing it, *before* you do it. Or I'll go back to

California and tell my supporters exactly what I think of your honesty. Do we understand each other?"

There was a silence. The driver was watching the governor's eyes in the rearview mirror. Merriman gave him a curt nod, and the car moved forward.

"Ken," Merriman said at last, "do you believe in divine appointment?"

"What does that mean?"

"It means that God never recommended democracy as His chosen pattern for government. He appointed a leader. Even those closest to Moses didn't always understand what he was doing."

"You're no Moses, Charles." He heard the echo of another politician in his voice, and Merriman smiled. He said, "I'm not crazy, Ken. I don't have delusions, or visions from heaven. I'm no Messiah. But I do think I've been put where I am, at this time, for a purpose. So that we can show the world what a country run by God's rules will look like. I have a chance to demonstrate the truth in front of the universe; and sometimes I have to make tough decisions and bear the full weight of them myself. Not spread the burden around to my cabinet."

"Then what authority do you obey?" Balder demanded.

"God's law constrains me," Merriman said, simply. "And if my cause is right, God's people will follow me."

They were almost at the airport. Kenneth Balder said rapidly, "I remember reading an article in . . . oh, the *Atlantic Monthly*, I think, about Hitler. Reviewing all the reasons Hitler became what he was. The writer finally said, 'The last victim of Hitler's rule is meaning, because we can't understand why he developed such hatred. This is the greatest mystery of modern times.' But it isn't, Charles. Hitler's hatred is the second-greatest mystery. The deeper mystery is: *Why did so many ordinary people follow him?* You remember that, Charles, when you see Virginia trailing along in your footsteps."

The car came to a halt. Charles Merriman, opening his door, said, "We'd forestall a lot of criticism if we were certain to appoint a high Jewish official. And an African-American. Make a note of that, Ken, and we'll get on it as soon as we get back. We're a bit too Anglo-Saxon for good PR, aren't we?"

He strode away toward the waiting helicopter. Kenneth Balder, moving more slowly, caught a glimpse of himself reflected in the windows of the black car; the brilliant blue eyes and blond hair, the tall Aryan figure. His father was Norwegian, his mother Dutch; his grandfather had spent seven years in a concentration camp for hiding a Jewish teenager. None of that would change his looks in the public eye. Merriman had turned his words back on himself, without even blinking to signal that the warning had been heard.

He walked toward the helicopter. For five days he had been part of a team. Now he was again on his own, as he had been for the decade before; balancing on a narrow path toward Paradise with a chasm on either side.

IN THE TWILIGHT that covered the North Carolina hills, he saw a brief flash, and then another. The blossoms of light were silent, drowned out by the noise of the chopper, but he felt Merriman's hand hard on his upper arm.

"Gunfire," Merriman mouthed.

Balder nodded. The pilot had seen the flashes also; he banked the helicopter sharply away. He shouted back over his shoulder, "Heading for the backup site, sir."

"Very good," Merriman called back.

The helicopter dropped through the dusk toward a large, open field beneath. Balder, reviewing the maps quickly in his head, placed them just south of Danville; he had seen the city lights pass beneath them a few minutes earlier. Route 29 ran across the North Carolina border here, straight south toward Greensboro. A logical place for a confrontation, an accessible and well-traveled road, but not a major interstate. The chopper bumped onto the ground. Balder ducked out under the blades, Merriman behind him.

"There," Merriman yelled, pointing. At the edge of the field, an uneasy little knot of men waited in front of a National Guard truck. In the middle of the whirling noise, they half-ran across the field toward the trees. Merriman's bodyguard trotted behind them.

"Who's in charge?" Merriman shouted, as soon as they were within earshot. All six men snapped to attention immediately. The captain, a stocky blond man in his thirties, shouted back, "Sir, I am. Michael Hines, captain, Twenty-sixth Army Guard."

"What's going on here?"

"Sir, we're supposed to escort you to the border. Governor Forbes of North Carolina is waiting for you."

Merriman jerked his head at Balder, and the two of them swung onto the back of the truck. The rest of the guardsmen—five men in battle gear, young and breathing fast—climbed up behind them, and the captain vaulted up beside them and barked an order to the driver. The truck started to move, bumping away from the field on uneven grass. Captain Hines said, "We'll take you to Route 29, sir, and move down to the border." His words were punctuated by the sound of shots, widely spaced and deliberate. Balder clutched the metal bench beneath him as the truck bounced through a rut.

"Who's shooting?" Merriman demanded.

"Sir, a North Carolina militia group demanded entrance. We told them to surrender their weapons and the situation deteriorated—"

"You're not fighting the North Carolina Guard?"

"Sir, we're not fighting anyone. We're at a standoff right now. Sir, the North Carolina Guard aren't posted at Route 29, I don't think they had enough turnout to cover all the roads—"

The truck jolted over a verge and onto a paved surface. *If this is Route 29,* Balder thought, peering out the back of the truck, *it's eerily empty.* Hines, intercepting his stare, offered, "We blocked 29 off at the nearest exit."

"This is my chief of staff," Merriman said. "Kenneth Balder."

"Yes, sir," Hines said. "They say they want to talk to the secretary of defense."

"Alexander Wade?"

"No, sir, yours."

"The adjutant general?"

"Yes, sir."

"Well, Joe's got his hands full with the Virginia Guard," Merriman said.

"Ken here's the closest thing I've got with me. They'll have to talk to the two of us."

The truck slowed. The shots had stopped, but the resulting calm was full of voices. Merriman had his foot on the bumper before the vehicle braked completely, and Balder followed him over the tailgate and around the front of the truck. Directly ahead of them, two more guard trucks were drawn together, hood-to-hood across 29. It was a four-lane highway here, and across a strip of grass two more trucks blocked the other side. A temporary wall had been erected across the grass, bridging the ditch that divided the verge. The scene was lit and shadowed by the headlights of a dozen trucks.

"Who ordered the wall?" Merriman asked.

"I did, sir," Hines said. "We had the material on hand—"

"Good work, Captain. Where's Forbes?"

"The governor's on the other side of the trucks, sir. We're parked right on the border. He doesn't want to come across."

Balder looked around him. It was an uncomfortable feeling, standing in the middle of a major highway; he half-expected traffic to come barreling over the hill toward him. On the other side of the trucks, a black limousine and three police cars sat in a flashing group, straddling the white lines. Another truck was parked in the grassy verge, its nose in the ditch divider. The headlights behind him lit up the red-and-blue of the North Carolina flag, painted on the side, and the gold letters *The Regulators* across the tailgate.

"Good heavens," Merriman said, mildly, "what happened to the militia truck?"

Captain Hines cleared his throat.

"Sir," he said, "the militia—they're a pretty big one, sir, based in Liberty, North Carolina, just south of Greensboro—they came up 29, saying they were ready to fight for liberty, all of them armed like they were going to war, sir. I had my orders, sir. I told them to disarm or go back. They said, er—"

"What?"

"Well, sir, they said I didn't have the guts to tell a true patriot what to do. I told them we'd fire if they didn't back off."

"And did you?" Merriman said.

"Yes, sir. They drove the truck straight at me, and I fired into the windshield. The truck went off the road."

"Anyone hurt, Captain?"

Hines' voice was expressionless.

"Driver's dead, sir. The rest of them scattered. They're in the woods now, taking shots at us." He motioned off the highway, toward the thin sapling woods that crowded up on either side of Route 29.

Merriman looked at him for a long moment.

"Did you have orders allowing you to use deadly force?" he asked at last.

"Yes, sir. In self-defense or in protection of the border."

"Lose your temper, son?"

"Yes, sir."

"Okay. Get on back there. We'll deal with this. Where's the body?"

"Greensboro ambulance, sir. Came and got him. Two police cars went back with it."

Merriman looked over his shoulder.

"Come on, Ken," he said. "Move that truck, Captain, so the highlights stay on us."

Balder followed him up to the barrier formed by the guard trucks. Behind them, the headlights moved until they lit a shining path all the way to MacDonald Forbes' official limousine. A loudspeaker crackled, and after a moment a voice came from the police car.

"This is Lieutenant John Davids of the North Carolina State Police. Stay under cover. Snipers in the woods. Police backup on the way. Maintaining radio silence."

"Hines," Merriman said without turning around, "get me something to talk through."

"Er," Hines said, and disappeared back behind the truck. They waited. The sun was completely gone, and the March night was turning cold. Outside the crisscrossing pattern of headlights, the blackness moved and whispered.

"If they don't hurry up," Merriman muttered, "we'll have enough TV cameras here to light up the rest of the countryside, radio silence or not."

Captain Hines arrived with a hand-held loudspeaker, and Merriman took it impatiently.

"What've those men got on them?" he asked.

"The ones in the wood, sir? Handguns. Nine millimeter. They had military assault weapons, sir, but we ran 'em out of the truck before they could get at them."

Merriman thumbed the button. The bullhorn crackled and spat. He said into it, "This is Charles Merriman, governor of the Commonwealth of Virginia." His magnified voice bounced from the sapling woods, back to where Balder stood behind him in the headlights.

There was a pause. The police voice said, "Governor, we suggest you stay on Virginia land. You're liable to arrest outside the state borders."

"Who says?" Merriman demanded loudly.

Someone cleared their throat. Merriman said, "Listen up. We've got a situation here where the Virginia National Guard came under direct attack from a North Carolina citizen. Now I suggest that we establish a neutral zone, on the road between these trucks and the governor's limo, there. Mac, you come out here and talk to me. I want the leader of the Regulators to get out of those woods and put his weapon down on the side of the road and meet us in the middle of the road. My secretary of defense is crucial to the operations of the guard and he must remain in Richmond. This man here is Kenneth Balder, my chief of staff. He has wide-ranging authority over all issues pertaining to the Reformed American States, including entrance. All right? Mac, that okay with you?"

Balder said, *sotto voce*, "You want me to walk out there with you?"

"They've only got handguns," Merriman said impatiently, twisting his head away from the loudspeaker. "Not too accurate at that range."

Kenneth Balder gazed out into the woods, feeling extreme reluctance to walk out onto the brightly lit stage of Route 29, no matter how inaccurate the enemy firearms. From the North Carolina side of the barrier, a different voice, younger and less assured, said, "The state police say the leader of the Regulators is liable to weapons charges."

"Tell the state police to sit on their hands for a minute, Mac. All I'm asking for is twenty feet of neutral ground. No one's watching, and this isn't going to make it onto any newscasts."

Another silence. The police voice came back on, finally, and said, "I can guarantee fifteen minutes of safety for the leader of the Regulators. The governor will have to be accompanied by two state troopers, but we'll take no action unless he's threatened. You and the militia leader will have to come out first."

"Great," Merriman said. "Here we come. Hear that, you in the woods? Don't shoot. We're not armed."

He put the bullhorn down.

"Let's go, Ken," he said. "Take your jacket off so they can be sure we're not carrying weapons."

Kenneth Balder shrugged out of his suit coat. The cold wind cut immediately through his shirt sleeves. Merriman was already without a jacket. They walked through the two-foot space between the guard trucks, past the green WELCOME TO NORTH CAROLINA sign, out into open space. Balder could feel the back of his neck prickling. He had been reckless by nature, because his young body had always seemed impervious to threat; but at forty-one the delusion had worn away. Somewhere, out in that dark, someone was sighting on him at this very moment, only a breath away from tightening slightly the finger that lay on the trigger. He mentally slotted Merriman into that class of fortunate people born without physical fear.

They stood, squinting into the headlights of the North Carolina police cars. In the dark at the edge of the trees, a shadow moved away from the blacker shades, toward the road. It resolved into a lean man in his forties, holding a nine-millimeter in his right hand, extended sideways out from his body. He laid the weapon carefully on the yellow line painted along the side of Route 29, stepped over it, and came toward the two of them. He had a neatly trimmed brown beard laced with gray, and a thin face with clear blue eyes and light eyebrows. He was wearing camouflage, and the shoulder of his green-and-brown jacket was spangled with blood.

"Governor Merriman," he said, "I'm Daniel Walker, captain of the Regulators Militia. Your man back there killed my second-in-command."

"Just a minute," Merriman said. Against the headlights of the North Carolina cars, three dark figures emerged and walked slowly toward them. Mac Forbes, white-faced and young; and two grim North Carolina state troopers, forming a wall with their bodies between the governor and the woods.

"MacDonald Forbes, governor of North Carolina," Charles Merriman said, "Kenneth Balder, chief of staff; Daniel Walker, captain of the Regulators. All acquainted? Okay. Walker, you drove straight at a border guard. What did you expect him to do? Shake his finger at you?"

"We expected free entrance into a free state," Walker snapped. "We were told we could join the fight for independence."

"There's no fight," Merriman retorted. "We're only defending ourselves against aggression. We're doing that by protecting our borders. The National Guard is our army, and you launched a hostile attack."

"Who told you?" Balder asked.

"What?"

"Who told you to come join the fight?"

Daniel Walker directed a long suspicious stare at him. He said finally, "Other fighters for freedom."

Mac Forbes interrupted, "He's not interested in freedom, Charles. He's interested in anarchy. We've dealt with this man before."

Walker said coldly, "I have eight men with their sights on you, Governor. Moderate your tone—"

The closest state trooper moved his right hand, very slightly. Balder, his heart beating somewhere high in his throat, saw Walker's head turn. The neutral zone had lasted for exactly two minutes. Without conscious thought, he moved so that Charles Merriman was behind his outstretched arm; and he felt the burn through his forearm before he heard the report. He saw, with odd slow clarity, that Walker was lying on the ground. His arm was immensely heavy. He heaved it back against Merriman's chest and saw the shorter man stumble backward onto the ground. He was the only man left standing. They were all on the ground, Mac Forbes under cover of one trooper's body while the other knelt, Merriman with a scarlet blotch on his chest, Daniel Walker crab-walking backward toward the darkness of the bordering woods. Behind the cluster of police cars, he could hear fresh sirens. They were running, the North Carolina Regulators, as police marksmen arrived and set themselves along the grass verge. Another state trooper was sprinting toward him. He clamped his right hand down over his lifeless arm, and Charles Merriman rolled over and felt his chest, incredulously.

"I thought I was dead and gone to judgment," he said.

"That's my blood, you fool," Kenneth Balder said. He sat down on the pavement, abruptly. He could hear Mac Forbes' high fast voice, and someone else's hand on his shoulder. It seemed very important that he stay in Virginia. He said, "Not Greensboro."

"The ambulance is already on its way," someone else said. There was too much light. He looked up, squinting into the dazzling brightness in front of him, and saw the red light of a recording TV camera. The press had arrived.

"Sit still," a voice said. Balder located Merriman and said, "Get me over the border."

"Come on," Merriman said. He put his shoulder under Balder's good arm and heaved. They went slowly backward until he felt the guard truck at his back. He leaned on it gratefully. Merriman's arm was removed, and he felt another shoulder: Captain Hines of the Twenty-sixth Army Guard. He said, "Sir, we can take you to the Dansboro emergency room—"

"Yes. Okay." Mac Forbes was standing right in front of him, just on the other side of the WELCOME TO NORTH CAROLINA sign, with two protesting state troopers behind him. Merriman went forward and said softly, so that only the six men at the border could hear, "Now what, Mac? You've got anarchy breaking out at all the seams. If you want to stop it, you know what to do."

"Sir," someone shouted from the woods, "we've lost them. We've ordered a helicopter—"

MacDonald Forbes stared back across the state line. He said, "Charles, it's too late. My guard is already federalized."

"Call them out, Steve. You've got more than half waiting for you already. You watch and see how many of the others come on back."

"I could start a war!" Forbes protested, his voice rising.

Merriman threw out both his arms, so that the blood across his chest and sleeves stood out bright and glossy in the lights of the TV cameras.

"What in the name of all that's holy do you call this?" he bellowed, and turned away.

CHAPTER 14

Friday, March 22, 11 P.M.

PROVIDENTIAL, that's what," Merriman said, four hours later. "You couldn't have made a better move if we'd planned this out for hours. You've drawn a thick line between my just revolution and the unjust rebellion of that militia, managed a heroic sacrifice which ought to polish your character right back up again in the eyes of the American people, and now Mac Forbes has a chance to stand with us against the forces of chaos. You're worth your weight in gold, Ken."

Kenneth Balder glared at him across the bedrails. He'd been put in a hospital room for observation, greatly against his will, and was registering his protest by sitting on the bed and holding his damaged forearm across his lap. His head was throbbing, his eyes hurt when he moved them, and he felt as though his entire right side had been pounded with a sledgehammer. Outside the hospital room, a guard complement kept the press at bay. Balder could hear the reporters shouting and shuffling down at the end of the hallway. Merriman was earning publicity points, hovering beside his wounded chief of staff while urgent matters awaited his attention.

"Why do they put the TV so high above the bed?" Merriman grumbled. He'd been channel-surfing from news report to news report, watching the confrontation with the Regulators and the accompanying commentary over and over. "Here. Look at this, Ken."

The TV cameras had shown up in time to catch the shot from the woods. Balder looked up and saw himself jerk under the impact of the nine-millimeter bullet, and Merriman go down while a gray North Carolina police uniform suddenly blocked the camera's lens. He grimaced and looked away. His forearm was broken. The doctor had looked at the x-rays admiringly and remarked, "You're a lucky man. A big mess of a compound fracture, but the bullet missed the major nerves and blood vessels. And only minor splintering at the break, see? Lots of times a bullet'll shatter that bone, just like smashing candy with a hammer."

"I don't want to hear about it," he'd growled. "Just fix it up. I have to go back to Richmond."

They had wanted to put him under general anesthesia, but he'd refused; and the ensuing hours were not something he wanted to remember. They'd put a plate into the arm, stitched up the entrance and exit wounds left by the bullet, and covered the whole thing up with a cast. Now the nerve block was beginning to wear off. Merriman said, "If that Regulator crackpot had shot at you with one of the M-16s they left in the back of the truck, you wouldn't even *have* an arm, so be grateful. Listen to this one. This is an Asheville station."

On the screen, a young local anchor said, "A state police spokesman has denied that Governor Forbes was ever in danger during the attack. But a bullet directed at Governor Charles Merriman was deflected by Kenneth Balder, Merriman's chief of staff. Greensboro police have not yet apprehended the shooter, thought to be James Walker, reportedly the cousin of militia captain Daniel Walker." A photo of the brown-bearded Walker, side by side with a clean-shaven man of the same height and coloring, replaced Merriman's picture above the anchor's right shoulder. "The other militia members have scattered. They are thought to be armed and very dangerous, and police are recommending that citizens along the Virginia-North Carolina border remain in their homes until the search concludes. The shooting tonight has led to demonstrations by two other militia groups in the southern part of the state. Governor Forbes has reportedly asked the president to return control of the North Carolina National Guard to the state, so that the guard can help bring the situation back under control."

Merriman chuckled to himself quietly.

"He'll get them back, one way or the other," he said. "If the president refuses, it'll make Washington stink for North Carolinians. We'll have the state with us in a matter of days."

"You really expect North Carolina to come in?"

"Of course," Merriman said strongly. "A decentralized population, largely rural and Bible-Belt in mentality. A history of two declarations of independence before the national Declaration. A long refusal to ratify the Constitution because Carolinians didn't want to grant power to a federal government." He paused. "Largest producer of tobacco in the United States, followed by Kentucky, South Carolina, and Virginia."

"I see," Kenneth Balder said, slowly. "And you expect Kentucky to be next?"

"Or maybe West Virginia," Merriman said. He looked out the window. After a moment Balder realized that he was humming to himself:

I have seen him in the watchfire of a hundred circling camps;
they have builded him an altar in the evening dews and damps.

THEY FLEW BACK TO RICHMOND just before daylight. Balder had swallowed a small army of pills, but every jerk of the helicopter sent a savage pain through the cast. He leaned his head wretchedly back against the headrest. The drugs, plus the chopper's motion, were causing him acute illness. He drifted into a doze filled with unpleasant colors and was roused, later, by Merriman's voice.

"Ken? We're coming into Richmond."

Balder opened his eyes and winced at the growing light.

"How's the arm?"

"Feels like I've been shot," Balder snapped, disagreeably.

"Look at the advantages. Cline will have to lay off you for a week or so."

"John Cline wouldn't lay off if I were paralyzed from the neck down and attached to a respirator. He'd just be glad I couldn't talk back. Why'd you bring him in, Charles? If you'd asked me, we could have asked Mark McKenna—"

"We've got to get some high-profile economic reforms going," Merriman said. "Popular ones, to keep our momentum. Cline's a hard-liner. I know that—"

"He can't exegete."

"Sure," Merriman said. "Your average Virginia taxpayer will stay up nights frettin' about that. Look at reality, Ken. John Cline's a brilliant man. He's got huge amounts of energy and he's got an enormous following; and most of all, he's got an economic plan all ready for implementation. We'll be making the first reforms by the end of next week."

"I thought criminal justice was the most pressing part of your agenda," Balder said wearily, closing his eyes again. "Why'd we spend all this time on justice laws if the economic reforms come first?"

"People want us to crack down on crime. They also want independence for their pocketbooks. The first issue's more emotional, the second more urgent. We work on justice reform and offer the promise of safer times; but we get economic reform on the books as quickly as possible." Merriman looked out the window, broodingly. *"Quickly,"* he said, "that's the key. Jim Macleod called the hospital this morning to tell me that economic sanc-tions are now on the House floor. We've got to put together a sweeping protest. Jim's getting a few churches together for me to speak to in the morning. I've got to put a mail service together, Monday morning, and then get out to the Newport News shipyard for a visit. Don't worry, Ken— I don't need you back at work until the middle of the week."

Balder was silent. Charles Merriman was still far away from the trans-parency demanded by the Mosaic ethic. He felt too sick to argue the point, and he disliked the idea of Cline's presiding over policy meetings in his absence. The helicopter sank through the air. He opened his eyes and looked down on the shining airport terminal beneath them. A little clus-ter of people waited beside the helicopter pad.

"Press?" he mumbled.

"Sorry," Merriman said. The chopper touched down, and Kenneth Balder gathered himself together. Every muscle and bone in his body fought against him. His left arm was a mass of pain; he hadn't bothered to shave, one-armed in the hospital bathroom, and he hadn't eaten for almost twenty hours. He concentrated on standing up, feeling Merriman's hand on his good elbow. The governor said in his ear, "Margaret Franklin's here."

He remembered, just in time, to stay crouched under the chopper blades.

"Why?" he gritted back.

"Because she's in love with you, I imagine," Merriman said, matter-of-factly. He propelled Balder out, past the helicopter's blades and off the concrete pad. Cameras were flashing and a reporter was calling, "Governor Merriman, do you think this shooting represents a breakdown in United States law and order? What will North Carolina do in response?"

"Governor, did you talk to Mac Forbes about the situation?"

"Governor, when can we expect mail service to resume?"

Kenneth Balder said through his teeth, "How did she know when we were coming in?"

"I called her," Charles Merriman said. He released Balder's elbow. "What do you think, Ken, I can't see what's right under my nose?"

He turned away to deflect the rush of press. Balder stood still. Maggie stood at the edge of the crowd. She was wearing jeans and an old flannel shirt; under the flannel, her shoulders were rigid with the effort of self-control, and her beautiful gray eyes were swollen with weeping. He put out his good arm, half-conscious that the cameras had turned toward him. He didn't care. He wanted comfort; he wanted a missing part of his soul back again. For the first time, she looked entirely familiar to him. The hostility that had walled her away from him was momentarily gone.

She came to him, and he wrapped his right arm around her shoulders and said, "I might fall over."

"I was watching television," she said unsteadily, "and they came on with the news reports, Ken, and I saw you. I can't go through this again. Not twice. . . . first Matthew and then you—"

"I'm all right," he said. Her hair smelled like soap and perfume. He touched his lips to her hair, and the memory of a hundred nights came back so strongly that Merriman's voice seemed to echo from miles away.

"That's enough, folks. Cameras off. Dr. Balder deserves a couple of days to rest in peace and quiet."

The press shuffled away, complaining. Kenneth Balder raised his head, realizing that every camera had probably photographed him kissing the top of Margaret Franklin's head. The painkiller cocktail had removed more inhibitions than he cared to realize. He rested part of his weight on Maggie's shoulder and said, carefully, "I'll be back at work tomorrow, Charles."

"Tomorrow's Sunday," Charles Merriman said. "We won't be working. And Wednesday's fine." His gaze flicked over Margaret. He said, "Spend a couple of days in the country. I'll see you Wednesday morning." Merriman turned his back and walked away toward his waiting car. Balder, squinting, could make out John Cline's strong profile on the other side of the rear window.

"The governor called and said you needed a rest," Margaret said, "and I have a guest room." She had regained control over her voice, somewhat to his disappointment. "He's sending you a bodyguard. Partly for safety, he says, and partly to guard your reputation. I thought you were dead, Ken, for a moment, and I didn't know how much I would want—" She came to a halt and then said, with a trace of the old defensiveness returning, "You can come. But that's all I'm offering—just the guest room."

"I am bound by the Ten Commandments," Balder said, allowing her to guide him across the grass. A guardsman fell into place behind him.

"Okay, then," Maggie said. "Step down. Here's my car. I have no idea what that means."

HE WOKE UP, AN IMMEASURABLE TIME LATER, with the smell of coffee drifting past him. Sunshine lay in wide bands across the bed. He was lying on his stomach, the cast on his left arm propped up on a pillow. Across from him, the bedroom door was cracked slightly. Next to the door a wood-framed mirror hung over an oak dresser and reflected the room back at him. Beyond the foot of the bed, wide double windows opened out onto the back garden.

He pushed himself up, and let out a short gasp at the shattering pain in his arm. Footsteps moved outside the door, and a young voice said uncertainly, "Sir? Are you all right?"

"Fine," he managed. The guardsman's shadow passed across the cracked door and disappeared.

He turned his head carefully. His clothes were neatly folded on an old table that stood under the windowsill, against the far wall. Next to them stood the opaque bottle of painkillers, and a full glass of water. He remembered the night before, as though it had taken place underwater; refusing to take the drugs until Maggie gave up in exasperation. He couldn't remember anything else. He heard her light tread in the hallway, and whisked the sheet across himself a moment before she pushed the door open.

"Ken?"

He said stupidly, "What time is it?"

"Ten o'clock on Sunday morning," Margaret said. She was carrying an old blue pottery mug with steam rising from it. He looked at it hungrily.

"It's for you," she said, and held it out.

"He said, "Er—"

"What?"

"I have to sit up."

"Yes?" Margaret inquired.

He looked ruefully down at himself. As far as he could tell, he had divested himself of everything but his underwear.

"Privacy?" he suggested.

"I've seen you with less on before," Margaret said, setting the mug on the dresser next to the door. "But if that's part of the Ten Commandments, I'll let you dress in peace. Breakfast is in the kitchen."

She went out without ever having looked directly at him, and pulled the door closed behind her.

Kenneth Balder sighed and worked his way into a sitting position, gritting his teeth against pain. Apparently he still had a long way to go. The mirror beside the door reflected him back to himself: a tall man in his forties, powerful chest and arms unbalanced by the white cast, fair hair rumpled wildly up and a two-day beard coming in. He rubbed at it and decided to leave it alone. He'd had a beard long ago, when Maggie had lived with him; so she would hardly be shocked at his present grubbiness.

Long painful minutes afterwards, he retrieved the coffee from the dresser, and drank half of it on his way to the table under the window. It was good coffee, crisp and fragrant. His clothes had been washed, but the sleeve of his shirt was in tatters. A green T-shirt was folded neatly beside the pill bottle. Garrett's, he decided, holding it up; too small for Matthew, and he wouldn't have worn Matthew's old clothes in any case.

He dressed with infinite care, stretching the sleeve of the T-shirt out to pass over the cast, and made his way out into the hallway.

All the windows of the house were open, and a cool, damp breeze blew through the hall. The guardsman was standing five feet from his door. Balder waved the empty mug at him and said, "Morning. You're not the boy who was here last night?"

"No, sir. I'm army guard. I have day duty."

"Did you have some coffee?"

"Yes, sir. Thank you, sir."

He shuffled around the corner, following the smell of hot bread, and found the kitchen on the other side of the stairway. The television was on, and Margaret was at the sink, slicing melon. She looked up and smiled slightly and his heart turned to water.

"Cantaloupe?" she offered.

"Yes. Thanks."

"Did you take your drugs?"

"No."

"Why not?"

"Because I can't think straight when I take them." He started on the long trek toward the kitchen table.

"You look like a nursing-home candidate."

"Yes," he said, "it isn't very dashing, but I need a clear head just at the moment." He managed to reach the table and lowered himself into a chair. The television, murmuring softly away, occupied the top of a bookshelf just across from the table.

"What's this?" he asked.

"'Sunday Morning with David Jones.' News and commentary. You've never seen it?"

"I'm not usually home on Sunday mornings."

"Ah." She put a plate of fresh cinnamon rolls in front of him and sat down, looking steadily at him across the corner of the table.

"Maggie," he said.

"What?"

He put his good hand out, carefully, and covered hers. At the touch, she began to change color. He watched her for a moment, and said at last, "I am sorry."

"For what?"

"Giving you another bad night."

She said, in an odd detached voice, "I didn't know, myself, until I thought you were dead. I . . . lost myself, for awhile."

He watched her beloved profile, and diagnosed that the rush of relief at finding him alive had subsided into guilt over the betrayal of Matthew's memory. He wanted to blurt out, *I still love you; I've never loved anyone else; all I want to do is forget the past and begin again.* Instead, he said, "I can't stay here, Maggie. I wasn't thinking clearly, last night. But when I see you I can remember all the times we were together, as though it were yesterday. And it is too hard."

She didn't answer, and after a moment he said, "Why don't you want to look at me?"

Maggie shifted her weight. She said at last, "I forgot how hard it is to lie to you, Ken. . . . For the same reason, I think." She cut off his answer and added, "Here you are on the TV again."

Together they watched the sketchily lit scene, the chaos on the pavement, and the shudder of his body as the bullet hit. She said thoughtfully, "What did it feel like?"

"A very hard blow."

"Painful?"

"Not right away."

"How long does that cast stay on?"

"Six weeks or so."

"How is it now?"

"Like my arm's on fire."

"You ought to take the drugs," she said, and withdrew her hand from underneath his. The news update ended and David Jones reappeared on the TV screen.

He began, "Last night's shooting was in stark contrast to the scene early this morning, when Governor Charles Merriman of Virginia held his largest rally yet. This is the Richmond Coliseum at ten P.M., Saturday." The picture flicked to the parking lot, jammed with cars and streaming with people. "The Coliseum was full of churchgoers from all over Virginia—"

"The Coliseum holds thirteen thousand people!" Margaret said incredulously.

"—Merriman adjourned the rally at midnight, thus preserving the sanctity of Sunday, and turned the meeting over to Earl Ferguson, pastor of Richmond's All Saints Reformed Presbyterian Church. After a two-hour worship service, the churchgoers disbanded to take the message back to local congregations. The only television cameras allowed inside belonged to right-wing Christian university, which supplied ABC with a twenty-minute tape."

The camera cut to the inside of the Coliseum. Charles Merriman stood behind a podium with the huge smoke-wreathed mountains of the Reformed American States flag hanging behind him. The Coliseum was packed full. The sound of applause from the audience hit like a solid wave. Balder found his attention directed sharply away from Maggie. He dug back through his memory. The day before was clouded; surely Merriman had said that he would address a few churches in the morning?

Merriman waited for the clapping to die down. He was well into his speech, already building toward a rhetorical climax.

"We have been told by the United States that if the citizens of Virginia cease to pay federal taxes—an unjust tax imposed by Washington, over and above the just taxes imposed by the Commonwealth—we will be treated as criminals. Out-of-state property owned by Virginians will be seized by the IRS. Whereas here in the Reformed American States, we have pledged to treat all property owned by United States citizens as foreign soil, protected by the laws of Virginia." He paused to let the contrast sink in.

"Why only out-of-state property?" he resumed. "Because Washington refuses to enter the Commonwealth. The president claims to be seeking a peaceful solution, avoiding any possible bloodshed. But the truth is: The government of the United States is afraid of the will of the people of Virginia. During my term as governor, we've built up a surplus in the treasury. We've contracted out schools to private companies, and test scores are beginning to rise significantly. We've removed restrictive regulations on business. Violent crime has plummeted. Virginians are safer, smarter, more prosperous than ever before. And Washington is scared to try and take it all away."

Merriman waited for the cheers to die down.

"We have asked you to file tax returns for the year that has gone by," he went on, "and also to pay taxes for the first three months of this year. But on April 1, you will find no more sales tax within the Commonwealth of Virginia. And on April 1, we will offer citizenship in the Reformed American States to anyone who wishes to pay the nine-percent tax we offer. We require no one to give up citizenship in the United States. Anyone who wishes to pay both taxes will be awarded dual citizenship. For those residents of the Commonwealth who want to leave, the R.A.S. government has pledged to purchase your property at full market value." He paused, smiling at the shouts of "We won't go!" erupting up from the mass in front of him.

"And to those outside," he finished up, "we welcome you. Anyone who wishes to enter the Reformed American States will be admitted. We ask only that you come peacefully, without bearing arms, and that you find employment within two months of entrance. And in doing so you will join a new world. . . . a just and prosperous country, where ordinary people can live in safety and in confidence, under the protection of Almighty God." He raised both hands. "Thank you," he said, simply, and let the roar of approval wash over him.

"I don't understand," Balder said. "There's nothing in that speech I would quarrel with. Why would he tell me a half-story about the rally and send me out here?"

"Maybe he wanted you to rest."

Balder frowned, pinching his lower lip between thumb and forefinger.

"Maybe he didn't want you to hear the early parts of the speech."

"Much more likely."

The camera angle drew back to show not only Merriman, but John Cline seated between Jim Macleod and the adjutant general, on chairs underneath the flag. An empty chair waited next to Macleod. A smaller flag had been draped dramatically across it.

"The chair of the fallen hero," Maggie said, amused.

"Cheap sentiment," Balder muttered. Merriman was a populist to the core. He was beginning to doubt that the sterner ethic of the law of Moses would ever really conquer that urge to hold a wetted finger to the wind. The tape blinked. Now the Coliseum was filled with worshippers, and "A Mighty Fortress Is Our God" swelled up to fill the concrete arches.

David Jones reappeared, with two men seated across from him in his carpeted studio. Balder said thoughtfully, "Mark McKenna. I wondered when he'd weigh in on this."

"Who?" Margaret asked. On the television screen, David Jones said, "My guests this morning claim the same God, but hold widely different opinions on what He requires. Mark McKenna holds a master of theology from Westminster Theological Seminary in Philadelphia—"

"Mark's a theonomist," Kenneth Balder said. "Pastor of a church in Alabama, puts out a monthly journal. A good man, but cautious. The other man is Christopher Dillard. Also a Westminster graduate, now teaching at Gordon-Conwell. Well-known expert on biblical hermeneutics."

"What?"

"Interpretation."

"Oh," Margaret said. Mark McKenna, portly and white-haired, was insisting, "No one believes more strongly than I that God's laws are meant to be obeyed today. I probably won't disagree with a single one of Charles Merriman's reforms. But I strongly oppose the way he's done this, and that's why I've remained in Alabama. Bringing out the guard is absolutely unjustifiable. It's a threat of armed revolt. We've been blessed with a democratic government, and in a democracy change comes from below, from the voters. Revolution is unacceptable."

"I agree with Mr. McKenna," Christopher Dillard said, "but I don't think he realizes that armed revolt is the inevitable end-point of his theological position." He was thin and clean-shaven, with white streaks in his brown hair; approaching sixty, still fit and energetic. "Mr. McKenna has written that God wants this country run exactly like Old Testament Israel, and he has insisted that we'll be judged if we don't comply. And given the fact that Washington is never going to agree with Mr. McKenna, his followers can only conclude that they've got to avoid judgment by putting those laws into effect by force."

"Plenty of people who aren't theonomists are joining in this revolt," McKenna pointed out. "Charismatics from around the state have flooded out in force—"

"The Charismatic emphasis on complete victory is heavily influenced by theonomist theology," Christopher Dillard retorted. "I don't imagine that most Charismatics realize that. But many of them are closet dominionists—people who talk about establishing God's reign in America and then in the whole earth. That sort of position leads directly to armed uprising, Mr. McKenna. Don't you find it ironic that all those people in the Coliseum are singing 'A Mighty Fortress'?"

"Certainly not. The hymn asserts the ultimate triumph of God over the universe. The Lord of Hosts must win the battle, just as the first verse says—"

"But you've forgotten the last verse: *Let goods and kindred go, this mortal life also; the body they may kill, God's truth abideth still: His kingdom is forever.* His kingdom has nothing to do with earthly power or political kingdoms. His kingdom is spiritual; and so it will last even after the earth is destroyed."

"That's exactly the sort of weak, faithless statement that led the church to withdraw from all political and social issues and prattle on about spiritual renewal without making a single concrete move toward holiness," McKenna snapped.

"So you admit that concrete action is needed?"

"Yes, but not revolution. Even just revolution will tend to feed the impulse to unjust rebellion. People will think: *If Merriman doesn't have to obey the United States, why should I obey Merriman?* Revolution is never an answer."

"Then what would you recommend—"

The telephone rang, and Margaret got up to answer it. "Hello?" she said absently, her eyes still on the television. Balder, half-listening, heard her voice change instantly and turned his head. Her face had gone white, her gray eyes wide. He started to get up, reflexively, and was brought to a crashing halt by pain.

"No," she said. "No, I won't." She paused. "I don't know exactly where Garrett is. I told you that before."

He could barely hear the indistinct voice on the other end. Maggie was listening. She said, finally, "Actually, he's sitting in my kitchen. Perhaps you'd like to speak to him."

The voice squawked in protest. She held the receiver out.

"His name's Allen Preszkoleski. He's an assistant to the secretary of defense. They want Garrett and me to come to Washington."

A familiar anger stirred inside him. He took the telephone, stretching the cord awkwardly over the floorboards.

"Kenneth Balder," he said.

There was only silence on the other end. In the distance he could hear someone shouting. He waited, and the shouting was replaced by black velvet.

"They've put me on hold," he said to Margaret. "You rate higher than I do."

"Huh," Margaret said, skeptically. The black velvet gave way to a click. A deep voice said, "Mr. Balder. . . ."

"Yes?"

"This is Alexander Wade, secretary of defense."

He was not entirely surprised; either by the voice, or by the loathing contained in it.

He said, "You're out of your sphere, Mr. Secretary."

There was a long pause on the other end. Finally the voice observed, "So you've found yourself a new cause."

"I believe we have terms to discuss, Mr. Secretary. You haven't yet given us terms for buying Camp Peary."

"When hell freezes," Alexander Wade snapped.

"When you're ready to negotiate, you might call my office directly. Do you need the number?"

Wade's voice was slow, as though he were translating his thoughts directly into words without the luxury of reflection.

"I didn't expect to find you there," he said, "but on second thought, it simplifies matters. I have a warning for you: Charles Merriman's going to use you as a scapegoat in case his revolution goes sour. If you're smart, you'll get out of there now."

"Why would that make me better off?"

"If you leave Virginia now, I'll arrange with the attorney general for you to be considered innocent of any crime. Any *additional* crime, I should say. If you stay, I can't guarantee you'll ever be able to leave the state's borders safely again."

"As everything I want is here," Balder said, "that's not much of a threat."

"You're going to have to face a greater threat than arrest, Balder. You may claim that this is a just revolt, but even a just revolt attracts carrion crows. I see on the morning news that you've already met a flock of them."

"What's your point?"

"You're likely to have a bloodbath on your hands if you don't crack down."

"Fortunately," Kenneth Balder said, "freed from the corruption of the United States judicial system, we'll be able to do that." He was simmering with fury; he had no doubt in his mind that Wade had orchestrated the public revelation of Mary Miranda's death, and had set his aides to pour fresh poison into Margaret's ear. Her abrupt queries in Charles Merriman's office made more sense now. In his cell, trying to come to terms with her desertion, he had finally decided that she was prone to believe the worst of those she loved. He said, biting out the words, "Mrs. Franklin has nothing to say to the Pentagon. There's no need to call her again."

Alexander Wade said smoothly, "I believe one of my assistants had some idea that we might put an FBI task force on the case of her husband's murder."

"We've already offered her justice."

"Allen also mentioned that he'd like to protect her son from his misguided choice to follow Charles Merriman's instructions."

"I have advised Garrett to take his present course."

"You sent Matthew Franklin's son away to plunge into war?"

"What do you think I am, Wade?"

"A psychopath with religious delusions?" Alexander Wade offered.

"Fortunately," said Balder, "my religious delusions assure me that it is unnecessary to tell you to go to your undoubted final destination."

He took the receiver away from his ear and discovered that the cutoff button was located on the wall set. In a sudden accession of rage he flung the telephone away from him. It bounced off the wall and clattered against the threshold of the kitchen door. Margaret went silently to the doorway, picked up the telephone, and hung it up. She said, after a moment, "You haven't changed all that much, Ken."

Kenneth Balder dropped his face into his hands. When he could speak again he said, "I have. I swear. Maggie, isn't there anything left of the past between us? If you remember, when you look at me . . . why can't you listen to what I say?"

"I do remember," she said. "I've tried to ignore it. I wanted you back here last night, Ken. And ever since I woke up this morning, I've known it was a mistake. All I would have to do is let go, and I would be as much in love with you as I was, all that time ago. But I don't trust you, Ken. I can't let myself fall."

"Then watch me, Maggie. Don't make up your mind yet. I've waited twenty-five years. I can wait a few more months." He paused, and added, "Don't worry about Garrett. I'll talk to the adjutant general. We'll make sure the Pentagon isn't able to contact him."

"They want to bring you down, Ken."

"If I do what is right, Washington has no power over me."

"Are you sure?"

"Yes, I am. God's law always works in favor of the righteous." He forced himself to his feet. "I've got to get back to Richmond. Merriman doesn't know what he's dealing with. Those Regulators were sent to the state line, and I want to find out who and why. And if I don't watch him, Cline will impose a gold standard and send Virginia into economic chaos—"

"You're not fit!"

Ken leaned his right hand on the table and looked down at her. He longed to kiss her. The tenseness in her shoulders suggested that kissing her would not be a welcome move on his part. He swallowed in an agony of frustration and said, instead, "Will you see me again?"

After a long moment, she put both her hands out, her palms upward.

"I don't know," she said. "I don't know. Don't ask me again. I'll . . . I'll call you. If I can."

HE DISCOVERED THAT THE GUARDSMAN outside his room had been assigned to drive him back to Richmond. He slid into the front seat of the truck, leaned his head back, and let out a long groan that was half despair and half sheer fury. The driver said anxiously, "Are you all right, sir?"

"In what sense?" Balder demanded, and then saw the boy's face. "Never mind. Take me back to the Capitol."

"I can take you to the hospital."

"No. The Capitol's fine."

He watched the rearview mirror as the farmhouse disappeared around the bend in the road. He felt entirely drained; his arm throbbed, his head hurt, and his stomach had twisted itself into a painful ball. And he had no enthusiasm at all for tackling John Cline about the gold standard.

CHAPTER 15

Sunday, March 24, 11 A.M.

ALEXANDER WADE thumped the receiver down with such force that the telephone at the edge of the desk toppled onto the floor. He kicked at it, and felt an infantile pleasure in the jolt against his slippered toe. Every time he heard Balder's voice, fresh hatred began to throb just behind his eyes, obscuring his thought, clouding his vision.

He was alone in the townhouse. His daughter Deborah had sulkily agreed to stay in Maryland. A telephone call to William and Mary had revealed that the school was in an uproar; the political science department was frothing with fury, the religion professors were gloomily predicting public stonings, the law school was up in metaphorical arms. But the division of town-and-gown had rarely been so complete. While the academic community bellowed, Williamsburg's service sector—the maids and restaurant workers and groundskeepers—had come out in strong support of Charles Merriman's brave new world.

Meanwhile, the college president left the state. He was new at his job; he'd been at it barely a year, he still owned a home in Vermont, and his wife was an obstetrician who had performed her share of abortions. The academic dean occupying the vacated presidential desk assured him that there was no danger in sending Deborah back to Williamsburg. But Wade had seen pictures of a militia group drilling on Yorktown land, and he was afraid that the daughter of the secretary of defense would be an immediate target.

So Deborah stayed in Maryland. Perri remained with her to sympathize and console, leaving him with the distinct impression that he could have prevented the secession, personally, if he'd been a bit quicker out of the starting gate.

A dial tone sounded loudly from the floor. He bent down to replace the receiver, and it rang instantly. He snatched it up.

"What?"

"Grant," the voice at the other end said. "Can you meet me at two?"

"Why?"

Ramsey Grant said grimly, "We've got a recording of the first two hours of Charles Merriman's rally."

"Ah," Alexander Wade said, "an agent who managed to carry out his assignment?"

Grant ignored this. "In the White House Solarium, with HM. George is finding Elizabeth."

"Would you say that Kenneth Balder could be classified as a psychopathic personality, Grant?"

Ramsey Grant said guardedly, "Why do you ask?"

"I thought you might be familiar with the FBI profiling techniques. Doesn't religious fanaticism fit into the psychopath pattern somewhere?"

"Kenneth Balder strikes me as a highly intelligent man following a well-thought-out course of action," Grant said, after a moment, "and as for the religious fanaticism, you'd need to ask an expert. I'll see you at two."

He hung up. Wade retrieved the phone and set it carefully on his desk. He was tired and chilly, but he shook himself and stood up. The anger seething through him would not let him sit still.

I will not let Balder get away with this, he thought, pacing back and forth behind the drawn blinds.

In his own mind, he was convinced that Charles Merriman would set Kenneth Balder up. The leader of a revolution inevitably took at least one false turn, made a dramatic reform only to find his followers ready to stone him in the streets. Merriman was no fool. He needed a lightning rod. Any necessary risks would be shuffled onto the new chief of staff. If the risks blossomed into success, well and good; Balder could stay. He was courageous and appealing, and he knew his Old Testament. If not, he could be blamed and jettisoned as no real loss to Merriman's fledgling cabinet.

But beyond that, Alexander Wade had no intention of allowing Kenneth Balder and Margaret Franklin and Charles Merriman to form a tight little alliance there in Richmond. People like them were a nexus, a conjoining point where the universe spun into chaos. Margaret Franklin—Margaret Keil—had been wide-eyed and bewildered, all through that trial. The jury had liked her and pitied her, trapped in her inexplicable devotion to the heartless murderer of Mary Miranda. He had always thought that, underneath that helpless fragile exterior, she knew exactly what she was doing. She'd listened to him, after all, the lovely forehead wrinkled. He'd caught up with her one night, just outside the courtroom.

"Miss Keil?"

She'd turned; and he'd held out those letters, the damning documents that the judge had not allowed. It had worked. She'd left that man and married the other, the quiet unassuming one who had spent the whole trial half-bent with pain, almost unable to face the horror of what he had done in blind discipleship. It had been worth a breach of professional ethics to see the cold curtain come down over Kenneth Balder's face, shutting out the pain he must have felt at his lover's betrayal. He wished he could have inflicted more pain on the man. Men like Balder, men who set themselves up as judges of right and wrong, were intolerable. They were dangerously willing to let individual lives fall into the gulf between reality and idea. Balder's conversion had been no surprise to him. It was a short step from knowing the direction a nation should take, to knowing what God thought. Anyone who claimed to know the mind of God was a threat to the fabric of society.

Well . . . he had provided the goads. With any luck, the puppets would move predictably on their strings. Balder was bound to want to prove himself to his lady-love now. He'd agree to prosecute Jerry Tindell. And when Balder and Merriman put those intolerably severe Mosaic penalties into action, the backlash would drive the revolutionaries out. Jerry Tindell's execution would save the Union. A phrase floated through his mind. *It is expedient that one man should die to save the nation.* He traced the sentence back into his memory; but it faded away, source unknown.

HE ARRIVED at the White House Solarium, freshly showered and bolstered by a pot of black coffee. The stuffed chairs nearest to the entrance were already occupied. The president was resting his head against the back of his favorite chair, wearing sweats and socks. Elizabeth Archer, the secretary of commerce, was clad in jeans and a sweater. The director of the FBI wore a sweatshirt with *I Supported National Public Radio* stenciled on it, and Ramsey Grant was resplendent in a charcoal suit and silk tie. Wade settled himself where he could see the shining blue sky through the Solarium's glass panels and cast his eye over the attorney general.

"Where've you been?" he inquired.

"Church," Grant said shortly.

"Let's hear this tape," the president ordered. Ramsey Grant nodded toward the director, who produced a briefcase and popped it open. The director was an influential man, and he looked it even in sweats; formidable jaw neatly shaved and the heavy gold watch on his wrist quietly boasting his salary.

"The agent in question actually had a small video camera, concealed in a diaper bag," he said, "but Charles Merriman had the guard searching everyone who went into the Coliseum. He claimed this was because of the attempt on his life, and no one protested. The agent stowed the diaper bag behind a trashcan in the outside hallway and used her tape-recorder, which we'd built into a makeup case in her purse. I've eliminated most of the rhetoric. Charles Merriman opened the meeting with the usual stuff about God's law and man's law, and then he turned the floor over to John Cline. This is the part he didn't want broadcast on national TV. I had Cline's main points typed up so you could follow along."

Wade accepted his document, stamped CONFIDENTIAL across the top. *Right,* he thought, settling himself more comfortably into his chair. *No one will know about this but the five of us—and thirteen thousand Virginia church-goers.* The director set his briefcase on his lap and started the tape. John Cline's deep Alabama voice began, "Inflation isn't an inevitable fact of life, as you've been told by those who control the economy of the United States. Inflation results from sin—from a direct violation of the Eighth Commandment. Putting unbacked paper money into circulation, brothers and sisters, is nothing less than stealing. We stand ready to reverse the dreadful mess caused by politicians who chose expediency over the principles of God."

The director paused the tape. He said, "The Eighth Commandment, in case you need refreshing, is 'Thou shalt not steal.' Cline gives eleven definitions of stealing. Theft, defaulting on a legal debt, extortion, failure to pay wages, and then seven other actions peculiar to his theology. They're the first paragraph on your summary."

Wade read John Cline's definitions of stealing.

Fraud, including unbacked paper money; passage of a law which deprives any individual or group of property; destruction of property by will or accident; restriction of property use; usury (exorbitant interest and loans designed to run more than six years); any form of gambling; failure to observe the land's sabbath year.

"As you can see," the director remarked, "economic reforms will have to include the reintroduction of the gold standard. By the way, Kenneth Balder has publicly said, in the past, that he doesn't support the immediate re-introduction of the gold standard." He restarted the tape, and Cline's voice went on.

"Brothers and sisters, we have all been forced by the ungodly system of government we now live under to violate the Eighth Commandment of God's law given on Sinai. Now we have graciously been given the chance to repent and reform. First and foremost, we must re-introduce the gold standard into Virginia's economy. The printing of unbacked paper money must stop. Other reforms will follow. Restrictions on wetlands must be lifted. Long-term loans must be paid off; twenty-year mortgages are a thing of the past. The lottery will end. Agriculture must incorporate the seventh-year rest into its land use."

"Now," said the director, "you'll see why Merriman wanted all this said to churchgoers—the core of the faithful."

"The next seven years may involve some sacrifice," Cline's voice admitted.

"Some of these reforms are straightforward. The full use of wetlands can be restored to unlucky property owners who have run afoul of the EPA. The Virginia Lottery has already been halted. As of tomorrow morning, Colonial Downs is prohibited from accepting bets. But the re-introduction of the gold standard is a complex reform. The Reformed American States has set a seven-year goal to accomplish this. At the end of those seven years, the citizens of this Commonwealth will possess a unit of currency which will never devalue. You can save for your children, brothers, without the worry that your savings may suddenly become worthless. Give us seven years, and we'll create an economy that will last for generations."

The director thumbed the stop button again. "See?" he said. "An appeal to their children, and few specifics. Merriman didn't want this broadcast across the United States; think what it might do to trade with Virginia. But he knows his audience. Most devout Christians are a well-known type. They enjoy sacrifice and self-denial, especially for the good of someone else. They get their psychological kicks that way. And he's going to let Cline hold that seven-year plan up in front of them—a guaranteed reward at the end. Plus, Merriman needs their help. Listen to this bit about welfare reform."

Wade turned the page. At the top of the next page was typed: WELFARE REFORM. John Cline's slow voice picked the thread of reformation back up.

"The Tenth Commandment bars any system of government which takes from one group to give to another," he droned on. "The welfare state is such a state. You have no responsibility to care for those who will not work, brothers and sisters." At this there was a low rumble of approval from the massive congregation. "On Monday morning, the Commonwealth will halt all welfare payments to those who are not physically disabled. We will continue government support only for those who are physically incapable of work, and do not live within fifteen miles of a church."

Wade asked, "Is fifteen miles somewhere in the Law of Moses?"

"No," Ramsey Grant said, "that came out of John Cline's busy brain."

"Now," Cline's voice continued, "we ask you, the churches of Virginia, to take up your rightful role as providers for those who have no help. When you go back home, pastors and elders, draw a fifteen-mile radius around your church. Make yourselves responsible for those within that radius who have no family, no health, and no resources. This is the true work of the church. In this way, the government can relinquish a responsibility it was never meant to possess, and the church can enjoy the blessings that come with fulfillment of God-given duties."

This was followed by a wave of clapping; and the director turned off the tape recorder and closed the top of the briefcase. He said, "He spends a good while after that talking about how property taxes deny God's ownership of the earth, and how he hopes the nine-percent tax can eventually be decreased even further, and how an open market as opposed to a government-controlled market allows for hard work to be properly rewarded. Then Charles Merriman took over. John Cline actually left the building at midnight."

"Why?" asked Elizabeth Archer.

The director looked at Ramsey Grant, who said, "According to our agent, Cline thinks that heating or cooling a building on Sunday breaks the command to rest. He also refuses to mail anything on Friday or Saturday, because he would be causing mail-sorters to violate the Sabbath. However, he allows that there may be differences of opinion on this subject, so he isn't going to try to write it into law. Apparently John Calvin himself used to go lawn-bowling on Sundays after church because he saw the Sabbath as a sort of allegory for the completed work of Jesus."

"Been reading up, Ramsey?" Wade inquired.

"Merely following a precept of modern warfare," Ramsey Grant said, unruffled. "Understand your enemy."

"So do you think Kenneth Balder is a psychopathic—"

"Not relevant," the president said loudly. "Elizabeth, how would you go about re-introducing the gold standard?"

"It's insane to think it could be done at all," the secretary of commerce said. She drummed her fingers on the side of the chair. Presently she added, "First you'd have to have a controlled unit of currency. If I were doing it, I'd create a gold-backed Virginia dollar and put it into circulation alongside the United States dollars. I'd require that all goods be priced in both currencies. The Virginia dollar price would inevitably be lower than the U.S. dollar price. . . . that would probably attract people toward using the Virginia currency, even if there were fewer units in circulation. That would mean creating a small army of advisers who would keep track of the relative values and continually advise people on how much goods and labor would be worth in Virginia currency. Complicated . . . but it could be done, over the seven-year period he's talking about. As time went on, more and more U.S. currency would be taken out of circulation. You'd have to continually adjust the exchange rate between U.S. and Virginia dollars, but the Virginia government's capable of doing that. They'd just have to treat commerce with other states as if they were dealing with Mexico, say, or Britain. I'll be darned. Yes, Mr. President, it could be done. Probably not by the United States, but a smaller and more controlled state economy could pull it off. But we can't make this public," the commerce secretary added, hastily. "Not if you want your economic sanctions to pass. That's going to be tough enough, dropping over one fiftieth of the United States economy into a black hole. If the market thinks Virginia will institute a stable and inflation-free currency in an open market atmosphere, it'll dig its toes in and refuse to sign on. Too much profit to be made, Mr. President. The bill comes up for vote in the House tomorrow. We've got to wait."

"So we can't use any of this information?" the president asked. "Here's a startling thought, Mr. Attorney General; why don't you bring me something I *can* use? Put that blasted tape away." He folded his hands over his carefully exercised stomach. "Even outbreaks of violence bring Merriman and Balder up smelling like roses. What've we got left?"

"The North Carolina and Maryland Guard," Ramsey Grant said. "You haven't done much with them so far, Alex."

"Did you see the latest polls?" Alexander Wade demanded. "Kenneth Balder's image with the American people shot up over twenty percentage points because he got wounded on national TV. If we march guard over the borders and some Virginia master sergeant with five children and a farm gets killed, the country will practically demand that we let Virginia do whatever it wants. No; if we're going to get the Commonwealth, we have to represent calm and peaceful reason. In fact, I think we ought to give control of the North Carolina Guard back to MacDonald Forbes."

"Surely you jest," the president said. "You want me to return the guard of a tobacco-producing state to a governor who admires Charles Merriman?"

"If you don't give him his guard back, he'll have a legitimate grievance against the presidency and an ongoing riot that will make North Carolinians long for Kenneth Balder's drastic peacekeeping techniques. If you do, he'll have no reason to revolt. Especially when the sanctions go through. Whatever he might gain by keeping tobacco producers happy, he would lose as a thousand other sources of revenue closed off."

"No," the president said decisively. "I will not weaken my stance."

"That worked in Russia, Mr. President, but we're on domestic soil."

"No. We may be hanging all our hopes on economic sanctions, but I'm not going to give away my only trump card. And that," the president said with finality, "is my last word on the subject. Now you'll excuse me. George and I have senators to see."

THE TELEPHONE, his private line to the White House, rang at three A.M. on Monday. Alexander Wade swore bitterly into his pillow, rolled out of bed, and staggered into the next room. The voice on the other end of the receiver said curtly, "It's not going through."

"Er . . . what, Mr. President?"

"The economic sanctions. They may go through the House of Representatives, but there's no way we can get them through the Senate. I've telephoned and pleaded and promised and cajoled until I'm blue in the face. They're not going to pass it. Either their states do too much business with Virginia, or they have relatives in Virginia, or they think that the Constitution gives Congress the power to regulate commerce but not halt it, and that we should shift the responsibility over to the Interstate Commerce Commission and let them study it for six months. The truth is, they don't want to be labeled as members of the Congress who halted trade to a state because the governor objected to overtaxation. If someone's going down over this, it isn't going to be a Republican or a Democrat. It's going to be *me*, Alex. Unless we take decisive action."

"Such as?"

"You don't want to risk attacking the Virginia Guard. What about the power stations? We could paralyze the state with two well-aimed hits."

"Mr. President—"

"You be in here at eight," the president ordered. "I want to hear about every legal option I have. Understand?"

The receiver clicked at the other end. Wade hung up and rubbed both hands through his hair. At this rate, Merriman wouldn't have the chance to incriminate himself with the American people. It would conceivably be legal to use the Maryland Guard to bomb a power station, provided sufficient warning were given; and the bombing might indeed end the Virginia revolt, but it would probably also close off the political career of the secretary of defense. Particularly if anyone were injured. He wandered restlessly through the house, avoiding the kitchen where the ever-present Secret Service agent waited. In five hours he would have to negotiate his way through this maze. He had to think.

HIS DRIVER ARRIVED at 7:30. He ducked into the back of the car to find George Lewis waiting for him, long face almost dragging the leather seat.

"Chin up, George," Wade said, flippantly. "It's only one state."

"We're taking a little detour," George said, disapprovingly. "The president would like you to see something." The car began to move. Wade took the folded *Post* from under his arm and shook it open.

"Where to? I see we're headed away from the White House."

"Just going in a circle," George Lewis said. "We'll have you there by eight."

Wade addressed himself to the paper, watching the scenery slide by out of the corner of his eye. The cookie-cutter row houses gave way to a less exalted neighborhood, which gradually resolved itself into a business sector. Ahead, the sidewalk seemed unusually full of people. George leaned forward.

"Right here," he said.

The car slowed. Wade gazed out through the window. Across the pavement, a wide-eyed worker was peering out from behind the locked glass door of a Maryland Social Services office. From the front step, stretching around the corner, a long line snaked away out of sight. The adults were chattering and drinking coffee, muffled up against the cold. Several were carrying bags. Children leaned dozing against their mothers or climbed around and through the legs of the adults, shrieking happily in the morning air.

"What in heaven's name is that?"

"Welfare recipients from Virginia," George Lewis said.

"But they can't get their checks here."

"Oh?"

"But Maryland can't afford—"

"Neither can the District of Columbia," George Lewis said sourly, "or Tennessee, if it comes to that. All the welfare offices near the Virginia border in those states are also flooded."

He nodded sharply at the driver, and the car picked up speed.

"The president will be waiting for your recommendations," George said. Wade watched the familiar cluster of Washington buildings grow larger ahead of him, the newspaper forgotten in his lap.

HE WALKED THROUGH THE West Wing entrance with George behind him and headed toward the Oval Office. Staffers scurried past him with unnaturally solemn faces, which was odd; the president would scarcely have let on yet that his request for economic sanctions was doomed. An aide was waiting. He tapped on the door and let them through, closing it behind them. The president was standing up, behind his desk, with his back to the door.

"Morning," he said, without moving. "Coffee?"

"No, thanks," Wade said. "The welfare situation—"

"George, will you excuse us for a moment?"

"But—" George Lewis began. The president whirled around and glared at him, and George backed toward the door set into the elegant molding. When the door closed behind him, the president said, "Do you know where this started?"

"On Mount Sinai," Wade said sourly.

"Nope. It started with Quebec. They finally got away from Canada, and it's given *our* states ideas. First Virginia, and now . . . Well, Alex, I'll admit I was wrong. I should have given the guard back."

"The North Carolina Guard?" Wade asked. He could feel a burning begin at the pit of his stomach. "Why?"

"There on the table," the president said.

He waved his hand toward the other end of the room, where two sofas stood across from each other, flanking the cold fireplace, with a low table in between. Wade walked to the table and bent over to look at the paper that lay there. It was a thick cream-colored document with a signature on the bottom.

Unless the president of the United States responds to these demands within forty-eight hours, I will declare the state of North Carolina to be separate and independent from the United States of America, and I will use all resources of the state to defend North Carolina's citizens from any further oppression.

- Return of the North Carolina National Guard to the control of the governor.
- Reversal of mandatory state funding for all Medicaid abortions.
- Reversal of legalized organ harvesting from anencephalic babies. . . .

At the bottom of the familiar list of demands was the signature: *MacDonald Jordan Forbes.*

The president sat down at his desk and folded his hands.

"Now, Mr. Secretary," he said, "what have you got for me?"

CHAPTER 16

Monday, March 25, 7 P.M.

"RICHMOND INTERNATIONAL AIRPORT," Davidson Smith remarked, his voice bored. "One set of escalators and two baggage belts. Why the international?"

"Flights to Mexico City?" Garrett offered.

"Not without changing planes at Dallas."

"Flights to Florida," Clint Larsen said, yawning, "and then you can get to Cuba by boat. Go get me a cup of coffee, will ya, Franklin? And not that flavored stuff for fairies. I've got a dollar somewhere."

He started to dig through his pockets. The three of them were leaning on the right wall, idly watching passengers trickle past the metal detectors. Traffic into Virginia had suddenly slowed; Mac Forbes' threat of secession had been broadcast at eight that morning, and the press had all gone south.

"It's gonna be more than a dollar," Garrett said.

"Says a dollar, down there."

"What about tax?"

"No tax."

"Oh, yeah," Garrett said. "I keep forgetting." He hoisted himself up from the wall and clattered down the silent escalators. His shift had been changed; he worked nine to nine, morning to evening, every day. For five days, the guard had kept watch at the airport. Two FBI agents had been relieved of their weapons the first day. After that, the rest of the watches had dragged by in peaceful monotony. He paid for the coffee at the quiet coffee-bar near the entrance and headed back to his post. He was halfway up the steel steps when he heard a rattle of feet, and looked over his shoulder to see the rest of the security police headed toward him.

"What's up?" he asked, reaching the top. Larsen shrugged and reached for his coffee.

"Ames's got something he only wants to say once," he said, jerking his head in the direction of the terminals. Captain Ames was striding toward them, the rest of the posted guardsmen following his thin, straight figure.

"Listen up," he said, arriving into the growing crowd between the glass walls. "New developments. In the morning we'll be leaving the airport. Those of you who aren't essential for protection of the base will be posted elsewhere. I'm authorized only to tell you that at noon today, the Pentagon promised to disrupt Virginia's infrastructure if North Carolina followed through on its pledge to join the revolution. No—" he shook his head at the instant rush of questions, "— we don't know exactly what that means. It was an indefinite threat. But infrastructure means roads, railroad tracks, power and water sources. We're going to supplement the army guard in keeping those areas secure. As you may know, our desertion rate these five days into the United States has been pretty low—about ten percent. But we started out with only seventy-percent strength, so that's weakened us enough to be spread thin. The R.A.S. secretary of defense, General Fletcher, has decided to supplement us with Commonwealth of Virginia citizen peacekeepers. They'll take over at some areas, including this airport, and we'll move into sectors which might see some action."

Garrett bit his thumbnail absently. He had not called home since Wednesday. He didn't want to go through the argument about leaving the guard again; he was half-afraid that if he were offered another chance, he'd be tempted to accept. Especially now, as the hazy prospects of fighting solidified. He'd probably do the same cowardly routine again: call until he got the answering machine, tell her he'd been moved somewhere else and he was fine. He had to stick with this. He had to stay with Clint Larsen. He had to find his father's murderer.

"You'll be given your new assignments at the beginning of your next

shift," Ames ordered. "Show up ready to move out. You won't be returning to your homes. Those of you with families, sorry, but assignments are
classified. This is temporary, men. Once North Carolina is firmly in, the
adjutant general plans to move the North Carolina border guards up to the
north and west, and then some of you can go back home. Okay? See you
in the morning. Back to your posts."

The crowd of guardsmen shifted and dispersed. Ames, drawn aside by
another officer, wandered off toward the terminals, deep in conversation.
Clint Larsen drained the coffee and tossed his cup into the nearby sand-filled
ashtray. He said abruptly, "Headed back home after your shift, Franklin?"

"Er . . . I was. Not in a hurry, though."

"Want to see something?"

"See what?" Garrett asked, striving for a bored tone of voice.

"Show you when we get there."

"Where?"

"Under an hour away," Larsen said.

Davidson Smith said sharply, "Leave him alone, Clint."

"You can come too," Larsen said.

"Not a chance."

"Hear you went to that rally, Saturday night. You don't talk like a
church man."

Davidson Smith sniffed and rubbed his nose. His brown eyes were
rimmed with red. He said, "My neighbor took me."

"Yeah? You heard all that stuff, then. About the gold standard and
opening up the parklands and stopping welfare payments. Think that'll all
happen peacefully?"

"I don't care whether it happens peacefully or not," Smith snapped.
"I'm gonna follow the law."

"What law?" Larsen demanded. "You've already broken the law."

"I haven't broken my National Guard oath, and I'm not going to."

"Laws change for the good of the people who make them. Haven't you
noticed? I'm just anticipating one particular change by a few months or so."

"You're going to get killed," Smith said unequivocally, "and you're
going to get *him* killed too. Garrett, he's a loose cannon, this guy. I don't

know why you hang around him, but you oughta get away from him now. Your dad—"

Larsen straightened up to his full height, bristling. Garrett felt the hairs rise on the back of his neck. With relief he saw a familiar shape walking back toward the escalators, and he hissed, "Captain!"

Clint Larsen threatened, under his breath, "You're running your mouth about stuff you don't know anything about, Smith. You watch your step."

Ames went by with an absent nod. Smith said, prudently, "I'm checking the radars again." He stalked off past them, headed for the radar room on the other side of the glass-fenced atrium.

Garrett ventured, "What about my dad?" He could hear his heart beating in his ears.

"Nothing," Clint Larsen said. "Your dad used to give me a hard time, Franklin. That's all. It was a crying shame he died the way he did. I was sorry for all of you." His voice held unexpected sincerity. Garrett swallowed, partly in disappointment and partly to rid himself of the choking grief that still swelled up over him at unexpected intervals.

"Go get me another cup of coffee," Larsen directed. "We're gonna have a late night." He shifted his weight against the wall, fretfully. "Most boring duty I ever drew," he said, "standing around this airport drinking coffee. Silly way to run a revolution."

GARRETT CHECKED IN HIS WEAPON and badge at the end of his shift, and followed Clint Larsen out into the air guard base parking lot. He slid into Larsen's old truck as the older man went around to the driver's seat. Excitement was turning his belly to water, and he was having trouble catching his breath. The truck pulled past the guard shack, and he caught sight of Jerald Williams peering suspiciously into the cab. He shrank away. Somehow he didn't want Williams, with his direct eyes and stern soul, to see him in this company.

"Settle in," Larsen said. "We've got a bit of a drive." His stolid face glinted with something stronger than anticipation. The truck roared past the old brick-walled graveyard full of war casualties, down East Williamsburg

Road, further and further out into the country. The highway divided, resumed its status as Route 60, and ran out of Henrico County into rural New Kent. Garrett held his tongue, waiting. Eventually they drove into Providence Forge and slowed. Late at night, the little crossroads was deserted and quiet. The traffic lights glinted green-and-red against the dark road; the country bank and auto-parts store on either side of Route 60 were silent and shuttered. A left turn here would take them toward Franklin's Plants. Larsen turned right and bumped over the railroad tracks, into deeper country. Sometime later they made another turn onto a small, paved, unlined road which ran through fields and woods, past an occasional logged-over waste. Garrett watched the trees rock by and thought, *You could be lost out here for days.* The few houses were sketchily lit and far apart.

"Where are we?" he asked.

"Charles City," Larsen said, uninformatively.

"Ah." Garrett had been down historic Route 5 a number of times, past the plantations and birthplaces of presidents, but on the other side of that well-known area the big county was an unknown maze of farms and secondary roads. Now they had turned off the narrow paved road onto a dirt lane that ran between two smooth fields of turf. Around a corner, out of sight of the road, Larsen slowed the truck to a halt. Garrett turned his head nervously, but the older man climbed silently out, went to the front of the vehicle, and bent down. Garrett peered out, watching him straighten up and head for the back bumper. A moment later he reappeared back at the driver's side and tossed two license plates into Garrett's lap.

"Stick those on the floor," he said briefly.

The motor roared again. The lane seemed miles long, and when the truck finally drew over to the side of the road, they were surrounded by trees and utter dark. Clint Larsen got out, and Garrett scrambled after him. Above them the stars were blue-white and strewn like sand across a pure black sky. There was a field over to the right of the road, blocked from view by a head-high pile of stumps and dirt left from the clearing of trees. Larsen unlocked the back of the truck and slung an M-16 over his shoulder.

"Sorry, Franklin," he said. "Nothing for you just yet."

"Aren't those National Guard weapons?"

"Not any more," Clint said. He flicked on a flashlight and strolled past the heap of waste. Garrett followed him along the edge of a planted field, his feet sinking into the soft cultivated earth. Ahead, he could hear the faint sound of voices. The glow of the flashlight led him through a tangle of brown weeds, around another pile of stumps, toward a faint scattering of lights.

"Halt! Advance and be recognized!"

"Captain Larsen," Clint said loudly.

"Who's that?"

"Franklin's son."

"Yeah?" The invisible voice resolved itself into a stocky man in his thirties, carrying an AK-47. "Come on in," he said. "Major's at the fire."

"Thanks," Clint Larsen said. They walked toward the scattered lights, which drew together into a cluster of lanterns, hung at the entrances of tents pitched in a circle among the trees. Men in camouflage sprawled at the tent entrances, sat around the large campfire in the clear space at the middle, and moved among the trees.

"Welcome to the Tri-County Hunt Club, Franklin," Clint said. "Otherwise known as the Tri-County Militia. Patriots from Charles City, New Kent, and Henrico. We're on alert."

Garrett stared around him, speechless. He had imagined Larsen to be engaged in some sort of illegal activity; he had briefly considered drugs and dismissed it in favor of illegal weapons running. Now the reasons for secrecy became apparent. Since the Oklahoma City bombing, regulations prohibiting National Guard soldiers from holding membership in hate groups had been expanded to cover unrecognized militias. The organization here was formidable. It looked like a regular military encampment, with sophisticated weapons and supplies.

"Have a seat," invited Clint, settling himself comfortably by the fire. "This here's Major Morrison. He commands the entire group. There's three captains, one for each county division. I'm captain of the Henrico division. Major Morrison, Garrett Franklin."

Major Morrison nodded curtly.

"Ex-Army Reserve," he said. "Army intelligence expert. I went to the army intelligence school at Fort Huachuca in Arizona." He turned his attention back to Clint. Garrett sat awkwardly on the ground, controlling the impulse to turn his head and gape at his companions. "Any new developments?"

"We're moving from the airport," Larsen said. "The guard's assigned to keep watch on the infrastructure threat, and Balder's bringing in peace-keepers to stand guard at the ports and airports. We've heard talk about combining the Virginia and North Carolina Guard into one group, after tomorrow."

"Mm," Morrison said. "Under whose command?"

Larsen shook his head. Morrison traced a pattern absently in the dirt with his forefinger, and then looked up at Garrett. He had the flat shoulders and short haircut of a military regular, unremarkable brown hair and eyes, heavy eyebrows that almost met over his nose. He was wearing a Glock nine-millimeter with the holster unsnapped.

"Know where you are?" he demanded.

"No, sir."

"Good," Morrison said. "Some of our members would face unpleasant consequences if the government knew we were here. Larsen here would probably be disciplined and then booted out of the guard. We're not popular any more, thanks to the media."

Garrett examined the faces around him covertly. They were all white, between his age and Morrison's apparent age of fifty. Two women in camouflage were deep in conversation on the other side of the clearing. Those who were listening to Morrison had their eyes full on him, concentrating on every syllable.

"Clint's been saying you might be interested in helping us defend Virginia's sovereignty," Morrison said, his fingers still moving in the dirt.

"Er," Garrett said, "well, that's why I joined the guard."

Morrison snorted. "The guard's turning into an arm of the regular armed forces," he said. "Pretty soon it'll be under the control of the UN and the Council on Foreign Relations, just like the army and navy and air force already are. Guardsmen'll be pawns in the establishment of one-world sovereignty. They'll have two choices: go along with the takeover, or end up in open-air camps with true patriots."

I don't believe this, Garrett thought. *I'm sitting in the middle of the woods with a crazy man and a hundred guys with assault weapons.* His heart was thudding again.

Clint Larsen leaned forward slightly, so that the fire illuminated his face. He said, "Know why we cooperate with these guys, Franklin?"

"White supremacy?" Garrett ventured.

Morrison grinned. On the other side of the flames, a young beefy man said, "Nah, we're not those types. That *other* group is."

"The ones camped down near the dam?" someone else put in.

"Yeah. Those guys are nuts. They sit around and eat survival food and drink out of Aryan Nation coffee mugs. No kidding. They all bought 'em at that Aryan World Congress thing in Idaho."

"The Pure Nations militia?" Larsen asked.

"Yeah, that's the one."

"They've got big-time guns over there. I went over last week. They've got those tactical rifles—"

"Hope they stay on our side, then."

"Why are they here?" Garrett asked.

The heavy speaker shrugged. He said, "You know, they hold their meetings at the Church of Jesus Christ Christian Aryan Nation. Anybody starts talking about Jesus Christ, they think they've found an ally."

"See," Clint Larsen explained, "that sort of thing gives militias a bad name. There was this survey done in Texas, and it found out that over half of Texans didn't like militias. But almost three quarters of the same people agreed that the federal government is slowly taking away more and more of our civil liberties. All we're doing is saying out loud what most people think. Me and Major Morrison, we've been worried for a long time about the federal government getting more and more power over the Virginia Guard. The way we see it, the state guards are the last shield between the people of the U.S.A. and the one-world forces."

"Um," Garrett said, cautiously, "who would *those* be?"

"The United Nations is the international agency," Morrison said, taking the conversation back over. "Nations get eased into the UN, just like the United States has been. The next step is to get them to ratify the World Constitution."

"What's that?" Garrett adopted the wide-eyed innocence that had served him so well with Larsen.

"Provides for a global economy, world disarmament, world courts. When twenty-five nations ratify it, we'll have full-blown world government. The World Parliament's already got an office in Colorado. The United States is the nineteenth nation on the list. Sooner or later, it's gonna ratify the World Constitution, and then good-bye to United States sovereignty. We think the World Parliament even has plans to wipe out some large U.S. cities, just to weaken us as a nation. They've got the Internal Revenue Service on their side."

"The IRS," Larsen chimed in, "even has a plan for collecting taxes after a nuclear attack. It's called *Fiscal Planning for Chaos*. Talks about imposing a flat-rate gross receipts tax right after the attack. It gives the IRS emergency powers to seize all resources to meet emergency needs." Morrison was nodding in agreement.

"So what does your—er—your militia *do*, Major Morrison?"

"We tell the truth," Morrison announced. "That's why we've got so many enemies. We're exposing the one-world plot, and powerful people don't like it. You gotta understand, when the UN talks about a speedy and final elimination of the terrorist problem, they're not just talking about the Armed Islamic Group and the Ulster Volunteer Force. They're talking about us. We've been yelling about the World Constitution for years, and no one's listened except Charles Merriman."

"You've talked to the governor?"

"Not personally," Clint Larsen said, "but he's obviously been reading our stuff, or why would he get out of the U.S.A.? Patriots are assembling all over Virginia to make sure that the revolution isn't sabotaged. We want Virginia to stay free, no matter what happens to Washington."

"So we've got to keep an eye on this merger business," Morrison ordered, standing up and dusting his hands against his thighs. "The North Carolina adjutant general's not trustworthy, you know. He's a member of the Council on Foreign Relations. That's the most powerful arm of the World Parliament within the United States. If he starts having any long conferences with General Fletcher, you get back to me right away, understand?"

"Right," Clint Larsen said.

"Good work, men. We're expecting another report in from Captain James. . . . that's probably him now." The sentry had just hailed another approach, from the darkness. A low murmur of voices gave way to a tall man in civilian clothes.

"Captain James commands the New Kent division," Clint Larsen explained, standing up and humping the M-16 back over his shoulder. Garrett got to his feet. The tall man glanced cursorily at the group around the fire. "Major," he said to Morrison; and his gaze returned suddenly to Garrett.

"Who's this?" he demanded.

"Garrett Franklin," Morrison said.

Captain James's gray eyes sharpened suddenly.

"Who brought him?"

"Larsen."

"You fool," Captain James said. "You've been here long enough. Get back to your base."

"Captain—" Major Morrison started.

"Major, sir, I've got news for you." The two militia officers moved away from the fireplace. Larsen blew out a short, exasperated breath.

"Come on, Franklin," he said. "You've outlasted your welcome." He started toward the field.

"Why?" Garrett demanded, trotting after him. "What'd I do?"

"I dunno, but I'm not arguing with Bill James. He's tough, that guy."

Garrett shot a puzzled glance over his shoulder. Through the trees, he could still see James and Morrison at the far edge of the clearing, their figures black against the glow of the lanterns. James, talking hard, threw a hand out in his direction. He tripped over a branch and scrambled for his balance, his breath coming short in the cold March woods.

Maybe, he thought, *there's something going on here that even Larsen doesn't know about.* He could feel prickles, running uninvited down the ridge of his backbone.

GARRETT FRANKLIN REPORTED to the Sandston base for duty at nine on Tuesday morning, with United Nations subterfuge and World Parliament skulduggery still swirling in his head.

He lined up with Larsen and got his orders. Selected members of the Seventy-eighth Tactical Fighter Unit's security police would be stationed at the newly-established border around the Yorktown Naval Weapons Station, two hours to the east. Inside the border were United States properties, the weapons station, and nine hundred trained military personnel. Outside the border was Virginia land, now under the authority of the Reformed American States. Their duties: to maintain order, check incoming and outgoing United States citizens for illegal weapons, and to watch for possible attack.

Garrett swallowed in a dry throat. He would be in the field, away from telephones; away from Margaret Franklin and any possible protection that her old friend, the chief of staff, could extend to him.

CHAPTER 17

ENNETH BALDER SPENT THE MORNING with the adjutant general, moving colored dots on a map in an attempt to shift the limited guard forces into place around vital elements of Virginia's infrastructure. The Pentagon's threat on the previous day had been curt, unspecific, and worrying. But he escaped the Capitol and Joe Fletcher in time to keep his noon appointment at the Richmond city police headquarters. Daniel Caprio had set aside a little room for him, with a table and two uncomfortable straight chairs, and a pile of pending murder investigations. The case file marked with Matthew Franklin's name was on top.

Balder pushed the other folders away and rested his cast on the table, shifting his aching shoulder. The folder held numerous papers dealing with Jerry Tindell. He separated those out and tried to ignore the rest: the autopsy report (*The bullet passed through the right chest and avulsed the aorta. . . . mechanism of death was loss of blood. . . .*) with its diagram of Matthew Franklin's body; the statement taken from Margaret Keil Franklin, wife of the deceased.

When asked whether she saw anyone near the crime scene, witness answered, "I didn't look. I thought if I got there soon enough I could. . . . but he was beyond talking, and I wasn't thinking. I ran back to the store and left him there on the road, and I don't know whether he was dead before I went or if he died alone while I ran down the sidewalk. I didn't see anyone. I didn't see anything. Where is he? Where did you take him?"

He and Matthew had shared a dingy apartment on a Berkeley side-street, countless pizzas and football games and an occasional all-night history session during finals. Matthew used to do sit-ups in the middle of the kitchen floor at sunrise, regardless of the time he'd gotten to bed the night before (*Maggie stirring beside him, mumbling, "Can't Matt do sit-ups without making those awful noises?" and drifting back to sleep again before he could answer*). Most mornings, Mary Miranda would arrive on the doorstep with doughnuts. She'd lived on pastry and coffee; thin, in constant motion, blonde hair swinging and fingernails bit to the quick.

He addressed himself grimly to the notes of the police interview with one Jamal Henderson, eyewitness and drug dealer.

In return for the statement, Jamal Henderson had been promised immunity from prosecution for his drug deal, which was a small-time affair of twenty bucks and a fragment of crack. Jamal Henderson, he gathered, was well-known to the police, and had a reputation for making exaggerated and impossible claims. But on the subject of Jerry Tindell, he was clear and very definite. He heard a shot and walked forward to peer out of the window of the deserted house where he was waiting. He saw a man lying in the middle of the road, and a white woman in a green coat running back toward the distant convenience store. The house was dark, and with his eyes adjusted to the darkness he had clearly seen Jerry Tindell standing on a doorstep across the way. Asked whether Tindell had been armed, he had said, "Couldn't see his hands." Asked whether he knew Jerry Tindell, he said, "Yeah, sure, I saw him around a lot. Man always had a gun. Crazy man, always yellin' about his brother and the cops." Tindell had started toward the body, and just then the client had come in the back door. Henderson and the client watched Jerry Tindell rifle the body, and when he disappeared back into the shadows, they concluded their deal and separated.

In a second statement taken the next day, Mrs. Franklin stated, "I saw someone move in the dark." Asked where, she replied, "Over to the left. I didn't see a face or anything, but there was someone there." When she was reminded that she had said both "I didn't look" and "I didn't see anyone" the previous night, Mrs. Franklin said, "Of course I said that. Matthew had only been dead an hour," and started to cry.

Kenneth Balder sucked his teeth, thoughtfully. The Mosaic guidelines

demanded at least two eyewitnesses for conviction, since a guilty verdict
mandated the death penalty. In this case, both Jamal Henderson and his
client had witnessed the robbery, and Margaret herself had identified the
presence of a murderer. No one had actually seen Jerry Tindell shoot
Matthew Franklin. But how many murderers, even in ancient Israel, committed their crimes in full view of an audience? He was inclined to believe
that fingerprinting, DNA testing, ballistics testing, and police searches
could all be contextualized as "eyewitnesses." The intent of the passage
was clearly to prevent conviction on inadequate evidence, and modern
criminal justice techniques practically eliminated the need for an eyewitness to the moment of murder itself. John Cline would no doubt disagree,
loudly and repeatedly. But from this report, Balder could hardly see how
anyone else could be involved in Matthew Franklin's death.

He flipped to the next page of the report and read the statements taken
from Margaret and Garrett. Garrett's story about his father's National
Guard worries was intriguing. But it was long on atmosphere and short on
details. Balder wasn't surprised that police had declined to stir up a fuss
within the National Guard over such a tale.

But this was a new era. They had an obligation to explore every possibility. He stood up and opened the door of the small room where he sat;
and after a moment a young police officer appeared from the office down
the hallway and looked at him inquiringly.

"Sir?"

"I'd like copies of these three case files," Balder said, exhibiting Matthew
Franklin's manila envelope and two others he had scooped up at random
and tucked awkwardly under his left elbow.

"Yes, sir." The young officer took the files off into the depths of the
station, and Balder waited impatiently by the door. Daniel Caprio was
away for the morning, attending a meeting of Virginia law enforcement
officers underway in Henrico County. Balder had come to Richmond's
police headquarters at this particular time so that he could review the
police files without anyone looking over his shoulder. Merriman wanted the
justice codes published on the next afternoon, and immediate application
of them beginning on Thursday.

The young officer reappeared with the copies in a very brief time and handed them over with a grin.

"We're not too busy today," he remarked, off-hand. "Violent crime's way down. All the criminals lying low and waiting for the new laws. Hope you make 'em stiff, sir. It's been a peaceful week."

HE ARRIVED BACK AT THE CAPITOL well before three, when Charles Merriman had planned yet another cabinet meeting to discuss North Carolina's pending independence; and so he dropped the files on his new desk and put in a call to the adjutant general.

"Joe," he said, "can you tell me where a particular guard unit has been posted?"

"Sure, if you're patient. Which one?"

"The Security Police Squadron, Seventy-eighth Fighter Unit."

"Yeah. Sandston. Just a minute." Joe Fletcher's voice trailed away, and after a short time resumed. "Part of the squadron is still baby-sitting the base. The rest of it went to stand guard around the Yorktown Naval Weapons Station. Who're you looking for?"

"Garrett Franklin and—" he consulted the file in front him, "Clint Larsen."

"I can have my secretary check on it for you."

"Yes. Thanks."

He hung up. It was still some minutes until three. He walked along the banistered walkway to Merriman's suite. The governor's receptionist was momentarily away from his post, and so he strolled past the desk and into Merriman's office.

Merriman was sitting at his desk with his elbows perched on either side of a hamburger and fries. He looked oddly young, less imposing, and much less sure of himself. Across from him sat a thin, erect man with white streaks in his brown hair: Christopher Dillard, who had obviously reduced his former pupil to a grubby college student once more.

"Sorry to interrupt," Balder said mildly. He realized for the first time, glancing around the room, that Merriman had arranged his furniture to evoke the Oval Office. Two chairs in front of the desk, the flag of the Commonwealth on his right, a small sitting area with a sofa and easy chair at the far end of the room, light yellow walls and bordered carpet. On the sofa, John Cline's iron-gray head was bent over a newspaper.

"No need to go," Merriman said. "Kenneth Balder, my chief of staff. Christopher Dillard—"

"Well-known opponent of racism and professor of New Testament hermeneutics, Gordon-Conwell," Balder said, shaking hands courteously. Christopher Dillard barely reached five-foot-six, and his hand was dry and light. Brown hair, brown eyes, a firm, generous mouth and eyebrows drawn close together; an intelligent and deeply troubled face.

"Dr. Balder," Christopher Dillard said, politely returning the compliment.

"I took New Testament Survey from Dr. Dillard, when I was eighteen," Merriman said, eating a french fry meditatively. "Two years of Bible college, before I transferred up to UVA. We've both come a good ways since then."

"You've come further than anyone expected," Dillard said, reseating himself. "I tried to get here before, but I couldn't get a flight, and I wasn't sure whether I'd be allowed through the borders if I drove, after that scene on TV last week. How's your arm, Dr. Balder?"

"It'll mend," Balder said. Merriman clearly wanted him to stay, and he momentarily dandled the idea of absenting himself for this reason; and then chastised himself for a lack of compassion, and folded himself into a chair.

"I saw you on 'Sunday Morning with David Jones,'" he remarked.

"Oh?"

"Trying to resuscitate the evangelical cause."

"Long dead," John Cline observed, apparently to himself. "Well past any CPR."

Christopher Dillard said bluntly, "What you're doing here is bringing everyone who claims to follow Christ into disrepute. You're discrediting all of us. Someone had to come and tell you so, Charles. I know it won't make any difference. You're achieving too much success. But for the sake of my conscience—"

"Sir," Merriman said, pushing a fry around with his forefinger, "power isn't my motivation. Righteousness is. I couldn't swallow the evangelical rhetoric about wanting a place at the table in American politics any more. It shows such a lack of conviction. God didn't tell us to ask nicely for a place at the table, along with the humanists and New-Agers and existentialists. He told us to exercise dominion."

"Over the physical world," Dillard said.

"Over all spheres," Merriman amended.

"Even Abraham was looking for a city with spiritual foundations."

"Whereupon God gave Abraham a plot of ground in the Middle East and supplied his descendants with five books of case-law," Cline rumbled, from the sofa behind.

Dillard ignored him. "Charles, the New Testament is very clear. We're fighting against the spiritual powers of darkness, not against the powerful men who govern politics. To do something like this, and claim that you're establishing God's kingdom on earth, reduces God's kingdom to a political entity, with all the corruption that inevitably involves."

"Sir, with all respect, your method of reading the New Testament back into the Old drastically reduces the importance of three-quarters of the Bible. When you do that, you don't show reverence for God's Word. You show a willingness to exercise your own judgment over it. You put your own reason above God's."

"Like most so-called evangelicals," Kenneth Balder put in, "which is why Christianity is so powerless in America today."

Dillard glanced over at him, the close eyebrows drawn together. He had the look of a man fighting a dangerous adversary; and Balder realized that the adversary was not Merriman, but himself. As if he held any sway over the governor. Sometimes he felt as though he were playing cards with Charles Merriman; and Merriman had dealt him a skimpy hand and then neglected to tell him the rules of the game.

"You know all my arguments already," Dillard said at last. "We could sit here and debate for days. I won't bother. Charles, I led you into the kingdom of God over fifteen years ago. I speak to you as your father in Christ. Please! I beg you not to go on with this revolution."

"I can't stop now," Merriman protested. "I'll violate my conscience. I did try to work with evangelical politicians, for three years. All I found was that they were perfectly willing to dismiss difficult parts of Scripture when they didn't like them. Like all American evangelicals. I'm done with evangelicalism, Dr. Dillard. I don't think it even deserves the name any more."

"Pure anti-nomianism," Cline put in from the sofa behind them. "Shallow feel-good lawlessness."

Christopher Dillard craned his neck around and said irritably, "I've read your stuff. You're the man who thinks stoning is the divine blueprint for execution. You have an absolutely blinding talent for ignoring basic principles of interpretation."

"God recommended stoning for a reason," Cline retorted.

"Yes. He was speaking to a people who had plenty of stones handy."

"The Master of the Universe is capable of seeing ahead. He could have prescribed another form of punishment if He'd intended us to use it."

"You're a literalist, Mr. Cline, and that's not a compliment. I daresay you expect the end times to bring an actual harlot with a post-office address in Babylon. Where did this nine-percent tax come from? It's not part of Deuteronomy."

"No," Cline drawled, "that was already in place when I was invited in. Dr. Balder was here first."

"There's nothing anti-biblical about an income tax," Kenneth Balder said. "I agree that a system free of internal taxation would be preferable. But until we can establish foreign trade—and be sure that the United States will trade with us—we have to have revenue."

"In God's scheme of things," John Cline remarked, "there are two taxes: the tithe, which the state can require but not regulate, and the head tax. The head tax is to support the state, military power, and the courts. Every other function—education, poor relief, and so forth—is to be paid for by the churches, out of the tithe."

"And do you recommend a return to ceremonial dietary laws?" Christopher Dillard asked.

"The word 'ceremonial'," Cline said, folding his newspaper onto his lap, "has become a convenient term for all God's principles that we don't like. Certainly our sanctification doesn't depend on the way we eat. But the dietary laws have definite principles of operation. They're God's rules for health and life. No animal fats except for poultry, no scavenger animals or pork, no restrictions on fruits, grains, eggs, and vegetables, wine in moderation—well, medical science gets around to it sooner or later."

Merriman covered his hamburger with a corner of his napkin.

"Tobacco?" Christopher Dillard inquired shortly.

Cline shrugged. "I wasn't consulted about the tobacco issue," he said, "and I think tobacco use violates the Sixth Commandment, but an argument could probably be made from the Eighth Commandment that government shouldn't legislate against it. My own convictions concerning tobacco come more from Adam Clarke than from the actual words of Scripture."

Christopher Dillard folded his hands.

"Well, Charles," he said, "considering that your government is founded on the explicit commands of God, your cabinet seems unusually divided over what those explicit commands actually say. You're going to have to create a separate governmental agency to apply all that clear and unambiguous Law to present-day Virginia."

Merriman's telephone rang shrilly, and he picked it up without answering.

"Yes?" he said, and listened for a long moment. Kenneth Balder shifted in his chair. His arm throbbed, his neck was unpleasantly stiff, and none of his visions of a God-administered country had ever included John Cline. Or the immediate re-opening of state parks. Or the instant introduction of the gold standard. The cast itched unbearably.

Merriman hung up, without closing the conversation.

"You'll excuse us?" he said politely to Christopher Dillard. "We have state matters to discuss. I'd be happy to offer you the hospitality of the Executive Mansion—"

"Thank you," Dillard said, rising from his chair, "I think not. I'm at the Holiday Inn downtown. I'll see myself out."

He marched out the door, his thin shoulders stiff and disapproving. Charles Merriman said curtly, "Enough of this. Apparently economic sanctions are stalled in the Senate. I imagine they're waiting to see whether the attack on our infrastructure materializes."

"Breathing room," Kenneth Balder said.

"I will *not* be intimidated," Charles Merriman announced. Judging from the tone of his voice, this encompassed both Christopher Dillard and Alexander Wade. "At today's cabinet meeting, the adjutant general will be presenting a plan to combine the North Carolina and Virginia Guards into a temporary defensive force. Mac's military strength is far lower than it ought to be, considering he's about to declare independence. So keep the gold standard to ten minutes, John. Plenty of time for that later. Let's stay focused on essentials."

"Speaking of essentials," Cline said, shaking out his newspaper again, "I notice the front page displays your chief of staff in a compromising position."

He held the paper up. Balder sighed, rubbing his eyes. The photo was of Margaret and himself, his weight mostly on her shoulder, in a wordless intimacy that needed little explanation.

"My chief of staff was chaperoned by the National Guard," Merriman said dryly. "I saw to it."

"You know, of course, that any relationship between the two of you is completely out of the question?" Cline inquired.

"Why?" Balder demanded.

"She's an unbeliever, to start with."

"At the moment."

"And of course, Deuteronomic law would forbid it in any case."

"Could you be more specific?"

"Twenty-fourth chapter. A sexual relationship interrupted by marriage to another man can never be resumed, without bringing a curse on the land. Cross-reference Jeremiah, the third chapter."

"That passage has to do with divorce," Kenneth Balder said. With an effort that seemed likely to burst his lungs, he managed to keep his voice calm and reasonable. He could hardly bear to have the photograph of Maggie under John Cline's eyes, much less under his judgment.

"Well," John Cline said, "and what is divorce but the ending of a one-flesh relationship? You lived with this woman in college, correct? The relationship ended, she married another man; you can't enter back into marriage with her now. I assume that is your eventual intention. *If* she comes to faith, of course."

Balder said, hearing the vibrations in his voice rise to the very edge of control, "We were not married. There was no divorce. And Matthew is dead. The situations are in no way comparable. In any case I lived with her when I was an unbeliever. When I became a Christian, the past was wiped away in the eyes of God."

"Insofar as your personal justification was concerned," John Cline said, "but it's absurd to claim that salvation erased the fact of the physical relationship."

"We live in the New Covenant, Cline. The life before conversion is forgotten—"

"You think that erases the demands of law? Balder, you're nothing more than a closet dispensationalist."

Charles Merriman stood up and kicked his chair over backward. He roared over the clatter, "Both of you, shut up! Cline: leave it! Ken, get out on the balcony and collect yourself before the adjutant general and ten aides show up. I am trying to conduct a revolution here. I won't have it sabotaged by pointless arguments." He glared at both of them and added, "I've had people in this room since six this morning, I've had no time for lunch, and I want my office clear. Go away!"

Balder strode out into the hallway under the rotunda. He was shaking with rage. He leaned on the railing and stared up at the seal of Virginia, surrounded by tobacco leaves instead of the traditional laurels. By the time Joe Fletcher arrived at Merriman's door, he was under some semblance of control.

But all through that cabinet meeting he was silent, unable to trust himself to speech. MacDonald Forbes had planned his declaration for eight the following morning; at which point the Reformed American States, that glowing collection of independent states with a cooperative central government, would be a reality. Balder found that he was having some difficulty keeping his mind on Merriman's plans for Virginia's defense. Merriman and the adjutant general had carefully mapped out for him every entrance point into the Commonwealth. He put his finger on the map and listened to the adjutant general's voice chatter on, and longed for Margaret with a bone-deep hunger that he dared not satisfy. *Almighty God*, he thought, *I'm not fit to hold any kind of office. If I thought it was wrong, I'd marry her anyway. How did my purpose get lost in such a tangle of wants?* He had once seized onto the law of God as his only still point in a reeling world. Now that reassuring certainty was slipping away from him; he was standing not on rock, but on thick and quivering mud. He looked across the table at John Cline's calm and settled face with a sudden unfamiliar pang of envy.

BACK IN HIS OFFICE, Balder checked his voice mail and found a message from Joe Fletcher's secretary. Garrett Franklin and Clint Larsen were both stationed at the Yorktown Naval Weapons Station. They could be reached by field telephone; she gave the number. Garrett Franklin was due for a weekend leave in ten days.

He started to dial, and then replaced the receiver. Suppose Garrett and Margaret were right, and Matthew had died because of corruption within the unit. A call to Garrett Franklin from the chief of staff, who was known to be considering re-opening the investigation into Matthew Franklin's murder, might be seen as a threat to someone who had already killed once.

He had one other option. He set his teeth and dialed Margaret's number, praying for the answering machine. The telephone rang once, twice, three times; and mercifully, her recorded voice picked up on the line.

He said carefully, "Maggie, it's Ken. We are officially planning to re-open Matthew's case. I'd like to hear from Garrett as soon as possible, but I don't want to call him in the field. When he contacts you next, please tell him to call me here at the Capitol."

He gave the number, cleared his throat, and could think of nothing to add. "Thanks," he added, miserably, and hung up.

IN THE BRIGHT SUNSHINE of Wednesday morning, Route 29 had lost the sinister aspect of an ambush and had become merely a flat stretch of pavement through budding hardwoods.

Kenneth Balder stepped out of the backseat of Charles Merriman's official car into a forest of cameras and microphones. He shielded his face with his left hand, hunching his shoulders, and thought irritably that he must look like a rock star emerging from a limousine. Across the border, North Carolina state troopers kept a cheerful crowd at a reasonable distance from a wooden platform with the North Carolina and Reformed American States flags hung along it like bunting. MacDonald Forbes had decided to declare independence on this spot, hoping to wipe away the memory of Regulator violence with a peaceful assembly.

And this was a happy group of North Carolinians. Virginia's declaration of independence had been played over and over again on TV until it had become as familiar as a toothpaste commercial, and as a result this second declaration had lost all sense of the ominous and turned into a party. Half the people in the crowd were wearing white T-shirts emblazoned with a large tobacco leaf and the motto which had spread rapidly from Richmond down to Raleigh: *Leaf Our Tobacco Alone.*

He said to Merriman, over his shoulder, "Do you know what Napoleon the Third said when he was asked to ban tobacco?"

"What?" Merriman mumbled, climbing out after him.

"'I will certainly forbid this vice at once, as soon as you can name a virtue that brings in as much revenue.'"

"A very practical point of view."

"Somehow I didn't expect to end up sharing the moral high ground with tobacco."

"There's nothing in the Old Testament about tobacco," Merriman said grumpily. After yesterday's cabinet meeting, he'd gone out to the shipyard and spent the evening making speeches, promising to drum up foreign contracts, and being mobbed by grateful Newport News residents. He'd returned with his hands sore and swollen from the enthusiastic handshaking. He had then dispatched Cline to Charlottesville to address an ultra-secret delegation from West Virginia and ordered Balder to accompany him down to the North Carolina line. His manner had suggested a mother separating two unreasonable toddlers.

"Not a word from the United States?" Balder asked.

THE REVOLT 215

"Not yet," Merriman said.

They stood shoulder to shoulder in the bright sun, waiting as Mac Forbes advanced toward the platform. His guard escort was sketchy—three young, nervous army guardsmen supplemented by state troopers. He had issued his orders contradicting the president on Monday morning. The 56 percent who had refused to be mobilized by the White House had instantly responded, and over the next two days almost 20 percent of the remaining guard installations had reverted back to him, one at a time. Forbes had supplemented their uniforms with a red-and-white patch sewn just above the insignia, so Balder could tell at a glance that the three guardsmen now standing around the platform were North Carolina-loyal, while the small silent outpost behind the crowd was controlled by Washington. He watched them, his eyes narrowed, as Mac Forbes climbed the platform and began to speak.

"Fellow North Carolinians," he began. "In this state we hold a rare honor—that of being the first Americans. In 1585, Roanoke Island saw the establishment of the first English colony in the New World. And although that colony came under misfortune, settlers returned again and again to North Carolina, until we could claim this state as our own. We have always resisted hostile rule. The Sons of Liberty were the first Americans to protest the oppression of the British. In 1776, we were the first state to vote for independence at the Continental Congress. And, because we knew that eventually Washington would seek to take our liberties away, we rejected the Constitution of the United States until the Bill of Rights was finally appended."

The crowd formed a human wall between Forbes and the federalized guardsmen, with their faces to the governor. In all that cheerful mass Balder saw only two heads turn nervously over shoulders. He thought, *We're only a generation away from our last war. Do they think we've moved beyond violence in so short a time?*

Mac Forbes' foray back into American history had reached the Civil War.

"We were slow to join the South, because our deep desire was the preservation of the Union. Only when Washington tried to force us to supply troops did we join the secession. And we paid dearly in the fight against federal aggrandizement. A fourth of those killed defending the South from Northern aggression were from North Carolina."

Merriman winced, beside Balder, and said out of the corner of his mouth, "Who wrote that speech?"

"I thought all you Southerners referred to the Civil War in that way," Balder murmured back.

"The shelf for that particular phrase lies just above the poverty line," Merriman said, displaying an unexpected snobbery. He returned his attention to the platform.

"Now we find that even the Bill of Rights cannot protect us from unjust legislation. The federal government has attempted to deprive us of both our protection and our livelihood; the National Guard, and the entire tobacco industry. It is time for North Carolina to stand with Virginia against this growing threat."

Forbes bent his head and, as Charles Merriman had done before him, read the familiar words of the Declaration of Independence:

"Prudence, indeed, will dictate that governments long established should not be changed for light and transient causes; and accordingly all experience hath shown, that mankind are more disposed to suffer, while evils are sufferable, than to right themselves by abolishing the forms to which they are accustomed. But when a long train of abuses and usurpations, pursuing invariably the same object evinces a design to reduce them under absolute despotism, it is their right, it is their duty, to throw off such government."

MacDonald Forbes raised his head and smiled nervously at the enthusiastic crowd. Beyond the waving North Carolinians, the federalized guard had not moved.

"Today we declare that it has become necessary for the citizens of North Carolina to throw off the despotism of the federal government and provide a new guard for our future security. Therefore, as the elected power of this state, I do solemnly declare that the state of North Carolina is, and of right ought to be, a free and independent state; that it is absolved from all allegiance to the United States of America, and that all political connection between it and the United States is and ought to be totally dissolved; and that as a free and independent state, it has full power to levy war, conclude peace, contract alliances, establish commerce, and to do all other acts and things which independent states may of right do. North Carolina now flies the banner of the Reformed American States, and will cooperate with the Commonwealth of Virginia for our mutual good and defense."

He stepped back from the microphone, and the crowd threw itself happily into applause. The three guardsmen and the state troopers stood at attention. Charles Merriman looked at his watch.

"Well," he said briskly, "that's done. Let's get back to Richmond. My secretary of commerce wants to see me; he's been talking to MCI about taking over responsibility for phone access, and he thinks he's firmed up plans for Federal Express to take over Virginia mail delivery. Apparently FedEx is slavering with delight over the prospect." He sounded as though he had just attended a routine ground-breaking.

"What are those guardsmen doing?" Balder inquired.

"Trying to intimidate us. Have you seen the latest polls? The rest of the country doesn't want to secede, but they'd like to think they *could* if they decided to. If the United States used force against us, the president and secretary of defense would both be out of a job tomorrow. All they can do is look threatening. Here comes Mac."

MacDonald Forbes was walking toward them, his face all smiles. He extended his hand. Merriman reached for it, and camera shutters fired off like a miniature round of artillery. The young North Carolina governor said in a low brittle voice, with the smile still pasted in place overtop, "Charles, I've got to talk to you. Right now."

"Washington?" Merriman murmured, shaking the hand for the cameras with cheerful unconcern.

"Washington? No. Durham."

"*Durham?*" Merriman's smile slipped, very slightly.

"Durham and Chapel Hill. I've got Raleigh, but the universities are full of social liberals—"

"You did this without securing the university centers?" Merriman's voice had dropped twenty degrees of welcoming warmth.

"They're incorporated cities with home rule. They've just done to me what you did to the United States—claimed interposition. They say that the duly elected officials of Durham and Chapel Hill have the moral right to interpose themselves between the residents of those two cities and a higher level of government that's run off the rails." He rattled all this out in a thin breathless voice, half-lost in the shouted questions from the press.

Merriman snapped, "Don't say anything to anyone. We may be able to isolate them."

"The federalized National Guard is keeping the roads open into Durham. I saw them myself. There's more guard headed to Chapel Hill—"

"Listen," Merriman interrupted. "Whatever you do, no force. Got that? *No force.* As long as this is a peaceful revolt, we've got the support of the rest of the nation."

"No force," Mac Forbes said reluctantly.

"Doesn't matter what else happens," Merriman said. "Better for you to lose another county than the high opinion of the nation. You stay put in Raleigh and talk about high taxes and high crime and unemployment until your face turns blue. And send your attorney general up to see me tomorrow morning. Why didn't you tell me this before?"

Forbes shook his head wretchedly.

"I thought I had them," he said, lost. Merriman released the younger man's hand and turned sharply on his heel, somehow managing to keep the victorious smile in place. Kenneth Balder followed him toward the black car. A quick look back showed the federalized guard still standing motionless behind the exhilarated crowd.

The car slowly outdistanced the press, and Merriman threw his dark head back against the leather seat and blew out a deep breath.

"John Cline would threaten to stone me for swearing," he said, after a few moments.

"Feel the need?"

"Yeah. This means we'll lose the northern counties of Virginia sooner than expected. I figured they'd work it out, eventually, that if we can interpose ourselves between them and Washington, they can do the same thing between us and their residents. I'd hoped it would come later."

"What do we do about Durham and Chapel Hill?" Balder asked.

"Durham and Chapel Hill . . . I'd like to skin Mac Forbes with a dull knife. We need 'em both." Merriman brooded for a moment. "We could offer financial incentives to some of the businesses within the city limits, try to get them out into the counties. We could impose an entrance and exit tax. . . . that might lead to a confrontation. Probably not a good idea. We could cut off United States mail service without too much trouble, though, and keep 'em from using the R.A.S. service. Better than nothing. I'll put Gerry and Tom onto the North Carolina attorney general and see what we can come up with."

Balder offered, "Want me to take a break from this criminal trial business?"

Merriman rubbed his chin. "Which case are you working on?"

Kenneth Balder looked straight ahead. He could glimpse Merriman's forehead and his clear blue eyes in the rearview mirror. Merriman knew exactly which cases sat on his desk.

"Jerry Tindell."

"Ah, yes. And you're publishing the justice codes tomorrow?"

"We'd planned on running the laws based on the Ten Commandments, yes. Macleod's got them scheduled for five pages in the front section. But we could wait until Durham and Chapel Hill—"

"No, you go ahead. I've got plenty of people to put to work on Durham and Chapel Hill."

"Charles, if the social liberals in Durham and Chapel Hill are behind the city secessions, running a murder trial and execution isn't the best way to bring them around—"

"Virginia's had the death penalty in place since 1975," Merriman returned. "There's nothing new or unusual in executing a convicted criminal." He closed his eyes, wearily. "We won't convert the social liberals anyway. We need to mobilize the uncommitted middle class that's following them blindly along. Maybe justice in action will tilt them away from the university centers. Sakes alive, I'm tired. . . ."

His voice trailed off, and he shifted his shoulders once more against the back of the seat. Balder was silent. His own inclination was to continue on with the arrest and trial of Jerry Tindell. But he was beginning to distrust himself. His motives were knotted and obscure, and he kept hearing Maggie's voice in his head. *If I thought you were all through playing God, I might not be afraid of you.* Merriman's arguments were reasonable and sane. He found them entirely unconvincing. Tindell's trial would lead him further down the unseen road Charles Merriman had planned for him to follow. He knew it; but he was at a place without crossroads or warning signs.

CHAPTER 18

Thursday, March 28, 11 A.M.

UNDER THE CONSTANT BRIGHT EYES of a hundred TV cameras, Richmond businesses were putting out flowers without regard for late frosts. As a result Margaret had entirely sold out most of her blooming stock. The three neat greenhouses were half-empty.

She had thankfully dropped the complex figuring and paying out of sales taxes. She'd made a startling profit this week, and if she could restock the pansies and find some impatiens slightly more mature than the tender seedlings in the third greenhouse, she could set a record for the next week's takings. John Cline's predictions about prosperity were coming true—for her, at any rate. But she had no idea where Garrett was, and she was increasingly worried. When she called the Sandston base, she got a recording. She'd stood in the kitchen two days ago and listened to Ken's recorded voice, fighting the impulse to pick up the telephone and tell him to come back. She had already thought this through. Twenty-five years ago, she'd left Kenneth Balder for Matthew Franklin because Ken had shattered her trust. And she would stay loyal to Matthew unless she was convinced that Kenneth Balder had changed. That was the rule she had made for herself; that was the rule she would follow, and the desperate loneliness of the last few days was irrelevant.

In a temporary lull of customers, she took a breather from the greenhouse and walked down toward the mailbox at the end of the rutted lane. The morning newspaper stuck out of the box, bright in its orange waterproof wrapper. The sky had been spitting early that morning, but the dawn clouds had slowly blown away and the day was unseasonably warm.

The mail, a single bill from Virginia Power, had arrived with the newspaper. Virginia's paper carriers were now paid a hefty sum to deliver mail along with the local dailies. Those who didn't subscribe had to retrieve their mail from the post office, but Merriman had promised a new privatized mail system within a month. She shoved the letter into a pocket and turned back to the house, shaking open the *Times-Dispatch* as she walked. The hard March wind whipped at the edges, and sun shone through the fragile newsprint. This morning Ken occupied the front page, above the fold. He was half-hidden behind Charles Merriman. MacDonald Forbes dominated the foreground, walking toward the two older men with his hand outstretched: *North Carolina Joins the Revolution*. A box at the side read *The New Code of the Commonwealth: Page 3A*.

The crunch of tires behind her warned that another customer had turned into the lane, and she stepped out of the road and quickened her pace toward the greenhouses.

Later, when a lunchtime quiet had descended, she retrieved the newspaper from its temporary resting place behind the cash register and went into the house for sandwiches and coffee. She carried the papers and her plate and mug into the side-porch office and sat down. Page 3A began with a dry paragraph signed by Kenneth Balder, chief of staff for Charles Merriman:

> This first part of the code, drawn up by a distinguished task force of scholars and criminal justice experts, is founded on the Ten Commandments, which contain the overarching principles of God's law. Five books of case-law accompanied the Ten Commandments and provided for the application of their broad principles in specific situations. We estimate that it will take at least a year to accurately relate the Old Testament case-law to present-day conditions. . . .

She skipped over the rest of the introduction and moved on to the new code.

THE TEN COMMANDMENTS

The first four commandments were capital crimes in ancient Israel. As they deal with the relationship of man to God within the community bound by the commandments, the Reformed American States has decided to interpret execution, in modern times, as exile from the community. Thus, the penalty for violation of the first four commandments is deportation to the United States of America.

I. YOU SHALL HAVE NO OTHER GODS BEFORE ME.

    A. Because education in the law is inseparable from obedience to the only true God, public education must be grounded in the laws of the Old and New Testaments.

    B. Because God rather than the state is sovereign over the lives and affairs of men, the state is prohibited from enforcing the following:

      1. Military conscription

      2. Compulsory labor in service to the state

      3. Seizure of private property

      4. Imprisonment, except in the case of those awaiting trial

      5. Taxes exceeding the tithe (10 percent)

    C. PENALTY FOR VIOLATION: Deportation to the United States.

Well, Margaret considered; any code that began by severely limiting the power of the state would increase its chances of popular acceptance fivefold, right from the start.

II. YOU SHALL MAKE NO GRAVEN IMAGES.

    A. To prevent the state from erecting itself as an image in the place of God, no one may participate in any state office who is not committed to obedience to the written law of God.

    B. Private and public citizens alike are prohibited from the erection of literal idols.

    C. PENALTY FOR VIOLATION: Deportation to the United States

III. YOU SHALL NOT TAKE THE NAME OF GOD IN VAIN.
  A. Defamatory, wicked, and rebellious language directed against God is prohibited.
  B. The breaking of an oath taken before God is prohibited.
  C. PENALTY FOR VIOLATION: Deportation to the United States.

IV. HONOR THE SABBATH DAY TO KEEP IT HOLY.
  A. Sunday, the day of the Resurrection, shall be a mandatory day of rest for all citizens, when no business may be transacted.
  B. PENALTY FOR VIOLATION: Deportation to the United States.

Here the text was broken by another paragraph of commentary.

The Fifth, Sixth, and Seventh Commandments have to do with the foundational relationships between men and the respect for life mandated by our Creator. Because of this, any citizen of Virginia who is duly convicted of a flagrant and deliberate violation of one of these commandments may be sentenced to capital punishment. Capital punishment has been legal in Virginia since 1975.

V. HONOR YOUR FATHER AND MOTHER.
  A. Parents must provide children with material needs, spiritual education, and training in a trade. Willful and continual neglect of the material and spiritual needs of a child may be deemed a capital offense.
  B. Children must return respect to their parents in the following ways:
    1. The public cursing of parents is forbidden.
    2. Grown children must contribute to the support of aged parents.
    3. Determined and intractable incorrigibility in children which leads to a violation of the Fifth, Sixth, or Seventh Commandments may be deemed a capital offense.

So much for Richmond's street gangs. The next commandment dealt with Jerry Tindell and Matthew's unpunished murder.

VI. YOU SHALL NOT KILL.

A. Any killing, with the exception of capital punishment administered by a legitimate government, just warfare carried out by duly enlisted military personnel, and self-defense, is a capital offense.

B. Suicide is a capital offense.

C. Abortion is a capital offense, except when carried out to prevent the imminent death of the mother.

D. Any form of euthanasia is a capital offense.

No "may be deemed a capital offense" in those sentences; they were clear and unambiguous. It was apparent to Margaret that the Reformed American States was determined to punish the shedding of blood. She forced her eyes to move on to the next commandment.

VII. YOU SHALL NOT COMMIT ADULTERY.

A. The following offenses may be deemed capital offenses, when fully attested to in a court of law:
1. Willful polygamy
2. Incest
3. Child molestation
4. Homosexual acts
5. Acts of bestiality
6. Transvestitism
7. Adultery
8. Forcible rape

After this grim list, it was a relief to reach another qualifying paragraph.

The final three commandments have to do with the assets on which a community is established. Violation of the last three commandments is punishable by restitution, ranging from the exact amount in question up to seven times the amount in question, depending on the degree of malice involved.

VIII. YOU SHALL NOT STEAL.

A. The state is prohibited from:

1. the issuance of unbacked paper money, which results in the theft of inflation;
2. the passing of laws which may deprive a particular group of property;
3. restrictions in the use of private property.

B. Both private and public citizens are prohibited from:
  1. direct theft;
  2. fraud;
  3. destruction of property by will or accident;
  4. usury, defined as exorbitant interest and loans that run more than six years;
  5. defaulting on a legal pledge or debt;
  6. extortion;
  7. any form of gambling;
  8. failure to pay wages fairly and on time;
  9. failure to observe the land's Sabbath year.

IX. YOU SHALL NOT BEAR FALSE WITNESS AGAINST YOUR NEIGHBOR.
  A. Deeds or words that injure the good name of another shall be compensated for by the assessment of monetary damages.
  B. Perjury shall be compensated for by the assessment of monetary damages; however, perjury that leads to the death of another may be deemed a capital offense.
  C. False statements with respect to men and events in everyday affairs shall be compensated for by the assessment of monetary damages; however, a false statement that leads to the death of another may be deemed a capital offense.

X. YOU SHALL NOT COVET.
  A. The state is prohibited from establishing any system which takes from one group to give to another.
  B. Both private and public citizens are prohibited from gaining an advantage over the property of another in a way not covered by the previous commandments.

Margaret's plate was empty; she'd eaten the whole sandwich and all the chips without a single mouthful registering on its way down.

Would Virginia accept these laws? The new code mingled the private and the public in a startling new way. Now the EPA couldn't take her farm away; and she couldn't play the lottery, or sell a plant on Sunday.

And yet the growing frustration around her—the exasperation with high taxes and nothing to show for it and lawlessness in every street and politician after politician talking, talking, talking without effect—inclined her to think that Virginians would give the code a chance. She understood the frustration of the age. She'd even been guilty once of calling into a political radio show to tell the story of a federal government that had forced her to remove her in-ground gasoline tank under the vague and terrifying threat of sending the EPA to test the soil around it and "recommend appropriate procedures." And when she looked over at the board on the left wall, she could see the yellow headline blazoned across the top: *No Arrests in Fatal Shooting of National Guardsman.*

They'll wait, she thought. *We've already seen how the old system works. Now Virginia will wait to see what happens under the new.*

And if it brought justice and peace, the new administration might just survive. . . .

THAT AFTERNOON, Margaret headed north on the interstate toward Falmouth, where her wholesaler was located. She was out of mature plants, and demand hadn't slowed. The sun was slanting blindingly through the driver's side window, and she barely noticed that traffic all around her was trickling off into exit after exit; or that an occasional dull green helicopter beat by overhead. She was hauled suddenly back from her daze by a row of orange blobs directly ahead of her. She stood on the brakes in astonishment. Cones stood across all four lanes of I-95, directing her through the nearest exit onto Route 17. Beyond the cones, a row of army guard trucks blocked the interstate. She pulled unwillingly over onto the exit and found herself launched into the middle of rural Spotsylvania County.

Margaret dragged the rattling old nursery truck to a halt by the side of the road. Little Falmouth, just on the other side of Fredericksburg, was barely two miles away by interstate. Whatever the guard was doing out there, it would cost her an extra hour in time maneuvering her way through winding country roads. She dug around in the side-door pocket for her old Virginia map and plotted her way. If she continued on 17 for a bit and then turned left onto tiny Route 608, it ought to take her right into Stafford County.

Route 60 proved to be an unlined rural road with the edges crumbling away into dust. She drove through a little stand of trees, just coming out in March buds, around a corner, and found a young inattentive guardsman standing in the road. He had his back turned to her, lighting his cigarette with his hand cupped against the wind, and he leapt out of the way of the nursery truck just as she slammed on her brakes. This was too much. She shoved the door open and climbed out and yelled, "What the blazes are you doing right in the middle of the road?"

The boy was barely older than Garrett, and she had trouble taking him very seriously despite the beret and the M-16 on his back. He recovered himself and dropped the cigarette and cracked his shoulders back into proper military posture.

"Ma'am, this road's closed," he said. "Didn't you see the signs?"

"What signs?"

"There's an orange sign back there—"

"There is not."

"Well," he said, "there oughta be. Stafford County's closed. This here's the county line."

"What do you mean, closed?"

"Ma'am, this morning the five northern counties of Virginia and the cities located inside their borders declared themselves independent of the Commonwealth and rejoined the United States."

"You're kidding."

"No, ma'am."

"Which side are you on?"

"The governor's," the boy said indignantly.

"So why are the roads closed?"

"Ma'am, we're guarding the Commonwealth from invasion by armed forces of the United States."

"But you were here before," Margaret said, recalling the maps on the evening news, with Tom Brokaw explaining that the red line running south of Quantico demonstrated Merriman's unwillingness to secede with that part of Virginia which contained a huge section of the federal government."

"Yeah," the young guardsmen said, "but we're on high alert now. That over there—" he pointed importantly to the innocuous black surface on the other side of the county line, "—is enemy territory."

"I see. So can I go through?"

"Better not, ma'am."

"Why not?"

"You might not be able to get back through."

"I'll risk that. I remember Charles Merriman saying on TV that the borders were to remain open to everyone except armed military forces."

They stood facing each other in the afternoon March sun, Margaret's shoulders stiff with indignation, the guardsman's young undefined features uncertain. He buckled first and stepped to the side of the road.

"Okay," he said, "but if you don't get back home tonight, I told you, remember?"

"Thanks," Margaret said. "I'll have a truckload full of flowers, not grenades." *And I'll come back another way,* she added mentally.

She got back into the old vehicle and bumped her way past the guardsman, into the United States of America. Around the corner another guardsman was leaning against his truck, but he waved her through without even bothering to straighten up.

The Falmouth wholesale nursery was in its usual spring chaos. She managed to place her order, pulled the truck up to have it loaded, parked it back against the stand of pines that divided the nursery lot from the neighboring railroad tracks, and waited in line to pay her bill. She had a charge account here, but with money in the bank there was no reason to go deeper into debt. The man in front of her signed his invoice and walked away, and she put the business checkbook down and waited for the invoice. The clerk at the counter glanced down at the checkbook.

"Wait just a minute, Mrs. Franklin," she said, and disappeared through the white-painted door behind her. Margaret was conscious of shuffling feet and impatient coughing behind her. The clerk came back through the door in the wake of George Jelsen, the nursery's owner.

"George," Margaret said, surprised. "Something wrong with my order?"

"No," George said, leaning his elbows on the counter. He was a big, quiet man in his sixties, his flattop haircut sprinkled with white and his upper arms bulging out the sleeves of his blue denim work-shirt. "Your order's fine, Margaret, and we've been doing business for a long time, but I can't take a Richmond check."

"But it's drawn on Crestar. There are branches all the way into Washington."

"Yeah, but it's headquartered in Richmond. I got to protect myself. They keep talking about sanctions on the news, and that means freezing up the banks."

"There aren't going to be sanctions. They failed in the Senate."

"Well then," George Jelsen said, "might be some kind of attack. Not just you, Margaret, I've turned down five or six Richmond checks today." His voice held the mild unshakable determination of a confused man. Clearly George didn't understand the maze of events unfolding all around him. Just as clearly, he wasn't going to take the check. She closed the checkbook up and said, "Can you put it on my account, then?"

"Rather not. If there's an attack you might be stuck there in Richmond, and I'm sure you'd be fine, but I wouldn't get my bills paid, would I?"

"George, I don't carry that kind of cash on me. Listen, you could take this check to any Crestar and get cash for it five minutes after I leave."

George gazed at her obstinately. She thrashed around for another option. "Visa? I could put it on my Visa card."

George wavered, visibly.

"Come on, George. My Visa bill comes from somewhere in Indiana."

George thought about this option for a long minute. He said finally, "Okay. That'd be fine." He pushed himself up from the counter. "Sorry for the inconvenience," he added. "Just tryin' to run my business here."

She handed the plastic card over and said, "I don't have to pay sales tax at my nursery any more, you know."

"Yeah, I heard."

"Things are pretty good."

"Yeah," George said, "I wouldn't have minded staying, but the county's in control of it, not me. I gotta say, I don't like all those guard trucks I keep seeing go by."

He left her with a nod, and she signed the Visa slip and collected her belongings and headed back to the parking lot. With the flats of flowers carefully secured in the two-tier bed of the truck, she pulled back out onto Route 608 and navigated herself east onto Route 3. This was a divided highway that ran from Stafford into King George, and would probably have an older and more reasonable guard post. Once out of United States territory, she could pick up 301 and head back south toward New Kent. Route 3 was virtually silent, no traffic around her.

As she approached the border she found her fingertips on the wheel tingling with apprehension. Around a corner, the National Guard sentry came into view. On this road there appeared to be two separate guard sentries, with a gap between them. She slowed to a stop and put her head out the window.

"There's just plants in the back," she said, and added in sudden surprise, "You're not Virginia Guard!"

"We're Maryland Guard," the sentry said politely. He was a sergeant in his late thirties, calm and professional. "We're going to have to ask you to turn around. This road is closed."

Margaret said in growing exasperation, "Governor Merriman promised that the borders would stay—"

"We're not under Charles Merriman's command. We take our orders from the White House, and the president is controlling access to the rebel counties of Virginia."

Across the gap Margaret could see the Virginia Guard across the county border, standing across the road and watching the confrontation.

"Would they let me in?" she asked, pointing at the silent line.

"Yes, but you're not getting that far. Turn around, please."

"But I live in New Kent. I've got a business there."

"You'll get a chance to go home eventually," the guardsman said. "Right now, you ought to go find some family and stay with them 'til things settle down."

"In San Diego?"

"Those are my orders. You can't go through."

The road itself was blocked by cones, insubstantial rubber made to bounce out of the way. She wiggled the toes on her right foot. The sole of her shoe was resting lightly against the accelerator. Another car had pulled up behind her. A second Maryland soldier bent to the window, and after a moment it reversed itself and idled away down the shoulder. A white van was approaching. The guard outpost here was five or six men with a green army truck, all of them wearing pistols but none with the combat M-16s slung over their backs.

"Are there more of you around here?"

She saw a sudden glint of caution in his eye and remembered something Garrett had told her about drill weekends. *I just hope nobody goes over the red line one of those Saturdays, 'cause all those guys have been training for years and they're just dying to shoot something.*

"Turn around and go back," he said.

"Is this a new order? I mean, did you just start doing this when the northern counties seceded?"

"The word is *returned*," he said. "Go back."

The white van in her side-view mirror had a logo on the side. It pulled off the pavement onto the shoulder, and two muscular young men in baseball caps jumped out of the side door. The guardsman at her window straightened up, suddenly alert, and his hand moved toward the pistol. The young men produced a video camera and hoisted it up. A red light on the lens flicked on. A slim woman in a skirt appeared around the back bumper, carrying a microphone and stringing yards of flex behind her. Margaret reached out and tilted the mirror slightly to read the logo. The van belonged to the film department of a large Christian university.

She slipped the truck into gear and drove straight for the cones. Behind her a chorus of shouts rose up. The Virginia guardsmen in front let out a yell of encouragement. She managed to think, in the three seconds when the Maryland Guard seemed likely to open fire, *Maybe the plants in the back will block the bullets.*

But under the paralyzing camera, the Maryland Guard proved unwilling to fire on an unarmed female civilian driving a truck full of pansies. She slammed on her brakes in the middle of the Virginia Guard. A grinning officer bent down and said, "Good work, ma'am. We've been wondering if they'd actually shoot someone who went through."

Margaret unclenched her aching fingers from the steering wheel.

"Glad I could help," she said, hearing her voice shake. Somewhere under the shooting terror of the last five minutes was an astonished recognition: *I'm still the same woman who went crawling into an air force base twenty-five years ago.* It had been so long since she'd done anything daring. The surprise of this self-discovery steadied her voice.

"Aren't you going to check the truck?" she asked.

"What? Oh. Yeah." He went around to the back, opened it and rummaged perfunctorily through the flats. "Okay. Go ahead, ma'am. Good luck."

She put her foot on the accelerator again. Ahead of her Route 301 stretched empty and welcoming, all the way down to the interstate, far away from the front lines of Charles Merriman's war.

THE ANSWERING MACHINE WAS flashing as she came through the kitchen door. She hit the button and heard Garrett's voice.

"Mom? I can't tell you where I am, but I wanted to let you know that everything is okay. I'll try to call again later."

The strain in his voice had increased. She played the message back again. He always seemed to leave messages; she hadn't spoken to him directly since the first day of Ken's visit. She picked up the telephone and told herself: *I've got to let him know.*

Unsparing honesty with myself.

And I want to hear his voice.

The telephone rang twice before a woman's voice said, "Office of the chief of staff."

"Kenneth Balder, please."

"He's in a meeting. Can I take a message?"

Margaret hesitated. "Tell him Margaret Franklin called. . . . and that I haven't been able to speak to my son."

"Very well, Mrs. Franklin. Should I have him return your call?"

"Only if he wants to."

"Thank you. I'll relay the message."

Margaret hung up, slowly. She'd already unloaded the pansies. She watered the geranium slips on the windowsill, made dinner, and turned the radio on. She chose the classical station this time, not the news, and she ate while listening to Bach.

The phone stayed silent all evening.

CHAPTER 19

Friday, March 29, 9 A.M.

ALEXANDER WADE sat in his office, reading the *Richmond Times-Dispatch*. The big polished room was silent except for the rustle of newspaper pages.

He reached the end of the front section and slowly refolded the paper so that the front-page picture lay upward. A rattletrap blue truck streaked toward the Stafford County line, the driver invisible inside. The photo, slightly blurred, was a still taken from the university-produced news film that had been plastered on TV screens across the nation the night before, and the story was headlined, *Washington's Border Closure Fails*. This particular frame had caught the line of Virginia Guard in front of the truck shouting happily, as though they'd just seen a Redskins touchdown. In contrast, the Maryland guardsman behind the truck was grim-faced, his nine-millimeter automatic drawn and aimed, his arms stretched out and both hands gripping the gun with clear intent to fire. And naturally the truck contained a woman—Margaret Franklin. The nexus of chaos; it was enough to validate that weird Eastern stuff about fate and karma and conjoined personalities, the way Kenneth Balder and Margaret Franklin met and made trouble for Alexander Wade, first on the West Coast, then twenty-five years later in the East.

Wade glanced at the phone. The White House line was still dark, but

that wouldn't last long. On Thursday morning the president had decided
to "control access" to Virginia by severely limiting all commercial traffic.
In the absence of economic sanctions, he hoped to put a dent in the loyalty of Virginia's small businesses. Wade had advised against it. The White
House was already cast as tyrant in this drama, and it wouldn't help
Washington's cause for the Virginia Guard to welcome travelers while the
federally-controlled Maryland Guard kept Virginians from going home.
He had been correct. Of the two groups of National Guard in the news
photo, there was no question which state guard would make better dinner-
guests; and most Americans were reacting to this conflict on just that level.

The telephone rang. He hit the speaker button.

"Yes?"

"George Lewis is on the line, Mr. Secretary."

"Put him through."

George Lewis had a cold. He snuffled twice and said indistinctly,
"The president would like to know if you've seen Virginia's new code,
Mr. Secretary."

"I read it yesterday."

"He'd like to talk to you about possible human rights violations."

"Mmm," Wade said noncommittally. This tactic had already crossed
his mind.

"The Solarium," George said, and coughed hollowly.

"He'd do better to talk to the attorney general."

"He instructed me to call *you*, Mr. Secretary."

Wade sighed, internally. "Right. I'm on my way. Take some syrup and
go to bed, George."

"I have work to do," George Lewis said distantly, and disconnected.

Alexander Wade remained at his desk, his hands folded on the *Times-
Dispatch* and a crease between his eyebrows. He had very little time. It was
now Friday, and he had stalled the president for five days.

The chief executive had demanded the use of force to bring Virginia back
into line on Monday, forty-eight hours before North Carolina's defection.
Wade had suggested that the United States wait at least until North Carolina's
secession was a reality; and the president had reluctantly complied. In the

meantime, Wade had attempted to energize the North Carolina legislature against MacDonald Forbes, and had failed. Forbes had wide support.

It was true that he had managed to rile the two university cities into rebellion. But that had proved worse than full secession, because now any attack on North Carolina's infrastructure would also punish Durham and Chapel Hill. He again begged the president to wait, pointing out yet again that Virginia was, in fact, proving no threat to United States security; and that Charles Merriman, legally, was in an unprecedented gray zone. But the president's patience had run out. Hence the "limited access" to Virginia; and the unfortunate photo of the opposing guardsmen, now being reprinted in every daily paper across the United States.

If Charles Merriman would take some drastic and unjustifiable action— some step that would set the whole nation against him—Washington could justify an attack. Wade longed for Virginia to do something stupid. Unfortunately Merriman had, so far, refused to play into Alexander Wade's hands. He had done his part, trying to tempt Margaret Franklin out of Virginia. He'd assumed that Kenneth Balder would authorize Jerry Tindell's arrest, simply to please his ex-lover. And then he could reveal the connection to an indignant America, and lean hard on the obvious corruption in Merriman's supposedly just government. But Balder hadn't acted yet. Tindell was still free, and the president was demanding action.

He shook his head over the prospects. This administration had played the troops card sparingly and with great success, in its foreign disputes. But the president had still not grasped the basic fact that it was the otherness of foreigners that allowed a few civilian deaths to pass as necessary with the American people. The enormous fuss over the death of any U.S. soldier demonstrated that America would not tolerate the sacrifice of its own. Injury to an American citizen, in the attempt to bring Virginia back under control, would turn the secretary of defense into a permanent political cripple. The warmonger, the movie-familiar military bureaucrat of limited intelligence, the scapegoat.

Alexander Wade leaned back in his leather chair and stared up at the ceiling. He was the son of a rural doctor who barely cleared the housekeeping. He had gone to college on a Pell Grant, achieved law school on a merit scholarship, clerked his way grimly through the bar exams, come east and married a Georgetown debutante (how long had it been since he'd seen Perri, anyway? . . . two weeks?) and clawed his way into a reputation as a scholar, an expert on international law, and the ethics of military intervention. He ran the Pentagon. He refused to return to that stuffy linoleum-floored office on the fourth floor of a crumbling academic building.

No matter how he looked at it, Wade couldn't see the mere publication of the code as justification enough for an armed attack. There were other tactics, of course. They could set Amnesty International howling on Kenneth Balder's trail, and pull out the hoary comparison of Charles Merriman with the Ayatollah. The religious character of the code, based as it was on the laws of Moses, would inevitably lead to abuses of human rights, no matter how often Kenneth Balder and Charles Merriman denied it. They claimed that worship and belief would not be regulated. That was absurd. Wade had been trained in ethics, after all. He knew perfectly well that the beliefs of a society shaped its actions. If Merriman and Balder really intended for Virginians to honor the law of God, they would have to convert most of Virginia to Christianity—by peaceful means, or by coercion.

But this was beside the point. They hadn't done it yet; and the president was still going to demand military action. He leaned forward and possessed himself of a pen, and printed DENIABILITY in big letters across a blank piece of Defense stationery, and folded the sign and tucked it into his pocket. The president was a visual thinker.

If only Merriman would do something stupid.

Alexander Wade reached into the locked bottom right-hand drawer of his desk and produced two file folders, labeled PRIVATE AND CONFIDENTIAL. One contained a summary of his information on Kenneth Balder, culled from his old files on the trial and supplemented with a series of newspaper articles and photos covering the decade of Balder's freedom. In that file as well were photocopies of those letters from Mary Miranda Carpenter that the judge had refused to admit—the letters that had driven Margaret Keil to the east coast. The folder also contained the police reports on Matthew Franklin's death.

The other file was full of puzzle pieces. The bald statement from Alexander Wade's highly placed private investigator, revealing Ramsey Grant's mysterious tour of duty in the FBI's criminal profiling division. A copy of Grant's charge-card records (he'd obtained those by trading in almost a year's worth of favors). A newspaper photograph. A microcassette containing a telephone conversation with the chief of police, Culpepper, Virginia. And a summary of Culpepper's startling crime statistics.

He spread the papers out and sat, staring at them with unseeing eyes. Presently he lifted the receiver, dialed a well-known number, and got Ramsey Grant's secretary.

"Sir, the attorney general is out of his office. I can give him a message."

Alexander Wade said carefully, "Tell the attorney general I'd like to buy him dinner tonight. At Benvolio's, eight P.M. I'll meet him there unless he calls and cancels."

"Yes, sir. Could I tell him what this is in reference to?"

"Tell him I'm getting ready to have a short vacation in Culpepper."

"Yes, sir."

He replaced the receiver and swept the newspaper into a drawer. Only a stupid man would walk into a rainstorm without an umbrella. Only an inexperienced or suicidal soldier would walk into gunfire at the front of his platoon. Alexander Wade was an old hand at battles; and his political life was of paramount importance. He needed a shield.

He replaced Ramsey Grant's file in the locked drawer, tucked the Balder-Franklin file under his arm, and headed downstairs.

THE CHINTZ-COVERED SOFAS in the Solarium were empty, and the president was alone. He was pacing underneath the bright glass, in shirt and tie with the collar loosened. He lifted his head as Alexander Wade came through the door, and every posture of his body and line of his face made clear: *I am done with conferences.*

"You've read the new Virginia code?" he demanded.

"Yes, Mr. President."

"Can't we do anything about it?"

"There's nothing about it that violates international law, Mr. President."

The president scooped up a nearby newspaper and waved it at his secretary of defense.

"You're telling me that they're threatening to execute rebellious kids and we can't do anything?"

"'Determined and intractable incorrigibility' could mean that juveniles could be executed for first-degree murder. That's not even a new idea. We can't send troops in for that."

"You may be the secretary of defense, Alex, but I'm the commander-in-chief. I make the final call."

Alexander Wade kept his voice level and disapproving.

"Yes, sir," he said. "I think we've tried every peaceful means possible."

"Well," the president said, "let the band strike up. You're actually agreeing with me." He flung the paper away. "I can't even set up a single blockade in the country I'm supposed to be governing without some woman in a pickup going through it like it's a tollbooth. Come look at this map of Virginia. I've had a few ideas."

The map of Virginia was spread out on the ping-pong table the president had introduced into the Solarium. The two men moved to it and bent over the Old Dominion.

"What are these marks?" Wade asked, cautiously.

"Power plants," the president said with satisfaction.

"Electricity?"

"Yes, of course." The president jabbed his finger against the thick paper. "I had the Department of Energy send someone over to explain all this to me. Virginia's got several different types of plants for generating electric power. These blue dots are hydroelectric plants—you know, electricity generated by water pouring over a dam."

"We can't bomb a dam. We'll flood whole valleys."

"Thank you, Alex. I'm aware of that." The president's voice was ironic. "We're not going to bomb the Surrey Nuclear Plant either, are we? Come back to reality. Let's hit one of the steam plants."

Wade scratched the back of his head.

"Where are they?" he inquired.

"Here, here, here . . . and there's this one, outside Richmond. We could throw the whole metropolitan area into a blackout."

"What about hospitals?"

"Hospitals have generators, don't they?"

"Yes, but if we take out an entire plant, it'll be weeks before power comes back on."

"Virginia has plenty of oil for the generators."

"It's a very large target, Mr. President. We'd have to attack by air."

"Yes? Why not?"

Wade took the folded piece of paper from his breast pocket and flattened it onto the map.

"Here's why not," he said.

The chief executive viewed the block letters for a long moment. He always spoke with a diagram of his speech in front of him, and he needed a photograph of any world leader before he could make telephone calls convincingly personal. The single printed word would convince him faster than all the secretary of defense's arguments.

He said finally, "You have an alternative for me, Mr. Secretary?"

Wade, thinking on his feet, said, "First, let's discuss timing—"

"Let me guess. You want me to wait?"

"I want you to look at something." Alexander Wade turned back to the cluster of sofa and overstuffed chairs. The president followed him reluctantly. Wade sat down and spread out the contents of the folder he had brought with him onto the coffee table in front of him.

"What's this?" the president demanded.

"Mr. President, I believe that the Reformed American States will arrest this man soon and try him on capital charges. We can use his arrest as our justification for mounting an attack . . . of some kind."

The president pulled his reading glasses out of his breast pocket and examined the file in silence. He'd come to the White House from industry, not law, which was another reason for his popularity. As he'd instantly surrounded himself with lawyers, Wade thought this a perverse attitude for the voters to take. But in deference to his boss's lack of specialized knowledge, he'd arranged the file to make the situation perfectly clear: Jerry

Tindell was suspected of having a hand in Matthew Franklin's death, but the evidence which would convict him was inadmissible under present interpretations of the Constitution. If Virginia arrested him now, it would be in defiance of United States courtroom law. And he hoped with all his heart that he had read the situation correctly, and that Jerry Tindell's arrest would indeed follow soon.

The president said dubiously, "How soon will they arrest him?"

"I suspect Monday," Alexander Wade said, gritting his teeth.

"And what sort of attack do we mount then, Mr. Secretary?"

Alexander Wade got to his feet and walked back across to the map. He bent over it, giving himself an extra moment to marshall his thoughts. He said, slowly, "The power . . . it goes from the plant through a number of generating stations, doesn't it?"

"Yes."

"And these stations are basically under remote control? Equipment, but no Virginia Power workers?"

"Yes."

"Mr. President, if we bomb from the air and something goes wrong, we could be facing dozens of casualties. And it's an incredibly aggressive move. If we fly a fighter into Virginia, we've stepped over a broad and important line. We could use a ground team of special-forces men instead. Send them in to disable . . . oh, say, five electricity generating stations, in and around Richmond." He was hitting his stride now. "I had a status report on the Virginia Guard early this morning. The army tells me that the best way to get into Virginia would be through the West Virginia border. The guard on the West Virginia line are only giving a cursory check to freight trains. We could put the special-forces men in a coal train. . . . it would be a long ride in, but we could time it carefully."

The plan was unfolding rapidly inside his head. When the attack force reached Richmond, they could act swiftly and decisively. Well-trained men could easily avoid security guards. They could use the precise and controlled Dartcord linear cutting charges to collapse the structure of the generating plants, and remove themselves swiftly from the area. Supplied with proper identification, the special-forces men could dump their military gear and become ordinary appalled Virginia citizens, who could then wander out through the permeable borders of the Commonwealth over the next week.

"It would hardly be devastating," the president objected.

"We could black out a hundred thousand Virginians."

"But we won't cause major damage. The stations could be repaired within a week."

"Yes, sir. But we'll have proved our point. We can threaten escalation if any more illegal arrests are made, and Charles Merriman won't be able to convince Virginians that war is impossible."

The president took a few steps away. He said, "So we cut the power if they arrest this guy, and that puts us on the side of civil rights for Americans?"

"We desperately need to be on the side of someone's rights," Wade said gloomily.

"Are you sure we want to hang our sympathies on this guy? He's not really an . . . admirable character."

"Mr. President, if we play this right, it'll be perfectly clear that we support due process and the full protection of the law for everyone—background notwithstanding. There's personal vengeance at work here; this is the man who killed the husband of the woman Kenneth Balder's been seen with over the past two weeks. We can stand for principle here."

The president said, "Got a picture?"

Wade was prepared for this. He passed over a newspaper shot of Jerry Tindell, attending the funeral of his brother, who had been killed by a Richmond police officer. The policeman, pulling the car over for expired tags, had approached the vehicle to find the younger Tindell rummaging under his seat for a weapon. The officer fired, and then discovered that the weapon was a steak knife. He'd spent a few months on desk-duty before being moved quietly back into the city.

Wade said after a moment, "It won't hurt our case any that Merriman is recommending capital punishment for this kind of offense, and Tindell is black. Won't help Merriman either."

"He looks white to me," the president said, squinting at the photograph.

"He's African-American, Mr. President."

"His skin's too light."

Wade pushed the newspaper page closer to the chief executive's eyes. "Look. There's his mother."

The president viewed Beulah Tindell, seated by her son's coffin, and conceded the point.

"Very well," he said. "They arrest him on Monday, we protest the violation of his rights, they ignore us, and we take out the generators with the special-forces men?"

"Yes. And the next day, we point out that we could remove the electricity plants themselves with just as much ease. We can use the Maryland Air Guard for that, so we won't be violating *posse comitatis.*"

"We're violating it with special forces, technically speaking."

"Sir, no one will ever know who carried out the attack."

The president brooded over the file for another moment. He said, "I wish we could find some higher ground, Alex."

"Sir, they're going to execute this guy on inadmissible evidence."

"Yes," the president said, "but I don't like him."

"Charles Merriman's too canny to execute anyone likable in his first weeks of independence," Alexander Wade said dryly.

The president looked at him sharply, but let the phrase pass. They both recognized the truth of it. For a full week, Virginia had behaved as an independent government with the apparent full support of its population, excluding the welfare recipients now clogging the systems of the surrounding states.

The president removed his reading glasses.

"Monday," he said. "And that's the last stall I will accept. With or without Tindell's arrest, Alex, the plan goes into effect Monday night."

Wade stood, gathering his files together. It was as great a victory as he had any right to expect. Now, all he had to do was guarantee Jerry Tindell's arrest.

And for that, he needed Ramsey Grant's cooperation.

CHAPTER 20

Friday, March 29, 8 P.M.

ALEXANDER WADE was at Benvolio's ten minutes early. The restaurant was expensive but not fashionable, a place which served good Italian food without frills and offered small, private dining rooms without question. He waited in one of these, sipping absently at his red wine, until Ramsey Grant's tall, thin figure appeared at the doorway. The attorney general stepped onto the scarlet carpet of the small room and cast a look around him.

"Wine?" Wade offered politely.

Grant regarded him with suspicion.

"Thanks," he said. "Whatever you're having." He sat down, stretching his legs out under the table. "And so how are things at the Defense Department?"

"Rather quiet, actually. I've had time to do a little extra research." Wade took another sip of wine.

"Oh? Something about Merriman?" The waiter brought Grant's wine. He left it untouched on the table in front of him. His voice was friendly, but Wade could hear the wariness behind it.

"No, I've been on a different track today. I have a friend in Culpepper who was telling me an interesting story—"

"Culpepper?" Grant's voice was noncommittal.

"Yes. Culpepper, Virginia. It seems that Culpepper had quite a little streak of law-enforcement excellence a few years ago. Coincidence," Wade said, "around the same time that a couple of years seems to have fallen off your résumé."

Grant said lightly, "Fortunately, I don't have to remember the details of my résumé anymore. I'm done job-hunting."

"Yes. I hope that remains true for you. Anyway, a few years ago Culpepper police solved local crimes at some phenomenal rate—something like ninety-seven percent success. My friend was so impressed with this statistic that he sent me a few newspaper articles on the subject. One of them has a photograph. A newspaper photograph of you and the Culpepper chief of police in deep conversation. You're in the background," Wade said, "but enhancement brings your face out clear enough for identification."

Ramsey Grant's tall, thin body had assumed a sudden deep stillness. "Yes?" he said.

"And this would not be unusual, except that I spoke to the Culpepper chief of police weeks ago and mentioned your name in passing, and he immediately remarked that the two of you had never met "

Ramsey Grant sat still, his long arms idle in front of him and his eyes wandering vaguely over the intricately carved molding on the far wall. Alexander Wade took another sip of wine and waited.

"Well," Grant said at last, "he has a short memory. I traveled down there on business a couple of times."

Wade leaned forward.

"I also know," he said, "that you spent two years working in the FBI criminal profiling division. I wonder why this wasn't made public? Funny, Grant, I now have two instances of things which ought to have been made public about you, and weren't. That agent you approved for Merriman's cabinet, and this strange missing period of two years. Do you think the American people would be inclined to resent this?"

"Possibly," Grant said. "Mind if I order dinner?"

He turned around and gave his order to the waiter. When he turned back, his face was perfectly composed.

"Naturally," he said, "if I can help you in any way, Mr. Secretary—"

"You can, actually. I need a profile of Charles Merriman."

Whatever Ramsey Grant had expected, this was not it.

"What?" he demanded.

"A profile. A psychological profile. And I'd also like profiles of Kenneth Balder, John Cline, and the Virginia adjutant general."

"Call the FBI."

"And the president."

"Oh, is that all?"

"That's all. My friend tells me that you can supply me with better profiles than the FBI. I need them."

Ramsey Grant drank the rest of his wine. Wade watched him, waiting. Grant was protective of his background; but he was even more protective of his public image. Moments later, the attorney general got up and yanked his jacket from the back of his chair.

"Come on," he said. "I'll show you something. But in return, Alex, you don't ever breathe a word of this to anyone. Waco'd be small potatoes, compared to the fuss this would kick up. Got that?"

Wade put the glass down and left fifty dollars on the table. He followed Grant out the door and through the dim, sparsely-seated restaurant, past the puzzled waiter with his tray full of food.

Grant had his own car parked at the curb. He was alone, having shed his Secret Service agent, as Wade had shed his on the plea that he was meeting Perri after fourteen days of absence for a romantic dinner. The attorney general produced a remote-control starter and thumbed it, from a safe distance. Wade waited, silently. The engine started with a smooth reassuring roar, and the two men approached the car. Grant unlocked the passenger side, and Wade climbed in. They pulled away from the curb and drove back through the city streets toward the FBI building.

The big, ugly concrete pile was silent and dark. Grant took him in a side door, down a series of halls and staircases, to a plain locked door. He pulled a key from his pocket, put it into the lock, and placed his hand flat against the plate beside the door. The palm-print and key combined opened the door. They were now in a small white room with another locked door and a more elaborate identification device.

"Infrawarm scan," Grant said briefly. He leaned down and presented his face to the camera. "It has an infrared print of my face. . . . as individual as a thumbprint. If I were dead and you were merely propping my corpse up in front of it, the scan wouldn't register."

"What if I were armed and just forcing you ahead of me?"

"The people who designed this assumed that I would prefer death to dishonor," Grant said dryly.

"Won't there be a record of our visit?"

"Yes, but the only people who'll see it have a vested interest in keeping any hint of what you're about to see from the public."

The door clicked, and he pushed it open. Wade half-expected, after all this secrecy, to find a corpse sewn together from pieces of criminals, waiting for a jolt of electricity. The cool windowless room contained a row of computer terminals and stacks of bins, stuffed to bursting with plain brown file folders. Grant strolled forward and flicked on one of the terminals. His hands moved quickly over the keyboard. The program blinked ACCESS CONFIRMED, and Wade found himself looking at a screen that read CRIME PREVENTION PROFILING RESEARCH. Below the headline, a tiny cartoon unfolded. A little black-masked burglar climbed out of a trashcan, whacked a glass-fronted door with his fist, and disappeared through the hole.

"Nice graphic," he said.

"This," Grant said, ignoring him, "is the FBI's highly illegal Crime Prevention Profiling Research program. I spent two years developing it. We call it Culpepper from the initials, and our original profiling information all focused on that one town. We predicted almost every crime that took place in Culpepper, Virginia, over an eighteen-month period. Robberies, rapes, domestic beatings, even the first murder of that serial killer who started work in January. Naturally, we had a completed profile of every citizen over the age of ten within the county limits. The crimes that we missed were all perpetrated by criminals passing through from somewhere else." He pushed a chair over with his foot. Wade took it, his eyes on the screen.

"I see why this didn't show up on your background check," he said slowly.

"There's no way we could make the program public. We've used confidential information to create psychological profiles of innocent non-criminal American taxpayers, and almost all the people profiled in our test run were residents of Virginia. Remember the thunderstorm Clinton stirred up when he proposed giving the FBI extra powers to fight domestic terrorism? This would've caused a hurricane. And now, of all times, with Virginia howling about civil rights and intrusive government."

"You wrote this?"

"The program content, not the computer code parts; we had a Georgetown grad student working on that. He did the graphics during lunch breaks."

"Where is he?"

"Having an all-expense-paid year of post-graduate study in Germany. Very happy. Want to see how it works?"

Wade nodded silently, and Ramsey Grant said, "Let's take a normal law-abiding citizen. You, for example. First we pull up the preliminary data screen." He hit ENTER. The computer displayed a screen full of coded boxes.

"Give me some information," Grant said, moving his hand on the computer's mouse. The cursor blinked in the first box. "Name, date and place of birth, social security number, mother's maiden name. . . . all the stuff we could get by looking at your birth certificate or driver's license."

Wade supplied the information, and Grant typed it in.

"Now," he said, "each entry in the preliminary data screen is cross-linked to the CPPR INFOBANK. Watch."

He typed a command. The computer meditated for a moment, and suddenly data began to scroll by. Ramsey Grant hit another key, and the screen froze.

"Pick any line," he said.

Wade leaned forward and read the entry under FOOD PREFERENCES. Halfway down the list of his favorite food and drink, he read: *Favorite restaurant.* Pizzeria Uno. *For romantic liaisons.* Hampton Inn Suites room service. *For illegal arrangements.* Benvolio's.

"The INFOBANK contains every scrap of known information about you," Ramsey Grant said.

"From what sources?" Wade asked. He was slightly shaken. He'd had one extramarital fling ten years ago, while he was still an unknown academic; and he had taken the young woman to a Hampton Inn and ordered champagne and chicken Provencal, delivered to the room. He rubbed his top lip. His fingers were cold.

"You name it. Anything you've ever filled out can become part of the INFOBANK. Your social security number, of course, pulls up your computerized IRS information, which gives us all the information on your tax return—salary level, deductions, all that stuff. Other parts of the data screen are linked to credit-card records, club memberships, those household surveys that come with warranty cards—you really ought not to fill those out, Alex—children's school records, court records, newspaper interviews, hospital records. You get the idea."

"You profiled every citizen of Culpepper?"

"Yes," Grant said.

"And found out whether they had criminal tendencies?"

"Look here," Grant said, turning back to the screen. His thin face was sardonically amused. "All I have to do is pull up the criminal profile screen. This is linked to different information, of course. . . . family records, personality profile, mother and father's personality profiles, place in family, medical records. The profile gives us a criminal index. These are merely preliminary, of course. To get an accurate profile would take the computer longer than I want to spend down here."

He punched ENTER, and Alexander Wade's preliminary criminal index appeared.

"You scored a PCI of eighteen-point-eight-point-two," Grant said. "Each number is scored on a twenty-point scale. You're a fairly law-abiding citizen, Alex. The first number is the likelihood that you'd break a civil law that endangers no one—speeding, for example, or coasting through a stop sign if no one's around. Almost everyone we profiled scored above ten in that category. The second category involves nonviolent felonies—white-collar crime, as it were. The third category involves bodily harm. You'd never murder anyone, Alex, but you might bend the rules a bit for your own benefit, and you'd almost certainly cheat on your income tax if you were sure you wouldn't get caught."

"Huh," Wade said.

"Each one of these numbers is introductory. If I key on one of these ratings—the bodily harm rating, for example—I'll get separate ratings for rape, all three levels of murder, homicide in self-defense, and so on. The older the subject, the more complete and accurate the ratings. In most cases we can predict weapon of choice, type of victim, likely alibi. If I key in a different code—" his fingers moved again—"I get a motivational profile that might impel you to any type of lawbreaking. You're easy, Alex, because you've been interviewed so often. According to Culpepper, you have an almost pathological need to preserve your dignity. Anyone who makes you look stupid, or humiliates you in any way, would be a likely victim for—"

"And this works?" Wade interrupted.

"In most cases. Sometimes it isn't specific enough to be of any use. But I'll tell you this, Alex. We ran all fifty state governors through it to see whether elected officials' parameters differed from private citizens' parameters. We're still fiddling with the effects of occupation on profile," Grant added, parenthetically. "We added another subdivision to that first number, the civil law violations: likelihood that the governor would defy a federal mandate. Charles Merriman had just been elected. He came out on top. MacDonald Forbes was fourth."

"Who came in between?"

"Sorenson of Montana was second and Masters of South Carolina was third."

"South Carolina!"

"Yeah," Grant said, "but he's an Episcopalian Democrat, so he might start his own revolution but he's not likely to join Merriman and Balder." He hesitated for a moment. "I came down here two weeks ago, " he said, "and asked them to do a surface run-through on Kenneth Balder. We got contradictory results, so the techs separated his pre-prison and post-prison information and did it again in a bit more detail. His ratings had almost flip-flopped."

"What does that mean?"

"Psychological trauma of some kind. We saw those sorts of results a couple of times in Culpepper. A woman in her early twenties lost her parents and brother in an auto accident and turned into a different person overnight. Man in his fifties had a heart attack and one of those weird near-death experiences and all his ratings changed."

"And the FBI isn't using these results?"

"Not legally," Ramsey Grant said.

Wade thought about this. He said, "So you already have the profiles I want?"

"Only the preliminaries. I can run you full profiles, in time."

"How much time?"

"When are you bombing Virginia?" Ramsey Grant countered.

"Monday," Wade said, after a long pause. "Probably. I need them before."

"You can have them Sunday morning."

Alexander Wade nodded in agreement. He had no more leverage with the attorney general.

"I have a private file folder of information on Kenneth Balder," he offered. "Any use to you?"

"Is there anything in it that wasn't made public at his trial?"

"Oh, yes."

Grant lifted an eyebrow at his tone. "It would help," he said. He leaned forward and typed in a row of symbols, and the screen disappeared.

"That erases the content of my search," he said. "There's a record that I've been here, but no proof of what I've done."

Alexander Wade rose. He said, "What if you know that a crime is about to be committed, but you can't legally use the information to arrest the criminal?"

Grant shrugged. "He's not a criminal until he commits the crime. You're a lawyer too, Alex. You know that."

"So you could predict a murder, but refuse to save the victim?"

"Technology creates moral dilemmas," Grant said, not answering the question.

"What would you do?"

"I have a conscience, Alex. I've broken the law three times to prevent homicides. But you'll never discover the circumstances."

"Ramsey . . . can you predict anything about how this revolt will end?"

Ramsey Grant watched the program go through the motions of exiting. He said, "We did expand our profiling project a bit past the borders of Culpepper. I'll just say this. There are a lot of people out there who have no brakes, Alex."

"In Virginia?"

"That was our pool."

"No brakes," the secretary of defense repeated.

"Loathing of the federal government. Almost pathological distrust of any authority. No sense of responsibility toward any higher moral standard, or Being, or whatever you want to call it. And we found some odd gaps too. In some rural areas we couldn't find all the population we *knew* ought to be there. There's been a movement underfoot for years to do away with social security numbers and drop out of the system. It's been gathering force in Virginia."

Wade thought this over. He said at last, "You're the expert. What does that add up to?"

Ramsey Grant's thin clever face sobered. The screen had reverted to a single blinking cursor. He leaned forward and flipped the power switch.

"Bloodshed," he said.

CHAPTER 21

Saturday, March 30, 3 A.M.

GARRETT FRANKLIN WAS SOUND ASLEEP in a tangle of blankets and sheets. He was dreaming, confusedly, that his father sat on the end of the bed cleaning his M-16. The gun lay in parts all around them. Matthew Franklin's shadowed eyes were intent on his work. Garrett sat up and said, "Dad!" with glad amazement. At the sound of his voice, Matthew Franklin raised his head, lifted his nine-millimeter army-issue Beretta to his temple, looked his son straight in the face, and pulled the trigger.

"Franklin!"

The thunder of the report jerked Garrett awake. He let out a muffled yell and discovered that a hand was clamped tight over his mouth. He struck out blindly at the shadow in front of him, and managed to grab onto an arm. Clint Larsen's voice whispered sharply, "Franklin! Shut up and pipe down! It's me."

He released his grip on the arm. Clint Larsen was wearing a heavy dark coat. His hand brushed across the strap of an automatic weapon.

"Awake?"

He nodded, and Larsen removed his hand.

"Come on," the older man said in a low voice. "Get dressed. We're going."

Garrett swung his legs over the edge of the cot. He was in Yorktown. He'd been posted to guard the Naval Weapons Station along with guardsmen from all over Virginia. It was a grueling test of endurance, standing watch for sixteen endless hours every day, while the Weapons Station went quietly about its business and submitted to the searches of incoming and outgoing personnel. Apart from the occasional insult, the navy was maintaining a lulling and deceptive peace.

He shook his head, ridding himself of sleep and the haunting remnants of that nightmare.

"Where?" he demanded.

"Shut up and don't ask questions 'til we're out of here."

His voice was heavy with significance, and Garrett felt a prickle down his spine. He had succeeded beyond his hopes in attaching himself to Clint Larsen, but Larsen had begun to worry him.

He hurried himself into off-duty clothes, the jeans and sweatshirt that had served him for the eight hours each day he wasn't on duty. He shared this tent with eleven other men. Five were in their cots, sound asleep against the far wall. Clint moved softly out the door ahead of him, and they walked quietly through the dark rows of tents toward the Colonial Parkway. The Weapons Station covered a sizable stretch of land between Interstate 64 on the west and the York River on the east. National Guard camps occupied every access point. Garrett's own camp was on the banks of King Creek, which marked off the northwest boundary of the navy's land.

"Halt," the sentry said, in a bored tone of voice. He was still ten feet away, half-visible in the dark. "Peace and—"

"Goodwill," Larsen said, supplying the countersign. "Larsen and Franklin, Seventy-eighth Fighter Squadron Security Police."

"Destination?"

Larsen said, "Seven-eleven. I'm dying for a Snickers."

"Yeah? Get me one too." His outline was clearer now, his weapon slung across his back and his pistol still in its holster. Garrett had just begun to wonder how Clint was going to explain that he needed his M-16 to venture into Williamsburg, when the older man swiftly unslung the weapon and brought the butt of it up into the sentry's jaw with casual shocking brutality. There was a sound like eggshell shattering. The sentry collapsed silently onto the grass at their feet. Garrett went down on one knee in panicked disbelief. The sentry's breath was gurgling through his throat. He put his hand down to the man's face and found wetness covering his fingers.

"He's gonna die!"

"No going back now, Franklin," Clint Larsen said. Garrett glanced up. The reflection from the parkway's streetlamps caught Larsen's light eyes until they shone like marbles, and he still held the M-16 like a club. Garrett drew his hand across the sentry's back, and felt the man's breath rattle and stop, halfway through the inflation of lungs and ribs. Garrett's teeth were chattering with fright and shock.

"Get up," Clint Larsen said, "and let's go."

Garrett scrambled to his feet. He was weaponless and cold and only twenty-two years old, and now he was party to a crime that could earn him execution under the code of the Commonwealth. He stumbled after the older guardsman, through the trees that fringed the parkway. A Jeep had been pulled to the side of the throughway, half-covered with brush. Clint pushed the pine limbs aside and climbed into the driver's seat. Garrett clambered in after him. The back of the vehicle was covered with a tarp. He didn't look closely; he could well imagine that Clint Larsen had squirreled away more guns and ammunition beneath the tarp for the use of the Tri-County Hunt Club.

THE MILITIA HAD MOVED ITS ENCAMPMENT into another Charles City field, this one mere steps away from the banks of the Chickahominy River. The sky was beginning to lighten, but the air was still black; Garrett could hear the invisible water washing against the banks in the pitch darkness. He sat down where he was told, put his head between his knees, and thought about not vomiting. The rough motion of the Jeep and the smashing echo of the sentry's facial bones had combined to make him violently ill. He could hear snatches of the argument going on in front of the fire. Captain Bill James of the New Kent division, the tall man who had objected to Garrett's visiting the first encampment, was shouting. Clint Larsen was protesting, "I couldn't have left him there. He's already been to the encampment. . . ."

"You should never have brought him in the first place. . . ."

"I didn't know that, did I? You never said—"

". . . a common murderer—"

"Enough," said a new voice. Garrett looked up. Major Morrison had arrived, trim in camouflage and carrying a weapon Garrett recognized only from photos he'd seen—the ACR or Advanced Combat Rifle, which fired the new caseless rounds in three different modes.

"Larsen and Franklin aren't under your command, James," Major Morrison ordered.

"Franklin's a New Kent resident," Bill James snapped.

"He's coming to us from Richmond, and I'm putting him under Larsen. Okay, Clint. What's the news?"

"Sir, they've done it. As of midnight, the Virginia Guard is part of a combined force, under the partial command of the North Carolina adjutant general. The Virginia adjutant general's been moved to a strategic post—secretary of defense for the Reformed American States. I think it's the North Carolina general who's been responsible for our present assignments. They're not even using us for Virginia's defense. We've been standing around doing nothing ever since independence was declared."

"Good enough," Morrison said. "Time to get on the move. What the guard won't do, we will. We can't trust 'em to keep the borders safe from invasion, men, not under such untrustworthy leadership, and the North-South Carolina line is the most likely place for attack now. So we're moving south. James, Larsen, Richardson—you captains get your men together."

In the rustling confusion that followed, Garrett saw Morrison turn toward Clint Larsen. Larsen spoke in the major's ear for a moment, gesturing toward Garrett with his hand. Morrison nodded and made his way through the hurrying men; and Garrett hauled himself wearily to his feet. Clint Larsen had already disappeared toward the tents, pitched near the bank and lit by lanterns hung on spikes driven into the waterside pines and cypress trees.

"Franklin," Major Morrison said, "glad to have you along."

"Looked to me like I wasn't welcome."

"Never mind Bill James. He's a firebrand. Good man in a fight. I'm going to put you under Larsen though. He says you're a fine marksman. We can use you."

"Marksman?" Garrett said. "Yeah. I did okay on my guard drills." A voice in his head said, *You're not far from finding the truth about Matthew Franklin's murder. Don't blow it now.* He wiped his nose on the sleeve of his sweatshirt, choking down more nausea.

Morrison looked at him narrowly. "Not convinced you want to join us?"

"I don't think I have any choice, do I?" Garrett asked.

"Don't worry about that sentry, son. You're beyond air force justice now."

"Sir, it wasn't necessary. Clint killed him for no reason."

Morrison examined him for a long, silent moment. He said, "Larsen says *you* swung the gun."

"No! No, sir! The guy was going to let us by, and Clint smashed his jaw in just so he could take his gun out with him. I didn't have anything to do with it."

"There's blood on your hand," Morrison remarked.

Garrett glanced down. Dried darkness caked the nails of his right hand. He could feel the contents of his stomach boiling up into his throat. He lunged for the fringe of woods around the camp and threw up into the dark grass. When he straightened, gasping, Major Morrison was still standing at the edge of the clearing, arms folded, fixing him with a clear straight stare.

"Don't you worry, Franklin," he said at last. "We'll toughen you up here. You've joined the *real* fight for independence now."

THEY BUMPED SOUTH over tiny secondary roads in a caravan of surplus army Jeeps and repainted pickups. Once past Hopewell and Petersburg, the Tri-County Hunt Club veered west. They crossed the Nottoway River when the sun was halfway up the pale blue morning sky. Two more hours to the North Carolina border, Garrett calculated. They saw no National Guard. Virginia's defenders were stretched thin, posted as they were around roads and electricity plants and water towers; it wasn't likely that any would be wasted on the line between Virginia and her sister rebel.

He sat in the back of an unfamiliar pickup, his hands dangling between his knees and his mind full of wretchedness. The shining spring morning was all blackness to him, and his thoughts were a frightening mix of terror and apprehension. Recurring with more and more frequency was the notion that his mother might ask Kenneth Balder to get him back. He liked the man. He knew his mother had told Balder about their suspicions of the guard. But he was chief of staff, the author of the uncompromising Virginia code: *You shall not kill.*

The pickup truck slowed suddenly and drew off the rural road into a deserted logged-over clearing. The caravan was drawing into a circle. He unfolded his legs and climbed down from the back of the truck. Someone offered him an MRE, but he shook his head. He couldn't have eaten prime rib at that moment, let alone army food. Major Morrison was sitting in the front seat of a Jeep at the other side of the clearing, eating jerky and surrounded by militia members.

He made his way cautiously over the scuffed uneven ground. Morrison, spotting him in the crowd, raised a questioning eyebrow.

"Sir," Garrett said awkwardly, "can I speak to you for a minute alone?"

Morrison shrugged and climbed out of the Jeep. They took a few steps away from the others, and Garrett said, "Sir, I ought to call my mother." Aware of how this sounded, he hurried on, "My mother's an old friend of Kenneth Balder. I'm afraid that if I disappear without her knowing where I am, she'll ask him to find me. He might put some of the regular guard on my track. If you don't want the guard to know where you are, sir, I ought to call and tell her not to say anything until she hears from me again "

Major Morrison considered the situation.

"Okay," he said. "I see the difficulty."

"Can I call? I mean, there must be a Seven–Eleven or something around here—"

"You can use my cellular phone," Morrison said. He strolled back to the Jeep. Garrett followed him, and found himself offered a mobile phone. Militia members were sitting on the Jeep's hood, on its bumpers, leaning against it, jaws moving steadily on the unappetizing rations.

"Number?" Morrison inquired.

Garrett gave it, and the major dialed for him. He put the phone to his ear and listened to the ring. Ten pairs of curious eyes fixed on him. *Please*, he thought, *not the answering machine this time.*

"Hello?"

He cleared his throat. His mother's calm voice had already gained an undertone of worry.

"Mom, it's me."

"Garrett!" The voice sharpened at once into near-panic. "Garrett, your unit called me this morning and said you were missing! Where are you?"

"Mom, I'm fine."

"Where are you? Son, they're saying another guardsman is dead. Garrett, if you're in trouble, I can ask Ken—"

"No! No, don't do that. I'm okay."

There was a long pause. She said flatly, "You can't talk, can you?"

"Er—no, I can't."

"You need help."

"Mom, please don't do anything until you hear from me again. I'm safe for right now."

"Garrett. . . ." she said helplessly. He held the phone, aching to say something reassuring. He was surrounded by a listening enemy.

"That's good enough," Major Morrison said, and held his hand out for the receiver.

"I've got to go, Mom."

"Garrett, darling—"

Morrison removed the phone from his hand and replaced it in the truck. Margaret Franklin's last plea would be met by a dial tone. Garrett cleared his throat and willed his voice into careless bravado.

"Thanks," he said. "She won't do anything drastic now." He trudged back toward his own vehicle, conscious of eyes on his back. He had cut himself off from both retribution and help. He was entirely alone.

IN THE MIDDLE OF THE AFTERNOON, they crossed the North Carolina border without incident. The truck he rode in was near the front of the procession now, and Clint Larsen had joined the driver in the front seat. Through the glass window at the back of the cab he could see them, absorbed in conversation. The little road wound on through a wilderness of pines, past a green sign announcing that Roxboro and Graham lay ahead.

The truck slammed on brakes suddenly. He clutched at the side and peered out. The Tri-County caravan was bunching up behind them. Ahead of the pickup were two other vehicles and then Morrison's Jeep. Over its hood he could glimpse two unfamiliar uniforms. Clint Larsen climbed out of the cab and walked forward, and Garrett scrambled over the tailgate and followed him unobtrusively along the graveled side of the blacktop.

The road was blocked by a bright red-and-blue truck, hood pointing toward them. He squinted at the gold letters painted along the side: *The Regulators*. The North Carolina militia whose marksman had broken Kenneth Balder's arm. He paid fast attention to the little knot of men between the two militia groups.

The two North Carolina militiamen were talking hard at Morrison. One of them had a bulky bandage around his right arm, his camouflage jacket torn and bloodied. He was waving his other hand north, toward Virginia. Morrison was nodding in agreement. The two, having carried their point, walked back to their truck and began the process of reversing it. Major Morrison turned around and walked back toward his own men. The captains of the three divisions waited at the front of the Jeep.

"Well," the major said, arriving, "we've missed some action." Garrett could hear him clearly over Clint Larsen's shoulder. "Balder marched a group of his new peacekeepers into North Carolina early this morning to help Governor Forbes round up the rest of the Regulators Militia. They got Daniel Walker and almost all the leadership. These two are the only ones left from the Liberty chapter. Good thing we came in. They need help."

His eye wandered past Larsen and James and lit on Garrett.

"Franklin!" he said. "Bet you're glad you put Balder off your trail. Marching Virginia forces into North Carolina to harass a group of citizens exercising their constitutional rights! Can you believe it? Looks like Charles Merriman's surrounded by conspirators. We've got work to do."

He rubbed his hands together. "We'll follow these men to a secure camp-site out near the Blue Ridge. The North Carolina militias are assembling there."

Larsen blurted excitedly, "Sir, what's our mission?"

"To save this revolution," Major Morrison answered. "No matter what it takes. The Reformed American States is the first time states have dared to stand up to Washington since the Civil War. We can't let this historic revolt be co-opted by corruption, creeping in from the outside. Even if it takes fighting."

He swung back into his Jeep, his shoulders straight and heroic. Clint Larsen let out a battle yell, shaking his weapon in the air. Garrett heard the yell echoed behind him as the news spread down the line. Larsen slapped him cheerfully on the back.

"Come on in the cab, Franklin. More comfortable in there. Now you're seeing action, eh?" Larsen's face was shining with excitement.

Garrett kept his mouth shut and climbed in between the two militia-men. He stared straight out the windshield, clenching his teeth until his jaw ached. *Balder should know about this,* he thought frantically. *These guys are about to start a war within a war. Nobody knows but me. And I don't dare tell him.*

CHAPTER 22

Sunday, March 31, 8 A.M.

KENNETH BALDER HAD BOUGHT FLOWERS, the evening before; an unusual indulgence for him, and probably completely unnecessary. Maggie was surrounded by flowers. But she didn't eat chocolate, and he no longer knew her taste in books. He wanted to convey the overwhelming love that possessed him more and more, and she had put words completely off-limits. Mingled in with this was pure pity, because she was about to hear the worst of news from his own mouth. He hadn't dared call first. He hoped she would let him in.

He scooped the expensive sheaf of daffodils off the front seat of his car and walked across the damp grass to Margaret Franklin's steps. She opened the door when his foot was on the bottom step. She was wearing jeans and a T-shirt and her ash-brown hair was still damp from the shower. Her face was white, the skin papery with shock and fatigue. The rings under her eyes were bruised with worry.

"You've already heard!" he said, in quick horror.

"From Garrett," she said. Her voice was empty of any emotion, drained of both blood and thought. "His unit called. . . . They said he'd deserted, along with some others. . . . and he called me, Ken. He's with those others somewhere. He's in danger. I *can't* lose Garrett. Not after you and then Matthew. I'll go mad."

He bounded up onto the porch and put his right arm around her shoulders. Her weight sagged against him, and he steered her through the door and into the kitchen. The big wood-floored room had lost its polish. The table was strewn with newspapers. Mud dirtied the floor, and used dishes filled the sink.

"Sit down," he said, tossing the flowers onto the counter. Margaret rested her weight into a chair, dropping her face into her hands. He felt her shoulder shake underneath his hand. He said, "Have you eaten anything?"

"What?"

"Where's your food?"

"Up there," she said vaguely, twisting her head toward the cabinets above the counter. He rummaged through the cartons and cans and found cooking brandy and instant coffee. Repulsive, but better than nothing. He made coffee in the microwave and poured a slug of the brandy into the mug. Behind a jar of popcorn, he found a stash of cookies and shook several onto a plate. Margaret protested faintly, but he said firmly, "Natural tranquilizer. Carbohydrates and caffeine. It'll help you think straight."

He sat down across the table and watched her. Two cookies and half-a-mugful of coffee later, a faint wash of color had come back to her face and her gray eyes had lost that stunned, oblivious look. He waited until she had eaten another cookie and drained the mug.

"Now tell me what you know," he said.

She said, rationally, "The guard called early Saturday morning and said that several men from the Seventy-eighth had deserted. Garrett was one of them. They wanted to know where he was. I didn't know, of course. But he called, around noon, and I could hear voices in the background. The line was scratchy, like it was a pay phone. . . . He couldn't talk to me. He was frightened of whoever was around him, and I was still talking to him when someone cut us off." She swallowed and said, "I saw the paper this morning. It said a sentry was killed out by the Yorktown Naval Weapons Station, and the air force thinks the deserters had something to do with it. They want to arrest him for murder, don't they?"

He reached out and covered her cold hands with one of his.

"Listen," he said, "and don't lose hope. We don't know the whole story yet. I was unable to speak to Garrett, and I didn't want to spook his friends, so I thought I'd wait until he came off on leave next week. I was wrong. Clint Larsen deserted and Garrett went with him. The man was killed by the deserters. There's no question of that. His jaw and Adam's apple were crushed by a double blow. From the butt of a gun, we think. Someone put a hand down on his face and then touched his back. Maggie, love, we've got one of Garrett's thumbprints from the back of the dead man's belt."

"Oh, Garrett," Margaret said. She put her head down on the table and sobbed. He sat where he was, his hand under her cheek, and thought, *You shall not kill. What do I tell Charles Merriman now?*

"Maggie," he said gently. "We still don't know what happened. Garrett didn't even take his gun with him; it was found with his other belongings, so there's a good chance he had nothing to do with the death at all."

"There's no lesser penalty for murder in your code, is there?" Margaret said dully.

"Come on," Kenneth Balder said, getting to his feet. "We're going to church."

"Ken! I'm not going to waste a morning like this—"

"Maggie, this is beyond us," Balder said. "It was beyond me from the beginning, dear heart, but I didn't know it." He half-lifted her from the chair. She objected again on the way down the front steps. But twenty-four hours of sleepless worry had weakened her will, and he was able to persuade her into the car and drive her out into the greening New Kent countryside. He had planned to convince her to go to church with him, and he had intended to bring up Garrett's thumbprint after worship and lunch, in a calm and rational manner.

Now the muscles in his neck and shoulders had tied themselves into wire knots, and he was feeling a ghastly, uncertain hollowness in his stomach. If he gave those misgivings concrete expression, the words would write themselves scarlet across his mind: *If God is in this, why has it begun to go so horribly wrong?*

He pushed the sentence away without allowing it to coalesce.

The call to worship was just beginning as they came through the doors. *Let all mortal flesh be silent, and in fear and trembling stand!*

He settled himself and Margaret in a back pew as the royal words rolled past them. *Ponder nothing earthly minded, for with blessing in his hand, Christ our God to earth descended!*

He welcomed the elements of the service like a traveler hailing a familiar landmark after wandering through strange and frightening streets. The Nicene Creed, the church's foundation stones, made of pure verbal light; the General Confession of a sinful humanity that fell sorely short of the perfection demanded by the Creator; the abject plea for mercy and the heartfelt assurance of forgiveness. *Five bleeding wounds He bears, received on Calvary; they pour effectual prayers, they strongly plead for me. Forgive him, o forgive, they cry; nor let that ransomed sinner die!* The old words flowed over him like a satisfying stream. He let himself go into the rich comfort of it, the knots in his mind and soul slowly untangling themselves. And all the while he could see the stiff misery of Maggie's shoulders as she fumbled through the unfamiliar service, and the awkward bend of her head as she waited for the final prayer to end. That plentiful, soul-healing assurance was nothing to her but so many tin-syllabled words. At the final benediction he reached for her hand. Her fingers were stiff and cold, and her eyes were distant. She was locked away in a world of private anticipation and torment, and neither the Word of God nor his own assurances could break in.

HE TOOK HER HOME AND TRIED TO FIX HER LUNCH. She refused to eat, and when she announced that she was going to take a nap he reluctantly left her. He drove back to Richmond, to the guest quarters of the Executive Mansion. He was unable to sit still. He wandered restlessly through the cool empty rooms, out onto the sun-saturated lawn. He had finally put into words a sentence that would serve him, for the moment: *The evidence which will execute Jerry Tindell is no more certain than the proofs against Garrett Franklin.* And, that being said, he had severe doubts about the wisdom of their present course.

Even deeper were other doubts he barely dared to look at: *What if this whole revolution is wrong? What if God never intended us to do this?*

What if I've been misled by my own desires?

He stared at the lawn with half-blinded eyes. Charles Merriman was sitting on a chair in the middle of the grass, asleep in the warm afternoon sunshine, with the Sunday newspaper scattered on the grass at his feet. Above the walls, the sky was the clear deep blue of a heraldic emblem. Balder walked toward the chair where Merriman lay dozing. The governor roused and lifted a placid hand.

"Hi," he said.

"Warm afternoon."

"Yes. Unusual for the last day of March in Virginia. Have a seat?"

Balder drew up a nearby wrought-iron chair and sat in it, his right elbow on his knee and his left awkwardly resting against his thighs. The cast had begun to strain his shoulder muscles, producing agonizing cramps at unexpected times. Charles Merriman shifted his head and looked at him through eyes narrowed against the sun.

"Where'd you go to church?"

"All Saints Presbyterian."

"Ah," Merriman said comfortably. He closed his eyes.

"Charles—"

"It's Sunday, Ken. I'm not working."

"*Charles.*"

Merriman sighed and sat upright.

"Okay," he said. "Let me guess. You're coming down to the wire on making an arrest under this new code, and you're getting cold feet."

"I'm only wondering whether I ought to be the one to choose this particular victim for the headsman's ax."

"That's not the reason you're hesitating," Merriman said. "You've got scholar's disease. You've been preaching on paper about the right thing so often that when it finally takes on flesh and features you gasp in horror and throw up your hands and say, 'Oh, I didn't expect it to look that way!' Well, get used to it, Ken. God says, 'He who sheds the blood of man, by man shall his blood be shed.' That's the true principle. Don't let details of individual cases pull you away from it."

"You know about Garrett Franklin?"

"I've been briefed about Mr. Franklin and fifteen other cases of desertion, yes."

"The proof of his involvement in the sentry's murder is the same type of proof that's at the center of the Tindell case."

"Then he ought to be arrested, when he can be found."

"That boy wouldn't kill anyone."

Merriman snapped, "You should hear yourself, Ken. I've heard this before. Feed the poor, but no homeless shelter in *my* backyard. Take care of the elderly, but don't raise *my* taxes to do it. Put God's law into effect, but don't enforce it on anyone I happen to care about."

Kenneth Balder shifted on the iron seat, uncomfortably aware that the accusation hit close on target. He said, "Washington's taken no action on that threat to wreck our infrastructure. But that doesn't mean it's gone away. They may be waiting for our first concrete move. Our first arrest might set off firecrackers."

"We've got to start arresting people under the new code sometime," Merriman said reasonably.

"But they may launch an attack."

"Well," Merriman said, "let 'em. I've got National Guard and volunteers covering every square inch of Virginia. There isn't anything Washington can do that we can't turn to our own advantage."

His voice was supremely confident. Kenneth Balder said, "You never have any doubts, do you, Charles?"

"About what?"

"About whether this revolution of yours scratches your own itch for power."

"No," Merriman said. "Do you?"

"Yes."

"Ken, if I were you, I'd spend some time on my face, wondering why I'm backing away from my duty. Is there some remnant of your old self in there, hiding behind the man of God?" He closed his eyes and leaned his head back against his lounge chair. After a moment he added, "In the meantime, we have an arrest to make."

MONDAY MORNING, bright and clear as glass; April Fool's Day.

Kenneth Balder came into his own office in the Capitol after an almost sleepless night. He arrived at eight, the back of his throat aching with fatigue, and found Christopher Dillard standing sober-faced outside his door.

"Good morning, Dr. Dillard," he said, and sidestepped the man to reach his doorknob.

"Dr. Balder," Dillard said, following him past the secretary at her desk, into the sanctum of his office. He stood on the threshold as Balder settled himself behind his desk.

"I've spoken again to Charles," Christopher Dillard began, "but he's wrapped himself up in his own purposes like a blanket, and he won't hear me. I want to speak once more to you."

"Well, Dr. Dillard, we've decided to rejoin the United States." Balder banged his top drawer open, looking for a red pen with which to tackle the stack of paperwork in front of him.

"What?" Dillard demanded.

"April Fool," Balder said, and was instantly ashamed of himself. He said contritely, "Please. Sit down. Would you like coffee?"

"No," Christopher Dillard said. He sat down on one of the green upholstered chairs, his thin body stiff and upright. "You've already heard all my arguments, Dr. Balder, but I have to make one more effort, for the sake of my own conscience."

Balder looked wearily down at his desk. A stack of papers already awaited his attention. The secretary of transportation wanted reinforced National Guard posts at the multiple railroad entry points into Virginia from Kentucky and West Virginia. Chief Caprio wanted final written authorization for the arrest of Jerry Tindell. An arrest warrant had been issued the previous Friday by the Richmond courts, Merriman's newly appointed judges happily sweeping the stables clean of corruption and delay. But the chief of police had spent a lifetime working under the old rules of search and seizure, and he wanted his tail well-covered. Merriman's newly appointed secretary for human services had spent Saturday compiling a report on the homeless and hungry who remained to Virginia, and the thick sheaf of statistics and recommendations awaited his comments. John Cline had sent him a copy of a memo to Charles Merriman, concerning state quarantines for infectious illnesses. The new secretary of defense wanted to know whether he or the North Carolina adjutant general should take responsibility for monitoring several Virginia militia groups reported as moving into North Carolina.

He said, "Okay. Go ahead," and braced himself for another diatribe on the difference between Old Testament Israel and Virginia after the incarnation of Christ.

Dillard merely said, "For if there had been nothing wrong with that first covenant, no place would have been sought for another." The words were from the eighth chapter of Hebrews, and Kenneth Balder knew well what would follow. He said, "You're going to tell me yet again that God's commands to Israel were peculiar to the ancient Middle East, the physical kingdom and all its regulations a mere picture of the spiritual kingdom that was God's ultimate goal."

Christopher Dillard leaned forward slightly. He said, "'It will not be like the covenant I made with their forefathers when I took them by the hand to lead them out of Egypt. This is the new covenant I will make: I will put my laws in their minds, and write them on their hearts. I will be their God, and they will be my people.'"

Kenneth Balder sat with his head half-bent, running his thumb along the edge of the paper stack in front of him. Dillard's voice went on.

"'No longer will a man teach his neighbor, or a man his brother, saying, 'Know the Lord', because they will all know Me, from the least of them to the greatest.'"

There was a little silence. Kenneth Balder looked up and said, "And do you see this happening in American Christianity today, Dr. Dillard?"

"No," Dillard said bluntly.

"Then why condemn our efforts to bring it to pass?"

"Because you're using the wrong methods, Dr. Balder. You've resorted to rebellion. Using physical means to bring in God's spiritual kingdom. The Inquisition tried it in Spain. John Calvin tried it in Geneva. The Puritans tried it in Massachusetts Bay. It didn't work then and it won't work now. Even Christ turned down a political kingdom when it was offered to him."

"Of course He did. Satan was the one making the offer."

"Are you sure that's not what's happening now?" Dillard demanded. Balder winced, but the smaller man swept on. "Haven't you been listening to the debates in Washington? You've already produced an immense backlash against anyone who professes Christ and holds public office. 'Religious Right' has become the equivalent of 'Nazi stormtrooper.' We're losing the hard-won gains of the last decade because of your experiment."

"The hard-won gains of the last decade? In the last decade Christian evangelicalism has held rallies, sent out millions of appeal letters, published thousands of books, and faithfully voted for the local pro-life candidate. In the meantime we've seen plummeting morality, complete loss of any concept of truth, legalization of infanticide and euthanasia and other perversions, while state governments have been denied any power to interfere. So what's the answer, Dr. Dillard?"

"I don't know. But this isn't it. Not an armed revolt."

The weakness of this argument was suddenly obvious to both of them, and they sat for a moment in silence. Kenneth Balder said at last, "Dr. Dillard, it's out of my hands now. I'm an appointed official in a government supported by the people of Virginia and North Carolina. I have to do my duty. At some point, even in the American Revolution, it became impossible for the revolutionaries to stand up and announce: *We were wrong.* Even if they felt it, in their private rooms late at night."

"Well then," Dillard said, "if that is true, then you deserve to be an object of my prayers rather than my reproofs." He stood up. For a moment he wavered. At the last, he decided, quite visibly, not to offer his hand.

"Good-bye," Dillard said, and let himself out through the secretary's office. The sound of his feet on the hard floor outside echoed and faded.

Kenneth Balder forced his eyes back to the papers on his desk. Halfway through the Transportation plea for guard reinforcements, he found his attention meandering away and returning to the words spoken in Christopher Dillard's clear, certain voice.

He got up from the desk and wandered to the small television Merriman had provided each of his cabinet officials. He generally watched the first few minutes of the news each morning, keeping tabs on the public face Washington presented to the world. He turned on CNN and stood, watching a well-known and respected evangelical speaker—a senator from a Western state—shouted down on the floor of the Senate.

Right, he thought to himself. *Let's put all the unthinkables into words. Am I sticking at Jerry Tindell's arrest because I think he's innocent? Am I doing this only to free Maggie from the past?*

He tried to peer down into the depths of his soul. It was mostly dark in there. To the best of his knowledge, he truly thought Jerry Tindell was guilty. The man deserved to be arrested and put on trial.

But in him was still a deep and profound reluctance to sign the final order.

I can't do it, he thought at last. *Let someone else put this man's life on trial. I do not know my own heart well enough to be sure that justice will be served.* Merriman had pushed all the right buttons, the afternoon before, suggesting that his reluctance came from a lack of dedication to the God he had so publicly embraced. It was enough to send him stampeding into action. Now he took an almost physical hold on himself.

"I will not be manipulated," he said out loud, and felt better.

His telephone rang, and he walked back to the desk and picked up the receiver.

"Sir, Mrs. Franklin's on line three."

"Thank you," he said hastily.

"She sounds very upset—"

"Yes. Thank you." He reseated himself at his desk and pushed the button.

"Kenneth Balder," he said.

"Ken!" Margaret's voice was past the edge of panic. "Ken, the United States wants Garrett. . . . They say he can be court-martialed and put in jail for decades. I can leave, and they'll straighten everything out for me. But I couldn't go without telling you. Not a second time."

"Maggie! Sit down." Her voice was so thick with tears that he could barely understand her. "Sit down and tell me slowly what's happened."

"He called again," Margaret said, with difficulty.

"Who?"

"The man from the Defense Department. Allen something. He said he was working under Alexander Wade's orders—"

Kenneth Balder found his hand gripping the hard wooden arm of his chair. He released his fingers and saw that the carved design was printed into his palm.

"What exactly did he say, Maggie?"

"He said that Garrett was in big trouble—he wasn't just involved in a murder, he'd also acted against the United States by being at the Naval Weapons Station at all, and he could be tried for treason and for being an accessory, just as soon as he was found."

"They can't do any of that as long as he's inside the R.A.S."

"But I don't know where he is. Ken, what if he's gone out into the United States? They said that if I come out, they'll take care of everything, they'll drop the charges—"

"You can't leave! Listen, as long as both you and Garrett stay inside Virginia or North Carolina, I'll do everything in my power to protect him. But if either of you go into the United States—Margaret, can't you see they want you to come out so that you'll be a weapon against me?"

He could hear her breath coming in rapid gasps at the other end of the line. He was terrified that she would put the telephone down, and disappear once again. He said, desperately, "Maggie, do you really think the United States will do right by you? How much justice have you received from the United States in your life?"

Margaret said bitterly, "None from your government either."

"These things take time—"

"How much more time, Ken? All I can see is that I've lost my son, and not found justice for my husband either. Have you done anything at all to investigate the guard?"

"Maggie, I have tried. Merriman has not . . . cooperated. But Tindell will be arrested this afternoon." He said it with certainty in his voice; and thought, *He is guilty. I know it.*

There was a little silence. She said, "You're going to investigate the guard?"

"I will do everything I can to follow up on Garrett's story." *And it would help if I had Garrett to tell it,* he thought. "But if you go into the United States and take your son with you, I won't have anyone to testify about Matthew's suspicions of the guard. The evidence is flimsy enough. If I lose both of you, the Richmond police will go right back to Tindell and stay there. If you want the guard investigated, you've got to stay."

Her voice had lost the edge of panic; but she sounded distressed and immensely weary. "Ken, what can I do? I've got to make sure that Garrett's safe."

"Maggie, I'll pile every power I have into a wall to protect him. But you have to promise that you'll stay in Virginia. I can't do anything if you leave me."

Another silence. He felt his heart drumming in his ears.

"Yes," she said at last. "Yes, I'll stay."

"I'll come out tonight—"

"No. Ken . . . not until I know that—not unil it's over."

He held the receiver, not knowing what to say; not daring to hang up. He heard a faint click, and said impulsively, "Maggie, I do love you. . . ."

He was talking to the dial tone. He put the telephone down and swiveled his chair around to the word processor. He rarely used it, but he wasn't going to dictate this memo to his secretary. He typed as rapidly as he could with only one hand:

> To Daniel Caprio, chief of police, City of Richmond.
>
> The Commonwealth of Virginia is in full agreement with the arrest of Jerry Tindell for the murder of Matthew Garrett Franklin, as authorized by the Third District Court, City of Richmond.
>
> Kenneth Balder, chief of staff, Reformed American States.

He printed the document out and signed his name at the bottom. After a moment, he attached a handwritten note.

> Dan,
>
> I think you ought to consider bringing Clint Larsen in for questioning as well. There seems to be good reason to suspect a guard connection. Let's make sure this investigation gets off on the right foot. This is our first case and we need to make sure that every angle is explored. And a wide-ranging investigation will prevent United States media from accusing us of racial discrimination.

That ought to do it. He put both papers in an envelope, and summoned his secretary.

"Send that by personal messenger over to the Richmond chief of police," he directed.

"Yes, sir."

She took the letter away. He turned back to his papers. Under the new guidelines, Tindell would be arrested this morning, a jury assembled tonight, and the trial would begin on Tuesday.

The peculiar mix of emotions coursing through him was somehow familiar. He put down his pen and let memory come back to him. Finally he put his finger directly on that place in his past where he had felt this contradictory combination of certainty and searing guilt before: on the witness stand, during the well-drilled close to his testimony, when his own defense attorney had fixed him with a cold eye and said, "Mr. Balder, did you intend to kill Mary Miranda Carpenter?"

"No, sir. I intended to keep her safe."

"No further questions," the lawyer had said, triumphantly; but in his own mind Kenneth Balder had thought, *Did I?*

He could clearly recall every one of Mary Miranda's pleading phone calls; and then the letters, arriving daily; and then the threats to tell Margaret of that one night he had spent with her. Even then, in a day when he had carried with him no standard of morality higher than his own wishes, he had been heartily ashamed of himself. He had yielded to an egotistical impulse, with no thought other than his own satisfaction. And he had incautiously mentioned to Mary Miranda his plans to take explosives to the air force base. If Maggie had known how far ahead he had planned, that he had been deceiving her about the purpose of the protest for months, she would have walked away from him.

Just as she had in the end, of course.

But Mary Miranda would have shattered it in a moment. And he had been terrified, all through the trial, that the missing letters would suddenly appear in the hand of the prosecuting attorney, giving him a perfectly good motive for second-degree murder, and confirming the weak case of the state of California in Mary Miranda's own words. *You won't talk to me, Ken, so all I can do is write. But you can't pretend it never happened. You told me about the bomb, and you trusted me. Now you can't suddenly make me go away.*

And here he was again, ordering people's lives, knowing to the best of his knowledge that he did so for the right reasons, and yet with the sneaking nasty suspicion that underneath the level of consciousness, selfish interest was at the core of all he did.

In sudden frustration he turned both his hands up to heaven and said out loud, "God, if this is not Your will, take me out of it. By whatever road You prepare."

He stayed there, with his hands outstretched and a plea for mercy in his mind, pushing away the thought that Christopher Dillard may have pointed him to the last exit before the highway fell away into a pit.

THE PHONE CALL CAME MID-AFTERNOON. Jerry Tindell was in custody. He had just been arraigned, had pleaded not guilty, and his trial was set to begin on the following Monday after his state-appointed attorney had been given ample time to prepare a defense. Subpoenas had already been prepared for all witnesses. Caprio had assembled a list of National Guard members to interview, and had sent a request to Joe Fletcher to authorize their temporary removal from duty.

Balder hung up and dialed Margaret's number, but the answering machine picked up his call and he replaced the receiver without leaving a message. He glanced at the clock. It was past five already, and the secretary would be gone. He opened his briefcase and piled the remaining papers into it. Tonight would be a working evening at the guest cottage. He'd scheduled a meeting with the secretary of defense and secretary of transportation for early morning, so that he could still be present at the opening of Tindell's trial; and he needed to have a proposal ready for them.

He walked out, past the secretary's empty desk. The first arrest was over, Maggie was still in Virginia, Christopher Dillard was gone. April Fool's Day had passed without catastrophe. He was grateful, and slightly surprised.

CHAPTER 23

☆ ☆ ☆ ☆ ☆ ☆ ☆

Monday, April 1, 9 P.M.

KENNETH BALDER HAD CHASED THE housekeeper out, fixed himself toast and coffee for din-ner, and spread his papers out over the kitchen table. Here, with no distractions, he made fairly good progress. He worked his way through the guard reorganization that would be required to tighten up the railway entry points, and put the papers into a neat stack, ready for his early morning meeting. He was be-ginning the first draft of a proposal to organize Virginia's churches into alliances, each responsible for the poor and homeless within carefully drawn districts, when the lights went out overhead.

Balder looked up, blinking. It was well past sunset. The windowpanes were dark. Without the electric light overhead, the stone-floored kitchen was all flickering shadows. The fire in the big kitchen fireplace cast a dim red light into the room, but he could barely see the words on the page in front of him.

He got up and put his head out into the cottage's front hallway. The rest of the cottage was all blackness. He felt his way through the hallway, out to the front door, and peered out. The Executive Mansion was dark, and the lights that illuminated the front of the Capitol had gone out. As he watched, the backup generator for Capitol Park kicked in and the mansion's windows lit palely up.

His heart suddenly began to thump against his chest. He left the door of the guest cottage open and sprinted out onto the grass. He'd left his shoes under the kitchen table, and cold dew instantly soaked through his socks. From Capitol Green he could see nothing. Ninth Street was dark. The towers of the Medical College of Virginia, the complex of tall buildings in Richmond's Church Hill district, all were completely blacked out. On the horizon, the reddish glow of Richmond was fading away.

Inside the guest cottage the telephone began to ring, the sound startling in the complete darkness all around him. He ran back toward the stone steps and fumbled his way into the kitchen. Apparently the guest cottage was not on the backup circuit. When he picked up the receiver Charles Merriman's voice said, "It's happened."

"What is it? Where did they hit?"

"I don't know yet. I've got Virginia Power on the other line. . . . I'm at the Capitol. I was still in my office. I'm going to send my car around for you right now."

"Where's the adjutant general?"

"I don't know. I can't get him on the phone. I've sent a state trooper to find him."

The line cut off. Balder went down on his knees to find his shoes under the table. The right lace had gotten into a knot. He clamped the shoe between his side and the cast and worked at it with his right hand, but it took agonizing minutes to get the shoe on his foot and retied. His hands were shaking—odd, since he felt clear-headed and full master of himself. He hauled himself to his feet, retrieved his jacket from behind the door, and went out to meet Charles Merriman's car. He slid into the backseat and waited.

Merriman appeared, breathless and disheveled, five minutes later and got into the backseat next to him with a curt direction to the guard driver. The car picked up speed. Merriman said crossly, "Joe Fletcher had a cold, so he went to bed early and took the phone off the hook, silly man. We've roused him now. He's sending out extra National Guard for each of the generating stations hit."

"*Each!*"

"Virginia Power says that five stations have been disabled," Merriman said soberly. "Power for this area's produced by two steam turbine plants east of the city. The power's distributed through the generating stations."

"How were they disabled?"

"Well," Merriman said, "we'll be there soon. We put most of our guard at the plants themselves. The stations just pass the power along. Joe put security forces at them, but not big ones. They sit in the middle of the city. We didn't think they were a high risk for attack."

"Can the hospitals manage without power?" Balder asked.

"I spoke to MCV two minutes ago. They've got generators going, so we don't have to worry about anyone's life support failing. They tell me most hospitals in the area could go indefinitely on generators if the oil supply keeps constant; and we've no worries on that front, the ports are still open. But using emergency power means they're running far below the usual level, of course. Everything cut off that isn't absolutely necessary, and the medical staff is miserable, already raising a huge fuss."

The car swung through the pitch-black streets. Balder, squinting out his window, caught a glimpse of a highway sign in the headlights: *Canal Street*. They were headed to mid-city, where the mirror-sided corporate centers rose up in a glistening cluster amid circling overpasses. He made an immense mental effort and dredged up a picture of the surroundings; a tangle of mysterious poles and wires, off to the side of the four-lane highway, surrounded by red-labeled chain fencing. So that was a generating station. The modern equivalent of the underhousemaid, ever-present and practically invisible, unnoticed until it failed.

Ahead of them, just off the road, a Virginia state trooper sat with his lights flashing. Merriman said curtly, "Behind the officer," and the driver pulled the black car to a stop on the shoulder.

On the other side of the highway, the dark poles of the generating station loomed up against the night sky. Shouts and running feet echoed across the median. Guardsmen milled around the base of the station. Two Virginia Power trucks were parked on the far shoulder and another sat in the median. The revolving lights of the power trucks and the moving beams of flashlights lit up the useless metal framework.

Merriman climbed out of the backseat and started toward the trooper.

Balder followed him. It was extraordinarily disorienting to be standing in the middle of a city with no lights anywhere, except for the flashing police lights ahead of them and the occasional headlights of a passing car. The guard driver, who was doing double duty as Merriman's bodyguard, emerged from the driver's seat and crunched along the gravel behind the two R.A.S. officials.

The trooper, walking back toward them, shouted, "Sir?"

"Merriman!" the governor shouted back. A car whizzed by, slowing curiously at the sight of the police lights. The trooper waved at it impatiently.

"Yes, sir. I was told you were coming," he called.

"Can we go up?"

"Yes, sir. They've secured the area."

"What's the ambulance for?"

"I don't know, sir."

"Okay. Come on, Ken. How do we get up to the station?"

They stood in a little cluster between grass and pavement, Merriman and Balder facing the state trooper with the guardsman slightly behind them. The trooper offered, "Access road's on the other side, sir. You can exit a mile up, take a right on Poplar, come into the station by a little gravel road that runs right up behind the station."

"Can't we walk across?" The station was only a few steps away, up a slight slope of grass.

The trooper looked both ways, but the highway was quiet. Kenneth Balder remarked, into Merriman's ear, "Seems to me we've done this before."

"What?"

"Walked happily into danger. *You* came out unscathed."

Merriman grinned, his smile white in the dimness. He said, "And look how well we did out of the last scuffle, Ken. No terrorist is going to hang around with all those guard swarming all over the station. I want to see what I'm dealing with."

The trooper walked them in tight formation across the highway to the gravel shoulder at the foot of the grassy slope on the other side. A guard captain met them halfway up the slope. Merriman demanded, "How was it done?"

"I'll show you, sir." The guardsman turned and shone his powerful flashlight against the chain-link fence ahead of them. The fence at the front of the station appeared whole. The light continued up the shining links, up to the poles and wires and hovered there. At eye level, facing them, a pole had been neatly sheared in half and telescoped in upon itself, ripping connections away. Ends of wire dangled above the shattered pole.

"Some kind of explosive charge," Merriman murmured. "Carefully placed. This was done by men on foot. Where was the guard detail?"

"Sir, this station sits right next to a heavily traveled road, in front of a school." The flashlight momentarily illuminated a jungle gym, sitting in the middle of the concrete yard behind the generating station. "It wasn't considered a high-risk target. We had four men guarding it."

"Well, where are they?"

"They were all on the same side of the fence when the charges went off—"

"You mean somebody got in there and planted the charge and got back out again without the guard seeing them? What were they doing?"

The guard captain cleared his throat. "Er . . . having a smoke, sir. They were on the far side, facing the school, so the saboteur must have gone over the fence facing the road. They say a Virginia Power worker came by and told them to all get out of the way while he checked the equipment. Two of them were burned, sir. There were sparks everywhere when this thing blew."

Merriman shook his head. "Let's see the other side, then."

They moved along the fence. Balder, scuffling through the grass, noted that the flashlight showed scorched and blackened places on the ground. At the explosion, electricity must have popped like fireworks. The guard captain turned the corner, and they stood looking at a gap in the wire fence. The chain had been cut from top to bottom as though it were string, and another wrecked post stood beyond it.

"They planted several charges," their escort said. He ran the light over the gap and the gravel beyond it. Two more guardsmen trotted up, with a Virginia Power worker behind them.

"Sir," one of them said to the guard captain, "this guy's ready to go in."

"I'll come with you," Merriman announced. The little group of men looked him over, and Balder saw recognition come into their faces. The Virginia Power worker said tentatively, "You ought to have a hard hat, Governor—"

"I just want a look," Merriman said.

"Well . . . okay, sir. If you'll follow me—" The worker stepped through the gap, with the governor behind him. Balder followed, watching the beam of the man's flashlight move over the shattered structure. The guard captain was breathing anxiously at his right shoulder.

The Virginia Power man halted, suddenly, and Merriman stepped on his heels. The governor demanded, "What is it?"

"Look," the man said, unevenly.

"What?"

"Over there—"

His flashlight's beam illuminated an incongruous bit of color. An orange safety vest, lettered with *Virginia Power* across the back. The flashlight traveled along it, down a khaki-colored leg, and stopped at a shoe. Merriman and Balder sprang forward simultaneously. Balder was first to the body. He knelt beside it and put his hand on the back and knew instantly that the man was dead. His head was out of sight in the shadows and a huge pool of blood had puddled beneath him. He put a hand on the man's shoulder and rolled him over. The head remained, face down in the gravel. The man's throat had been cut so thoroughly that the head was attached to the body only by a flap of skin at the nape of his neck. Behind them, the Virginia Power worker gagged, clapping his hand over his mouth, and made for the fence. Balder straightened up and turned quickly away, wondering if his face was as white as Merriman's. The guard captain was already yelling to his men on the other side of the fence.

"Get over here and bring the rescue squad guys. And a stretcher—"

"And a TV camera," Merriman said, his voice shaking slightly.

"Sir!"

"Tell 'em to call Channel Twelve. Now!"

The guardsman sent him a shocked glance and relayed the order.

Merriman met Balder's eyes. Underneath the horror was pure satisfaction.

"*Charles*," Balder said, quietly.

"The man's dead, Ken. There's nothing we can do for him. We've got to think about Virginia now."

"What happened?"

"I think Washington sent combat-trained men into a civilian area, and one of them overreacted. You didn't serve in Vietnam?"

"No," Balder said.

"That's a commando-type killing. Ambush from behind, yoke the guy under his chin, yank his head back, and cut the windpipe and carotid artery. Silent and fatal. The special-forces men must have already been in there when this poor guy went to check the equipment. He must have startled one of them in the middle of setting a charge. Washington can do anything they want to the culprit, but it won't make any difference. The United States killed an unarmed citizen of Virginia."

"You can't broadcast pictures of that!"

"Why not?"

"What about his family?"

"We'll notify the family. Ken, this'll paralyze Washington."

The rescue-squad men had arrived with the stretcher. Balder turned his back on the whole scene and went to the fence. Below him, a Channel 12 van skidded onto the verge.

"Press," he said, over his shoulder.

Merriman brushed past him and advanced to meet the TV cameras. He spoke into them, rubbing his hands wearily through his hair and gesturing back at the clump of dark poles and wires behind him.

Kenneth Balder leaned on the fence and watched, silently. He thought, *If I were that special-forces man, I wouldn't get out of Virginia. I wouldn't go back to Washington and face my commander and explain why I lost control. I'd stay put.*

Hard on the heels of this came another thought.

If this is Washington's response to Jerry Tindell's arrest . . . what will happen after his execution?

PART III

★

WAR

CHAPTER 24

Monday, April 8, 10 A.M.

MARGARET FRANKLIN sat outside the Third District Court, waiting to be called to testify in the trial of Jerry Tindell. The hallway was dim and cold, and it smelled of wax and April air. Inside the courtroom, the jury was hearing from the forensic pathologist. She'd excused herself, unable to bear any more of the clinical description of Matthew's shattered chest.

The minutes ticked past. She shifted wearily in her seat. She had been waiting for this trial for a week, eating little and sleeping less. Thinking about Matthew's death and Garrett's absence, and Kenneth Balder, waiting for her to fall in love with him for the second time. Waiting in vain to hear that the guard connection had been investigated. Waiting for the phone to ring again, and hoping to hear her son's voice, no matter how distant.

The subpoena had arrived on Tuesday, the day after April Fool's. She had gotten up, turned on the morning news, and discovered only snow on the Richmond channels. Switching to a Norfolk broadcast, she learned that Richmond was in the throes of a blackout engineered the night before by the United States.

And then the pictures of the murder had begun to come in—the mutilated Virginia Power worker sprawled under the wires of the transmitting station, rolled carefully onto a stretcher and loaded into an ambulance while Charles Merriman's cold voice condemned Washington.

She spent most of that morning inside, watching the news with fascination. Her own community, out at the rural end of New Kent, was served by a separate power station. But Richmond, Henrico, Chesterfield, and the suburban end of New Kent itself were all paralyzed. It might take days for electricity to return.

She knew that the warrant was due to be issued on April 1. *There's no way they've managed to arrest him,* she thought, *no matter what Ken says. They'll have to wait. They'll have more time to investigate the guard.* She felt a wash of relief and turned off the TV and went out to work. But in the afternoon, while she repotted pansies and carefully separated the seedling impatiens, the sheriff's deputy had arrived with subpoena in hand. She wiped the dirt from her hands and signed it and said, "How can the courts carry on without power?"

"We have generators. We're going right ahead with preparations for the trial, Mrs. Franklin. We're going to keep everything on schedule. Washington can't push us around."

And that was the voice of Richmond. The evening news, broadcast from Norfolk's Channel 3, unfolded the whole story in front of her. The sprawled body of the Virginia Power worker—a young man, twenty-six, with a wife and toddler—had whipped the city into a fervor of indignation. From Fredericksburg down to the South Carolina border, the rebel states were suddenly united against an oppressor that could now be accused of greater crimes than mere greed and incompetence. North Carolinians organized an impromptu blockade of the university cities. Guardsmen serving the Reformed American States cleared the crowds away, gently and reasonably, and Charles Merriman appeared in front of television cameras to declare, "We will not react in anger to this immense injustice. We will allow the United States citizens in Durham and Chapel Hill full access to all Reformed American States. Including electricity." Significant pause. "We call the United States before the bar of international opinion. A peaceful demand for separation has been met with military infiltration and murder."

The national news showed Alexander Wade entering his car at the Pentagon, his face drawn, wearing dark glasses at dawn. He refused to be interviewed; but an unnamed Defense Department aide incautiously told the press that Wade had never approved of the attack on Virginia's infrastructure, for fear of just such a catastrophe. The president had insisted.

And the president of the United States, facing a roomful of blood-scenting reporters in front of the Great Seal of the United States, had visibly wavered between his options. If he condemned the special-forces man who had apparently killed a bystander while carrying out the destruction of the station, he would have to admit that the United States had launched an attack on Virginia. If the president ignored the attack, he would imply approval of what had been done. He settled for a beautifully turned passage about the tragedy of violence in America, and the reporters streamed out to savage him in their morning stories.

This had ushered in a week of stalemate. Silence issued from the White House and rhetoric from the Virginia Capitol. Margaret waited for Jerry Tindell's trial to begin, and the rest of the world watched in fascination. Virginia Power had thrown itself into the task of restoring electricity. Now, a week later, Richmond was back to full power; and still the White House maintained that noncommittal silence. Margaret had called Ken's office three times, always hearing the same news: Guard personnel had been interviewed by two Richmond police detectives. No leads had been uncovered. Clint Larsen and Garrett Franklin, the most likely sources of information, were still missing without a trace.

"Mrs. Franklin?"

She recalled herself to the present and stood up.

"They're ready for you, ma'am."

She followed the courtroom officer through the doors. The room was packed. Reporters and public alike were curious over this first trial of the new administration. The jury—the first twelve people drawn, she had been told, minus those dismissed by the judge because of prior obligations or mental disability—turned their twelve heads to stare at her curiously. She let herself look back at them for a moment; divided almost equally into men and women, seven black and five white, business suits and sweatshirts and one orange-beaded headdress. She walked up to the witness stand and was presented with a Bible. The days of non-religious affirmations were over.

"Do you swear to tell the truth, the whole truth, and nothing but the truth, so help you God?"

"Yes," Margaret said, and sat down. The public prosecutor rose. She fixed her eyes on him, aware that Jerry Tindell sat behind the other table.

"Now, Mrs. Franklin," the prosecutor began, "please tell us in your own words what happened on the night of February twenty-second."

She told the story yet again. Matthew's request that she should get up out of bed and come out to Oregon Hill. Leaving the car at the convenience store, buying coffee because Matthew seemed to think they were too early for their mysterious appointment. The walk down the street, Matthew slowing as though looking for a house number, the shot, Matthew's collapse. She heard her voice shake. The door at the back of the courtroom cracked open, and Kenneth Balder's tall figure came quietly through it. He slid unobtrusively into a backseat. Half the heads in the courtroom turned to look at him and a whisper ran around the room and died. Margaret drew her eyes away from him. His physical presence imprinted itself on the drab room, like a colored seal on gray paper.

"Order," the judge snapped.

"Mrs. Franklin, did you see anyone else in the street?" the prosecutor asked.

"I saw someone move in the shadows across the way."

"Across from where Sergeant Franklin was lying?"

"Yes."

The prosecutor moved to the open space in front of the witness box, where he had propped a large diagram of the Oregon Hill street where Matthew died. He said, pointing, "You were here, and this mark represents Sergeant Franklin's body?"

"Yes."

"And you saw this movement here?"

"A little further up."

"Here?"

"Yes."

"This spot has been identified by Richmond city police as 551 Oak Street," the prosecutor said to the jury. "Mrs. Franklin, is it possible, that the movement was made by a dog or cat?"

"No. It was above my eye level."

"And you are how tall?"

"Five-eight."

"So—six feet or so?"

"Yes."

"Your Honor, I'd like to ask the defendant to stand up," the prosecutor suggested.

"Objection!" the defense attorney said, immediately.

"Nonsense," the judge retorted. "Your client's height is a matter of public record. Stand up, Mr. Tindell."

The defense attorney heaved an exaggerated sigh, and Jerry Tindell pushed his chair back and unfolded his thin body from behind the table. The courtroom was silent for a moment, as the jury examined his six-foot frame. Margaret allowed herself to glance at him. His light-skinned face was calm, but a thin sheen of sweat stood across his forehead.

"You can sit down," the judge said.

"I have a question," said the man in the beaded orange cap. Margaret turned her head, startled. The judge said kindly, "The jury has been given permission to ask questions of clarification, Mrs. Franklin."

"Yes, sir," Margaret said. The juror was a dark-skinned man in his early forties, thin and cleanshaven. He asked, "Mrs. Franklin, did you ever find out why your husband wanted you to go down there with him?"

Margaret told the story of Matthew's last request. The jury listened, but at the end their faces had not changed. The man settled back.

"No further questions," the prosecutor said, and sat down. The defense attorney rose. He said, "Mrs. Franklin, could you describe this movement more thoroughly?"

"I was running toward Matthew, and out of the corner of my eye I saw something move. There's a little house there with a front porch, and whoever it was stood on the front steps in the dark."

"You say 'whoever,' Mrs. Franklin. In the statement taken by the police just after Sergeant Franklin's death, you say—" he adjusted his glasses on his nose and peered at the paper he held conspicuously in front of him, "'I didn't look, I didn't see anyone, I didn't see anything.' Am I to understand that this statement is incorrect?"

"That statement was taken three hours after Matthew died. I could barely remember anything except for Matthew lying in the middle of the road."

"So the next day, when you told Detective Stott—" the defense attorney retrieved a second paper from the table and held it up in front of his nearsighted eyes, "'I didn't see a face or anything, but there was someone there,' you had . . . remembered?" The word was thick with irony, and she saw Ken shift in his hard seat, propping the cast on his left arm more comfortably on his lap. She paused, recreating the scene in her mind. She said at last, "When I was able to think rationally, I remembered seeing movement from the corner of my eye, just across from Matthew's—where Matthew was lying."

"Just movement, Mrs. Franklin?"

"Yes."

"So this movement could have been porch awning, flapping in the wind? Or a stray dog?"

"No," Margaret said, refusing to be drawn. "The movement was definitely human. But I can't say that it was Tindell. I saw an arm and a shoulder, but not a face."

The defense attorney said insistently, "So you can't say with certainty *what* you saw, can you, Mrs. Franklin?"

"No," Margaret said. "I've always thought there was a possibility someone else might be involved. My son—"

"Objection!" the prosecutor protested. The defense attorney turned away with an irritated motion of his hand, and the judge said, "Sustained. Mrs. Franklin, you cannot testify as to your son's theories."

Margaret said stubbornly, "He would be here himself, but the National Guard seems to have kidnapped him."

"Objection!"

"Disregard that," the judge directed the jury. "Mrs. Franklin, you may step down. Let's break for lunch. Reconvene in one hour."

The courtroom rose in a hum of conversation, and the jury filed out. Margaret stood up in the witness box and found her knees trembling. She walked carefully down, and the prosecutor glanced up at her and frowned.

He was a thick energetic man of her own age, and the last time she'd seen him he had explained to her with great regret why Jerry Tindell could not be successfully prosecuted under the Constitution of the United States.

He snapped, "Are you trying to sabotage the case?"

Margaret shook her head wearily. "We've been over this before," she said.

"Indeed we have. Your testimony puts Tindell right on the spot where Jamal Henderson identifies him. We'll have Henderson up after lunch, and get to the physical evidence against Tindell tomorrow. We could hand this thing to the jury by Thursday. I just hope you haven't confused them. Afternoon, Dr. Balder." He stood up and shook hands with Ken over the wooden rail. Margaret met his blue eyes, and felt her breath catch, and once again tried to ignore the effect his mere presence seemed to have on her. Ken leaned on the rail and said, "What's on your schedule for this week, Mr. Prosecutor?"

"If we can get this Tindell case out of here by Thursday, we've got two grand larcenies and an attempted rape. No more capital cases until next week."

"One's quite enough," Ken said dryly.

The prosecutor said, "Any news from Washington about the murderer of that Virginia Power guy?"

"Washington hasn't even admitted that special forces came into Virginia, let alone that one of them blew it. We think they came in by railroad. I shuffled guardsmen around to tighten up the borders."

"A little too late, eh?"

"As you say," Ken agreed.

"Well," the prosecutor said, philosophically, "the attack could have been a lot worse."

"Yes. That was just a warning. Later, we may see a stronger move on the part of the United States, but judging from the news this past week, I'd bet no one in office wants to stake his political future on another attack just now. Not without great provocation."

"Like an execution?"

"Time will tell," Kenneth Balder said. He didn't look at Margaret again. She watched the side of his face, the well-known slope of jaw and the close-clipped fair hair at the nape of his neck. A muscle twitched intermittently at the corner of his eye. "Speaking of provocation," the prosecutor said, lowering his voice, "I heard a rumor." He glanced around. The three of them were alone at the front of the courtroom; Tindell had been escorted to his lunch through a back door, the judge was gone, and the spectators had clumped into chattering groups.

"What rumor?"

"I heard that we were about to quarantine AIDS."

"Where did you hear that?"

"From my secretary. I figured someone at your office's been talking."

Ken hesitated. He said, "John Cline has recommended quarantine, yes. But as secretary of the treasury, it doesn't fall under his authority."

"Seems a bit extreme."

"It's an extension of the same Commandment you're prosecuting Jerry Tindell under now. The sixth. *You shall not murder* mandates preservation of life. We preserve life by executing those who snuff it out . . . also by protecting the uninfected from dangerous diseases. That's why the Old Testament banished lepers." His voice was slightly flat, as though he felt obligated to defend quarantine. He added, "Quarantine in modern times wouldn't necessarily mean confinement. We know more about how germs spread than the Israelites did. But the matter's still in discussion. No action's been taken."

"Well," the prosecutor said, "*my* office has already got plenty of criminals to run herd on. If you intend to keep tabs on sick people, I hope you'll create another agency to do the job." He scooped the files up from his table. "Excuse me, if you will. I want to run over this testimony one more time before we call Henderson."

He headed for the back door of the courtroom. Margaret cleared her throat uncomfortably. Ken suggested, "I can buy you a hot dog in the hallway."

Margaret shook her head. Her voice seemed to have caught somewhere in the back of her throat.

"Maggie. I know we don't have any evidence about the guard. But I tried." His face had developed unfamiliar lines, as though stress had become an unremarkable part of his daily life.

"Yes," she said. "It didn't help though. Your revolution isn't going to discover the truth, and now I've lost my son as well." She was aware that her voice was flat and listless. After the last week, she seemed to have no energy left for protest. She wanted all this to be over; she wanted Garrett back, and deep down she wanted Ken back as well. He said gently, "Maggie, you don't have to do anything to atone for Matthew's death."

She was silent. He had put his finger right on the most painful spot in her soul. He went on, "Even if there is some guard connection here, isn't it enough that Tindell was involved?"

Margaret said, making an effort at logical thought, "All I can see is that your new revolution is bringing justice, . . . but not the *whole* justice. Tindell might be convicted, but his guilt isn't the whole truth. This is the last chance I have to do something for Matthew."

"And you think that when the trial is over, you'll be free from whatever guilt is driving you?"

It was a rhetorical question, and she suddenly saw the truth of it. When the trial was over, she would still feel the weight of guilt over her loveless marriage, over her emotional unfaithfulness to Matthew. She was so tired that she could no longer stand the thought. She turned her eyes away from the future and thought: *I have to hold on for the rest of the week.* Ken was still standing in front of her, and she felt a sudden savage impulse to push him away. She wouldn't be bearing this burden if it weren't for Kenneth Balder; she could have married Matthew and loved him as she had wanted to, if her heart hadn't been trapped. She lashed out, "What do you know about guilt? You had an affair with Mary Miranda and told her all about your plans to use violence in that protest. You betrayed me and never told me about it. Not in the trial, not afterward. You don't have any right to talk about atoning for guilt. If you were really changed, you would have told me the truth as soon as you saw me again. But you were content to leave that lie between us."

To her horror, she found her eyes filling with tears. "I saw her letters, in the hallway, right after you were sentenced. Alexander Wade had

them. He asked the judge to admit them as evidence, and the judge refused because the envelopes were never found and it couldn't be proved
that they were from Mary Miranda, or when she'd sent them. But if your
jury had seen those letters, they'd have convicted you of *murder*, not manslaughter. You'd still be rotting in jail. I never loved Matthew the way I
loved you. Never in all the time I lived with him. But he never betrayed
me the way you did. It's no wonder you got converted and found yourself a new life. You ruined the old one with your own hands." She was
almost too exhausted to finish the attack, but desperation drove her on.
"The only thing I can do for Matthew now is try to get justice for him
until it is too late. So go away, Ken. Go away until I do this."

He had gone very white. He said, "*Maggie*. I didn't mean to kill her. It
was an accident."

"You can look me in the eye and tell me that? In front of the God you
say you believe in?"

Ken looked at her, wretchedly. The muscle in his face leaped again. He
said, "I did *not* kill her on purpose."

"But you slept with her. And you lied to me. You killed any chance that
we could ever live together again."

"I was a selfish fool," Kenneth Balder said. "I have paid for it."

The prosecuting attorney reappeared behind Ken, a clutch of file folders
in his hand. Margaret pushed past both of them, down the aisle and out of the
courtroom. The smell of wax, the flickering lights, and the bone-numbing
April chill had combined to make her violently sick. As soon as she was outside the door, she bolted for the ladies' room. She stayed there a long time,
staring at herself in the mirror over the sink, willing tears away; and when she
finally nerved herself to re-enter the hallway, it was cold and empty. She had
no desire to go back into the courtroom and listen as Matthew Franklin was
finally laid to rest. Instead, she walked down the hallway, through the
courthouse's main door, and found herself under the cloudy spring sky.

She reached the bottom of the stone steps. Pigeons scattered from in
front of her. She looked around her, illogically longing to see his tall, broad-
shouldered figure. But Kenneth Balder had taken her words at face value;
he had gone.

CHAPTER 25

Wednesday, April 10, noon

GARRETT FRANKLIN sat under the flap of a tent and watched rain drip steadily off the edge, onto the pinetags below. His fingers were ice-cold and his nose was running. Clouds lay over the top of the North Carolina mountains, and shapeless chunks of mist drifted through the clearing. He had nothing to do until he took his turn to monitor the short-wave radio news at one P.M. It was a brand-new assignment; a definite step up from the KP duty he'd been on for days.

He was somewhere in the middle of the Pisgah National Forest, sharing his sleeping quarters with a maniac. The Tri-County Militia had traveled through fields and woods, along unmarked dirt roads, with the Blue Ridge Mountains growing larger and darker in front of them. Finally, bumping along mountain fire roads, they had arrived at a rock-walled clearing where the remnants of the Regulators Militia huddled.

Garrett had conceived a grudging admiration for Major Morrison. Within two hours, the ex-army soldier had transformed the clearing into a well-guarded fortress with neat rows of tents and campfires and a duty roster which included monitoring police frequencies, checking the short-wave news reports, and walking sentry. Catching sight of Garrett's worried face, he had also allowed another carefully monitored phone call to Margaret Franklin. But the answering machine picked up after the first ring, and

Garrett hung silently up. He still thought Morrison was paranoid, but he was less frightened of the man than he had been.

On the other hand, he had slipped into pure terror of Clint Larsen. Larsen shared his tent, and Garrett never slept until he could hear the older man's breathing slow and deepen. Nights when Larsen had watch duty, Garrett didn't sleep at all until his tentmate had come back and peeled off his clothes and rolled himself in his sleeping bag. The brutality of the murder and the casual unnecessary lie about Garrett's own part in it had shaken him almost into panic.

Garrett heard voices on the other side of the tent and peered around the edge. He was immensely bored. He had no weapon to clean, and the day was almost too dark for reading, even if he'd been interested in the gun magazines stacked up next to Clint Larsen's cot.

Major Morrison emerged from the mist, with Larsen behind him. Both men wore billowing, knee-length plastic capes that covered their weapons, and Morrison looked oddly humpbacked. Garrett hoisted himself to his feet and ducked out from under the tent flap. Immediately the rain poured down on his head, the squall gaining sudden strength.

"Franklin!" Morrison hailed him. "Get back under the tent. We're coming in."

The two men ducked in, out of the spattering water, and Garrett settled himself back on the pinetags. Major Morrison squatted down on his heels and grinned.

"Congratulations," he said. "You've been promoted."

"To what?" Garrett demanded. He added, "Sir," as an afterthought.

Morrison shrugged himself out of the cape and revealed two M-16s, slung across his back under the waterproof fabric. He unslung one of the weapons and held it out.

'For you," he said. "I've added you to our security detail. You'll relieve Larsen at sentry duty tonight."

Garrett took the M-16, not entirely pleased. Even though he'd resented the caution which kept him unarmed, he was uneasy about being given an armed post. He had an unpleasant suspicion that he'd been awarded a gun because the Tri-County Militia needed additional firepower for its future plans. He wanted no part of those plans.

"Thanks," he said.

"I'd have gotten you a weapon sooner, but I had to pacify Bill James first," Major Morrison added.

Garrett checked the clip silently, and rested the gun across his knees. His fright of Clint Larsen was nothing compared to his terror of Bill James. James made it an occupation to watch him, with a dark, hooded look that made Garrett want to crawl under the nearest rock.

"Might as well clean mine," Larsen said, philosophically. "Too wet to do anything else."

He disappeared into the tent and clanked around for a few minutes, emerging with cleaning rods and patches and his cache of Hoppe's powder and gun oil. He settled down in the driest corner of the little canvas-shielded porch and started to take his weapon apart. Morrison straightened his knees and said, "Well, men, back to duty."

"Sir," Larsen said, running a rod down the barrel, "maybe I could have a chance at radio duty, now that Franklin's got a gun. I'm sick of walking around on top of the rocks. I swear, if we stay out here much longer I'm gonna lose my mind. Nothing but squirrels and dead leaves for company, and it's so quiet at night, I can hear my blood runnin' all the way down to my toes. I'm ready for some action." The seclusion had made him chattier than usual, and Morrison smiled. He said soothingly, "We'll get moving soon."

"Back into civilization, I hope."

Morrison lowered his voice and said, "I'll tell you what we're getting ready to do. We've got men coming from all over who want the new country to stay free, but we're running low on ammo. I'm planning a raid. All we're waiting for is a break in the weather."

Larsen said eagerly, "A raid? On what?"

"Army guard weapons depot at Fletcher. Still U.S.A. loyal, not very heavily guarded. The guard that stayed loyal to North Carolina haven't tried to get the weapons back—"

"Why not?" Garrett asked.

Morrison shrugged. "They say it's not ethical to attack other citizens of North Carolina. But we know that the North Carolina adjutant general's corrupt. He's systematically weakening the guard so the U.S.A. can take us back over."

Garrett thought, in the ensuing silence, *Now I'm a deserter, an accomplice to murder, and part of a plot to attack federal property.* He bent his head over the M-16, pretending to examine the clip. Larsen said, "Here, boy, you might as well clean that thing as long as you're admiring it," and passed him a rod.

Garrett started to disassemble the gun, cautiously; the skill wasn't yet second nature to him. Morrison lingered; the rain had suddenly intensified, and he peered out at the drumming water with a grimace. Larsen said, "Get your thumb under that spring. Well, I hope we can move back out of these mountains when we're done. I thought it was quiet in Windsor Shade, but this beats the county hollow."

Morrison said idly, "You out in a subdivision now?"

"Yes, sir. We lived in the city for a long time—551 Elm Street. It was a dump, but we were taking care of my wife's parents, and it was all we could afford. Then we got a little inheritance from my uncle, so I could finally get my wife and family outta there. New house, safe, nice green grass for the kids. We've been there a little more than a year. Amy loves it."

"Where's Elm Street, anyway?"

"Oregon Hill. Real dangerous area."

Garrett let the spring slide back, incautiously, and gave a yelp of pain as it pinched a wad of skin off his thumb.

"Hope you shoot better than you break down," Morrison remarked.

Garrett sucked on his aching thumb. Larsen gave him a quick glance and said, "Sorry, Franklin. I wasn't thinking. . . . His dad got killed in Oregon Hill, remember?"

Morrison snorted. "How could I forget? Bill James talked about it for weeks."

"Shock to all of us, it was. James was at my house when it happened."

"He was?" Garrett demanded. He heard his voice soar up, and prudently put his wounded thumb back into his mouth. Clint Larsen inserted a cleaning rod into the barrel of the M-16 and said, "Yeah."

"At five in the morning?"

"Yeah. See, Amy and his wife were in this food co-op, and he was working for this city construction company. He used to drop the food on the back porch on his way in. Real early, of course, so he never knocked, but it was nice. Otherwise Amy'd have to drive out and get it. . . . anyway, he came up to the porch to leave it and he saw the lights were on, so he knocked to see if everything was okay. Amy'd been up with Kristen all night with her asthma." The cleaning rod clicked softly against metal. "He offered to take Kristen to the hospital 'cause I was late getting off duty and Amy couldn't leave the other kids, but I got back just in time, so he went on to work. We didn't find out about your dad 'til the next morning. About three streets over, it was, where he got killed."

Garrett removed his thumb from his mouth. He thought, *I can't rush this.* He ran the cleaning pad over the same spot until it shone. When a little silence had passed, he said casually, "How long you been in this militia, then?"

"Oh, a couple of years," Larsen said. He didn't appear to connect the question with what had gone before, and Garrett relaxed slightly. Major Morrison, pulling his hood up in preparation for plunging out into the weather, said, "Not formally, that is. He didn't actually sign on until last year. I was certainly glad to have him. Real leadership material, Larsen is. He's got a cooler head than my other two captains."

"Like Bill James?" Garrett suggested. He waited for the conversation to end abruptly, but both men chuckled.

"Bill takes some getting used to," Morrison said, "but he and Clint between them have gotten us a good number of guns and ammo. We couldn't manage without 'em. Well, I'd better get back to work."

He gave a short salute and headed out into the rain. Clint Larsen started to put the mechanism back together. After a moment he said, "Amy likes Bill's wife, but I wasn't ever much on Bill. Good soldier, but he's always thinking people are after him. He kept telling me your dad was gonna blow the whistle on me," he added. "Your dad was a sharp one, Franklin. He knew I was going to militia meetings, before I actually joined. Used to worry James. But I guess your dad finally decided I was a patriot, 'cause he never did say anything about it. He let it go. That's one of the reasons I thought you'd be a good recruit. That, and you were always so interested."

"Yeah," Garrett said, after a moment. His hands were shaking. He put the gun down and cracked his knuckles to conceal the tremor.

If the National Guard had prosecuted Clint Larsen for militia membership, what would have happened to the Tri-County Militia? He had a vague idea that most militias were tolerated by local authorities unless they had illegal weapons. But if Clint Larsen, under direct orders from Bill James, had stolen National Guard weapons . . .

Bill James. Bill James, tall and hawk-eyed and cold, had had good reason to fear Matthew Franklin's interference.

Maybe Matthew Franklin had been headed for Clint Larsen's house that last night, to warn him what was about to happen. He'd have expected to find Larsen at home, just back from his shift, not yet sleeping. Clint Larsen had four small children, and a wife who might have known nothing about his illegal activities, and his association with the Tri-County Militia had still been casual, loose enough to be repudiated. He could have distanced himself from the militia before the ax fell.

"Don't you have radio duty?" Larsen asked.

Garrett said promptly, "Yes, sir," and scrambled to his feet. As he headed toward the command center Morrison had set up in a large central tent, Larsen yelled after him, "Try to catch a weather report, would ya? If it rains much more I'm gonna melt like the Wicked Witch of the West. My kids watch that movie over and over. Now I know what she felt like."

His kids, Garrett thought. *His kids and wife. I bet that's why Dad wanted Mom with him.* Matthew Franklin had gone to Oregon Hill off-duty, as a private citizen. He had taken his wife along with him to show that he came as a friend, one family man warning another of danger. . . . and met Bill James somewhere between his car and Clint Larsen's house.

He hadn't realized that Bill James and Clint Larsen were both capable of murder.

In the command tent, he sat down at the makeshift table in the corner and fitted the earphones onto his head. The headset wasn't necessary to hear the short-wave radio, but it kept the noise from annoying Morrison in his meetings with his officers. Garrett liked it; he'd be able to linger on news items that weren't necessarily of military interest. He'd been cut off from the outside world for a week, and he was beginning to feel that his universe consisted only of this circular patch of forest enclosed by the rock walls of the mountain.

Sanders, the listener before him, had filled out two pages of news in neat fifth-grade handwriting. Richmond had restored power to most of the city, a Pentagon insider had leaked the fact that one special-forces man was still missing somewhere inside Virginia. Garrett picked up the pen and recorded his name and the time at the top of a fresh log sheet, as he'd been instructed. Sanders had been listening to Richmond's WRVA, but news had given way to a call-in talk show. He followed the arguments until the callers began to repeat themselves, and then wrote under his name, "WRVA call-in show, 1:30 P.M. Listeners say Richmond needs extra National Guard to protect the city limits. Most of them think armed attack from Washington is very likely. Ninety-eight percent indignant over what the Pentagon is doing."

He trolled through the bands, his thoughts still fixed on Clint Larsen and the ominous figure of Bill James. A sentence from the radio jerked his attention back to the news. A voice was concluding "—for the murder of National Guard Master Sergeant Matthew Franklin, two years ago."

Garrett leaned forward, his mouth dry. It was a Delaware station, coming in clearly by some trick of the weather.

"Secretary of Defense Alexander Wade, speaking on Monday before the disastrous attack on Richmond, insisted that Tindell's arrest was a violation of the Constitution. 'This is only the first in a long, inevitable series of human rights abuses,' Wade said in a Pentagon news conference. Secretary Wade made no reference to the attack, and he is refusing further comment. Attention around the nation is fixed on Richmond during this first trial under Governor Merriman's new administration. An unnamed aide at the Defense Department says that if Tindell is executed, Virginia can expect further retaliation." Pause. "In other news, Montana governor James Sorenson has turned down a federal education grant. Sorenson said, in a speech televised this morning, 'We don't need the money, and we don't need Washington telling our teachers what to teach'—"

Garrett turned the knob, skipping across bands of interference. *If Tindell is executed!* Last he heard, the man hadn't even been arrested. Almost an hour passed before he found a full report on Jerry Tindell's trial. A woman's voice with a faint Southern lengthening of the vowels said, "The country is watching Richmond's Third District Court this week, as Jerry Tindell of Oregon Hill becomes the first Virginian tried under the new code of the Commonwealth. Tindell, accused in the death of a National Guard sergeant two years ago, will testify today in his own defense. To discuss the case, we have legal expert Jeremy Fowler with us from his New York office. Mr. Fowler, how does the case look?"

"Well, Marianne, the prosecution has a great deal of very strong evidence against Tindell. Charles Merriman chose his first case carefully. Tindell would probably be convicted in any United States courtroom if all the evidence were allowed in. And the Reformed American States is doing just that."

"Is there any possibility that the evidence was planted by police?"

"That's always a possibility. We'll find out more when Tindell testifies this afternoon."

"What about the possibility of execution?"

The lawyer's voice said cautiously, "Well, capital punishment has been legal in Virginia since 1975, so an execution wouldn't exactly be a startling development. . . . except that under the old system, this particular homicide would probably have been prosecuted as second-degree murder, and Tindell wouldn't have faced the chair. Lethal injection, I should say, as that was the method used in Virginia's most recent execution."

"If I could ask one last question . . . what would have happened to O. J. Simpson, if he'd been tried under these new rules?"

"Can't say for sure, Marianne. But I suspect Mr. Simpson fared better in L.A. than Jerry Tindell will in Richmond."

"Thank you, Mr. Fowler."

"My pleasure, Marianne."

"That was legal expert Jeremy Fowler from New York, with us via telephone. Now for the weather. The Atlanta metropolitan area will see clearing this afternoon, with lows tonight dropping to the forties—"

Someone tapped Garrett on the shoulder, and he sprang up out of the chair.

"Take it easy!" the man behind him snapped.

"Sorry. I can't hear anything with these on."

"I'm taking over for you."

"Right now?" Garrett recognized the face; he was a member of the Charles City division.

"Yeah. Morrison's assembling the Henrico and New Kent divisions outside."

Garrett handed over the earphones and went outside. Rain still came steadily down. He pulled his waterproof cape up around his ears. Raindrops drumming down on the hood made hearing difficult.

In a clear spot between the tents and the rock wall of the hollow, the Tri-County Militia was assembling into neat rows. Clint Larsen met him at the edge of the clearing.

"We're going out," he announced. His voice had returned to its usual hostile tones.

"In the middle of a storm?" Garrett asked.

"It's gonna clear by tomorrow. Shut up and get into line."

Garrett obeyed. Major Morrison was standing with his back to the upthrusting mountainside, waiting for the militia to quiet, his thumbs hooked into his belt and his feet planted wide apart in the damp leaves.

"Men," he announced, "we can't fight for freedom without weapons; and there's no excuse for guns and ammo to stay in the hands of soldiers who've forgotten their loyalty to the state of North Carolina. We've just confirmed that the weather is about to clear. So we're going to liberate the weapons depot at Fletcher."

He grinned, hearing an excited murmur spread through the ranks. Garrett turned his head nervously toward Clint Larsen. Bill James, ramrod straight at the front of the New Kent militiamen, was looking sideways at him along the lines of men. Garrett turned his eyes forward at once, pulling his head back into the shell of his hood. Water blew into his face. He could feel James's gray stare boring into his temple.

"The Charles City division will guard this camp," Morrison went on. "We've got a couple of Regulators to guide the rest of you. You'll travel all tonight and the raid will take place just before dawn tomorrow. Now I'm going to turn the briefing over to your captains. Men, this is the first campaign in the true war for freedom—"

Garrett detached himself from the remainder of the rhetoric. Panic was beginning to balloon up inside his chest. The lines swayed and moved, and he followed Larsen blindly toward the vehicles, parked off the mountain fire-road, well away from the clearing. He supposed that he would discover what he was supposed to do, closer to Fletcher. Unsuspecting Fletcher, with a legion of zealots preparing to assault it. He stumbled over a root. Someone gripped his shoulder and hauled him up. He twisted his head around and looked directly at Bill James. The older man hadn't bothered with a hood. His close-clipped hair glistened with rain. Above the strong bony planes of his face, his gray eyes were implacable.

"Watch your step, Franklin," he said.

Larsen had disappeared into the fringe of trees. Garrett recovered his voice.

"Don't worry," he said, "I'm going to watch my step."

James's strong fingers still pressed into his shoulder. He said, "I hear you're a good shot."

Garrett was silent. The other man leaned slightly forward and said, "So am I."

Garrett looked unwillingly into the steel-gray eyes. He might never find proof for his suspicions; but he saw confirmation in that steady gaze. Bill James said, "Morrison and Larsen insisted on bringing you along. Said you'd do your part. I said you weren't reliable. I've been overruled, Franklin."

"I'll do what I have to," Garrett said. Even terrified, trapped in this mad enterprise, he still could not keep loathing out of his voice. James released his shoulder, and Garrett stepped hastily away from him.

"You run away," Bill James said, his voice lazy and confident, "and you won't get far past me. Understand?"

Garrett hunched his shoulders and hurried after Clint Larsen. The array of Jeeps and trucks, coming into sight through the trees, was as welcome as a fortress. He climbed into Larsen's old truck and clenched his teeth to stop them from chattering together. The caravan of vehicles pulled slowly into the fire road, one by one, heading east.

AND SO HIS EFFORTS to find Matthew Franklin's murderer had brought him here: lying on his stomach at the crest of a hill on a gray April morning before sunrise, sighting an M-16 on the United States Army National Guard Weapons Station, Fletcher, North Carolina. He'd had militia men to his north, south, east, and west until this very moment. He was aware of a whole layer of emotions, each giving way to another: *I'm supposed to fire on United States property. They're going to execute Jerry Tindell, and he didn't do it. I can't get away and tell them. We're about to start a real war. Bill James is right over there, and all he has to do is lift his barrel and I'm right in his sights. One way or another, I'm gonna get shot.*

The weapons depot was a gray building surrounded by the usual forbidding, red-tagged wire fences. Major Morrison had rejected plans to simply storm the depot. It was easy enough to fire down on the building from the surrounding hills, but the United States-loyal National Guard inside could simply stay under cover until the Tri-County Militia ran out of ammo. Instead, Morrison dressed himself and a volunteer in two North Carolina Guard uniforms, supplied by the Regulators, and put a colored patch on each to approximate the North Carolina-loyal mark instituted by MacDonald Forbes at the time of North Carolina's secession. He then tied a handkerchief on the barrel of his M-16 and walked down to the front guard shack with the nervous Henrico boy behind him. To all appearances, the two militiamen were members of the North Carolina National Guard who'd finally come to their senses.

Garrett was too far away to hear the conversation. He saw Morrison put the gun gently onto the pavement on his feet and raise his hands. The sentry emerged from the shack, fully cautious against the two men in front of him but oblivious to the hundred armed militiamen in the hills around. Garrett heard a burst of fire. The sentry crumpled. Another guardsman, sprinting toward the shack across the dark pavement, stumbled and fell. Morrison leaped for the guard shack. The front gate was his, and a line of yelling men burst from the hills and stormed down on the depot. Garrett leapt to his feet and, with a sudden sixth sense that saved his life, ducked immediately to the right and rolled. Dirt and grass spurted up in a muddy fountain from where he had stood the moment before. He lost his footing on the slope and slid, scrambling for a foothold. When he finally came to a stop, the wire fence was right before him. Inside the compound came yells and the sound of firing. He hauled himself up and sprinted along the wire, away from the front gate. Morrison had massed his men on three sides of the depot; the fourth side of the surrounding fence, containing the windowless backs of the army buildings, gave onto a rocky field clumped with dead grass and young gum trees. He left the shelter of the fence and ran out into the open space. The tree just beside him shivered and splintered, and he threw himself down onto his stomach and wriggled frantically for the woods. The shoulder strap of the gun caught on a tough clump of grass. He left it on the ground, pushed himself up on his hands and feet, and ran the last few steps. Now he was in a pine woods, heavy with tangling underbrush, and the sounds of firing were fainter. He thought he could hear footsteps. He was too terrified to look behind him. He crashed through the scrub maples and poplars, tripping and gasping and stumbling, until all he could hear was his own sobbing breath and his heart pounding in his ears. When he finally collapsed onto the dead leaves, red sparks danced in front of his eyes. He rubbed them away, and found that his hands were streaked with blood from beating through the brush. He was alone. The woods were wet and still dark.

Garrett hauled himself to his feet and stumbled blindly through the water-soaked trees. He walked for a long time before the woods began to thin. He could hear the occasional sound of a car, far ahead. He slowed his step, drawing closer and closer to the road, until finally he could look out unseen from the brush along the edge of the woods. It was a big road, a divided six-lane highway almost empty of cars. The woods he stood in were slightly below the ridge of the road, with a gravel shoulder sloping down toward him. He squinted up into the sky. It was starting to clear into day, and on his left the sun was rising.

He turned his face toward the sunrise and trudged through the brush, until a blue shield-shaped marker came into sight, up there on the shoulder just above him. This was Interstate 40, running eastward toward the ocean and the north-south corridor of I-95. It was against the law to hitch-hike on an interstate, but perhaps that too had been suspended. It was Thursday morning, early. Garrett didn't know whether anyone would dare pick him up, tattered and streaked with blood. He'd left his wallet under his cot at the Yorktown Naval Weapons Station a lifetime ago. He had no identification, no credit cards, no money. He'd been looking for the truth about Matthew Franklin's death for two years; and now the wrong man was on trial. He would go home and tell his mother the truth, and then leave the farm before the chief of staff could find and prosecute him.

He climbed up the gravel slope onto the interstate itself, and set his face toward Richmond.

CHAPTER 26

Thursday, April 11, 10 A.M.

ON THURSDAY MORNING, Alexander Wade climbed out of
his car and walked wearily into the Old Executive Building.
He ignored the yells of the press clustered on the sidewalk.
The jury in Jerry Tindell's trial was expected back momentarily, and the
president required his presence in the military situation room. The location was ominous. Wade had ridden over from the Pentagon, with one
thought shouting over and over in his mind: *He's made up his mind to attack.*

The president had been in virtual seclusion for the last week. The last cabinet meeting had been before dawn on Tuesday, the day after that ill-starred
attack on Richmond's electricity. Defense and State and Treasury and Transportation had wrangled over the options for hours, while those first appalling
photographs of the butchered Virginia Power worker began to drift out over
the United States. The president, facing the united opposition of his staff to
any military intervention, had finally stormed out, directly into his badly-sched-
uled press conference. There, still seething with fury and conscious that any
approval of the raid would certainly condemn him, he had bungled what was
meant to be a soothing and reassuring speech to the nation.

By Wednesday he had withdrawn into the Oval Office, refusing to grant
the press secretary's pleas for an address to the indignant nation. "Let 'em
wonder what will happen next," the president said grimly when Alexander
Wade protested. "Merriman does exactly what he pleases without explaining

himself, and he's turning into the most heroic figure in America. I've explained everything and I'm pulling an eleven-percent approval rate. Let 'em wonder."

"It's a little late for a dignified silence," Wade snapped. His patience was running short. If the chief executive had followed his policy from the beginning, Washington would have continued to respond with reticence and diplomacy to Merriman's rebellion. But the president had waited only with reluctance, then insisted on armed response. Now he was mulling over methods of further attack, while stonewalling the press. Dignified silence while conducting behind-the-scenes diplomacy made eminent sense. Dignified silence while planning for war made the American public intensely nervous. Alexander Wade was already hearing rumblings from the Hill about hearings on the deployment of those expurgated special forces.

Wade stepped through the door, scratching irritably at the back of his neck. His hair was too long, but he hadn't had time to sit down to a meal recently, let alone get a haircut.

The long table was half-full. Besides the cabinet officials who had met with the president throughout the crisis, the president had summoned the chairman of the Joint Chiefs of Staff. Beside the chairman sat the adjutant general for the Maryland National Guard, ramrod straight and apparently suffering from nerves in this exalted company.

"Morning," Ramsey Grant said, from across the table.

Wade nodded coldly and sat down. He was beginning to resent the attorney general, who had managed (so far) to sail above the fray. On Monday, Ramsey Grant had mentioned to the press that Charles Merriman could no doubt be prosecuted on any number of federal charges by this point, if he could only be brought into custody; but as sending the FBI in to arrest him would only risk additional bloodshed, he really couldn't recommend it. The press had immediately labeled him the Voice of Reason.

The president came briskly in. He was immaculately dressed, and the belligerence of the past days had settled into decision. Alexander Wade thought again, *We're going in.* He had spent the drive rehearsing arguments, and settled on the one most likely to sway the president. He had very little faith that he would succeed. He could feel a prickling of sweat around the back of his collar.

"Sit down," the president said, doing so himself. He was followed by George Lewis and his press secretary, who settled themselves into the empty chairs at his right "I'd expected to know the outcome of the trial in Richmond by now, but they've hung up on a procedural question. We should be hearing the verdict any minute."

Wade looked at him sharply. His voice was supremely confident, as though he knew a secret that would bring Virginia back in line. Wade held his tongue, waiting.

"Let me review the situation for you," the president said. "Since Virginia's declaration of independence on March nineteenth, the federal government has received none of the taxes due to us. According to Treasury, the state is now in arrears to the federal government." He nodded to the treasurer, who began to give the figures. Wade allowed his mind to wander, his eyes politely resting on his colleague. He had listened to most of the previous day's testimony in Jerry Tindell's trial. The judge had gleefully booted television cameras out of his courtroom, but he'd allowed wiring for sound, and several Virginia AM stations had carried the testimony live.

Wade didn't think there was much doubt about the verdict. The defense had argued that Jerry Tindell was guilty of robbing a dying man, but not of murder. The defense lawyer had also attempted to discredit Jamal Henderson. It was true that Henderson, high-voiced and inarticulate and stuttering in the throes of withdrawal, was not an impressive witness. But the physical evidence, admitted in defiance of all United States courtroom rules, was practically incontrovertible: the gun that killed Matthew Franklin had been discovered in the suitcase of Tindell's girlfriend. According to the defense, the real gunman had simply pitched the weapon out into the street and disappeared. Jerry Tindell had stubbed his toe on it, on his way back from manhandling Franklin's body, and had scooped it up as part of his loot. Wade, turning off the radio, thought: *Tindell's a dead man.* He'd meant to use Jerry Tindell's trial as a justification for the inevitable invasion. But the man was so clearly guilty that America would probably cheer at his conviction. Another good plan gone west.

He returned his attention to the conference table. The treasurer, still chronicling Virginia's debts to Washington, was interrupted by an aide who came into the military situation room and silently placed a single sheet of white paper in front of the president. The chief executive glanced down, and then placed his hand lightly over the black type. Into the silence he said clearly, "Jerry Tindell has been convicted of murder."

A slight rustle ran around the long table. Ramsey Grant leaned forward and asked, "Mr. President . . . what degree?"

"Just murder," George Lewis answered. "They've classified homicide into murder, accident, and self-defense. No mitigating degrees."

"And has he been sentenced to death?"

The president folded the paper in half. He said, "The judge cleared the courtroom for sentencing. But I refer you back to the code of the Commonwealth. There are no exceptions to the capital punishment clause. We have a serious case of human rights abuse happening right across the river. Alex, you said you wanted Merriman to make a mistake. Well, he's done it. We'll get Amnesty International to condemn this, and . . . oh, find some religious groups that object to capital punishment. George, get me a list."

George Lewis was scribbling solemnly on the pad of paper in front of him. The president looked over at his secretary of defense. His handsome face became suddenly dangerous, his eyebrows drawing together.

He said, ominously, "Tell me you're not going to say it again, Alex."

Alexander Wade could feel the eyes of the rest of the cabinet fixed on him. He scowled around the table. Treasury, Transportation, the NSA, the director of the FBI, Ramsey Grant himself—all waiting for him to point out the flaws in the president's logic. All of them, like spectators around a coliseum ring, electing him to fight the lions single-handed. The chairman of the Joint Chiefs of Staff was staring at his hands.

Wade said, "Mr. President, did you *listen* to the trial?"

"Yes. Why?"

"The man's a lowlife. He's guilty. There's no doubt about it. America's probably going to be thrilled that he's out of the way."

The president snapped, "*You* told me to wait until his trial."

"That was before I heard the evidence. And it was before we killed a Virginia civilian."

The president pointed an impeccably manicured finger at him.

"You know why that went wrong?" he demanded. "Because I listened to your advice. You told me to hit civilian targets. Well, we're not going to do *that* again. If Merriman proceeds with this execution, we'll strike directly against his armed forces. If they decide to execute, they'll give him Friday and Monday to appeal and schedule the death for Tuesday. That gives us a long weekend to prepare."

"What are you going to do?" Wade asked sourly. "March troops into Fredericksburg?"

"No. I'm going to take back the Richmond National Guard bases—the army and air guard bases in Sandston. They went with Merriman almost a hundred percent. We'll fly Maryland guard into Richmond International Airport. There's nobody there but Kenneth Balder's peacekeepers."

"And then what?"

"Liberate Richmond."

"How, exactly? There's not much liberating to do. Richmonders could all leave, if they wanted to."

"Not the Richmonders in quarantine," the president said with satisfaction.

"What quarantine?" Wade was aware of a sudden sharpening interest around the table.

"Listen carefully," the president said. His voice had the free relief of a man who had finally found a foothold on a very steep cliff. "This morning, I was informed that Virginia is planning to quarantine all infectious diseases. That includes AIDS, Mr. Secretary. Charles Merriman is going to restrict the freedom of HIV-positive patients. Can you imagine what a stink there'll be? It's tailor-made for us. Merriman's already instituted unconstitutional capital punishment. By taking back the guard bases and moving from there into Richmond, we can save AIDS victims from being the next group on Charles Merriman's hit list."

Wade said slowly, "I haven't heard anything about this. Who told you?"

"My information comes from a confidential source," the president said, virtuously. Wade glanced at the attorney general, whose face was studiously blank. "This hasn't hit the Virginia media yet, because Merriman's keeping it under wraps. I want it leaked to the national media today."

"And when are you planning this . . . attack?"

"As soon as we're sure the execution will take place. I want a preliminary plan from you and the chairman by tonight. I want to be able to move troops into Richmond at six hours' notice. General Johnson—" he inclined his head toward the Maryland officer, "assures me that the Maryland Guard will be proud to serve in the preservation of the freedoms enjoyed by all citizens of the United States. I'd prefer to use regular active duty forces, but the attorney general feels this would be a blatant violation of *posse comitatis* and give Merriman something legitimate to complain about."

Wade looked speculatively across the table. He said, "General, will your Maryland Guard be proud to march into Richmond and impose martial law on their neighbors?"

The adjutant general said, "Sir, that's their job."

"Yes, I'm aware of that. That's not what I asked. Are they willing to kill Virginia guardsmen who look like them and think like them and talk like them, except that they happen to be facing north while your men are facing south?"

George Lewis protested, "There's no need to take such an apocalyptic tone. We're not talking about a full-blown civil war."

"You are indeed," Alexander Wade said. "Because I'll tell you what'll happen when you march Maryland troops into Richmond." He held up one finger. "One. Your Maryland guardsmen get down there, sight their M-16s on the enemy, and then discover that some vestige of decency prevents them from killing the guy who was their fellow American three weeks ago. Anyone ever tell you, Mr. President, that ninety percent of the weapons retrieved from Civil War battlefields after the battles were *still loaded?* We'll have guardsmen staring at each other in the streets, in a stalemate even uglier than the one we have now. . . . because they'll be surrounded by civilians and any small incident, any accidental firing, could set off bloodshed." He held up a second finger. "Or they might get down there and start shooting without any moral dithering at all. In that case, we'll probably get Richmond back. We can arrest Merriman and force Virginia to pay its debts to Washington. And then we can settle down in Washington and go back to normal. Of course, to the south we'll have a sullen resentful Virginia under martial law, full of widows and orphans of guardsmen. Oh, and to the north we'll have a sullen resentful Maryland with its own war victims, demanding to know why other guardsmen from across the nation didn't share the dangers of dragging the prodigal Commonwealth back home. And I haven't even touched on North Carolina. . . . which, according to all the latest reports, is swarming with rural militiamen spoiling for a fight."

There was a short silence. The president said, "Alternatives, Mr. Secretary?"

"*Instant* alternatives?" Alexander Wade said, throwing his hands out in frustration, "I don't *have* any instant alternatives for you, Mr. President. You wanted this secession settled twenty-four hours after Merriman announced it. That man's been planning this for years. I think we *could* get Virginia back. But we'll have to retool the federal government's involvement with the Commonwealth. That will lead other states to want the same. It's going to be a long and delicate process, and there aren't going to be any immediate rewards." He added, mentally, *And your reputation as chief executive is based on immediate and decisive action.*

"There's no precedent for any of this," George Lewis snapped. "The Civil War settled this whole question. No state can hold the federal government hostage to its own peculiar demands. You're suggesting that we pitch out the Constitution and start over!"

"No, I'm not. Unlike Charles Merriman, I don't think the Constitution is fatally flawed. But it may be time to clear the accretions away. Have you ever considered that a nation might require a major overhaul, every hundred years or so?"

"Accretions!" Ramsey Grant said, in a tone of incredulity. "You're talking about a century's worth of constitutional law, Alex, not a disputed reading of Shakespeare!"

Alexander Wade shook his head, silently. He could see the president's mouth set in a straight grim line, and he could predict the next words out of the man's mouth. The prickle under his collar had turned into droplets of sweat, rolling down his back between his shoulder blades. The heaters in the Old Executive Building were going full blast, April sun notwithstanding.

"Mr. Secretary," the president said, "we have neither the authority nor the leisure to amend the Constitution of the United States in order to make Virginia happy. It's time to take Richmond back. You have two choices. You can support me in this venture. Or I will accept your resignation."

The cabinet members, the aides, the hovering staffers, all turned their heads back toward the secretary of defense. Wade thought, distinctly, *I should resign*. Somewhere underneath the knowledge that ground troops in Virginia would create a political nightmare was the conviction—unspoken, almost unformulated—that it was simply wrong to send American soldiers in to subdue other American soldiers by force, on American soil. Immediately after this, he thought, *Troops are going in whether I resign or not. I just need to shift this over onto different shoulders. Let Kenneth Balder and Charles Merriman appear the aggressors.*

He stood up.

"Sir," he said, "if you are determined to follow this course, I will do my best to present you with a workable plan. You've given me a very tight deadline, and I'd like your permission to return to the Pentagon immediately." The stifling air was beginning to distress him. He was having difficulty swallowing.

The president said cordially, "Certainly. No need to ask permission. I'd like to see you at six P.M. I'm addressing the nation at eight tonight." He rubbed his hands together. "And then we can finally show the American people some leadership."

BACK IN THE PENTAGON, Wade slammed the door of his office and ripped off his tie. He sat down and put his head in his hands. A bevy of aides and a handful of the Joint Chiefs of Staff and the Maryland adjutant general and Ramsey Grant were all waiting for his presence. He needed a quiet week to think this through. He had approximately ten minutes.

Freeing AIDS patients from confinement might be a noble cause, but it had two huge warts. He wasn't convinced it was true, to begin with. That tidbit had undoubtedly come from one of Ramsey Grant's informants, and the move for segregation could merely be at the rumor stage.

But even if the rumor turned out to be true, the deliverance of AIDS patients would only appear noble to that segment of America which was already frothing over Charles Merriman's fundamentalism. The conservatives who supported Merriman would probably be thrilled to see HIV infection subject to some sort of regulation.

His aide tapped on the door and said, "Sir, the Joint Chiefs of Staff are waiting—"

"Come in here and close the door," Wade ordered.

The aide stepped in. Wade said, "I've got a job for you."

"Sir?"

"Find me a fundamentalist to condemn Jerry Tindell's execution."

"Er . . . what *kind* of fundamentalist?"

"A religious one," Wade said impatiently. "A Christian. Someone who's well-known and respected and popular with conservatives. I want him making a strong anti-R.A.S. statement on the evening news."

The aide, who obviously had only a passing acquaintance with Christians of any kind, ventured, "You mean like a priest or something?"

"No, blast your eyes, someone like Billy Graham. Get on it. Ask Martha to help you; she's a Methodist. And get our press liaison to make sure the major networks cover it. Now I'll go see the joint chiefs."

He reached for his tie and reknotted it. A protesting evangelical would serve merely as a weak finger in a crumbling dike, but it was better than nothing at all. The joint chiefs would be waiting for him in the large conference room on the second floor. He was halfway down the hallway when the aide reappeared, puffing slightly.

"Find someone already?"

"No, sir, there's a report for you—"

"From who?"

"The Department of the Army. They think the Reformed American States Guard has mounted a takeover of an army guard weapons depot in North Carolina—"

"They *think?*"

"Sir, they lost contact with the depot six hours ago."

Wade halted in his footsteps and read the dispatch. The Fletcher weapons depot had abruptly broken off all communications at five-thirty in the morning. The army had been unsuccessfully trying to raise the base. No other Washington-loyal National Guard were nearby, but rumors of disturbance—yells and other odd noises at dawn—had already seeped out of Fletcher into the nearby towns.

Wade stood in the hallway and pondered, aware of the shifting impatient aide and the minutes ticking by him. A plan was beginning to percolate through the layers of caution in his mind.

"Okay," he said abruptly. "Tell the Joint Chiefs of Staff that I'll be right with them."

"Sir—"

"Take them some doughnuts. No. No, first find Allen for me and send him in."

He spun on his heel and went back to his office. By the time the assistant secretary arrived, the plan had taken full shape. Allen came in with his quick, decisive step and closed the door. He was holding a corned beef sandwich in his right hand.

"Listen," Alexander Wade said. "If we march all the Maryland Guard out of Maryland, like the president is insisting, what does that do to Maryland's defenses?"

Allen inquired, reasonably, "Who's going to attack Maryland?"

"Theoretically, then."

"Well theoretically, Washington itself would be more vulnerable without the extra layer of protection on the north—"

"So we'd be putting the capital in danger?"

"Yes, but there isn't any danger."

"Doesn't matter. Here's what we do. Tell the president that we'll march the Maryland National Guard into Richmond, but before we do that we've got to move some of the manpower still in Virginia back up to Washington, in case some Middle Eastern potentate decides that all the domestic confusion provides the perfect opportunity to launch a terrorist attack."

"Go on," Allen said.

"Then we move some of our military personnel up to Washington."

"Fly them?"

"No. Use ground vehicles."

"Why?"

"If you were Charles Merriman," Alexander Wade said, "would you let a heavily armed army division or two tromp through Virginia, up to Maryland, in clear preparation for an attack?"

"I might," Allen said. "Merriman's established a pretty clear policy of peaceful resistance, so far."

Wade held out the dispatch. "It appears that he's moving on to more forceful strategies," he said.

Allen read through the dispatch silently. When he reached the end, he said, "You're going to have to ask for volunteers, Alex. You're using these boys like goats on tethers."

"I don't for a moment think Charles Merriman will order a slaughter," Alexander Wade said impatiently. "I imagine that depot was taken without bloodshed. All I want him to do is mount some kind of a roadblock."

"That would be in line with his actions so far."

"The letter Merriman sent at the time of his declaration clearly stated that he would not block access to United States defenses located inside Virginia," Wade said. "If he won't let us take men out of our own bases, that's clear justification for moving on Richmond. Much better than Jerry Tindell's trial. We've got to protect our own national interests, after all. The American public will agree with that."

"What if Merriman doesn't block the convoy?"

"We've got to make the troops movement ominous enough so that he does." Wade thought of his psychological profiles with satisfaction. Merriman was most vulnerable on the point of his personal popularity. Wade would make sure the troop convoy went right by a major population center; Merriman was bound to stage a dramatic roadblock if he had enough audience.

"The president isn't going to like any more delays."

"No. And he won't accept them from me. I want *you* to propose this to the Joint Chiefs of Staff, and let *them* point out to the president that Washington needs additional defenses. Today's Thursday. The president wants to act on Tuesday. Let's move the men on Monday and hope for the best."

"What if you've read Merriman wrong?"

"The worst that could happen is that the troops would march straight up to Washington without interference, and I'd be in the same mess I am now."

"That's not the worst thing I can think of."

"What, then?"

"One of those militia groups might start taking potshots at your convoy."

"We've had almost no reports of militia activity in Virginia. Most of it seems to be restricted to North Carolina. Some in the Blue Ridge, but we'll plot the convoy path well away from the mountains. I'll go give the joint chiefs a lecture about the dangers of Middle Eastern terrorism. Go brush up on Fort Monroe. Or Fort Lee. Or Fort Pickett, maybe. Those are your best bets."

Allen said, accepting the commission, "You've got to give me at least half-an-hour."

"You've got it."

The younger man hesitated at the door. He said, again, "I'd check on those militia groups, if I were you—"

"I'll put someone on it," Wade said, absently. Allen disappeared, and the secretary of defense headed for the conference room. His mind was already working through its store of convincing tales about terrorist near-misses in and around Washington D.C.

WADE TOOK A COFFEE BREAK at six-thirty, and went back to his office to watch the evening news. Whatever strings his staff had pulled, they had successfully animated the proper marionettes. They had found him an articulate and deeply distressed Christian, a well-respected academician named Christopher Dillard, previously known for his strong stand against any form of racism. Dillard had been interviewed at his son's home in South Carolina. He stood, spare and strong and white-haired, in the neat suburban front lawn, as the news cameras rolled.

"Charles Merriman and Kenneth Balder have betrayed the true gospel of Christ. They have covered it over, drowned it in a legalistic sea of commands and regulations, and set themselves up as God's regents on earth. Only Christ has that authority. Yes, of course I believe in the law of God.

And I know that it can be enforced only by those who are pure themselves from any ambition or self-interest. Who can say that with honesty?" He shook his white head and said, "The Crusades have come to America. This is nothing but a blatant search for power, fronted by the cross of Christ."

In his office, Alexander Wade smiled with satisfaction. If he were any judge of character—if those profiles on his desk had any validity—those words would set Kenneth Balder and his chief even more firmly on their path toward destruction. And with any luck at all, evangelicals watching all over America would begin to doubt Merriman's righteous cause. It was a very small beginning, but small seeds produced great plants.

He hauled himself up, and prepared to face the half-convinced Joint Chiefs of Staff yet again. Two more hours, and he would carry his point. And the president's Tuesday morning invasion would be forestalled by Merriman's attack on a United States convoy on Monday.

CHAPTER 27

☆ ☆ ☆ ☆ ☆ ☆ ☆

Friday, April 12, 6 p.m.

MARGARET FRANKLIN STOOD IN THE LITTLE office at the back of the farmhouse, ripping newspaper articles off her bulletin board. Tacks detached themselves from the corkboard and rained onto the floor around her feet. She crumpled the photos and stories and all her careful records of Matthew's suspicions, one at a time, and stuffed them into the trashcan beside her.

Jerry Tindell had been convicted the day before. This morning, she had skipped her meditation time. It was hardly necessary. She'd been up all night, making cups of tea that cooled on the counter undrunk, pacing through the empty house and wrestling with her soul.

She hated what she was becoming. The conviction should have brought an end to her struggle. She had failed to prove the guard connection, but some logical part of her mind told her that she had done everything humanly possible. A jury of Jerry Tindell's peers had found him guilty of murder. Kenneth Balder had done what he could to bring justice about.

And yet she was still captive to the same throbbing guilt and weariness as before. The story wasn't over. It ought to be, but Matthew's ghost still haunted her. She had to face the truth. Kenneth Balder was right; her obsession over the case hadn't been because she wanted justice for Matthew, but because she wanted atonement for herself. And she could never atone for that lack of love. Her rules no longer worked. Fidelity, even after death, was never going to remove the guilt she still felt. She was helpless, and in that knowledge she had lashed out unjustly at the only man who had listened to her story. Twice now she had done that, wounding Kenneth Balder with her words because of sheer sick anger.

She went on destroying the board. *You thought the system could be reformed. You thought just laws would bring you peace.* Well, it hadn't worked. Peace was located somewhere else, not in the laws of the Commonwealth of Virginia.

The telephone on her desk began to ring. Margaret threw another crumpled ball of paper into the trash. For two days, reporters had been calling her for quotes. She'd quit answering the phone, letting the machine screen all her calls. Most of the time they hung up without leaving a message. The machine clicked on. Through the door that connected her office with the kitchen, she could hear her own muffled voice begin, "You've reached Franklin's Plants. I'm probably out in the greenhouses—"

The line disconnected. The machine whirred and reset. She wrenched the headline out of the board. *No Suspects in Fatal Shooting of National Guardsman.* Into the trashcan.

"You've reached Franklin's Plants. I'm probably out in the greenhouses—"

This time the caller did not hang up as quickly. A calm, recorded voice said, "Caller, you have reached an answering machine. Please hang up and try again. You will not be billed for this call."

Click. The words slowly registered on her. Taped operator assistance; someone was trying to place a collect call.

A collect call. She ran to the desk and grabbed for the telephone, but it buzzed in her ear. The caller had already hung up. She put the receiver hastily back on the cradle and watched it, her hand hovering nearby and her heart suddenly thumping. A minute passed, and another.

"Come on," she muttered. "Don't give up! I'm sitting right here. Dial it again."

The ring shrilled at her, and this time she snatched at it.

"Hello? I'm here—"

The taped voice said with maddening slowness, "You have a collect call. Caller, state your name."

"Mom!"

"Garrett, where are you?"

"If you will accept this call, press one or say 'Yes' at the sound of the tone."

"Yes!" Margaret yelled into the receiver. The voice said, politely, "Thank you."

"Garrett!"

"Mom, where have you been? I've called every time I could get to a phone, but I don't have any money or credit cards—I had to call collect—"

"I'm right here. Where are you?"

There was a little pause. Garrett said, "I'm at a Seven–Eleven in somewhere called—er—Gaston. North Carolina. A town and a lake, somewhere near the border. I've been hitchhiking, but hardly anyone wants to pick me up—"

"I'll come get you."

"No! Mom, if anyone's watching you, they might follow you. They might arrest me. I didn't do it, Mom."

"What happened?"

"I can't tell you here. I'm on a pay phone. Someone's waiting."

Margaret thought rapidly. She said, "Listen, I can get away and be sure that no one's following me. I'll wait until after dark. I could go around to the interstate through the back roads. Are you near 95?" She propped the telephone between shoulder and ear and rummaged frantically through her drawers. Surely there was a map in this bottom drawer somewhere? It seemed to be stuffed with every other sort of useless paper.

"I think so," Garrett said uncertainly. "But what'll I do? I'm a fugitive. If a guard patrol sees me—"

"Wait a minute," Margaret said. "Wait. Hold on." Old seed catalogs, an election mailing from last year's delegate race, a county map of New Kent . . . here it was. She snatched the Virginia map out and flattened it on top of the receipts. Fortunately it had a narrow slice of North Carolina at the bottom. She ran her finger down I-95 and found Gaston, on the shores of Lake Gaston just below Virginia.

"I've got it," she said. "It would take me two hours to get down there, and it won't be dark for another hour. Three hours. Can you wait three hours?" She could hardly bear that he should hang up and disappear again.

Garrett said, "I don't want to stay here, Mom. I need to get moving again."

"Is someone chasing you?" Margaret said, incredulous.

"Yes—"

"Can you get another ride, do you think?"

Garrett's voice, exhausted and hoarse, was starting to edge toward hysteria. She recognized the sound; she'd been there herself, this past week.

"I don't know. I can try—"

"Okay, darling. Listen to me. Route 48 runs northeast out of Gaston, goes across 95, and joins with Route 301 at a place called Pleasant Hill. Got that?"

"Pleasant Hill."

"Okay. If you can get a ride, hitchhike to Pleasant Hill and go north on 301 to the Virginia border, and ask them to drop you off right at the state line. That'll keep you off the interstate. I'll get off 95 at Emporia and drive south on 301." She took a breath. "If you can't find a ride, start to walk north along Route 48. Stay on the left-hand side of the road. If I don't see you at the Virginia border, I'll drive toward Gaston on 48. I'll look for you. I'll be in the nursery truck."

"Yes," Garrett said, sounding slightly dazed.

"I'll find you," Margaret said forcefully.

"Yes. Mom . . . you won't tell Kenneth Balder where I am, will you?"

"No, darling."

"I'm going to have to leave Virginia."

"Then I'll help you." She remembered the words of that Defense Department aide, reassuring and concerned. *The Virginia Guard isn't a good place for your son right now. We'll see that he gets out of the guard and well-launched on a second career. Or college, if he'd prefer.* She would do anything necessary to see that offer renewed. She pushed away the memory of Ken's voice, begging her to stay in Virginia.

Garrett said, "Mom, there's one more thing. Jerry Tindell—he didn't do it. He didn't kill Dad. We've got to tell Balder about it."

"*What?* You found proof?"

There was another silence. She could faintly hear cars passing by in the background. Garrett said wearily, "I can't talk. There's someone waiting for the phone. I've got to go."

"I'm on my way, son."

"Yes."

"I love you."

"Okay, Mom."

He hung up. She put the telephone down and stood up. She could still see the distant pines, although they'd grown darker. It would be at least half-an-hour until full night. She needed shoes, a jacket, her purse. She headed through the kitchen toward the stairs. She had her foot on the bottom step when the telephone rang again; and she turned at once and ran back through the door and caught the receiver off the hook.

"Garrett?"

She had just enough time to realize the error. Ken's voice said, "Maggie?"

Margaret stood with the receiver in her hand. He was waiting on the other end. She wanted nothing more than to say: *I'm sorry. I accused you because I wanted to hurt you. It was inexcusable.* Garrett's voice had been close to panic; if the R.A.S. knew where he was, he would be arrested at once.

After a long moment, she put the receiver gently back. She was in her room when the telephone rang for the fourth time. She put her jacket on, hunting for her billfold, and eventually the ringing stopped. Her eyes were full of tears.

IT WAS FULL NIGHT in Emporia. Margaret exited onto Route 301 and slowed, her eyes searching both sides of the highway in case Garrett had decided to walk. She was terrified that she might miss him in the darkness.

She drove along 301, straining her eyes for the sign that marked the state line between Virginia and North Carolina. When her headlights finally illuminated the WELCOME TO NORTH CAROLINA message, she slammed on her brakes and pulled to the side of the road and jumped out of the truck.

The black air was cold in her lungs.

"Garrett?"

This was a deserted stretch of road. She was conscious of her own breathing, loud in the silence.

"Garrett?"

There was no answer. She swallowed down the sick feeling in her throat, and turned back toward the truck, when a movement in the trees beyond the sign caught her eye. Garrett stepped out of the brush. He was just beyond the light cast by the headlights. She could see the familiar expanse of his shoulders and the shadow of his dark hair. He seemed to be swaying slightly on his feet.

"Garrett!"

He came slowly into the light, and attempted a smile.

"Mom, he said, "I'm kind of a mess."

Margaret stared at him, her hand to her mouth. His arms were scratched and bruised. He was wearing his guard camouflage without the insignia, but the shirt was torn and another rip gaped below his right knee. He was limping, and there were traces of blood in his hairline.

"Are you hurt? Should I take you to the hospital?"

Garrett shook his head. "I washed the worst of it off before I tried hitchhiking," he said. "None of the cuts are very deep. I got most of them running through brush."

"Your leg—"

"Just bruised," he said. "Someone shot at me, and I dived into the ground and hit a log with my knee. Don't hug me, Mom, I hurt all over."

Margaret drew a deep breath. "Get in the truck," she said. "Let's get out of here."

Garrett climbed stiffly in and slammed the door behind him. She got in the driver's side. Closer to him, she could see that his skin was white with exhaustion, and his young face was dragged into deep lines. He leaned his head back while she restarted the truck and reversed direction, heading back toward Emporia.

"Are you hungry?"

"I'm starved. Mom, I've been hitchhiking since dawn yesterday, I haven't slept, and I didn't have any money to buy food. Some guy who drove me to Roxboro bought me a cup of coffee and a ham biscuit this morning. I could've eaten twenty of them."

She bought him three hamburgers at an Emporia drive-through, and got back on the interstate, listening to him tell the story between huge bites. Bill James was a new name to her; Garrett's stumbling description drew a picture of a man without fear or conscience, a man with an almost fantastic intolerance for authority. By the time he told the story of the raid on the guard armory, she was physically shaking with fear for her son.

"You took part in a raid on a United States military installation!"

"Mom, that's nothing compared with murder."

"I know you didn't do that."

"But I touched him. I must've left a mark on him somewhere."

"Yes . . . a thumbprint on his belt."

"Well, I didn't even fire on the armory. I was just there." Garrett wiped his mouth on the back of his hand. He said, "What are they going to do with Jerry Tindell?"

"He was sentenced to execution. Thursday afternoon."

"Were you there?"

"Yes, I was."

Garrett gave her a quick glance, unreadable in the dark.

"They didn't investigate the guard?"

"They interviewed everyone except for you and Clint Larsen. But without either of you, nothing useful came out."

"When are they gonna do it?"

"Tuesday, unless the judge grants a retrial. The defense had Friday and the weekend to prepare an appeal, and the judge considers it on Monday."

"That's pretty quick!"

"Ken says capital punishment is only a deterrent when it is carried out swiftly." She dragged her mind away from Kenneth Balder. Garrett said, "You've got to go tell the judge what I told you. All about Bill James and the militia and what Dad was going to do."

"I already tried. It's only hearsay. *You've* got to tell him."

"I'm not going anywhere near a judge. If they'll execute him, Mom, they'll execute me."

"But Tindell—"

"I can't!"

They drove in silence for a while. Margaret began to see signs for Petersburg, and pulled into the right-hand lane to take advantage of the 295 bypass.

She said, concentrating on the road, "Garrett . . . are you sure of this? About Bill James?"

"Yes. I was there. He tried to kill me, and I *know* he killed Dad. You've got to find a way for me to testify without actually showing up in court."

She glanced over. His face, in the intermittent gleam of oncoming headlights, was intent and serious; Matthew's face. She sighed, looking back at the road.

"Well," she said. "I could call the judge tomorrow. I won't tell him I know where you are. I'll make it a hypothetical question. I don't know if he'll see me on a Saturday. You can stay at the farm tonight. No one will know you're there. I will try to get you out of Virginia. But you're guilty in the eyes of the United States too. I'll have to call the Defense Department. It may take some time."

"What if Kenneth Balder comes out to the farm?"

"He won't," she said. Her voice was unexpectedly sharp. Garrett didn't answer. When she looked back over at him a few minutes later, he had leaned his head back against the seat and his face was lost in shadows; he had gone to sleep.

SATURDAY MORNING SHE PLACED A CALL to the judge's chambers. An answering machine was on duty. She left three messages, one after the other, and was rewarded by a phone call at noon. Garrett had awakened early, showered off his grazes, eaten a tremendous breakfast, and staggered back to bed. She'd put him in the small upstairs room with all the shades drawn and the door locked.

"Mrs. Franklin? Judge Straus here."

"Sir, I've got to see you right away. About the Tindell execution."

Children were shouting behind the judge's voice. He said, "My family's here. Three grandchildren. Can we discuss this on the phone?"

Margaret stretched the cord across the kitchen and sat down. She'd built a fire in the old wood stove and the sun poured down outside the windows, but her teeth were chattering with cold.

"I don't know how to start this. . . ." she said, ". . . it concerns my son."

"Yes? He didn't testify, as I recall."

"No, sir. He deserted from the air guard last week and disappeared. I— well, I heard from him, and he's found out that someone else was involved in Matthew's murder."

"Who?"

She repeated Garrett's story. There was a long, thoughtful silence on the other end. Judge Straus said, finally, "Where is your son?"

"He's on the run," Margaret said evasively.

"He was involved in the murder of that guardsman at the Yorktown Naval Weapons Station?"

"He didn't do that, sir."

Another silence.

"Mrs. Franklin, while we want to make sure that Jerry Tindell is treated justly, I can't allow you to accuse another man on the basis of a theory proposed by your son, who won't testify because he is himself suspected of a crime."

"No, sir, I understand that. But couldn't you at least delay the execution, until this other claim is checked out?"

"If your son comes and gives a sworn deposition, certainly."

"He's afraid he'll be arrested."

"I'm sorry, but he probably will."

"There's no chance of . . . some kind of deal?"

Judge Straus' voice gained a sudden edge.

"Bargaining away guilt," he said, "is an unjust process. It has nothing to do with guilt or innocence. Bargains don't belong in any trial. It was my understanding, Mrs. Franklin, that you were ready to see such travesties of justice done away with. Are you telling me that you're now ready to go back to the old ways of American courts?"

"Sir—"

"If you have contact with your son again, tell him to give himself up. If he's innocent, the truth will come out. If he's guilty, he has no right to accuse another man of murder."

Margaret was silenced. The judge said, "You'll be informed of the outcome of any appeal, Mrs. Franklin. Is there anything else?"

"No, sir." She was aware of an unfamiliar feeling of shame.

"Good-bye, then."

He hung up rather abruptly. Margaret sat for a long time with the receiver in her lap, thinking hard. If she could reach that aide . . . he had left his name and telephone number on the answering machine message that she had erased. She stood up and went to the telephone on the wall and dialed for directory assistance.

Half-an-hour later, she had been shuttled through the Pentagon switchboard, from receptionist to secretary and through several aides. She was on hold. She heard footsteps on the stairs. Garrett came warily around the corner, barefoot and wearing his old sweats. Margaret watched him check carefully out each window before he went to the refrigerator, and her heart twisted painfully in her chest.

A voice said in her ear, "Mrs. Franklin?"

"Yes. Margaret Franklin. Er . . . are you the person I talked to last week?"

Garrett retrieved an egg carton and went to the stove for a frypan. The voice said "This is Allen Preszkoleski, Mrs. Franklin. I'm an assistant to the secretary of defense. I apologize for the delay, but I had to review the details. You were offered refuge two weeks ago, is that correct?"

"Yes. You said you'd help my son get out of the guard."

"I see from the information we have here that, at the time, your son—Garrett Franklin, is that correct?—was innocent of any offense, apart from obeying Charles Merriman's orders in defiance of the United States."

"That's all he ever did. You promised to help us."

"Yes, but the situation has changed somewhat. There are two warrants out for Mr. Franklin's arrest on suspicion of homicide."

"I can tell you how it happened—"

Allen Preszkoleski said apologetically, "At this point, Mrs. Franklin, there's really nothing the Defense Department can do. When the illegal call-out of the guard began, the Defense Department was naturally concerned to help service personnel get out of Virginia. Now, of course, your son is involved in a criminal proceeding. I can refer you to the attorney general's office. They would be the ones to handle any sort of plea bargain."

"If you were to ask Secretary Wade—"

"I can have the receptionist transfer you," the voice said, inexorably. The live sound of connection was replaced by silence. Garrett stirred his scrambled eggs, watching his mother apprehensively. Margaret attempted to keep her face blank. *They don't need us any more*, she thought, *and I've lost any leverage I had. I've sacrificed my son by staying in Virginia.*

"Department of Justice."

Margaret swallowed and said, "My son needs to get out of Virginia."

"Another one?" the voice said wearily. "Is he accused of a crime?"

"Yes, but he didn't do—"

"In Virginia or in the United States?"

"Er—well, both, actually—"

"I'm going to give you the name and extension of one of the attorneys in the Office of Legal Counsel," the voice said mechanically. "You can call on Monday morning and discuss your case. It will take approximately three to five days to arrange for extradition. They're very busy. In the case of arrest by the Commonwealth, the United States will request that the accused be extradited to Washington for trial—"

"But he has to get out *now!*"

"Ma'am, the Commonwealth doesn't process arrests on Sunday, and even if your son is picked up he won't go to trial for a week. So far Virginia has granted all extradition requests. Please call on Monday morning."

The Justice Department representative hung up. She replaced the receiver slowly.

"Well?" Garrett demanded.

"I can't get you out. Not legally. You could try to sneak out. . . ."

"And get shot? And what would I do then? Stay on the run for the rest of my life? If I ever say who I am, I'll get arrested."

"Better by the United States than by the Reformed American States. The U.S.A. won't execute you."

"No," Garrett said, "they'll just throw me in jail for the rest of my life for desertion and treason and second-degree murder. And I can't sit here and do nothing while they execute somebody who might not be guilty. I've got to say what I know." He yanked the pan off the burner. His chin was set into a stubborn line. The dogged determination to do right was Matthew's. When he was in the grip of that emotion, the likeness to his father came strongly out.

"Mom," he said, "you've got to go see Kenneth Balder Monday morning."

"You think he'll help you get off? He's in charge of enforcing those laws, Garrett."

"Yes. But he'll listen to *you*. He'll believe you if you tell him about Bill James. He'll know what we can do."

Margaret looked at her son, despairingly. She had read passion in Ken's eyes, but she was frightened of the streak of ruthlessness that she had known in him. She was not at all sure that the passion would overbalance the ruthlessness. She said slowly, "Ken is different than he was. But I don't know how deep the change goes. He has never been a man who made exceptions."

"It's the only way out I have left," Garrett said. "Did, er—did you two have a fight?"

Margaret laughed despite herself. He said, "Sorry, Mom. None of my business."

"No. Garrett, darling, I wish I were still twenty and I could describe all my mistakes as a lover's quarrel. It goes far beyond that. I was exorcising an old ghost, and I said the cruelest things I could. It didn't work. I am . . . ashamed to go ask him for help."

She had always resisted the temptation to make a confidant out of her son, and Garrett was turning red over this sudden revelation. He said awkwardly, "Mom, I'm sorry. I really am. But it's the only way."

"Yes, I know." She watched him dump the scrambled eggs onto a plate. "I'll go talk to him," she said at last. "Monday morning. If he'll see me."

CHAPTER 28

☆ ☆ ☆ ☆ ☆ ☆ ☆

Monday, April 15, 8 A.M.

KENNETH BALDER SAT IN HIS OFFICE with work stacked around him, and two secretaries taking his telephone calls, and a line of Virginia officials waiting outside his door. After years of writing and wishing and speech-making, he finally had the power to enforce the laws of God. He held righteousness in both hands. Even the adjutant general had asked his permission before sending troops down to investigate that rumored disturbance at Fletcher, out near the North Carolina mountains. He was second only to Charles Merriman; and it was a horrifying success, dry as chalk-dust to the fingertips. He had been entrusted with God's kingdom on earth. He had corrupted it with his own selfish wants and fooled himself into believing he was acting for justice.

And all the time he had thought he could win Maggie back. Even after the trial's start last Monday, he'd held onto that dying hope. But hope had drawn its final breath late Friday afternoon. He'd dialed her number one more time. She had finally answered the phone. He said her name, and she paused for a long moment, and hung up with finality.

Sitting behind his desk, listening to the dial tone, he knew with horrible clearness that he had authorized the arrest of Jerry Tindell for Maggie's sake. He had acted improperly, against his conscience and against God's standard of righteousness, and he wasn't worthy of his position.

He dragged himself back to his duties, and blinked at his appointment

schedule. The superintendent of the Surrey County school system was first
on the list. He buzzed the secretary and said, "Alice."

"Yes?"

"Send 'em in."

"Yes, sir."

The door swung open onto the anteroom, already lined with people.
He hauled himself to his feet and saw Margaret in the far doorway, her
eyes drawn to him by the opening door. He was almost deafened by the
sudden drumming of blood in his ears, and he was afraid he had turned
scarlet. The secretary's voice drifted in behind the Surrey superintendent.

"The chief of staff already has a full schedule today. If you'd like to
leave your name, I could work you in tomorrow."

"Alice!" he called through the open doorway.

"Yes?"

"I'll see Mrs. Franklin this morning."

"Yes, sir." Alice's voice was martyred. "Take a seat, Mrs. Franklin. I'll
try to squeeze you in."

The Surrey superintendent held out a friendly hand. The door swung
closed behind him, blocking Margaret and the anteroom from view.

"Dr. Balder, I'm very pleased to finally meet you. I'd like to discuss our
educational goals with you. I have a few specific questions about these
religion classes—"

He shook the man's hand and forced himself to focus. He thought, halfway through the Surrey superintendent's first question: *What an incredibly
boring man.* He used far too many words. Balder could see the questions coming a mile off, and he had to sit here and wait courteously until the
superintendent squeezed the final drops of honey out of each ornate long-
winded phrase. He could never remember, afterward, anything he had said in
answer. . . . something about absolute morality and the necessity of teaching children their responsibility to a transcendent standard. . . . words he
could reel out by now with absolutely no mental effort involved. It seemed
hours before the man thanked and bowed himself away. He was on his feet
a split second before the superintendent had quite finished saying good-bye.

"Alice, I'll see Mrs. Franklin now."

"But the clerk of the Seventh District—"

"I'm sure the clerk will excuse us. We're still preparing to respond to the appeal from Jerry Tindell's trial."

He gathered that no one was quite sure what this meant; but no one argued with him. He held the door open for Margaret. She walked into the room past him, and he closed the door and came back to stand behind his desk. She remained in the middle of the floor. She was wearing a navy blue coat and skirt, much more elegant than anything he had yet seen her in. Silver jewelry almost the same color as her eyes lay against her fine skin.

"Will you sit down?" he said at last. A wild expectation was leaping up inside him. Margaret looked around her and selected a chair, and sat down into it. Her whole body was stiff with tension.

"What is it, Maggie?"

"Garrett," she said. "It's about Garrett. Ken, I need your help."

She still hadn't looked directly at him; her gray eyes were fastened steadily on a point beyond his head. Kenneth Balder took his own seat, slowly. He felt the unreasonable surging hope begin to seep out of him. When it had entirely gone, he said, "Do you know where he is?" He was amazed by the matter-of-factness in his own voice.

"That's not the problem," Margaret said. "He has proof of the guard involvement in Matthew's death. Ken, I know you must be sick of my telling you this—"

"Go on," he said.

"He was asleep in his tent out at the Naval Weapons Station—"

Kenneth Balder listened to the story of Garrett's militia recruitment, and his suspicions of his militia companions. Margaret's clear low voice was temporarily empty of any hostility, as it had been for those brief days before Jerry Tindell's trial. He had almost managed to win her back. He let his eyes stay on her face, a growing misery inside him. He could barely keep his mind on the narrative.

"So they marched him off to Fletcher," Margaret said, "and mounted an attack on the weapons depot—"

Balder's attention abruptly returned to her story.

"They did *what?*"

"Took the depot back," she repeated. "But Garrett didn't even fire a shot. He ran while they were all shooting, and got out to the interstate and hitchhiked north."

"Was anyone killed?"

Margaret hesitated, twisting her hands in her lap.

"I don't know," she said, finally. It was clearly a lie for Garrett's sake, but Balder refrained from comment. His mind offered, *She doesn't trust you, of course. She never did.* He pushed the barbed thought away and picked up the telephone.

"Excuse me for a moment," he said. "Alice, get me the adjutant general, would you?"

Margaret watched him silently. The adjutant general answered his telephone almost at once. Balder, conscious of Margaret's stare, said, "Joe, has the guard reached Fletcher yet?" The adjutant general had asked two days ago to send guardsmen to Fletcher. Balder had delayed authorization until this morning, reluctant to thin their border force so close the first R.A.S. execution.

"They ought to be there momentarily," the adjutant general said. "Glad you called, Ken; I've got another problem—"

"Hold onto it for a minute. I have an eyewitness to the depot disturbance."

Margaret half-rose from her chair, protesting. He shook his head at her and mouthed, *Trust me.* She settled back into her chair, her hands twisted in her lap.

"What happened?" the adjutant general demanded.

"A militia group took it over. Apparently a combination of the Regulators from North Carolina and a group from rural Virginia, acting together."

"Took it over? Bloodshed?"

Balder said, temperately, "I don't know. I suspect so. But they've got more firepower than your guardsmen. You get hold of them right away and tell them to tread carefully, unless they want a bloodbath down there."

"We might try starving them out first," the adjutant general offered.

"That's not all. There's another nest of them up in the mountains."

"The same group?"

"Yes."

There was a little pause. The adjutant general said, "Ken, if you *want* a bloodbath, the best way to get one is to send the National Guard up in the mountains to run a well-armed militia out of a hiding place."

"No need to root them out. But I want to know where they are, and what direction they move in next. We can't let them wander at will all through Virginia and North Carolina."

"I could send a chopper up to look," the adjutant general said dubiously. "Carefully, though. These men have military weapons and supplies."

"Right. I'll get on it. The other problem—"

"Yes?" Balder said, restraining his impatience.

"I'm getting reports from the National Guard posted around Fort Pickett. Pickett's on the move. Trucks have been going in and not coming back out. We've searched the vehicles. No weapons. Sometimes food and supplies, but sometimes the trucks are just empty. And lots of activity inside the base."

Balder swiveled his chair around to look at the map posted on his right. "Can you supplement the Fort Pickett border guard at all?"

The adjutant general sighed audibly. "It'll spread us even thinner," he said, "but I'll see what I can do."

"Let Charles know. And keep me informed."

"Yes, of course."

Balder hung up. Margaret was still watching him anxiously. He said, "The Regulators are a violent unpredictable group, Maggie. We've got to keep tabs on them, but Garrett doesn't need to be named. The other problem ought to be presented to Judge Straus."

"I called him Saturday. He won't listen unless Garrett appears and makes a sworn statement."

Kenneth Balder scratched absently at the edges of his cast. His mind leapt instantly to the far end of this dilemma. He knew already that Garrett would be arrested as soon as he showed his face in Richmond; and he and Merriman had written strong language into the code that would bar any sort of plea bargain.

He said abruptly, "What do you want me to do, Maggie?"

Margaret flushed. She said, producing the words with difficulty, "I thought—if you spoke to the judge yourself—"

"I might be able to pull some strings?"

He was suddenly enormously angry with her. She had spent two years fighting the elaborate system of string-pulling that had set Jerry Tindell free. He had cut the strings for her, and ruined his own prospects of happiness in the meantime. She ought to trust him now. Instead she had accused him of living a continual lie, and now she was asking him for one final intervention. It was wrong, unjust, unfair, and unlike the woman he had known. He whirled his chair abruptly away from her and bent his head over. He wanted to lash out at her with the truth: *You were never interested in justice for Matthew. Only in satisfying yourself.* He ached to say it. His tongue was tied by the knowledge of his own untrustworthy motivations, his own selfish graspings. A slow, calm stream of thought gradually penetrated through the raging torrents in his mind. *If she loved you, would you be so angry?* And in a single moment of clarity, he saw the answer. He was infuriated not by the request, but because she had come to him only for his help. In that brief unclouded glimpse of himself, he asked, *Do I think Garrett Franklin is innocent?* and found a true answer.

Behind him, Margaret's voice was thick with tears. She said, "Ken, I can't turn Garrett over to the courts. He can't stay here; I'm afraid someone in that militia may find out where he is. I'll—I'd do anything to get the charges dropped. If you want, I'll—"

"No!" he snapped. "Don't say it. You'll shame us both." He fought for control over his face and voice. In another moment he was able to turn his chair back toward her, with some semblance of normality.

"He's at the farm with you, isn't he?" he asked.

Margaret met his eyes. Her own glance changed as she read his face.

"Yes," she said baldly.

"Go home and watch over him. Judge Straus may still grant Tindell a retrial for another reason. I won't know the outcome of the appeal until this afternoon. But if he upholds the execution, I'll do what I can to get Garrett's testimony into the record without bringing him to Richmond. I promise you. If nothing else, I'll get both of you out of Virginia." He didn't trust himself to say any more than that. He could send the two of them into Washington, and get every federal charge against Garrett dropped, with a single word to Alexander Wade's office. But he could barely bring himself to consider the sacrifice that would be demanded in return.

"Go home," he said again. Margaret rose from her chair, silently. At the door she hesitated.

"Ken," she said, "are you doing this just for me?"

"No," he said wearily. "I'm doing it because this whole revolution has gone wrong, somewhere. I'm just trying to put things right."

"Ken, I—I never gave you the chance to tell me about the letters. I was too angry. I had no right to carry that same anger against you for twenty-five years."

He quelled the words that rose to his lips. It was all over, all gone; he could never recapture those days before his conviction. No promised land waited for him. He said, "Go home, Maggie. It doesn't matter anymore."

He didn't watch her go out. He lifted his telephone and said, "Alice, I want half-an-hour of quiet."

"But I've got the clerk—"

"If he doesn't want to wait, reschedule him."

"But I've already—"

"Alice!"

He hung up on her final protest. They could all wait for half-an-hour, while he had his own encounter with Apollyon. Pilgrim had been lucky. The Evil One was an easier enemy than one's own soul.

HE HAD WATCHED Christopher Dillard on the evening news Friday night, and recognized the strategy. Washington was determined to change public perception before attempting to change reality. If he were to walk out of the Reformed American States now, Washington would welcome him with open arms as a spokesman against Merriman's revolution. The Justice Department would certainly grant Garrett's freedom, if he asked it as a condition. And that would be the end of the kingdom and the power and the glory for Kenneth Balder. The end of God's kingdom on earth.

A whole series of remembered doubts rose to his mind. Merriman's efforts to manipulate him from the very beginning. John Cline's inclusion in the administration—done solely to muster another level of support, regardless of whether Cline's viewpoint actually lined up with the law of God. Even Tindell's arrest; Merriman wanted capital punishment, and he knew Balder had good reasons to authorize the arrest. Merriman's refusal to tamper with tobacco production. Merriman's grandstanding on the North Carolina border that had ended with a bullet through Balder's arm. Merriman's insistence on broadcasting the pictures of the bloody corpse sprawled under the generating station.

He had continually pushed away the thought that this kingdom had at its core not the Almighty, but simply Charles Merriman, bent on carrying out his own righteous purposes at any cost. Was all this worth protecting?

And yet the thought of leaving it caused him physical pain, like a crushing weight on his lungs. With one part of his mind, he thought: *No human leader can be trusted with God's kingdom on earth.* And yet another voice kept insisting: *We almost did it. If we keep trying, we can still set everything right.*

He couldn't bear the silence any more. He leaned forward to call for his next appointment.

AT NOON, HE WAS ABRUPTLY SUMMONED to the governor's suite. He pushed away his lunch with a grimace and went around the gallery, toward the gold lettering that read *The Governor's Office.*

The adjutant general and Merriman were both waiting for him. As soon as he stepped through the door, Merriman said, "They're trying to forestall the execution, Ken. Washington's determined to interfere."

"What've they done?" He moved to the small sitting area at the far end of Merriman's office and lowered himself onto the sofa. His bones ached with weariness.

"They're preparing to march out of Fort Pickett," the adjutant general said. He sat down on one of the armchairs, facing Balder across the coffee table, his hands knotted on his knees. "I moved two guard divisions north of Pickett—"

"Why are they marching out?" Balder demanded.

Merriman remained standing, his hands clasped behind his back. He said, "According to the Department of Defense, Fort Pickett will be evacuated at six P.M. tonight, and the personnel moved north."

"For what purpose?"

"We guaranteed the United States full access to its defenses," the governor said. "Apparently they've chosen the day before our first execution to exercise this option."

Momentarily sidetracked, Balder said, "Was the appeal denied?"

"Haven't heard yet. I wouldn't think there's much doubt. As to Fort Pickett—"

"I say we close them down until after the execution," the adjutant general said. "Tell them they can evacuate all the personnel they want on Tuesday night."

Balder shook his head and said reasonably, "If you guaranteed the United States access, Charles, you've got to let them shift their personnel."

Merriman took a turn on the carpet.

"Or you'll violate your word," Balder added. "And the Ninth Commandment."

"Huh," Merriman said, sounding unappreciative. The adjutant general protested, "But we can't let five hundred United States soldiers come out of Fort Pickett, armed to the teeth. There's no guarantee they're going north. I haven't noticed that Washington pays much attention to the Ninth Commandment."

Merriman walked to the window and looked out at the April landscape.

"Dogwood's finally coming out," he said, absently, and lapsed into silence. Balder gave him an apprehensive glance, but Merriman appeared sunk in thought.

He said instead, to the adjutant general, "What did you find at the weapons depot?"

"A right mess," the adjutant general said gloomily. "Four dead North Carolina guardsmen in a pile outside the front gates; and it's only a matter of time before that hits the national press, although we've managed to keep it out of the news so far. As a press secretary, Jim Macleod's worth his weight in diamonds. We've sealed up the whole area tight. But there's a slew of militiamen holed up inside, and sooner or later some reporter's going to get a whiff of it. They're making a lot of noise. Occasionally they pitch a grenade over the fence and yell something about treachery and world domination. We're sitting at a healthy distance waiting for them to get hungry. Unfortunately they've got a warehouse full of MREs. As for the rest of them—" he shook his head, "—we're still looking. I drew a straight line back from Fletcher to the mountains and started the choppers there. Nothing yet. They've got better camouflage than I expected—or else they've run."

"Four dead guardsmen," Merriman observed, from the window. "That could be catastrophic for us."

"Not to mention their families," Kenneth Balder remarked.

"Yes," Merriman said, "well, that's a bit out of our power to heal."

He turned around from the daylight. His dark mobile face was drawn into lines of concentration.

"Listen," he said. "Our best option is to cooperate. First of all, Joe, we let the Fort Pickett guys out—"

The adjutant general made a noise of protest, but Merriman waved an impatient hand. "Ken's right," he said. "We've got to honor our agreement. We let them out. But we tell the Department of Defense that we have a known militia group on the prowl for weapons, and so we won't allow Washington to bring weapons out into Virginia until we have these guys under lock and key. They can remove all the personnel they want, but they've got to leave the weapons under lock and key in Fort Pickett so that the militias don't try to waylay them and steal the weapons on the march out. Then we make sure that we don't pick up the militia until Wednesday morning, after the execution." He paused. "Then we'll ship the armaments out—"

"The Defense Department isn't going to let us anywhere near their weapons," protested the adjutant general.

"We'll work it out. We'll ask for an independent observer from Britain or Canada. Or the United States could appeal to the UN."

Balder said slowly, "Why would they march unarmed personnel through R.A.S. territory? Surely they don't have that level of trust in our word?"

"Why shouldn't they?" Merriman demanded. "I haven't made an aggressive move since we declared independence. I'm fully committed to a nonviolent resolution of our differences."

"Will you pull the guard back and let them out?"

"I'll pull back the western line, yes. I won't let them march straight north; that would take them right past Richmond. But I'll let them go west out 460 and then north on 29, all the way up to the border. The Defense Department can bring in all the impartial observers it wants. We're not going to take them prisoner on the way."

"You'll make them sitting ducks," Balder warned. "We have no idea where the rest of that militia division is."

Merriman shook his head. "The Regulators are on the run. They'll stay in the mountains, not come east. Joe, get back on the line with Pickett and give them our conditions. If they want to move out at six P.M., we'll have to arrange the terms right away."

"Washington will never agree to those terms," Balder said.

"We'll see," Merriman said, with supreme confidence.

"Perhaps we should delay the execution."

"Why?"

Balder glanced at the adjutant general, who took the hint and rose at once. "I'll get to it," he said.

Merriman waited until the door closed behind him and demanded, "Now what?"

"Margaret Franklin's son called her from some unknown place, and told her the guard deserters had joined up with this same militia, and that one of the leaders as good as admitted he was involved with Matthew Franklin's murder."

"How so?"

Balder told the third-hand story. When he reached the end, Merriman shook his head.

"Hearsay and speculation," he said decisively.

"Reasonable doubt," Balder countered.

"No. Tindell's case is as close to airtight as I've ever seen."

"But there's no harm in delaying while we check this out."

"No harm? Don't you understand what swept this revolution into popularity? The promise of swift justice and a sure standard. The people are tired of laws that constantly shift and change. They're sick of leaders who perpetually change their minds and platforms. They've welcomed the law of God because it is the same forever. It can be counted on. Delaying the execution while we chase a rabbit would be an admission that the code is no more efficient than the system we've rejected."

"I didn't think efficiency was our goal," Balder said sharply.

Merriman twitched a dark eyebrow up.

"God's law always works with efficiency," he said. "Truth never produces delay and confusion. I've already delayed the quarantine legislation until next week, Ken, and I refuse to delay the execution." The eyebrow returned to level. Merriman's voice softened.

"I wasn't sure you'd authorize the arrest," he said. "I thought you'd lost your commitment. I was relieved and glad to find I was wrong. Where's your certainty in the law of God gone, between last Monday and today? Do you really think that God's law is so flawed that an innocent man could be executed under it?"

"The law isn't flawed," Balder said, and hesitated over his next words. "But *we* are, Charles, you and I. . . . "

"And that is why the law has been exercised by an impartial judge and a twelve-person jury," Merriman retorted, "and not by you and I."

He went back to his desk and reseated himself. Kenneth Balder stood, silently. He waited for a moment. If Merriman were to show a single self-doubt, a moment of humility, a glimmer of compassion—but Charles Merriman looked up from his desk and said, "Scholar's disease, Ken. Rejecting the truth when it is translated from the written page to the living world. Don't let it get the better of you."

BACK IN HIS OFFICE, two messages awaited him. Judge Straus had rejected the appeal, and confirmed Jerry Tindell's execution at 8 A.M. on Tuesday, April 16.

And Christopher Dillard had been murdered on the front steps of his son's South Carolina home. Shots from a passing truck had tracked upward from his chest to his head as he stooped down for the morning paper.

CHAPTER 29

Monday, April 15, noon

THE FIRST SHOCK WAVE from Christopher Dillard's murder hit Alexander Wade at lunch. He was sitting in the White House mess, waiting for the Reformed American States to agree to the second round of conditions for emptying Fort Pickett. He would have preferred his office at the Pentagon; but the president had summoned him to the White House. *To hold the chief executive's hand,* Wade thought sourly. The president, less than twenty-four hours away from his airport takeover, had developed nerves. He had listened to Wade's plan to provoke Merriman's guard into the position of aggressor, and agreed to it with the caveat that the Tuesday morning attack was to continue if the Virginia Guard didn't blockade the Fort Pickett procession. His manner made clear that he had little confidence in the guard's cooperation.

Wade picked at his roll, watching the television in the corner of the paneled room. Beside him, Allen Preszkoleski was eating hungrily. The TV was tuned to CNN. The screen showed the blue drapes and empty podium of a White House press briefing before the president arrived. Wade had helped finalize the speech less than an hour ago, working in the Roosevelt Room, with the press secretary and George Lewis and a dozen fluttering aides filling the air with tension.

"Here he comes," Allen said, putting his fork down. The chatter in the small paneled room died away. Wade leaned forward. He'd been exiled from the press conference, reluctantly agreeing that the secretary of defense ought not to be publicly visible at such a time. The president walked across to the podium and adjusted his glasses. He excelled at public grief.

"This morning, I was brought terrible news," he said. His face was set in familiar distressed lines. "A great man has been taken from us. Christopher Dillard, who bravely stood against the forces of hate and division masquerading as Christianity, was murdered this morning in front of his son and his grandchildren." He paused. In point of fact, the grandchildren had been sound asleep upstairs; but they had awakened at the sound of the blast, and had seen their grandfather sprawled in his blood with the morning paper in his hand.

The president resumed, "From the beginning, this administration has stood against the unprincipled rebellion of Virginia and North Carolina. We have condemned the divisive and hate-filled motivations of its leaders. We have asked, repeatedly, for a peaceful solution to this situation. Until this moment, we have refused to send our own guardsmen to fight the Virginia Guard—hoping to avoid a second war within these once-United States."

Wade had objected to that last sentence. Every listener would think, "Yes, but . . . ", and the murder of the Virginia Power worker would immediately eclipse Christopher Dillard's death. The president had penciled it back in twice, determined to set the stage for the next day's top-secret invasion.

The president leaned forward. He said, "Now we see that the spirit of lawless violence is spreading beyond the borders of Virginia and North Carolina, out into the rest of this great country. It has been clear from the start that Charles Merriman, the so-called chairman of the Reformed American States, and his chief of staff, Kenneth Balder, are determined to quench free speech within the borders of the two unfortunate states under their power. Now we see that violent repression overtakes anyone who dares to speak against their authority."

"He's riffing," Allen said, warningly. Wade crumbled more bread onto his plate. As written, the speech sent a clear message to Charles Merriman: *Military action is just around the corner.* It was meant to provoke Merriman into barring the way of the Fort Pickett convoy. The speech also delicately implied that Merriman was morally responsible for Dillard's death—that was for the sake of raising indignation in the heartland. Now the president was blissfully expanding on this theme.

"You're all aware of the circumstances of Dr. Dillard's death," he said. "The South Carolina police have issued a suspect description: two men in a pickup truck without plates, last seen heading toward the North Carolina border. Inside North Carolina, they will be free from any reprisals. Merriman's new order is providing a haven for the violent. And make no mistake—Virginia and North Carolina will remain a boiling pot full of lawless rebels until Charles Merriman and MacDonald Forbes return the control of these two states to the elected legislatures. Charles Merriman is encouraging, justifying, and sheltering violent rebellion." He adjusted his glasses and returned to the text of the speech.

"The United States has tried every peaceful means of resolving the situation. We regret that every overture has been rejected by Merriman and Balder—"

Wade gritted his teeth. He was aware of eyes on him from every corner of the mess. Charles Merriman would be a fool to block the convoy now. He could prove his dedication to peaceful resolution by letting Fort Pickett march past. And he could easily crack down on the in-state militias, which would only boost his public image. Sure, the president had provided plenty of justification for the Tuesday invasion; but that was sixteen hours away, and Merriman could do a lot between now and then.

He stood up and left the mess, Allen trotting behind him. When they were safely in the hallway, he ordered, "Get on the phone with Pickett, and find out what that convoy's up to."

Barely twenty minutes later, Allen returned to the assembled officials in the Roosevelt Room to report the results of his telephone consultation with Fort Pickett. The Virginia adjutant general had agreed to all of Alexander Wade's conditions. The front and rear guards of the convoy would be allowed to carry weapons, as long as the rest of the soldiers remained unarmed. Fort Pickett would retain a complement to guard the on-site weapons until a UN team could be summoned to supervise the transfer.

The president shrugged, unsurprised. He said, "Told you it wouldn't work, Alex. We'll have to depend on re-taking Richmond."

Wade stared across the table. The set calmness of his face felt like a cracking mask. The president was sucking a cough drop to ward off incipient hoarseness, and the sickly sweet smell permeated the room. Wade's stomach turned.

"You came on too strong," Wade snapped. "There's no proof that Merriman was involved in Christopher Dillard's death. The man was his mentor. If you hadn't said that, Merriman might've blocked the Fort Pickett convoy and we'd have a better justification—"

"Let him try and disprove it," the president interrupted. "And we've got plenty of justification. I've received reports that the Medical College of Virginia is designating a wing for the confinement of infectious diseases. A prison, in fact."

"You're going to provoke them," Wade said, "slinging accusations around like that." The tang of that nauseating cough drop was filling his nostrils. "This is a man who walked out with Virginia right under all our noses. He's not done yet."

"Excuse me if I don't shiver with fear," the president said dryly. "We've won out over Middle-East terrorists, Oriental dictators, and Latin guerrillas. Charles Merriman isn't going to beat our armed forces. The rest of the country's busy filing income tax returns and swearing at the federal government; and there's no way I'm going to let Virginia go more than a day past the tax deadline. Get the Fort Pickett guys out, post them in Washington like you promised the Joint Chiefs of Staff, and let's get on with it."

THE SECOND SHOCK WAVE came on the ride back to the Pentagon. Wade had left Allen with the president, and he welcomed the silence of his official car. He put his head back against the seat. He would have no opportunity for sleep until after the invasion; he filed his misgivings away with the discipline of long practice, and fell into an unpleasant and highly colored doze. A fire alarm was going off. He struggled up out of flames, disoriented, and grabbed for the ringing phone.

"Wade." The Pentagon loomed ahead of him.

Allen said urgently, "Turn on NPR. Merriman's making a speech."

"Already?"

"He's accusing the CIA of Dillard's death."

Wade swore briefly and hung up. He turned on the worldband radio he'd had installed, and switched over to the local public radio station. Merriman's strong Southern voice came clearly into the backseat.

"—further proof that the United States justice system is broken beyond mending. The foundational principle of guilt in America has always been: Innocent until proved otherwise. We've already seen that principle disintegrate in trial. Now the president has proved that anyone who disagrees with the dictatorship of Washington can also be convicted without indictment, without trial, and indeed without proof.

"Minutes ago, the South Carolina police updated their suspect description. They have eyewitness accounts: A pickup truck without plates pulled up in front of the house, just as the victim bent down for the morning paper, and fired. The blast was originally thought to be from a shotgun. The ammunition has now been identified as an unusual military issue, used primarily by the CIA. Certainly a civilian could obtain it, but only with difficulty. Furthermore, the shots—and I regret having to give such distressing details in public—tracked upward from Professor Dillard's chest to his head, in a pattern taught to CIA assassins. I remind my listeners of political assassinations benefiting United States interests, carried out in Cuba and in Moscow, using the same ammunition and the same method of killing. The assassins in each case remain undiscovered.

"The truck in question has been found abandoned near the North Carolina border. Its registration number has been filed away. I submit to you that any militia members involved in such a crime would have used easily available ammunition; and, the crime completed, would simply have driven the truck into the mountains to rejoin their companions.

"I need hardly say that myself, my chief of staff, Kenneth Balder, and North Carolina Governor MacDonald Forbes are innocent of any involvement with the tragic death of Christopher Dillard. Professor Dillard led me to the cause of Christ, twenty years ago. And although we parted in our theological convictions, I held a deep respect for Christopher Dillard's faith, his integrity, and his goodness. I mourn his death. His comments on my actions entangled him in affairs of state, and it appears that this cost him his life. For that I apologize to his family, with all my heart. And if his murderer is indeed anywhere within the Reformed American States, we will prosecute this crime to the full extent that justice allows. Arrest, fair trial, conviction if warranted, and execution . . . removing another violent and unprincipled criminal from American society so that the rest of us can live quiet and peaceful lives under the law of our land. Thank you."

Halfway through this speech, Alexander Wade knew that Charles Merriman *must* take some unjustifiable action against the United States. The CIA, faceless and heartless, was a better villain than Charles Merriman, dark and charming and weeping over the death of an enemy. Unless Merriman attacked the Fort Pickett convoy, the presidency was going to totter and fall. They'd attack on Tuesday, and men would die, and America would turn in revulsion from such a solution. The White House would go back to Republican or Democrat. The experiment of an independent chief executive would be deemed a failure, and closed. Alexander Wade would be shredded by the press. He'd be lucky even to get a teaching post; he might end up hosting a talk show, just to keep creditors from the door.

When the speech was three-quarters over, he knew he would break the law to prevent that.

SIX IN THE EVENING. Alexander Wade sat in a Pentagon conference room—a war room, in his own mind. He was surrounded by his aides and deputies, and listened by radio to the Fort Pickett convoy move through the gates. Allen was making notes beside him. The two-way radio had a tendency to pick up a local CB radio conversation, and the voices of the Fort Pickett officers were continually overlaid with crackle and static. Down in Virginia the convoy was creeping west.

At four-thirty, Wade had finished laying his game pieces. If any of this ever came out, Watergate and the Iran Contra scandal and Whitewater would be tiny muddles in comparison—mere tempests in teacups, compared with a howling city-wide hurricane. He had two sharpshooters on Route 460, just outside the city of Lynchburg and its outlying border of protective guardsmen. Certain contacts within the CIA had been cooperative; the CIA was ticked off at Charles Merriman.

He had modified, by necessity, his original conception. *It is expedient that one man should die to save the nation.* That man had originally been Jerry Tindell, but Tindell was going to die for his own sins, and his death would spark no indignation from an America weary of murderers released. *It is expedient that several men should die to save the nation.* There was no doubt: some of those Fort Pickett men were going to fall. But not by his hand. Or by the hand of the sharpshooters, who had been chosen because they were capable of breaking a truck mirror, kicking up dust in front of the convoy, without harming an American soldier. No; they would fall at the hands of the National Guard who stood around Lynchburg. The Virginia Guard was already nervous at the thought of the approaching convoy. They'd be more nervous by the time the Fort Pickett parade drew near. He'd seen to that.

Wade found himself tearing at a cuticle. He put his hands in his lap and thought: *If I don't do this, civilians will die in Richmond tomorrow. I'm sacrificing a few soldiers to guard the greater good.* The telephone in the corner of the room rang, and an aide picked it up. He went on waiting.

"Mr. Secretary?" The aide held out the receiver. He rose and took it. His secretary's unemotional tones said, "The attorney general wants to speak to you, Mr. Secretary."

"What?" Wade had a moment to savor the terror of the guilty, who flee when no one pursues. He took a breath and managed to sound normal. "Of course. Put him on."

The line clicked. Ramsey Grant's sardonic voice said, "Afternoon, Alex. Biting your fingernails over your convoy?"

Alexander Wade felt a thump inside his chest. "What d'you mean?"

"I need you to help me arrange a rendezvous with those Fort Pickett men. I've just cut a deal, and I'd like to get the subject out of Virginia."

"Who is it?"

"Garrett Franklin. Name sound familiar to you?"

"*What?*"

"He's turned up in New Kent County. The Justice Department is arranging for all charges against young Mr. Franklin to be dismissed, providing he leaves Virginia at once. Apparently he's under the impression—or his mother is—that he's being pursued by militia members bent on his blood. Margaret Franklin wants protection for him."

Alexander Wade found his palm wet on the receiver. He had a little over an hour before those sharpshooters went into action.

"Where does he want to join the convoy?" he demanded.

"Wait," Ramsey Grant said. "I haven't gotten to the best part yet. Who do you think arranged this?"

"Who?" Wade snapped, impatiently.

"The chief of staff for the Reformed American States himself. Kenneth Balder." Ramsey Grant was savoring his words. He said, "I'll say this for Kenneth Balder; he's no fool. He's got a California lawyer who could tie a garter snake in knots. We've been on the telephone with him for an hour, providing for Balder's safe exodus from Virginia. He's offered to come out in return for Franklin's safety."

Alexander Wade felt a burning surge of adrenaline. His voice was hard in his own hearing. He said, "You're letting him off, Ramsey?"

The attorney general said, "The president has decided that Kenneth Balder is of much more use to us free and speaking against Merriman, than convicted of—er, whatever—and silent. Franklin will need an honorable discharge. I've already got someone arranging it with the air force. There's one more wrinkle, Alex."

"Yes?"

"Balder insists he has some sort of private business to settle with you before he comes out."

Wade could hear the minutes ticking off on his watch. He said, "I'm in the middle of a major military operation here, Ramsey. Afterward—"

"No. *Now.* He won't send Franklin toward the line until he talks to you. Franklin and his mother are somewhere west of Richmond, and as soon as you do whatever Balder wants they're going to head toward a rendezvous with the convoy at Appomattox. I've got him waiting on a private line now. We had his lawyer on a conference call, but he made the guy hang up. Alex—" Grant's voice carried an overtone of command, "—I don't know what he wants. I know you loathe the guy. *Don't block this deal.* Do you understand?"

Wade strangled the sharp retort that rose to his lips. He said instead, mildly, "Don't give me orders, Ramsey. I'm in a roomful of people here and I'm going up to my office so I can speak in private. Have him transferred over to my secretary."

"Yes. Alex—"

Wade hung up on the attorney general and said to Allen, "Take over for a minute."

Allen Preszkoleski nodded absently, his eyes on the map in front of him. To Wade's racing mind, Lynchburg was ringed in scarlet. The gap between the red line and the convoy narrowed, moment by moment.

He walked out the door and down the hall toward his office, forcing himself to travel with the measured dignity of a cabinet official. Inside his office he slammed the door and sprang for the telephone. To the unnamed CIA voice that answered the accommodation number, he snapped, "This is Jonah. Tell 'em to wait."

"What?"

"The sharpshooters. Tell 'em to wait. We've got a problem."

"The convoy's due in eighty-nine minutes."

"I know. I'll be back to you in ten minutes."

"Better be," the voice said.

Wade depressed the receiver and buzzed for his secretary.

"Do you have that call from the Justice Department?"

"Waiting for you on line five, sir."

"Thank you." He sat for a moment, collecting himself; and then reached out and pushed the glowing button where Kenneth Balder was waiting to surrender.

"Alexander Wade," he said curtly.

On the other end of the line, a living pause was finally broken by that deep, familiar voice.

"Balder," it said.

Wade discovered a sudden deep well of pleasure inside him. He said, "Ah, Mr. Balder. Dropping the flag and scuttling out of the line of Christian

soldiers marching to victory? How does that hymn go? *One in hope and doctrine, one in charity. . . . "*

Kenneth Balder's voice had lost the vibrations in the lower register. It was
flat, strained tight as a rope across a chasm. An odd rustling noise filled the
background. A distant horn blew. *Traffic,* Wade diagnosed. Kenneth Balder
was not in his plush office at the Capitol.

"I need something from you," Balder said.

"The charity is to be on my side, then?"

"Shut up and listen to me," the voice snapped, losing its anchor to
calmness. "I'm not doing this out of any love for the United States or its
government. You're a crew of self-seeking power addicts, and you're leading this country straight to chaos. I'm caught in the middle of it, and I'm
doing this only because Garrett Franklin's life is worth more than my own
position. Understand?"

Alexander Wade paused. He had spent hours over those psychological
profiles. The FBI's illegal project had yielded a virtual blueprint to the soul;
every string he twitched had produced a corresponding jerk in the subject.
He was faintly surprised that Ramsey Grant put such faith in Kenneth
Balder's surrender. Lawyer or not, this man wasn't leaving his chief of staff
office and authority for the sake of a young guard misfit.

"So what is it you want, Mr. Balder?" The hand on his watch had moved
an alarming distance. He pulled a sheet of paper toward him and began to
draw while he listened: Lynchburg, Route 460 running straight toward it, a
convoy of stick figures and a car containing a woman and a boy and labeled
with a large question mark.

"I want those letters you showed Margaret Keil at my trial."

The letters. Mary Miranda's desperate pleas to the man who had slept
with her and planned violence with her and then turned his back. He
sketched out Richmond, surrounded by a row of horrible gargoyles, and
considered his work with his head to one side. The letters were still in that
file, faded and almost worn through at the creases after twenty-five years.

"I only have copies," he said at last.

"You have the originals, and I want them in my hands before I step over
the line into North Virginia."

Wade penciled in two sharpshooters with improbably huge weapons, standing on either side of 460 and firing down as the convoy thundered toward them. He could hardly tell Ramsey Grant that the convoy was coming under attack. Of course, there was a good chance that Garrett and Margaret Franklin would be unharmed, even if the situation did escalate into full-scale battle.

"Why do you want the originals? I could make copies."

"I don't want them used against me in any legal proceedings."

"I thought there weren't going to *be* any legal proceedings."

"You'll excuse me for not having ultimate confidence in the word of the United States government," Kenneth Balder said. "If I do end up in court, I don't want those letters showing up as proof of my utter callousness for human life."

"I tried to have those letters admitted once. It didn't work."

"Yes. Well, you won't get a chance to try it again. Another judge might decide differently."

"Mm." Wade added a small cartoon explosion, directly in front of the convoy. "I won't be able to get them to you in time."

"I'm not coming out until Tuesday night. I have loose ends to wrap up. The Justice Department has already arranged all that. But I won't come out at all until I have those letters."

Alexander Wade spun the pencil around absently. Ramsey Grant's order, annoying though it was, had come indirectly from the president and he was bound to follow it. He didn't actually think the letters would be of use in a court of law. If they were, Balder would still be in jail and the United States undivided. He could afford to cooperate in this. Garrett Franklin wasn't getting out of Virginia tonight in any case.

He said with magnanimity, "I will oblige you in this, Mr. Balder. As you're losing so much in the next twenty-four hours."

Balder's voice was barely under control. "By courier. The United States can stand the expense."

"I look forward to seeing you face to face."

There was a brief silence. He braced himself for a retort. Kenneth Balder said merely, "I've already seen your face in a thousand other public officials. You all look the same. All worshipping the same god. The spirit of the age."

"The spirit of the age?" Wade said, faintly startled.

"Yes. His creed is: To bow for grace is shame, and to be weak is miserable."

"There's nothing wrong with that!"

"Lucifer," Kenneth Balder said, "*Paradise Lost*, Book I."

He hung up, having achieved the last word. After a moment, Alexander Wade shrugged and crumpled up his paper. He had come to a decision almost without knowing it. Margaret and Garrett Franklin would have to take their chances in that convoy. The attack on the Fort Pickett men was the pivot point in this struggle; it would turn public opinion toward Washington, away from Merriman, and make stronger measures permissible. In any case, Ramsey Grant was deluding himself if he thought Kenneth Balder was going to sacrifice his future to get the son of his ex-lover's husband off any legal hooks.

But he had no wish to antagonize the attorney general unnecessarily, and so he unlocked his bottom drawer and drew out Mary Miranda's letters. Kenneth Balder's folder had been close to hand for the last weeks. He left the letters in front of him while he called the mysterious number again. The voice, less composed than before, answered sharply.

"Jonah," he said.

"Ten minutes!" the voice snapped. "What have you been doing? We can't raise one of the sharpshooters—"

"It's all right."

"What is?"

"Everything's underway. Stick with the plan."

"As before?"

"Yes," Wade said soothingly, "the original plan. There was a bump in the road. I smoothed it out."

"Good," the voice said, "because we can't call it off now."

The line disconnected. Alexander Wade rose with the letters in his hand, and took them to his secretary.

"Get me notarized copies of these right away," he said. "The copies are to be returned personally to me. Send the originals by courier to Kenneth Balder at the Virginia State Capitol. I want them there before midnight."

The secretary stared at him with her mouth open.

"Understand?"

"Er—yes, sir."

"Good. Get on it. Then you can go home," Wade said, suddenly conscious that the sun had set.

"Yes, sir."

He strode back down toward the war room. Inside, Allen lifted his head and said, interrogatively, "Sir?"

"All's well," Wade said. He settled back into his chair. "Allen, the attorney general wants to arrange a rendezvous with the convoy at Appomattox. I'll leave it to you."

"The convoy's only half-an-hour from Appomattox," Allen said dubiously, his finger on the map.

"Yes. I suspect his subjects are already there."

Allen shrugged. Wade watched him go through the motions of contacting the convoy commander, his fingers steepled together. He had less than an hour to wait before Merriman's empire came crashing down. When the notarized copies of the letters arrived, he tucked them away inside his jacket. He'd held onto the letters for a final weapon. He might use it tomorrow, when Kenneth Balder was safely out of Virginia. The *Washington Post*, unlike the California court system, wouldn't demand postmarked envelopes.

CHAPTER 30

☆ ☆ ☆ ☆ ☆ ☆ ☆

Monday, April 15, 6 P.M.

T HE CHILL OF THE SPRING evening gathered and strengthened as the shadows reached slowly across the parking lot. Margaret shivered, pulling her jacket closely around her neck. The heat in the diner did little to ward off the clouds of cold that billowed in every time the door opened. The booth that she sat on was hard plastic, the table spotted, the glass window in front of her smeared and cloudy. Garrett sat across from her, shoulders hunched and his fingers playing restlessly with the silverware. He'd already shredded his napkin. He was wearing a knit hat that covered his short military haircut, and an old padded jacket with the collar turned up to his chin.

She transferred her gaze back to the window. Ken was still standing at the pay telephone across the parking lot, his head bent into the inadequate glass shield that served as a booth. The phone stood in a narrow strip of brown grass on the far side of the lot. Cars in the road beyond had begun to flick on their headlights. The light changed, and a truck roared past. She saw him wince and bend his head further down. After another long moment he straightened, and replaced the receiver. He had been out at that pay phone for nearly an hour, standing almost perfectly still. Occasionally his left hand had moved in a gesture. She and Garrett sat where they were told, drinking coffee and picking at the food Ken had ordered while they watched him through the window.

Ken was still standing at the telephone, his back to the diner. He was staring out across the busy little road that served the outskirts of Appomattox. Margaret tried, unsuccessfully, to analyze the set of his shoulders. He turned and walked back toward the diner, and she looked down at the table. Garrett had started to disassemble Sweet 'n Low packages, piling the white powder in little heaps around his plate. The door jingled as it opened. More icy air curled around her ankles. A shadow fell on the table as he came between her and the glaring light. He slid into the booth beside her, and she noticed with irrelevancy that his knuckles were red with cold.

"The Justice Department has agreed to drop all charges," he said.

The sounds were incomprehensible at first. Slowly the words began to make sense. Garrett was safe. She kept her eyes on her son, willing herself away from the sense of Ken's nearness. It was unforgivable that, at such a time, she should be so absurdly aware of every movement he made. A slow relief came over Garrett's face. The uncharacteristic lines in his forehead smoothed, and his eyes lightened.

"They have!" he exclaimed.

"Yes. Provided you and your mother are out by midnight, you will receive an honorable discharge from the air force. You'll be required to make a deposition about the murder of the National Guard sentry, but no charges will be filed against you. I've arranged for you to meet the convoy from Fort Pickett—"

He halted with a grimace, as the waitress appeared with fresh coffee. No one had recognized him as Merriman's chief of staff; he wore a dark billed cap over his conspicuous light head, and a heavy oversized coat covered the cast on his left arm. But Margaret saw that the waitress was perfectly aware of him as an attractive man without a wedding ring. She glared at the woman, willing her to go away.

"—at the 460–26 interchange on the other side of town," Ken continued, as soon as the waitress had sashayed away. "You'll be safe then. I spoke to the Virginia adjutant general this morning, Garrett. Air checks haven't located the Regulators or the Tri-County Militia anywhere. They're not chasing you."

Garrett nodded eagerly. For him, the nightmare was almost over. Ken drained his coffee cup and fumbled for his wallet.

"Let's go, then," he said. "The convoy's due at the interchange in half-an-hour."

Margaret said slowly, "What did you trade?"

"For what?"

"For Garrett's freedom. When I tried to call the Justice Department—"

"I was able to get past the secretaries," Ken said, tossing a twenty onto the table and standing up.

Margaret slid out of the booth after him. He wouldn't look at her. She'd asked him to do something that circumvented the code of the Commonwealth, the code he believed in, and he had done it. She'd asked him to sacrifice his own future, and he had agreed. He must loathe the sight of her.

She trudged after him toward the sleek rental car. She had looped the strap of her purse across her chest. The deed to the New Kent farm was zipped into the inside pocket; Ken had taken her by the bank so that she could remove all the papers from her safety deposit box.

HE HAD ARRIVED AT THE FARM in the early afternoon, dressed in the dark casual clothes he was wearing now and carrying an odd-shaped duffel bag. She opened the door as he mounted the front steps. He had said immediately, "Maggie, I've got about four hours to get the two of you out of here. Trust me and do what I say and I'll explain it all later. Where's the best light in this house?"

She opened her mouth, closed it, and thought, *Well, you asked for his help.*

"My office?" she offered. "The door just off the kitchen."

"Okay. Get Garrett and bring him down."

She went up the narrow stairs, hearing him thump through the kitchen and open the squeaking door to the narrow porch office. Garrett was dressed and peering out the door.

"Mom!" he said, aghast.

"It's all right. He's going to get you out."

"Are you sure you trust him? If he turns me in—"

"He won't turn you in," Margaret said. She knew that with certainty; although she wasn't quite sure how the Kenneth Balder she held in memory, brilliant and erratic, had developed this solid core. She went back down the steps with Garrett treading nervously behind her. In her office, Ken was unpacking a brand-new video camera and mumbling over the settings.

"Stand over by the wall," he ordered, and then caught a glimpse of Garrett's face. He said, more gently, "Do what I say, son, and I'll get you out of this mess."

Garrett examined him carefully, and then walked over to the bare white wall.

"Did you get a paper this morning?" Ken asked.

"A newspaper?" Margaret said, puzzled.

"Yes. Go get it."

She went in and retrieved the unopened *Times-Dispatch* from the kitchen table. The Monday papers, these days, held Saturday news; the papers were printed up on Saturday night so that the plants could stand idle over Sunday. She could hear the soothing murmur of Ken's voice, making conversation. Garrett had visibly relaxed by the time she returned to the porch. As she closed the glass-paned door behind her, Ken was finishing up. "I picked this up right after lunch, on Charles Merriman's credit, and I think the price doubled when I walked through the door." He squinted through the eyepiece and said, "Okay. Hold the paper up and say the date." The red light blinked on. Garrett said awkwardly, "It's April fifteenth, Monday—"

Ken focused in on the newspaper headline. He paused the recording and said, "Now give your name and your date of birth, and after that tell the story."

The light reappeared. Garrett began, "Garrett Joseph Franklin . . . "

Ken nodded silently. Wordless, he watched through the filtering glass as Matthew's son went through his enlistment, his suspicions, the meetings with the Tri-County Militia, Clint Larsen's killing of the guard sentry, and the hostility of Bill James. He showed no impatience, even as Garrett stumbled and backtracked and cleared his throat. At the end of the story, he flicked the stop button and removed the tape and slid it carefully into his pocket without comment.

"Go get whatever clothes you need," he said. "Where's the deed to the house, Maggie?"

"At the bank in Providence Forge."

"I'll take you by on our way out."

"Where are we going?"

"Appomattox," Kenneth Balder said, "and then Washington, with any luck. I'm going to ask the Fort Pickett convoy to take you out."

"What convoy?"

"The first crack in the United States front," Ken said. "They're moving most of the men out of Fort Pickett."

So, after hurried preparations, they had driven the two hours to Appomattox. And she and Garrett sat in a third-class diner and watched Kenneth Balder arrange their futures on a greasy pay phone on an anonymous side street. On the way out, Ken had warned her that it might be some time before she could arrange a sale of the farm. She had yielded to fear of the unknown, and withdrawn the entire contents of the nursery bank account.

THE SIGN DECLARING 460 EAST was quickly followed by 460 WEST. They drove past a cluster of gas stations and a McDonald's, the front wreathed by elaborate climbing play tunnels. The on-ramp slanted in front of them; they left the two-lane road and circled around onto the divided highway. A Virginia state police car was pulled halfway across the merge lane. The trooper opened his door and stepped out. Ken rolled the window down, pulling his hat off and tossing it onto the dash. The trooper came around to the driver's side. The interior of the car was too dark for him to see, and he shined a flashlight carefully into the car, and caught Ken's face in the beam. Ken shielded his eyes with his right hand.

"Four-sixty's temporarily closed, sir. We're expecting a convoy from Fort Pickett to go by. . . . "

"I'm Kenneth Balder. I've got official business with the convoy."

The trooper squinted at him, and suddenly lowered the flashlight.

"Sorry, sir," he said. "Didn't know it was you. I wasn't told about this—"

"No, it came up in a hurry. I've got an authorization from Charles somewhere." He started to undo the buttons of his coat, struggling one-handed. He was making heavy weather of it, Margaret thought, considering that he'd gotten his coat off and the video camera going with relative ease, earlier.

The trooper shook his head. "That's all right, sir. I recognize you. Go ahead, but be careful out there. They've got weapons in the front and back trucks, and my buddy posted down the road says he saw other guns too."

"Yes," Ken said again. The trooper stepped away from the car, and he pulled onto 460. It was empty and dead-quiet. A scant mile ahead, a green sign proclaimed 26 NORTH, OAKVILLE, BENT CREEK. Ken pulled over onto the shoulder, and the car slowed to a stop. He turned off the motor and huddled into his coat, staring through the windshield.

Margaret said tentatively, "Do you really have an authorization from the governor?"

Garrett shifted awkwardly in the backseat. She could barely make out Ken's profile in the darkness inside the car.

"Charles Merriman doesn't make deals," he said, invisibly.

"How did you arrange this?"

"I gave the Justice Department something they wanted. Maggie, stop asking questions. I did what you asked me to do."

"At what price?"

Ken twisted his head around. "You didn't kill anyone, did you, Garrett?"

"No, sir."

"See, Maggie? The spirit of the law has been preserved."

"Is Charles Merriman going to see it that way?"

"Almost certainly not."

"Ken—"

Ken overran her words. "The Justice Department will probably keep both of you in custody for twenty-four hours, but I have a legally binding commitment from them that you'll be free as soon as certain conditions are met. I've arranged for a lawyer to represent both of you. Don't say anything unless he's present." He paused, and Margaret was aware of a faint rumbling sound.

"Convoy," Ken said, economically.

Garrett seized at the words. "I'll look," he said, and slid hastily out of the backseat and slammed the door behind him.

Margaret said, with difficulty, "Will I see you again?"

"In person? I don't know. You'll see me on TV. I'll be splattered all across the news, after this." His voice was suddenly bitter, as though he had wound himself up for self-sacrifice, and then caught a sudden glimpse of the future laid out in front of him.

"Merriman will fire you, won't he?"

"I'll resign."

She thought : *I've ruined his chance to change the world.* The dream had gone sour. Any apology would be meaningless; there was no way she could offer to stay, to bring Garrett back under the ruthless code that would end his life. Tears were running down her face. She forced herself to breathe regularly, without any sound of weeping, but he reached out and touched her face. His fingers lingered on the wet streaks across her cheeks.

"Maggie," he said. "Garrett was only the last step on a long road. It's all crumbled away—ambition and selfishness all mixed up with my love for God. I don't even know how it happened. I failed. I'm paying for my own sins, not Garrett's. And I'm not doing this for your sake. I'm doing it because this kingdom I wanted to bring about is corrupted. I think *any* kingdom I might try to build would be corrupted. I'm done playing God. Don't cry over it."

He moved his fingers away. She put her own hand out blindly, and drew him back. She could feel his head turn sharply toward her. He leaned over and cupped her chin in his hand and kissed her. His mouth was warm and inexpressibly familiar. Margaret put her hand up against the back of his head, and felt the short crisp hair at the back of his neck. Twenty-five years of suppressed longing had come to this. His mouth left hers, and he pulled her against him and rested his cheek against her hair. His breathing had quickened, and she could feel the muscles in his arm trembling, very slightly.

She said in a low voice, "I've been nursing the past for so long that I couldn't let go of it. I *was* afraid of you. I didn't lie, during the trial. "

"I know," he said. "You should have been. I was willing to let everything fall victim to my own plans. I thought that was behind me. . . . but even when I believed I was following God, I was only carrying out my own purposes. I don't blame you if you don't trust me. I no longer trust myself."

"But you're a different man than you were," she said.

A distant light cast a faint gleam over the inside of the car. He said rapidly, "Maggie, I don't know what's going to happen now. I will come find you, when it's all over. If you want me to."

"Yes," Margaret said. Living with him would be like walking across melting ice, never knowing which seemingly solid patch would crash down underfoot. Past and present touched in so many places. . . . But across the melting ice she could faintly see solid ground. Not the Garden of Eden, but still with patches of green; and without him, the ground was empty of any color—nothing but dry thorns.

He kissed her again, lightly, and opened his door, reaching for his cap. In the rush of night air she could hear the noise of the convoy, blazing down Route 460 toward them. The approaching lights were gathering strength. The line of trucks stretched back over the horizon. She climbed out of the car, and the three of them stood at the side of the road while the army roared past. The noise was overwhelming. She gritted her teeth against it and waited, until one truck slowed and pulled onto the shoulder ahead of them. Ken put his right hand on Garrett's shoulder and his left hand on Margaret's, and they walked up to it in the glare of the moving headlights behind them.

The truck door opened, and a young blond crew-cut man in uniform jumped out and strode back to them.

"Franklin?" he yelled.

"Here," Garrett bellowed back.

"I was told to pick up you and your mom. You're to ride in the cab." Even in the noise and confusion his voice was curious. "I don't know who you are or why you're comin' with me, but let's get going, okay?"

Ken gave her shoulder a slight shake and let go. With his back to the light, his hair looked dark under the baseball cap, and his face was obscured in shadow. The young officer gave him a curt nod, dismissing him as the driver.

"Come on," he ordered.

Garrett started toward the truck. She followed him, glancing back over her shoulder. Ken was still standing on the side of the road. The last truck in the convoy had slowed to an idle, waiting for them to fall into line. She put her foot on the running board and climbed up into the warm cab next to her son. The man in uniform slammed the door behind her and walked around the front of the truck. The cab smelled of sweat and metal and old cigarettes. The driver vaulted in. The wheels grated against the gravel. The truck pulled onto the road, picking up speed. The headlights from the rearguard behind them glinted into the side mirror, and Ken's tall dark figure disappeared in the blaze of reflected light.

SHE COULD NEVER REMEMBER exactly which came first, the deafening rattle of gunfire, or the searing pain that sliced across her face. She had slipped into a daze, as the truck jolted interminably through the night. Her ears popped once, and she thought dimly: *We're going up, we must be near Lynchburg. It must be after nine. It'll be midnight before we get to Washington.*

Then the side window of the truck exploded into a razor-shower of glass. She could hear shots coming from behind them, and a chorus of yells from the men in the back of the truck. The young soldier at the wheel swore, slamming on his brakes, and the big vehicle slewed across the road. She put her hand to her face and felt exquisite agony underneath her eye, and blood running down her face. A piece of glass had cut her. Garrett grabbed her shoulder and pulled her down off the seat, below window level. Her knee hit on another piece of glass, and she cried out and jerked away from him.

"Stay down!" Garrett yelled.

She lurched against the door and crouched there, sobbing with the pain in her face. She could hear running feet behind her and more shots. The truck lurched back into movement. The two-way radio fed a stream of shouts into the cab.

"—Guard posted at the Lynchburg city limits were supposed to let us past. Somebody fired on us—"

"—flat tire and two broken windows. Guy in the back has a broken arm. . . . fell against the side."

"Only one shot?"

"Yeah, Captain—"

"Maybe up there, but we just had a whole—"

Another voice broke in with a stream of profanity punctuated by gunfire. "Captain, we got a whole army back here! There's a truck up on that side road—there it goes—"

"Says *Regulators* on it—"

She gave up trying to disentangle the voices, and let them flow past her. Someone was screaming, horribly, in the distance.

"All they got to do is hide in the dark!"

"Blackout the trucks—"

They were sitting ducks, target practice for whoever was out there in the dark; trucks on a slightly elevated section of highway, surrounded by dark trees and a maze of side roads. The young soldier at the wheel was yelling for instructions, but no one was answering him. She felt, ridiculously, for her purse. The deed to the farm was safe. Garrett was shouting into her ear.

"Mom, the guy driving told me, while you were sleeping. They've got weapons. They were supposed to come out with just a front and rearguard, but they didn't trust Merriman's promises, so a lot of these guys are armed—"

Margaret put her hand blindly out and held on to her son's shoulder. The streetlights around them had gone off. Dawn was hours away. They were in the middle of a pitch-black battle. A whine outside the truck exploded right in her ear, and she found herself at the center of a brilliant expanding sphere of silent light.

CHAPTER 31

Monday, April 15, 7 P.M.

K ENNETH BALDER could never afterward hear "The Battle of Lynchburg"—the phrase which passed quickly into the common language to describe the carnage at Route 460 on April 15—without memory plunging him instantly into the mix of exhilaration and pain and sheer despair that governed him, all that evening.

He stood on the verge, watching the red taillights of the Fort Pickett convoy disappear into the dark. The videotape was still in the pocket of his oversized coat, the hard corner digging into his hip. The rumble of truck motors diminished into the distance, and the road was again quiet and completely still. His blood burned in his face, sang in his ears. He could feel the hard gravel, lumpy and uneven beneath the soles of his shoes, as though his feet were an impossibly long distance away. He had expected Margaret to feel gratitude for Garrett's sake, and resentment because she was forced to leave her farm and business. Her hand against his wrist, drawing him back to her, had astonished him. After that, all was swallowed in the great leaping spring of joy that still ran all through him. He felt slightly drunk.

Sterner business waited. He got back into the car and reversed it, driving the wrong way down the closed road until he could exit past the watching state trooper. He had saved Garrett. Another man's life still hung on his words.

IN THE PRIVATE ROOMS of the Executive Mansion, Charles Merriman was alone. His voice answered Balder's knock. The opened door revealed him on the sofa, his sock feet stretched in front of him and his head sunk back against the pillows. Seen in profile, he had lost flesh; the skin was stretched tightly from the bridge of his nose across the bony structure of his face.

"Ken," he said, not moving.

Kenneth Balder shut the door behind him. It was imperative that Charles Merriman should believe in his absolute and total loyalty until Tindell was safe.

"By yourself tonight?" he asked. "Where's Cline?"

"In his office. He and Joe Fletcher are monitoring the Fort Pickett transfer. They'll be over afterward. Want something?" Merriman waved a languid hand toward the kitchen.

"Thanks. In a minute." Balder sat down on one of the stuffed armchairs. He was exhausted and cold, and the chair was soft underneath him. The mending bone in his arm twinged at him. The room was warm and bright with lamplight. Stacks of papers and books occupied the table in front of the windows. Charles Merriman yawned and said, "Got any room on your schedule tomorrow?"

Tomorrow I'll be in Washington, facing a hostile Justice Department with an army of hungry reporters waiting to rip me apart.

"I could adjust it," he said, with an effort. "Why?"

"Remember we sent out copies of that plan of yours to run a welfare net through the churches? Well, there's a coalition of churches out near Lynchburg that's been trying to put something like it into effect. They're all excited. They want to come tell you that they can spread their network over the state if we give them some administrative support. Counseling, job training, food and clothing banks." Merriman lifted his head from the back of the sofa, a spark of energy returning to animate his tired body. "I know we've had our differences, Ken, but when I see something like this, it's like the New Testament coming back to life and I get excited all over again. We've got great things ahead of us."

He subsided back into the cushions. Kenneth Balder, sitting in soft warmth, almost dizzy with lack of sleep and facing the hardest week of his life, found himself suddenly overwhelmed by the last and most powerful temptation. In the dark cold drive back to Richmond, the memory of Maggie's mouth beneath his had lost some of its immediacy. He had the vague promise of an uncertain future, and the guaranteed hostility of the United States, to set against Merriman's continuing offers of power. All he had to do was sit still. Garrett was already out of the reach of execution. If he didn't appear to fulfill his part of the bargain, Garrett could be convicted and imprisoned under United States law, but his life would be spared. And God's work would go on, here in Virginia. It was flawed, yes; but what government of men was without error? Warmth on one side of Virginia's border, arctic cold on the other. Maggie would be disappointed. He had been disappointed, sitting in his cell on visitor's day, waiting for the magic words: *You have a visitor.* He could feel the rectangular shape of the videotape against his thigh. Maggie's image was faint, ghostly in his mind. All the knowledge of his own untrustworthy soul was fading into weariness.

"Where've you been?" Merriman added. "I called you late this afternoon, and your secretary said you'd been gone since before two."

"Long lunch with the clerk of the Seventh District. I made him wait for me all morning, so I gave him most of my afternoon."

Merriman said, casually, "I hear you had Margaret Franklin in to see you this morning?"

Gossip pervaded the halls of the Capitol like air, ever present and the source always invisible. Balder had ceased to be surprised by it. He said, "She was in some distress." And the memory of Maggie's tear-stained face hit him so vividly that it almost qualified as hallucination.

Merriman went on, "Judge Straus sent me a note asking of any reason why I should intervene in Tindell's execution. Had she spoken to him, then?"

He could still hear her voice in his ears. The memory led him inexorably onward, to that terrible struggle with his own soul, when he had tried and failed to convince himself that he could remain outside the tangled drama he had created and watch it play to the end. He thought: *No. I've won this fight already. I will not battle through it again.*

He said steadily, "Margaret called Judge Straus, yes, but without any success. She's been in contact with her son. She wouldn't tell me where he was, but she took a videotape of him and brought it to me. I think you ought to watch it."

Merriman asked, irrelevantly, "Where is she?"

"Now? I don't know," Balder said. He was aware that his voice was curt, but Merriman probably knew already that Margaret had left his office in a hurry, and if he concluded that the relationship was ended, so much the better.

"Well," Merriman said, "let's see it."

He turned his head slightly toward the VCR across the room. Balder extracted the tape from his pocket and awkwardly disentangled the coat from the cast on his left arm. He got up, popped the tape in, and returned to his seat as Merriman reached for the remote control.

Garrett appeared on the screen. His dark hair stood up in a shock against the white wall behind him, and the frame of the kitchen door was just visible at his right shoulder. He said, "It's April fifteenth, Monday—" and the picture closed in on the newspaper headline. The film abruptly changed to a slightly different angle, and the face on the TV said, "Garrett Joseph Franklin . . . Right now I'm running away from both the United States and the Reformed American States, because they think I murdered a sentry. It isn't true." Pause. "Two years ago, before my father died, he told me that he suspected someone in the National Guard of doing something illegal. He was killed not long afterward, and I always thought it had something to do with what he knew. I enlisted in his unit. . . . "

Merriman watched, his face drawn into lines of concentration. Told from beginning to end without interruption, the story was heartfelt and convincing. The silence from the camera operator suggested that Margaret Franklin was concentrating on the operation of the equipment. Balder was only half-listening; his mind was ranging through the possible futures that were closing in on him. The sound of Garrett's voice paused, and he glanced up at the TV to see that the boy had shifted position. The camera lens followed him, catching a bit more of the glass-paned door at his right. Kenneth Balder felt his mouth go instantly dry. He had glimpsed himself, reflected in the glass. His right eye was obscured by the camera, but his fair hair was unmistakable and the left side of his face clearly visible. After an agonizing moment Garrett put his weight onto the other foot, and the camera moved back away from the reflection. Merriman's face had not changed. Balder thought frantically: *Maybe he didn't see. Maybe that transparent image isn't clear, unless you're looking for it.* The tape rolled on. Kenneth Balder sat still, itching for its end. But when Garrett had finished his story, Merriman reached for the remote and sent the tape into rewind.

"Interesting," he murmured. "Quite possible, isn't it? I'd just like to hear that part about Bill James telling guardsmen to get weapons for the group. That seems to be the crux of the story, don't you think?"

Balder swallowed. Garrett's face ceased its backward motion.

"John said that Bill James was always after them to get weapons for the militia, and that Clint Larsen used to do whatever Bill James told him." Pause. Shift. A millisecond glimpse of the reflection, and then the movement back away from the glass. "He says that on the night my dad was killed, Bill James came by their house to drop off food. . . . "

Balder clenched his hands against the soft fabric of the chair. Merriman gave every appearance of watching the tape right through to the end a second time. It was already after nine, and Tindell's execution was scheduled for five A.M. If Merriman suspected he was shielding Garrett Franklin from justice, he wouldn't be allowed to resign; he'd be fired, and that could jeopardize his deal with the Justice Department. They wanted a heroic turncoat, not a disgruntled ex-employee.

A tremendous knock on the door brought both men to their feet. The door burst open and John Cline catapulted in, the adjutant general behind him. Cline's iron-gray hair was rumpled wildly up, and his arched Roman nose was quivering with indignation. He roared, "They've attacked the convoy! That perfidious smiling chicken-souled crew of politicians attacked their own men! They're fighting it out in the road in front of Lynchburg, and we've lost contact—"

"*What?*" The tape was forgotten. Merriman's weary frame was suddenly filled with tense energy.

The adjutant general said urgently, "We heard from our National Guard outposts that the convoy was approaching the Lynchburg city limits.

It's right at the bottom of a hill, in front of a lot of trees. The guard saw the convoy headlights, and then there was a series of shots from *behind* them."

"Your National Guard didn't fire on them?"

"I guarantee it. I've half-killed myself talking to officers personally and promising them I'd skin them if any guardsmen ever fired on any citizen of the United States without extreme provocation. They've been set up, Charles. But the convoy started shooting back, and some of the guard had to fire in self-defense. Then something else hit the convoy from behind and then we lost the blasted connection."

Merriman protested, "But we've watched the other bases. There's no other military force in Virginia. Who's attacking them from behind? Cut off that tape, Ken, what's wrong with you?" Garrett's voice was still earnestly telling his story. Merriman grabbed the remote impatiently and cut the sound off himself. He whirled around suddenly.

"The militia!"

"*What* militia?" John Cline demanded.

"The Tri-County Militia and the Regulators! They're running around together, somewhere between Virginia and Carolina. Joe sent a chopper up to look for them. We didn't find anything—"

"I didn't look much east of the mountains," the adjutant general said. "Didn't have time."

"I'll bet the farm they've come up behind that convoy. They've been targeting U.S.A. forces, right? What d'you think, Ken? You know more about this situation than I do."

Kenneth Balder felt as though he were moving in a nightmare. Every time he pulled a thread from the tangle, the knot only tightened; and Garrett and Maggie were at the center of it. He'd sent them straight into an ambush. John Cline's face seemed to float up and down in front of him.

"Sit down," Cline said, practically. "You look terrible. Been taking those painkillers again? You can get addicted to those."

Merriman snapped, "He's been working, John, that's all."

Cline shrugged, dismissing the subject. "So what if it does turn out to be the militia?" he demanded. "The convoy's still getting shot up. Last report, a dozen men were down and grenades were flying around—"

"Any guardsmen killed?"

"Three," the adjutant general said curtly.

Balder could have predicted Merriman's next words.

"Television cameras?"

"On their way."

"Good. We're going. Joe, bring as many guard units up from Danville and Roanoke as you can spare. Get them now. We're going to hunt that militia down and *crucify* them." His voice vibrated with anger. "Ken! Come on. We're going out there. If the United States is trying to cast me as a villain, I'll show them villains. What is wrong with you, anyway? Need something to eat?"

Balder shook his head. He said hoarsely, "What about Tindell?"

"Plenty of time for that."

In seven hours Jerry Tindell would be strapped to a table and sedated, and a concentrated solution of potassium chloride would run into his veins. Balder looked at Merriman, his hand already on the telephone, and knew: There was nothing in this world that would save Tindell's life now. He longed to say it. He was sick of evasions and tact. A faint glint in Merriman's dark eyes warned him that any objection on his part might bring up the subject of his reflection in the glass door; and that would be the end of his tenure as chief of staff. He had to hold onto that position until Garrett had escaped. If Garrett was still alive.

Merriman said softly, "We're going to Lynchburg. You're coming in the chopper with me. We're going to face this situation down, just like we did before. We'll deal with the other issues afterward."

"What issues?" Cline demanded loudly.

Merriman turned his head and said, "Is videotaped testimony admissible in a court of law?"

"Under what conditions?"

"If the witness is frightened to appear."

Cline snorted. "God commanded that witnesses in a capital case be responsible for throwing the first stones in the execution," he said. "That's to assure the truth of their testimony. If a witness can't even show his face, he's certainly not telling the truth."

Merriman removed the receiver from the telephone. In two minutes the room was full of aides. The helicopter would be ready momentarily. State troopers were summoned to protect the governor. Balder heard someone over in the corner of the room, arranging for a Channel 12 cameraman to accompany Merriman to the battle site. He found John Cline at his elbow and growled, "What is it now?"

"You'll be present at the execution in the morning?"

"Why?"

"You signed the order for the arrest."

"Do you want me to insert the IV needle?" Balder said tartly.

"No," Cline said, apparently giving the matter serious thought. "Your presence will fulfill the intent of the law. Charles did send someone out to summon Mrs. Franklin, but she hasn't been home."

Balder turned his back. He was sick, his insides consumed by an empty loathing of his companions. The clock was inching toward ten. His imagination conjured up Jerry Tindell, sitting in a cell on death row, watching the hands tick away his last hours of life. And then Maggie rose up in his thoughts, real and warm and promising a future, and he thought to himself: *If she is dead, I hope they shoot our helicopter down.*

CHAPTER 32

THE DARKNESS that surrounded Lynchburg was broken by a shocking blaze of light. An army truck sat burning in the middle of Route 460. The huge pyre cast a circle of light all around.

Balder, squinting down at the ghastly scene from the helicopter, could see other red patches glowing in the darkness beyond. Someone had been pitching grenades around with happy abandon. No lights showed on the Lynchburg side of the convoy, and for the moment quiet reigned. The gunfire had temporarily halted.

The helicopter sank down below a ridge, and he lost sight of the blazing truck. The trip had been silent, with Merriman hunched on the other side of the cabin, listening intently to a headset. Behind him, the Channel 12 cameraman was checking his equipment. He said in an awestruck voice, "Was anybody in that truck?"

"They don't know," Merriman answered, straightening up. "The guard has set up a secured headquarters for us, behind the Lynchburg line—"

Balder said, "You're not going to be able to charm your way through this, like you did on the North Carolina border."

"Charm?" Merriman said, scathingly. "I'm not going to charm anybody. I'm going to set the guard on that militia group and *eradicate* them."

The chopper touched down. Merriman threw the door open and

scrambled out under the blades. Balder followed him, with the cameraman at his heels.

According to his glimpse from the helicopter, the truck sat burning at the foot of a long hill, in front of the WELCOME TO LYNCHBURG sign. Lynchburg was still country out here at the edges; and the sign announcing the entrance to the city had been erected at the bottom of the slope, with trees thick on either side of it. But he found himself heading down the far side of the hill, toward the secured headquarters. This turned out to be a tent erected at the edge of Route 460 behind a barrier of parked trucks. When he tried to look out from the tent, he found himself facing an upward slope of tarmac, with the battle scene on the other side of the crest. He said, interrupting the flow of words from the guardsman in command, "Can we look down on the site?"

"It isn't safe, sir." The guardsman, middle-aged and curt, made a visible effort to marshall his thoughts. He said, "When that truck started burning, the rest of 'em pulled back into the dark behind it. We didn't set it on fire, sir, someone threw a grenade from behind. We haven't fired off a shot in twenty-five minutes. But every time things get quiet and we think we might be able to talk to the convoy, another volley shoots off from one side or the other of those trees. Then the convoy starts firing all over again. If you put your head above that hill you might get it shot off."

Just at the moment, Balder didn't care.

"Not in the dark," he said. "I'm going up to look."

"Doesn't do any good to stand in his way," Merriman said, bent over the map produced for his inspection. "See if a volunteer will go up with him. Then get me somebody who knows something about these radios. If that *is* a militia they're bound to be monitoring one of the channels, and if we broadcast that I'm here and willing to talk we might get an answer. And show me the alternate roads. The adjutant general is busy sending guard up from Danville and Roanoke. We've got to bring them up from behind—"

Merriman's voice died away as Balder walked toward the parked trucks. Two young guardsmen were waiting for him. The sky above was filled with stars, but there was no moon. He looked around for the glint of the guardrail, found it, and followed it up toward the top of the hill.

"Better get down," the guardsman behind him murmured.

He crouched into the shadow of the trees. The hill's crest was right in front of him. He moved silently forward on hands and knees until he could see down the other side of the hill. The dark road sloped away from him, with the burning truck at the bottom. The night air was filled with the smell of melting rubber and glass. Beyond the fire he could faintly see the bumpers of two more trucks, and an occasional wary movement in the dark. A faint moaning sound floated up to him. Down in that invisible cluster of trapped men, someone was weeping in pain. He clenched his fingers against the cold grass and remained where he was, straining his eyes into the dark.

"Sir—"

The whisper from behind him was fearful.

"Sir, you shouldn't stay here too long—"

He crabwalked backward away from the top of the hill. When he was well down the slope he stood, brushing grass and dirt from his hands.

He murmured, "And you don't know who was in the truck?"

The young guardsman beside him said, "We don't know anything, sir, except that a bunch of men at the back of the convoy were killed when the shooting started from behind. That truck was one of the last in line."

From behind. He had a sudden vision of Maggie climbing into that truck at the convoy's tail-end.

INSIDE THE TENT, Merriman was the center of a tense knot. He was sitting in front of the guard radio equipment, his elbows on his knees and his dark face fierce with concentration. Balder inched his way through the crowd toward Merriman's side. Someone said in his ear, "He finally raised 'em. He went on every channel and said he was personally willing to listen to their complaints."

"Raised who?"

"They say they're the Tri-County Militia."

"Of course," Balder said. He arrived at the governor's side and crouched down to hear. The thin certain voice on the radio was saying,

"And you may not even know it, Chairman, but the adjutant general's been a member of the Trilateral Commission. If you don't get those tentacles of the New Order out of Virginia—"

Merriman turned his head and said softly, "As long as I'm listening to them, they won't fire on the convoy."

Balder nodded. The voice went on.

"—He arranged this convoy to go through. We have information to the effect that the Fort Pickett men have been mining the railroad track along 460 the whole way, and they were planning to take Lynchburg out, burn City Hall to the ground, and recapture that naval nuclear facility east of the city to scare Virginia into submission. We're defending our fellow Virginians. We didn't fire those first shots. The convoy started shooting at the guard around Lynchburg. It was the first stage of their attack—"

Another officer appeared at the edges of the group, holding a map marked in red. Merriman waved him over. While the voice from the radio went on, the two examined the paper. The hurriedly mobilized guard divisions were coming up Route 24, which intersected 460 behind the battle site. The adjutant general, listening in from Richmond, had already plotted the location of the Tri-County Militia and set up an attack plan. The guardsmen from Roanoke were already in place, awaiting orders; the Danville Guard was barely twenty minutes away. The heavily penciled letters at the top of the map said: *Keep talking to them and warn the convoy.*

Merriman turned back to the radio and interrupted the flow of accusations. "Major Morrison—"

"Yes?" the voice said grudgingly.

"Just a minute. I've got to consult my chief of staff."

"I'll wait."

Merriman closed the channel. "You've got to find me a way to speak to the convoy without Morrison listening in," he said intensely.

The radioman was shaking his head before the sentence was finished. "Anything the convoy can hear, they can pick up."

"We have to tell the convoy the guard is coming. If they'll sit tight we can chase the militia out of there. But if the guard starts shooting it'll set the whole fireworks off again."

"I know, sir, but you can't do it by radio. The militia's gonna hear it. It'll be like broadcasting over a loudspeaker that the guard is comin' to kill them all."

The commanding officer offered, without enthusiasm, "Someone'll have to walk down there and warn them."

"Walk *down* there?" his second demanded. "Nobody's gonna walk down there. Go down in a tank, maybe."

"I'll ask for volunteers."

This created an instant uneasy silence in the tent. Kenneth Balder got to his feet.

"I'll do it," he said.

The state trooper behind Merriman said instantly, "No, sir!"

"Charles can't go, but I can. Give me a white flag. I'll go down the hill at the side of the trees, so Morrison and his crew can't see me, and come out just at the truck."

"Someone's going to drill you right through the chest," another voice protested.

"Well," Balder said, hearing his voice harden, "let them. It's either me or fifty more guardsman before dawn." He was suddenly aware that every eye was on him. The guard officer was wearing a look of awe. The expression was repeated in every face around the circle. He realized at once that they thought he was being incredibly courageous. It was an illusion; he wanted to go down there and find Maggie so badly that he could barely manage to stand still.

Merriman looked up from the map.

"You can go," he said. "Take your coat off. That cast's as good as an ID. Maybe when they see who you are, they won't shoot you."

"I can give him a vest—" the commanding officer began.

"I don't want one," Balder said, pulling his coat off. "A vest makes it look like a hostile approach." He was warm anyway; a trickle of sweat ran around his neck. He was still wearing jeans and a dark shirt, inconspicuous clothes he had put on to drive Maggie to meet the convoy. He'd be able to fade into the dark.

"Sir," the guard commander said, "let me clue you in. This will look hostile no matter how you do it. We can't warn them that you're coming. You're going to come out of the dark right into the light of that burning truck. For all they know, you're the point man in an attack force."

"So be it, then," Kenneth Balder said.

Merriman quenched any further protest. "Let him go," he ordered. "I'll talk to the militia while you're on the way down, Ken, but I can't guarantee no one will be looking your way. Keep out of sight as long as you can."

"Yes," Balder said absently, hunting through his coat pockets for the dark cap to cover his hair. "When's that reenforcement guard coming?"

"They're twenty minutes away," another officer said.

"Listen, Charles, don't wait for me to come back. The convoy's going to think this is a trap. I'll offer to stay down with it while the guard rounds up the militia. And if they shoot me on the way down, there's no way we can contact them in any case. You'll just have to risk attacking the militia without informing the convoy."

There was a brief silence in the tent. He discovered the cap and pulled it on. When he looked up, Merriman's expression had changed slightly.

"Yes," he said. "Godspeed, Ken." Some missing undertone—warmth, or respect—had come into his voice.

Balder, surprised at the alteration, found himself suddenly face-to-face with the Channel 12 camera. He turned away with a grimace. Someone handed him a white flag—a threadbare towel—and he tucked it into his shirt. Merriman had reopened the channel to Major Morrison. Balder was aware of the camera tracking his path, and he welcomed the dark at the edge of the trees.

He walked softly up to the top of the hill and peered over. On the other side, the truck still burned. All else was quiet. The sound of moaning had ceased.

Halfway down the slope, a distant report sent him to his hands and knees. After a moment he realized the sound had come from far away. He stood back up, his heart racing.

Now he could feel heat on his face. Twenty feet in front of him, the darkness began to thin. The fire gave off an unpleasant, putrefying odor, acrid and more piercing than the smell of burning metal and oil. He pushed away thoughts of its source. He had come to the edge of the dark. The truck would be between him and the militia, which was ranging along the north side of the highway.

Balder pulled the towel from his shirt with his right hand and held it up above his head. With the cast on his left arm, he was incapable of making a hostile move. He walked steadily past the fire, toward the shadows beyond. Someone shouted, and feet shuffled loudly in the darkness. He felt a wave of terror, waiting for that familiar paralyzing burn to rip through his chest this time.

He hissed into the shadows, "This is Kenneth Balder. The Virginia Guard is not shooting at you! Got that? The guard has not fired on the convoy. *You are not under attack!*"

He heard a faint scraping noise behind him. Before he could turn a cold ring pressed into the nape of his neck, between his collar and the dark cap. A voice behind him shrilled out, "Who are you? What are you doing down here?"

He stood still. That was not the voice of a man with a steady trigger-finger.

"Kenneth Balder, chief of staff to the chairman of the Reformed American States. There's a renegade militia behind you. They've been firing on you, not the Virginia Guard."

The army man let loose a string of oaths, in apparent amazement.

Balder went on, "We've got more guardsmen coming to get the militia under control. I came to warn you. You'll hear gunfire across the road. If you stay put and still, we can get you moving again."

The voice remarked on the improbability of this, in no uncertain terms. The hand holding the gun steadied slightly, and Balder started to breathe again.

"Look," he said, "I've got a bath towel in my right hand and a cast on my left arm. Take the gun off my neck."

He was rewarded with a quick and not very gentle patdown, but the ring of metal above his collar was withdrawn. He turned around. The Fort Pickett soldier had the white wide-stretched stare of someone plunged into a nightmare. He was young, in his late twenties, and his hands were shaking. He said, "I've got a guy back there bleeding to death, and every time we try to move somebody pops a round off at us. Get us out of here."

"Who's in command here?"

"I am. The captain died twenty minutes ago."

"Can you move out?"

"I think so. We lost three trucks—that one and two more with all the tires blown out. The others have broken glass and dents, but we can drive 'em." He paused and said, his voice suddenly hardening, "How do I know this isn't part of some trap?"

Balder snapped, "Why in the name of all that's holy would we attack a convoy heading *out* of Virginia? We want you guys back where you belong. Didn't anyone see who was attacking from behind?"

The young army officer nodded, briefly. "Someone said they saw a truck with the *Regulators* name on it," he said. "It's the only reason I might believe you."

"I'll stay down here with you as a guarantee that Virginia isn't attacking the convoy."

The soldier looked him over. After a long moment he said gruffly, "Come back here and tell the others, then."

"Who's been killed?" Through the roaring in his ears, he barely heard the answer.

"The captain. Five men in the back of the truck that got hit, and the driver. Two guys in the truck behind them. We had two civilians with us. One of them's been bleeding—cut artery in his thigh. We stopped it, but he's drifting in and out. Either he's still bleeding somewhere inside, or he's already lost too much blood." He swallowed. "Come see for yourself. Hang onto my coat. We can't use lights outside the trucks."

Balder clutched onto the back of the man's coat and stumbled after him through pitch darkness, past the looming black shapes of trucks. The soldier turned his head as they passed one.

"We put the bodies in there," he said, briefly. Ahead of them a very faint chink of light showed. The back of a truck had been turned into a makeshift infirmary. The soldier climbed in, past the blankets that masked the work area, and Balder followed him. The truck bed was already crowded with makeshift pallets. Three white-faced men lay on the boards, gritting their teeth against pain, and over against one side Maggie sat with Garrett's head in her lap. He could feel tears sting his eyes; the relief was so great that he could not even grasp it. He blinked rapidly. Behind him the soldier was murmuring orders to another man. "Go around to the trucks, tell them to keep down and quiet, don't shoot back when you hear firing out in the woods. . . ."

The side of Maggie's face was cut. Blood smeared her cheek, and a bruise was already forming under her eye. Garrett was lying perfectly still, his gaze fixed on some point above his head.

Balder made his way gingerly across the truck bed and knelt down beside Margaret. She turned her head, startled, and her mouth opened slightly. No sound came out; her eyes were glazed over with fear and shock.

"Maggie?" he said gently.

After a long moment she managed to get his name out, her voice barely audible. He said, "Okay. It's all right. We're going to get you moving again." He leaned over Garrett and said, "Can you hear me, son?"

Garrett moved his head slightly. He murmured, "Can't stay awake."

"I'm going to get a chopper in, just as soon as it's safe. You need to be in a hospital. We can send you to UVA."

"No. Not in Virginia," Garrett said. His voice was a thin whisper, but the determination came clearly through.

"If you don't get to a hospital, you may die."

"Better die here," Garrett mouthed, "than be executed in Virginia."

"You haven't been tried. You can still be proved innocent."

The boy whispered, "Did you show them the tape?"

He nodded, reluctantly.

"What—"

"He's still scheduled for execution," Balder said roughly.

"I'll stay here," Garrett muttered. "Not as bad . . . as I thought it would be."

Maggie put her hand against his face, and he closed his eyes. She stayed huddled over him, clearly past reasoning.

Balder wasn't entirely sure he wouldn't have made the same choice. He rose to his feet and made his way back through the truck. Maggie didn't even twitch in response to the movement; her universe had been narrowed to the prostrate figure of her son. He slipped out of the truck and found the commanding officer right outside, waiting for his troops to be notified of the coming attack.

"What happened to the boy?" he murmured.

"They were in the truck that burned," the officer answered. "A grenade went off right beside it. Killed the driver, and a piece of glass went into the guy's leg. The blast threw him up against the woman. They were both stunned when we pulled them out. . . . We couldn't get to the driver before the truck burned." His voice was flat and hopeless. "I think her collarbone's broken, but she won't leave him. You'd better get back in the truck."

"I'll stay with you."

The soldier shrugged. "Cigarette?"

"No. Listen, he doesn't want to go to a Virginia hospital, but I can get a Medivac helicopter for the other wounded—"

"Mr. Balder," the army officer said, "I don't want anything from the Commonwealth of Virginia. The medic says the other guys are stabilized. They're miserable, but they'll be safer once we get over the line into North Virginia." He spat the cigarette out and drove it into the pavement under his heel. "Noble of you to serve as hostage, so I guess I have to believe you when you say the guard's not gonna shoot at us. But as soon as the way is cleared, I'm driving this convoy up 29 and out of this hole as fast as I can. If you want to help, send a couple of troopers in front of us to make sure the way stays clear. I'm taking these guys home. The army can sort it all out after we're safe."

Balder ducked suddenly as a fusillade of shots went off, over to his left. The officer joined him on the ground, and the two of them stayed crouched down below the bumper, listening. Shouts and yells broke out in the woods. A sudden faint explosion sent a glow through the trees. The guard was routing the Tri-County Militia; but not without resistance. He couldn't see into the dark alleys and pockets created by the massed trucks around him, but he could hear a faint rising murmur. The Fort Pickett men were watching. Another explosion threw light up above the trees. Whoever had those grenades was making good use of them.

Come on, he said to himself. *Move away from the road.*

After several interminable minutes, he was almost sure that the center of the conflict was shifting away. The next volley of shots was certainly fainter. Another explosion, noticeably more distant. The army officer grabbed Balder's arm and hissed, "They're running!"

Balder shook the man off. "Can you get these trucks moving?"

"Right away."

"Let me go, then. I've got to get back up to the top of the hill and tell them you're on your way."

"I want state troopers ahead of me," the officer said. "And a rearguard."

"I'll see to it," Balder said impatiently. He hauled himself to his feet and looked around for the red glow of the flaming vehicle. The fire was beginning to burn itself out. He resisted the impulse to go back inside the truck behind him. Maggie was oblivious to his presence, and there was nothing else he could say. He was afraid of finding Garrett dead; the possibility of saving the boy's life lent urgency to his mission. By the time he took five steps, he had completely forgotten the army officer.

He made his way out of the maze, and sprinted up the hill toward the crest. The cast dragged at him. When he mounted the top of the hill he was gasping for breath and sweat was dripping into his eyes. Someone posted at the roadside gave a shout as he approached. In a minute he was surrounded by men. At the edge of the tent Charles Merriman met him. His dark face was alight with victory.

Balder gasped, "Is the road clear ahead of us?"

"Yes. Except for the guard stationed on the other side of the Lynchburg limits—"

"Well, move them. That's all we need, one more accidental shooting." He drew another breath. "The convoy's got wounded men. They're getting underway now. I promised they could have two police cars ahead of them and two guard trucks behind."

The advantages of Merriman's personal presence immediately became obvious. He turned around and ordered, "Do it now." Instantly the crowd thinned out, as the guard and the state police surrounding the governor jumped into action.

"Come in and sit down," Merriman ordered. Balder followed him into the tent and lowered himself onto a nearby chair. He could still hear gunshots, but at an increasing distance.

"Did you get the militia?" Balder asked.

"Twelve men, so far." Merriman said. "Five of them are up here. We picked them up right away. The guard has seven more confined, further down, and we're still chasing the rest of them through the woods."

"Any injuries?"

"Minor for the guard, except for the three killed earlier. A few dead on the militia side."

"Who?"

Merriman hoisted himself to his feet.

"Come with me," he said.

He led the way out of the tent, through the fringe of trees that lined the road. On the other side, in the clearing where Merriman's helicopter waited, a miserable little band of militiamen stood huddled under guard. Two Virginia guardsmen were crouched over a stack of weapons, sorting through them. Their powerful flashlights illuminated three long blanket-covered shapes, lying on the cold ground at the edge of the open space.

"We've got temporary identification of the dead men," Merriman said, jerking a thumb at the wretched captives. "That guy there is from the Charles City unit, or whatever they call them. He says these two were from Charles City too, brothers—George and Gerald Davis. And this, he says, is the captain of the New Kent arm of the Tri-County Militia. William James." He bent down and twitched the blanket away before Balder could protest. William James stared sightlessly up at the stars; dark hair, hawknosed, the prominent bones in his face imprinted on the waxy skin that covered them.

Merriman pulled the blanket back over the dead face.

"A man unable to defend himself against charges," he said mildly. "And the charges are farfetched, Ken."

"I hear you," Balder muttered, through gritted teeth.

"I wouldn't allow Tindell's execution, Ken, if I didn't think he was guilty."

"You didn't *think*? What happened to the law being exercised by an impartial judge and a twelve-person jury, not you and I?"

"A jury convicted Tindell," Merriman said.

Behind them, sirens announced the approach of the convoy. In a moment the creak and roar of the trucks came clearly over the hill. Balder was visited by the sudden temptation to resign on the spot, throw Garrett's escape in Merriman's face, and ride the convoy out of Virginia with Margaret and her son.

He clenched his teeth over the words and followed Merriman silently back toward the tent. He had one more duty before he could leave. On the road ahead, the two Virginia Guard trucks rumbled past, bringing up the rear as the convoy disappeared from sight.

Merriman watched the tailights of the last truck disappear into darkness and drew a deep relieved breath.

"Time to go," he said, over his shoulder. "It's already past two in the morning. We'll leave the National Guard to mop up the mess."

AT TEN MINUTES TO FIVE on the morning of April 16, Kenneth Balder stood in the glass-paned observation room and watched as Jerry Tindell fought against the restraints. Merriman had retained lethal injection as the legal method of execution, over John Cline's protests. Tindell had been given the customary sedative. The sweating doctor explained that an idiopathic reaction was possible, producing agitation rather than drowsiness. They were having trouble running the line that would send Tindell into unconsciousness.

Cline was holding the fort back at the Capitol, waiting to hear from Washington about the condition of the Fort Pickett convoy. Kenneth Balder stood next to Merriman. Jamal Henderson was at the other side of the room, breathing hard and looking at the ceiling. It was a sound principle, requiring hostile witnesses to confront the results of their actions. Kenneth Balder had forced himself to this place as a final reminder that he was not worthy of power. He had enough energy left to sneer at himself. *You think this act of penance means God will erase your guilt? It doesn't work that way.*

"The police couldn't find Margaret Franklin," Merriman said. His voice was curt—proof that he wasn't unmoved by the scene on the other side of the glass. The IV had finally gone in, and Tindell lay still. His eyelids flickered once, then closed.

Balder looked over at Merriman. The governor had given no further sign that he was aware of Balder's role in Garrett's testimony. He was beginning to think Merriman had no idea of what he'd done. It didn't matter. Garrett might be dead, and the little voice in the back of his head had already suggested that, if there was no deal to be cut, there was no point in his leaving the R.A.S. He had rejected the temptation; it was easier, this time.

Merriman gave a curt nod, and he realized that the warden had looked over to check for the last time that no clemency would be offered. All of a sudden he was unable to look. He had intended to watch, to blaze across his mind the horrible consequences of his own arrogance. He kept his eyes on Merriman. The potassium chloride would be running into Tindell's veins. When he saw the slight relaxation of the governor's shoulders, he knew that Jerry Tindell was dead.

IN THE CAR, heading back toward the Capitol, he leaned forward and closed the soundproof glass window between the driver and the backseat. Merriman said drowsily, "What are you doing?" Exhaustion had begun to drag at the governor. His shoulders slumped and his face was set and weary.

"Charles," Balder said.

"What?"

"I quit."

Merriman opened his eyes wide, and watched three more streetlights flick by. The sun wasn't up yet; Richmond's streets were still dark, almost deserted.

"Try a few days off first," he suggested at last.

"No," Balder said. He was sick to death of evasions. "I have to resign, because I've broken laws of the Reformed American States. I helped Garrett Franklin tape his testimony, and then I arranged with the Justice Department for him to leave Virginia with his mother. He's already gone. I'm going out too. It was the only way they would agree to drop all charges against him."

He saw incredulity in Merriman's face, and then dawning understanding.

"I saw you in the tape. I thought you had him hidden away somewhere. I thought," Merriman said, his volume rising, "you would do the right thing eventually, and turn him in. I was going to give you time to come to that decision. And instead you've sent him to Washington? What makes you think he's exempt from the laws that you just saw executed? Just because he's *her* son? Ken, I could prosecute you. I could prosecute you under the Ninth Commandment and take everything you own." His voice was tight with fury, and his right hand had curled into a fist. For a moment Balder thought he was going to swing it. But Merriman seemed to make an immense effort at control. His fingers opened. He laid his hand on the door and stared straight ahead, his fingernails white with pressure.

"Charles."

"What?" Merriman spat.

"I could have left without telling you."

"Oh," Merriman said, "and so this is a noble gesture?"

Balder leaned forward and said, "There's been far too little truth between you and me. How can you expect to build a government on God's laws when the truth is constantly bent for your sake?"

"When have I ever lied?"

"Lied? You never told me Cline was coming in, because it suited you. You used me to have Tindell arrested, because you wanted a case that the American people could sympathize with. You told National Public Radio that the CIA was responsible for shooting Dillard—"

"Well?"

"Do you really think the CIA had anything to do with it?" He was aware that his own voice was rising. Merriman looked at him sideways.

"*Do* you?" Balder demanded.

"It's possible," Merriman said defensively.

"It was one of those half-whacked militia offshoots, probably the white supremacy branch—they've never liked Dillard—and you know it. You said that to get America on your side."

Merriman said in sudden anger, "What did you expect me to say? They were accusing me of setting up a murder."

"And so you fight back by using the enemy's rules? Since when?"

The car drew through the gates in front of the Capitol, and veered right around the statue of George Washington and the heroes of the American Revolution. Balder said, "Admit it. Just here, between us. No one's listening, and in twenty-four hours I'll have less credibility than Nixon right after Watergate. You wanted to found a new nation, and you were willing to bend the rules to make it work."

Merriman snapped, "Look at the results. We've got God's laws in place all over Virginia."

"They're good laws. It's a pity we just used them to execute an innocent man."

The car halted in front of the Executive Mansion. Kenneth Balder peered out the window at the gleaming bulk of the Capitol on his left, a stone's throw from Merriman's front gates. Merriman remained silent.

"So here we are?" Balder said. "Are you going to have me arrested, or should I collect my things from the guest cottage and leave quietly?"

Merriman turned his head and looked directly at his chief of staff. For the first time, Kenneth Balder saw in his face a completely unfamiliar glimmer of pity.

"You saved this revolution last night," Merriman said. "If you hadn't gone down there, we'd have a full-scale meltdown on our hands, right now."

Balder swallowed uncomfortably. The night before was a jumbled chaos in his mind, but when he remembered what he'd done he felt the hairs stand up on the back of his neck.

"You can go," Merriman said.

"Go—"

"I could fire you. But I'm going to allow you to resign on your own terms. I'm not going to tell the citizens of Virginia about the laws you've bent. You have done more to establish the success of the Reformed American States than I have. There's no way you can stay in office, but I'm not going to have you arrested and tried." He paused. "What you make public about your actions after this is up to you. I'm not going to say anything about it. Get your stuff out of the guest cottage and go."

Kenneth Balder reached for the door handle.

"Oh," Merriman said. "This came for you." He reached into the inside of his jacket. "It arrived at the mansion last night, just before you came in with that videotape. By personal messenger, from the Department of Defense."

"And you didn't give it to me?"

"I forgot," Merriman said. He produced a thin packet and handed it over. Balder ran his thumb under the flap. It had been unsealed.

"You read this?"

"Of course I did," Merriman said. "You've been acting very odd, Ken. I had to make sure you weren't cooperating with the Department of Defense to undermine the security of Virginia. I don't understand what those letters have to do with your deal, but after looking at them I'm not sure you're qualified to be my chief of staff in any case."

Balder shook the letters out onto his palm. Mary Miranda's looping handwriting struck his eyes, shouting up from the creased disintegrating paper.

> *All I can do is write, Ken, but you can't make me go away. What did it mean for you? Were you just scratching an itch? Or do you still want me, and you're afraid to say so? I wonder what Maggie would say. I happen to know she's never slept with anyone but you. She doesn't know you want to bomb the base. I think she must still trust you.*

He folded the letters over and shoved them into his pocket.

"I expect you're right, Charles," he said. "I'm not qualified to be your chief of staff. It's a good thing that God is more forgiving than the Reformed American States."

Merriman got out of the car without answering, and slammed the door behind him. Balder could see the driver's head crane curiously after him. He leaned forward and slid the glass panel open.

"What's your next assignment?"

"Be on call," the driver said promptly.

"Good. Take me to Fredericksburg."

"Er—the border, sir?"

"Yes."

The driver shrugged, philosophically. Balder leaned back and felt the car move beneath him. He'd left all his possessions in the guest cottage. He didn't want them. It was easier, somehow, to go straight out of Virginia and leave the whole thing behind.

He could see the sun, rising red on his right. When the car had reached the interstate, with concealing trees on either side, he pulled Mary Miranda's letters out of his pocket and shredded them into tiny bits, and then opened the window and let her words blow away.

CHAPTER 33

ALEXANDER WADE, back at the White House Solarium with his feet up on an ottoman and a White House steward hovering at his elbow, was enjoying a rare moment of leisure. He'd managed to snatch three hours of sleep on his cot at the Pentagon. The Fort Pickett convoy had crossed into North Virginia at 4:30 A.M., and at the moment of safety he'd thankfully handed the whole chaotic jumble over to Allen Preszkoleski and his aides.

He'd monitored the escalating battle with sickening dismay. His original plan had worked to perfection; the snipers had set off an exchange of shots, and if the fight had ended there, with a minimum of bloodshed on either side, it would have been easy to get on national TV and storm in righteous indignation about the Virginia Guard attacking unarmed United States men.

Unfortunately, it hadn't ended there. That cursed militia had appeared out of the Lynchburg foothills; and when they opened fire it became perfectly clear that the Fort Pickett convoy had not adhered to his original deal with Merriman. They were armed. The bloodshed escalated. And it came to an end only with the help of the Virginia Guard he had intended to vilify. As a pretext for invasion, the Battle of Lynchburg was a non-starter.

Wade woke up from his short sleep clear-headed and ready for action. He'd had so little rest recently that three skimpy hours refreshed him like a week's vacation. He called in an aide to brief him while he shaved, and was relieved to find that the president had issued a curt fiat: The airport takeover was postponed, pending further consultation with cabinet officials.

He arrived at the White House to find the president red-eyed, eating breakfast on a TV tray. He settled himself into another of the stuffed over-sized chairs, ordered a second breakfast, and leaned his head back with a sigh of relief.

"You've heard the convoy information already?" the president inquired through a mouthful of wheat toast.

Wade nodded. He slept at the Pentagon these days. He hadn't been back to the Beltway townhouse for a week. Perri might be leaving messages on the answering machine there. In any case, she hadn't called him at the office. He accepted his fresh orange juice from the steward.

"Not as bad as we thought at first," he said, bringing his thoughts back to his job. "Nine dead, four wounded. Four trucks lost. Everyone else safely out."

The president dabbed at his mouth, silently. He had called for a meeting to be held at ten A.M., in the military situation room at the Old Executive Office Building. Apparently he wanted to consult his oldest friend and adviser first. The steward set a breakfast tray in front of Wade and left the two men alone.

"Ready for the show?" the president inquired.

"What show?"

"George has had people monitoring every news network since midnight. He put a tape together for us. I want you to see it before we go over to the Old Executive. Clips from all three broadcast networks, plus CNN and a couple of other cable channels. It'll give you a clue to public opinion. And they call *us* masters of the spin," the president said, parenthetically. "Charles Merriman's got that *Dispatch* editor working for him. His TV technique would be the envy of any good Communist propagandist."

"I wouldn't say that in public."

"I wouldn't dare," the president said. He picked up his remote and flicked the TV in front of them into life.

The tape began with an early-morning ABC news report on the Fort

Pickett convoy. At the time of broadcast, the convoy had already moved into United States territory. Military personnel in full battle gear surrounded it in a ring, faces outward toward the press and their backs toward the battered trucks. The images on the screen swung up and down as the frustrated cameramen struggled for a clear view of the catastrophe. Wade caught a sudden glimpse of sheeted bodies, being carried to a waiting helicopter.

"Apparently a civilian accompanying the convoy was killed in the attack. . . . Must have been two civilians with them, Bob." The camera zoomed in on the disheveled figure of a non-uniformed woman being helped out of a truck by two men with U.S. MARSHAL printed prominently across the backs of their jackets.

"As a matter of curiosity," Wade said, "why is the U.S. Marshal's Office trying to escort Margaret Franklin?"

"You never saw such a mess in your life," the president said gloomily. "There were at least nine federal agencies trying to take responsibility for the survivors. Those two must have gotten to her first, that's all."

Wade hadn't seen Margaret Franklin for over two decades. She had been a thin girl with intent gray eyes set wide apart in a round, serious face. The camera, tracking her into a close-up as she walked toward a waiting black car, showed those same eyes netted around with lines and glazed over with fear and pain. The round face he remembered was thin and drawn, and disfigured by a wide crimson cut across her cheek. She walked unsteadily, and as she stumbled sideways against one of the marshal's men the camera cut away. The reports from the other networks showed much the same scene, with widely varying guesses as to the number of casualties and the probable reaction of the Department of Defense.

The CNN broadcast, dating from slightly later in the morning, took the story further. Using footage from Richmond's hometown station, WWBT, the news network ran a twenty-minute behind-the-scenes piece, showing Charles Merriman at work to straighten out the convoy mess.

It was riveting theater. The Channel 12 film began with a shot from Merriman's helicopter, showing the blazing army truck at the foot of the 460 hill. The microphone picked up the steel resolve in Merriman's voice:

I'm not going to charm anybody. I'm going to set the guard on that militia group and eradicate them.

And from then on, the broadcast was a pure exposition of Merriman's innocence in the assault, his determination to hunt down the culprits. The guard attack on the militia was fully documented, along with Kenneth Balder's heroic journey down to warn the Fort Pickett convoy. When the camera recorded Balder's refusal to wear a vest, Wade lost his appetite. He pushed his breakfast away and mumbled, "Why didn't he just announce, 'I regret that I have only one life to lose for my country?' The man's a walking sentimental cliché."

On the screen, Kenneth Balder was insisting, "If they shoot me on the way down, there's no way we can contact them in any case. You'll just have to risk attacking the militia without informing the convoy." Merriman, looked up, his voice filled with warmth and respect: "Godspeed, Ken."

"I'm going to throw up," Wade announced.

The president watched Balder walk down the hill and disappear into the shadows. He said, "It won't do us any harm for him to look like a hero. He's going to be on our side in a matter of hours."

"You think so?"

"That's what Ramsey Grant and the rest of the Justice Department keep telling me."

"Well," Alexander Wade said, "we'll see." He doubted it. The news reports were broadcasting Garrett Franklin's death; why should Kenneth Balder sacrifice himself for a corpse? He thought with renewed gratitude of those letters. He could pop Balder's bubble with the American people, and he intended to. There was no way that man was going to parade around like God's gift to an America starved for heroism. The CNN report went on broadcasting distant pictures of the guard attack, complete with shots echoing in the distance and the glow of an occasional grenade.

The CNN report ended, and the picture changed back to a broadcast station: a soft-news morning show, which had already managed to get hold of an opinion poll. The anchor announced, "Seventy-six percent of American adults believe the members of the Tri-County Militia should be prosecuted under the strict Reformed American States laws. This morning,

Virginia executed the first man to be condemned under the new penalties for murder: Jerry Tindell, convicted of shooting a National Guard officer two years ago and robbing the body."

More footage. Kenneth Balder and Charles Merriman after the execution, emerging from the maximum-security facility into a crowd of reporters. Both men were drawn and grim in the artificial lights, brushing away questions as they ducked into Merriman's official car.

The president thumbed the stop button.

"And there you have the pictures America is seeing," he said. "Now you know why we're not going in to take over the airport. We'd look like bloodthirsty tyrants. Anyway, Merriman appears to have postponed the move to segregate HIV-positive patients."

"Have you heard anything privately from Merriman? Apart from all this public grandstanding?"

"I have," the president said, "but I'm not supposed to be talking to him at all, so you'll kindly keep this to yourself."

Wade nodded, unsurprised. After the events of the night before, he had assumed that the president would be in touch with Merriman in some way; George Lewis talking to Merriman's press secretary, most likely, while the president and Merriman listened to the conversation from their respective office chairs.

"Charles Merriman had three items of business for me," the president said. "First, he's offered to extradite some members of the Tri-County Militia for trial in the United States, since their offense was against United States personnel. He wants to keep those who were guilty of killing the North Carolina men at that Fletcher depot. I've referred the whole question to the Justice Department." Wade opened his mouth, but the president said firmly, "We can discuss it in this morning's meeting."

"Very well."

"Secondly, he wanted me to know that the South Carolina police suspect white supremacists of engineering Christopher Dillard's death, and he has authorized his own people to cooperate with South Carolina authorities to determine whether the culprits have fled to Virginia or North Carolina."

"Ah," Wade said, "a matter of both of you having opened your mouths too wide? Neither Merriman himself nor the CIA was involved, I gather."

"I made a justifiable assumption," the president retorted.

"I hope you're going to let it drop now."

"Er—well, yes. The third item," the president said, hurriedly, "is more important." He paused, tilting his head backward to inspect the sunlight pouring through the Solarium's glass panels overhead. Wade felt a prickle of apprehension.

"What?" he demanded, irritated by the delay.

"He's threatened to close the Virginia entrance to the Chesapeake Bay if we don't leave him alone. His very words. All he wants, he says, is separation from Washington and peaceful relations between the two countries."

Wade thought rapidly. The entrance to the Chesapeake Bay lay between Virginia Beach and the southernmost tip of Virginia's outer banks. It was not a large stretch of water, and Merriman could easily patrol it. He could cut off the main access to the United States military installations that lay on the bay.

"A brilliant move on his part," he said thoughtfully. "It'll be an incredible inconvenience to us, but we can't accuse him of cutting off all access."

"The Chesapeake Delaware Canal," the president said, nodding. "Two hundred miles out of the way. Can you imagine sending ships all the way up to the canal and then down the Delaware Bay, every time we need access to the Atlantic?"

"What was your response?"

"I told him I needed to consult my cabinet."

"Your cabinet's going to tell you it would be political suicide to try to break a Bay closing by force, when you still have access. You can't attack Merriman's National Guard. Especially after last night." Wade hesitated, feeling the weight of the words he was about to say. The president watched him expectantly. He took a deep breath and said, "Sir, the American people know you're a leader. They know you can mount a military operation. They've seen you do it. Let's show them the other side of your character. Let's make peace with Charles Merriman."

The president steepled his fingers together under his chin.

Wade went on, "We don't have to recognize him as a separate nation. We don't have to cave in on all his demands. But let's stop demanding tax payments and provoking fights—"

"That's enough," the president said abruptly.

"Sir?"

"Bring a plan for peace to the meeting," the president ordered. Wade felt himself gape with astonishment. He closed his mouth quickly and said, "In twenty minutes?"

"A broad outline."

"Can I mention the threatened Bay closing?"

"If it's relevant. I'll consider your proposal," the president said, "along with my other options. That's all I can promise you."

His eyes went back to the blank television screen. He said, with a very faint wistfulness in his voice, "They both looked heroic. Both of them. Those pictures convinced *me* of it. I refuse to look like a tyrannical bureaucrat in comparison, Alex. Do you hear me? Find me a way out."

IN THE MILITARY SITUATION ROOM, the cluster of high officials had expanded. Every cabinet member had brought company; the treasurer had two aides with him, the secretary of transportation and the secretary of commerce had one each; Ramsey Grant and the director of the FBI were accompanied by two pinstriped attorneys from Legal Counsel. The director of the CIA and the national security adviser sat together. Wade himself had brought Allen Preszkoleski and an armful of papers, and the broad strokes of a plan that would allow Virginia to go its own way. . . . for a time.

The president, as was his habit, entered slightly late. He said curtly, "Everybody sit down. We've got work to do."

He sat down at the head of the long oak table and looked down its crowded length. His mouth curled, ironically. This morning he was very much the Lord of the Manor; which meant, Wade thought, that he had again made up his mind. He hoped that it was in the direction of peace.

"My," the president said, "a full house this morning."

He put his reading glasses on and glanced down at the paper in front of him. "Legal problems first. Let's start with the Justice Department, please. The attorney general has spearheaded an effort to bring Kenneth Balder out of Virginia." This information—not yet general knowledge—produced a murmur from the table. "I'd also like your reaction, Ramsey, to the possibility of asking for extradition for the Tri-County Militia, which is guilty of crimes against the United States." He cocked a distinguished eyebrow up, and Ramsey Grant responded.

"Extradition would be a bad move," he said. "Let Merriman have 'em."

"Why is that?"

"Same reason Jerry Tindell's execution didn't create much in the way of public indignation. Nobody likes those guys. And furthermore, most people don't think the American justice system does a good job removing violent offenders from the streets. If you announce that you're saving the Tri-County Militia from Merriman's just wrath, the heartland is going to start yelling about preferring offenders over victims. That's off the cuff, sir."

"Taken into advisement," the president said, making a note. "I'd like a written recommendation from your office, Mr. Attorney General."

"Yes, sir."

The director of transportation said eagerly, "What's this about Kenneth Balder?"

That was the tone of the meeting, Wade judged; forget about the dry details and get on to juicier matters. Ramsey Grant said, deliberately, "The Justice Department has arranged for Kenneth Balder to leave Virginia. Dr. Balder agreed to return to the United States and condemn Charles Merriman's revolution in return for the dismissal of any charges against Garrett Franklin, a national guardsman who joined Merriman's revolution and was then suspected of having a hand in the murder of another guardsman at the Yorktown Naval Weapons Station."

"And you agreed to this?" someone said in disbelief. Wade twisted his head around. The question had come from a Treasury aide, a young man standing against the wall.

"We have reason to believe Mr. Franklin was framed," Ramsey Grant said, in the tone of a realist forced to throw a sop to idealism. *Any moment now*, Wade thought, *someone is going to connect the name of Franklin with the execution of Jerry Tindell.* And a breath later, someone on the other end of the table did.

"Wasn't Franklin the name of that guard sergeant—"

"This has been a complicated deal," Grant interposed, "and it's not necessary to go over the details now. What's important is how we can use Balder to our advantage."

"Just a minute, sir," said Allen Preszkoleski. Wade looked at him with real gratitude. It was high time someone brought up the possibility that Balder would not in fact fulfill his half of the deal. "Weren't Garrett Franklin and his mother in the Fort Pickett convoy? It seems to be general knowledge that one of them was killed."

Grant gave a brief, reluctant nod.

"Yes," he said. "Both of them were wounded in the attack. Mrs. Franklin escaped with minor injuries, cracked ribs, and so forth. Garrett Franklin suffered a cut artery in his thigh. He was immediately taken to a Warrenton hospital. He is in critical condition, but as of fifteen minutes ago he was still alive."

Allen persisted, "But the rest of the country's been given the impression that a civilian was killed. If Balder thinks the boy's dead, will he still come out?"

Ramsey Grant's dry tone made his next announcement even more startling. He said, "Kenneth Balder surrendered to United States authorities in Fredericksburg at eight o'clock this morning. His first question was whether Garrett Franklin had survived. We told him that we didn't know."

"Well," the president said slowly. "Well. Ramsey, this seems to be our first bit of luck. Alex here has already suggested—"

Grant held up a hand. "Sir," he said, "I take it that our purpose here is to decide how we will continue to deal with Virginia. Since Dr. Balder's condemnation of the revolution will play a big part in our strategy, may I suggest that we first hear just what he is willing to say?"

"Do you have a statement from him?"

"No," Grant said, "but I've got him, right outside the door."

This produced a sensation all over the room. The president removed his reading glasses.

"Then bring him in," he ordered.

The door at the end of the room opened. Alexander Wade was barely aware that he had risen, until he found himself looking up at his rival. Twenty-five years ago, he had savagely resented the other man's greater height. Kenneth Balder had used it to stare down his nose disdainfully at the young Alexander Wade, groping frantically for a question that wouldn't make the courtroom laugh.

There was no disdain in the blue glance now. Balder was between two Secret Service men, and Wade imagined that he had been strip-searched before the agents allowed him into the same room as the president. He appeared to be at the very edge of debilitating exhaustion; lines in his forehead made him look older than his actual age, which Wade knew to be forty-six. The striking fair hair was marred by a glint of gray at the temples. A spare, cautious-eyed man had followed Balder into the room, with another Secret Service agent close on his heels. Alexander Wade felt for the chair behind him and sat back down.

Ramsey Grant said, "Mr. President, ladies and gentlemen: Kenneth Balder. Dr. Balder, the president of the United States."

"Who's this?" the president demanded, looking past Balder's level gaze.

"Dr. Balder's lawyer," Grant said dryly. The spare cautious man said, "Joel Adams, J.D., Mr. President."

"Ah." The president sat motionless, examining Kenneth Balder from head to toe. At last he said, "So you're willing to condemn Merriman's revolution?"

"I'm willing to express my concern over Charles Merriman's methods," Kenneth Balder said, after a slight pause. His voice was flat.

"Meaning his oppressive laws?"

"His laws are based on God's Word. I was in charge of drawing up the Commonwealth's code, so you can blame the laws on me, not Charles Merriman. I'm willing to say that the carrying out of the laws has been corrupted by personal ambition."

"Merriman's?" the president persisted.

"All of us," Kenneth Balder said.

"The specifics, please, Dr. Balder," Ramsey Grant directed.

"I presented Merriman with an alternate theory which would have proved Jerry Tindell's innocence. He declined to use it."

"Why?" the attorney general asked.

"He wanted Tindell's execution to proceed. He wanted to show the United States that he couldn't be intimidated into changing the penalties. I'd like to say that I authorized the arrest in the first place for personal reasons which had nothing to do with justice."

The thin lawyer cleared his throat. "That is the substance of the statement the Justice Department agreed upon," he said. "I feel it would be unwise for Dr. Balder to go beyond it at the present time."

"Mm," the president said. He sat for another minute, staring at Balder. The rest of the room followed his example. They were looking, Wade thought, for some clue to Kenneth Balder—something that might show on his face, some reason why this intelligent and charismatic man had just set a torch to his own chances for power. Kenneth Balder looked back at the room, steadily.

"Very well," the president said at last. Ramsey Grant nodded at the Secret Service agents. One of them opened the door.

"Mr. Attorney General—" Balder's voice had cracked, very slightly. "Yes?"

"What do you know about Garrett Franklin?"

Grant shrugged, noncommittally. Wade cast him a surprised sideways glance. He knew Ramsey Grant to be ambitious and occasionally ruthless, but he had never seen this cat-with-a-mouse side of his personality.

"We'll let you know," the attorney general said.

"Oh," Balder said. The faint sound was painful. Wade looked away, embarrassed by the man's face. Behind him, the same young treasury aide said impulsively, "He's still alive at a Warrenton hospital."

"All right, all right," the president said, annoyed by all the raw emotion seething around him. "Let's get on with it."

The door closed behind Kenneth Balder. Ramsey Grant turned his head around and skewered the young aide with a single glance. Wade collected himself. He said, "I have a proposal, Mr. President."

"Let's hear it," the president said.

Wade got up and moved to the small podium with the map screen above it. He was visited by a sudden sensation of weary repetition. He had done this at the beginning of the revolution, and recommended peace, and the president had refused to listen.

He slapped the map of Virginia down onto the overhead projector.

"Charles Merriman," he said, "has threatened to close the Virginia end of Chesapeake Bay unless we cease attempts to get Virginia back. He could easily do so, using a minimum of guard resources. Given the current public temperature, we can hardly mount an attack on the guard. I suggest we do as Merriman says."

He waited for the brief clamor to die down.

"We can't fight our way out of this," he said, when the room was quiet again. "I've been saying so from the beginning. Our first task is to reestablish an atmosphere of reason and sensibility. We won't get anywhere until we move away from the suspicious panic we seem to be operating under. First of all, we ask Merriman for a major concession. We ask him to return Virginia Beach, Chesapeake, Norfolk, and Portsmouth to United States control." He put the tip of his red pen on Fort Story, at the southern end of the entrance to the Chesapeake Bay and ran a thick red line down to the North Carolina border, west to Lake Drummond, and up through the Great Dismal swamp until the line met the James River. "This is a major United States military complex. Merriman's bound to see that as long as he tries to hold onto it, friction is inevitable. If he yields it to the United States, both the U.S.A. and the R.A.S. can be assured that the Chesapeake Bay will remain open."

"What do we offer in return?" the president asked.

"In return, we move Camp Peary. Merriman can't be expected to settle down as long as the CIA is sitting on his front porch."

The director of the CIA remained poker-faced. This was a matter to be discussed in private.

"We also offer a ten-year plan to shift the military operations at Fort Eustis and Camp Pendleton to Maryland locations." He could see the political advantages to this flit quickly through the president's thoughts. "We'll also ask to redraw the North Virginia line so that it includes Fort A.P. Hill. Then we rename this little chunk down here East Virginia. Mr. President, you suggest to Congress that under the circumstances East Virginia and North Virginia should be considered separate states and given one senator each. The sections of North Carolina that remain separate from MacDonald Forbes will be considered North Carolina proper and will retain their representation."

"You're talking about a constitutional amendment!" the president exclaimed.

"If necessary. Plenty of time for that later. Right now, I'm just aiming to restore some sanity to the debate."

"What do we get out of all this?" the national security adviser asked.

"*Time.* We get time. Listen, Charles Merriman has been in power for *one* month. Anybody can govern successfully for thirty days. We let the Reformed American States tick along. Let the furor settle down. Gain points for making peace out of a dicey situation. Then, slowly, we start to make things harder for the residents of Virginia and North Carolina. Require passports when they come over the border. Make it as difficult for them to move into the United States and claim full citizenship as it is for any Mexican or Peruvian. When they get sick in the United States, we ship them home to a Richmond or Raleigh hospital. When they marry United States citizens, we conduct stiff naturalization investigations. We impose the usual trade restraints and requirements on Virginia and North Carolina goods. If we wait," Wade said, "if we're patient, they're going to get fed up with it. They're going to get tired of blue laws, of those draconian penalties for theft and slander, of creationism taught in every school. The lost sheep will come home."

A little silence lay over the room. The president shifted in his seat. Wade looked around the room. When he saw Ramsey Grant nod, he knew that he had won.

Grant said, "Balder's condemnation of Merriman's methods will help shift public opinion. We ought to put him in touch with Bob Woodward. Or somebody who'll write an exposé of Merriman's government."

"We'd do better if he wouldn't insist on including himself in the condemnation," the president said.

"I'll see what I can do," Grant promised.

The president looked over toward his secretary of defense.

"Well, Alex," he said, "let's have details of this plan. I'll give you a week to coordinate it. All of you are to make this top priority in your schedules, understand?"

Alexander Wade reached for his map with hands that trembled very slightly. The next two years were going to be tricky ones. But he could see the road he needed to walk on. He could keep the president on it. He could see re-election for the president, and a long and glorious career for himself, at its end: the men who fought those foreign battles and domestic troubles with force and tact combined.

HE FOUND HIMSELF NEXT TO GRANT, later in the day, listening while the president spoke to the press. Under cover of the insistent questions, Grant said softly, "Use those profiles?"

He nodded slightly.

"Useful to you?"

"Merriman's."

"Not the other?"

"Nothing in it suggested that Balder would actually come out."

"No," Grant said, meditatively. "I was surprised myself. The profiles are accurate ninety-eight percent of the time. Kenneth Balder *would* be in the mysterious two percent that act unpredictably. On the other hand, Wade, you've acted true to type. You've preserved your dignity."

"And what else have you predicted about me?"

Grant said, "That you're capable of holding a grudge for twenty-five years."

Wade stilled his face into blandness, aware of the occasional lens swinging his way.

"I am," he said at last.

"We need a hero, Alex."

Wade grimaced, despite himself. He saw the intent. That Lynchburg display of physical courage—the most impressive and least important of the virtues—would allow Kenneth Balder to be rehabilitated as an American hero in order to drag Merriman down. Even by Wade's exacting standards, it was a reasonable strategy. But he knew he was capable of managing relations with Virginia without Balder's anti-Merriman sentiments to reinforce his authority. And he could not bear to see Balder turned into a shining knight.

"You'll get a hero," he said, and thought to himself: *A classic hero, with a tragic flaw.* It was high time the *Post* saw Mary Miranda Carpenter's last words.

CHAPTER 34

Monday, April 22, 8 P.M.

THE TOWNHOUSE PROVIDED by Washington was tastefully decorated and completely blank: beige walls, neutral carpet, recessed lighting, and a meaningless sea scene on the bedroom wall. Margaret's scattered belongings merely cluttered the rooms, doing nothing to personalize them.

She prowled restlessly through the living room, past the cream-colored sofa and chairs and the silent television. Her mending collarbone ached, but the crack had been minor and she had gone back to driving herself. The hospital had called an hour before. They expected to release Garrett in the morning; she could come pick him up and take him home. She thought briefly of the deed to the New Kent farm, now locked in the safe she had found, unexpectedly, in the bedroom wall.

Garrett had been in the hospital for almost a week. The weakening blood loss had been followed by a dangerous infection, and for two days she'd sat outside intensive care with a single horrible fear dominating her whole person. By then, Ken's face had been plastered all over the TV screens and newspapers. The images of his walk down the hill had been replayed a thousand times. He appeared at least once a day, speaking against Merriman's motives with dogged determination. For every treacherous speech, two pictures of courage flashed out at the American people.

In the hospital waiting room, flipping drearily through the morning TV talk shows, Margaret became aware of a confused rumble from the American people. Was this man a hero or a traitor? Did he share the responsibility for Jerry Tindell's death, or did he fight Merriman until the moment of execution? Had he saved the convoy, or set it up?

By Saturday the momentum seemed to be swaying toward the hero side of the equation. Saturday night, trying to sleep in her government-provided bed, she thought, *But he'll always be in the middle of a storm. Experts will still be arguing over this in years to come. No one will ever look at him and think, 'This is a brave man,' without a creeping doubt behind the praise. No one will ever be able to condemn him without wondering why he sacrificed his own power, just as the United States had finally agreed to negotiate with the renegade states.* Chairman Merriman and his new chief of staff, John Cline, had celebrated by publicly declaring victory on the evening news. She'd turned it off at once.

And now it was Monday night. There was nothing on TV, nothing to read in the townhouse. She'd quit buying newspapers two days ago. She was saturated by the story. Ken was constantly surrounded by government officials, so it was no wonder that he had not called.

She wandered into the kitchen and stood staring at the spotless refrigerator. When a bell rang, she looked around at the microwave in confusion.

The doorbell, of course. She left the kitchen and walked across to the front door, expecting to find another polite government aide who wanted to discuss her future. She hooked the chain and cracked the door open.

"Yes?"

On the dark doorstep, the porch light gleamed down on Ken's fair head. He said tentatively, "Maggie?"

It was raining lightly, and the shoulders of his jacket were frosted with water. After a moment she realized that he was getting wetter. She unhooked the chain. Her mind, suddenly kicking into working order, was beginning to exult.

"Come in," she said.

He stepped through the door, glancing over his shoulder at the curb. A black car sat silently in the dark. Two more sets of headlights shone suddenly at the end of the little suburban road. She shut the door on the scene

"More press," Ken said. "They haven't gotten tired of me yet."

He stood uncertainly, dripping on the elegant carpet. His blue eyes were fixed on her face. Margaret held her hand out. As she did, she glimpsed herself in the entranceway mirror; her hair loose, the bones of her face distinct—she had lost ten pounds, this week—and an angry scar across one cheek. The Warrenton doctor had referred her to a plastic surgeon.

"I'll hang your coat up," she said.

He hesitated. Her blood was still singing with joy. She said, "Don't you want to stay?" and wondered why he looked so grim. He shrugged his way carefully out of the light raincoat. The cast on his forearm had been replaced by a light plastic shell, held in place by Velcro straps.

"Go into the living room," she said, and took the coat to the hallway closet. When she came back, he was sitting on the cream sofa with a thick folded newspaper on his knees, looking around him.

"Very elegant," he said.

"I hate it. It has nothing to do with me."

"No," he agreed. He was avoiding her eyes. After a moment he sighed and separated the front page from the paper in his lap, laying the rest carefully on the floor at his feet.

"Do you read the papers?" he asked.

"I haven't this weekend."

He held the sheet of newsprint out to her. Sunday's *Washington Post*, she saw, with yet another picture of him below the headline. She felt a strong surge of caution.

"I don't want to see it," she said.

"Read it, Maggie."

"Why?"

"You've got to know everything."

Margaret eyed the paper resentfully. She was just beginning to learn how to live, tentatively, with a whole new way of thought. The careful rules she'd set up for herself hadn't worked. Kenneth Balder had forgiven her for the past, and she was discovering how to do the same; the rigid order of the universe was being replaced by something else, something more personal and infinitely more merciful.

"I know the story already," she said. "I don't remember much about the attack on the convoy. But I've seen the news reports. I know you saved our lives."

"I'm no hero," Ken said bluntly. "I've managed to uproot you from your life, and I almost got Garrett killed. But one day I want you to marry me, Maggie, and before you answer you need to know that I'm in a heap of legal trouble, I'll likely be penniless in less than a year, and the whole nation probably thinks I killed Mary Miranda on purpose. Read this."

"I don't want to, Ken. I'm still trying to let go of the past. Don't make it harder for me."

"Please, Maggie. I don't want there to be any lies between us."

She took the paper with reluctance. Under his picture, a *Post* writer had covered his latest public appearances. On the right-hand side, another, luckier reporter had written up the details of his manslaughter conviction. The story began with a sickeningly familiar line.

Dear Ken,
This is the fifth letter I've written you this week. . . .

It was the fifth and sixth letters, she remembered, that Alexander Wade had shown her in the courthouse hallway two-and-a-half decades ago. She hadn't seen them since. She recalled every word. The two letters—"supplied to the *Post* by a reliable source"—appeared in their entirety on the third page. She didn't bother to turn to it; she refolded the paper so that those over-familiar lines were hidden, and put it on her lap.

"What else?" she said.

Ken, thrown off balance, said rapidly, "The Justice Department agreed not to press any criminal charges, provided that I was willing to make public appearances to condemn Merriman's revolution."

"That was the condition of Garrett's escape."

"And my own." He was determined to show the blackest side of the matter. "I also promised to forgo any contact with elected officials of any state for the rest of my life. And I resigned from the California Institute for Theonomic Law, so that they could appoint another director. I could live with all that. But someone in the Justice Department's been busy making phone calls. I found out this morning that the families of the army men killed at Lynchburg are filing civil suits against me. My lawyer says he'll do his best, but he doesn't sound hopeful. Those letters can't be admitted in court, but they'll sway public opinion. Everyone's read them."

"The families want your trust fund?"

"They want twice as much as my trust fund could possibly supply. Joel Adams wants to settle out of court. It would clean me out. But otherwise, he says, I'll be tied up in legal proceedings for two years, and probably lose at the end of it." An echo of dark humor appeared suddenly in his voice. "He wanted to know if I had any salable skills besides starting revolutions."

"Do you?"

"Nothing spectacular. I can write," Ken said. "I can get a job as a newspaper reporter at a small-town paper. Maybe."

"Is there anything else?"

"Isn't that enough? I'm going to be broke and notorious."

"What about Merriman?"

Ken said, meditatively, "If Charles Merriman can keep his cabinet from pulling in different directions, he may well bring it off. I see he's already agreed to hand the eastern military complex back to the United States. It was a smart move. His future all depends on whether the people of Virginia and North Carolina chafe under the laws. I think it'll be years before we begin to see whether the experiment works."

Margaret looked at him narrowly. His tone was academic, with no trace of regret in it.

"Ken," she said, "don't you want to be part of it? You spent years talking about God's laws. Aren't you longing to be back in a state where God's laws are enforced?"

Ken got up from the sofa and walked to the window. He peered through a crack in the masking drapes. The rain had steadied; Margaret could hear it drum down on the sidewalk outside.

He said at last, "Have you ever read Revelation?"

"The book with all the dragons and plagues in it?"

Ken chuckled and turned around. "That's the eye-catching part that nobody really understands," he said. "The good stuff is later on, when

God promises His people a new heaven and earth. That's what I wanted. For thirty days, I've been trying to make myself believe that a shadow was the real thing. I've been trying to convince myself that Virginia and North Carolina could equal the kingdom of God." He shook his head. "I was wrong. When I finally admitted it to myself, leaving it behind was easy enough."

"What did Charles Merriman want, then?"

"The same thing I do," Ken said, "but he still has hopes of bringing it to pass in Richmond."

"And he won't succeed?"

"Oh, he may succeed in establishing a country with just punishments and rewards. I hope he does. But it'll slide toward compromise, eventually. Maybe in thirty years; maybe in two hundred." He paused. "I wanted more than that," he said, and his voice had changed. "I wanted the old order of things to pass away . . . but there's no mortal man who can do that, not until God comes to live with us." He cleared his throat. "The politicians win in the end, Maggie. They won this time. The old rules will always work best, in the old order of things. It's all in the Epistle to the Hebrews."

Margaret said gently, "You'll have to read it to me."

He looked down at her. The preoccupation in his eyes gave way, slowly, to amazement.

"You'll listen?" he said. Margaret nodded. He took two steps toward her. She stood up, hastily, and held the newspaper out to him.

"Take this away," she said. "I've quit buying papers. This is all the past, Ken. I'm so weary of it I can taste it. We're going to have to start over, you and I. . . . somewhere else."

"Australia?"

"Well," she said temperately, "I was thinking of Colorado maybe. Will the Reformed American States buy my farm? They offered to buy property of people who went into the United States, back at the beginning."

"I think we could arrange it," Ken said. He dropped the newspaper on the floor and took both her hands and bent his head down. When she came back to herself, an unknown time later, she pulled away from him and laughed shakily.

"It's a good thing the curtains are drawn," she said. He was looking down at her, and when she met his eyes she could feel her heart pounding in her chest. She said, "When can we get away from Washington?"

"As soon as I settle these lawsuits."

"That could be months!"

"It's been twenty-five years. I can wait a few more months. . . . if you will."

"I can wait for you. I'm not sure how much longer I can stand this townhouse."

He glanced around the immaculate room with distaste.

"I don't blame you," he observed. "When does Garrett get out of the hospital?"

"They're releasing him in the morning."

Ken said decisively, "I'll have Joel Adams meet you at the hospital. I can't show up there with reporters trailing at my heels. But I can ask him to help you through the sale of the New Kent property. Will Garrett mind?"

"I don't think so," Margaret said slowly. "He knew two weeks ago that he wouldn't be able to live in Virginia again. And he likes you. Anyway, the United States is going to pay for his college. He can't wait to go."

Ken put his hand gently against her face.

"I'll leave it to you," he said. "Find us a farm out in the country somewhere. Near a small-town newspaper. I'll get a job, and you can show me how to grow geraniums."

"Back to the garden?" Margaret said, amused despite herself.

Ken shook his head. "It's not possible. But we can look forward to something better."

"Is *that* in the Epistle to the Hebrews?"

"Yes," he said simply. "Don't worry. I'll read it to you." The elegant little clock on the living room wall struck nine, and he lifted his head sharply.

"I have to go," he said apologetically. "I have another speech to make."

She got his coat from the closet, and helped him slide the sleeve over his arm. At the door, he turned around and kissed her again, and laid a finger against the scar on her face.

"I am sorry," he said.

"It will fade," Margaret said. She was strangely unconcerned with the scar. Her soul had undergone such drastic change in these last weeks that it would have seemed incongruous for her face to appear the same as always.

She looked up at Kenneth Balder, standing reluctantly in the doorway, and was overcome with a wave of longing. She had glimpsed this future once. It was like landing on shore after a difficult journey, and finding the land choked by weeds with a few green patches crying out for cultivation. She was ready to undertake the labor. But the longing she felt was for another country—a country with a summer sun that shone night and day. Ken's words had given her a glimpse of it. She was soul-sick of the shadows around her.

She managed, "Don't be long, Ken."

"I'll come as soon as I can," he said gently. He went quickly through the opened door. She closed it behind him, shielding herself from cameras, and turned off the living room lights and walked over to the window. She cracked the drapes and watched as the door of the black car opened from the inside. He slid in, and the car drew smoothly away from the curb. The headlights of the car behind it showed government plates.

The street emptied, and she let the drape fall back into place. The shadows of the townhouse lay all around her. This whole block was a place of dark and secrets, but that time was almost past.

She scooped up the newspaper from the dimness of the living room floor, went out onto the back stoop, and stuffed it into a trashcan. Someone's dog started barking. She dusted her hands with satisfaction and went back inside.

"There," she said, out loud. She was suddenly ravenously hungry. She thought of Garrett, lying in a dim hospital room and waiting for morning. She would go buy him something to eat, something solid and appetizing, and sit up with him and tell him about the Colorado farm.

Margaret retrieved her purse from the bedroom and turned the lights off. She locked the door behind her and headed for the rental car parked at the curb. When she looked into the rearview mirror, she could see the dark townhouse sitting forlornly between its neighbors; all its tasteful luxury shrouded in shadows.

She pulled away from the house and turned east, toward the horizon. The lights of the city cast a red glow up into the air. In a few hours the sun would come up. The strong morning light would drive the false sunrise away.

These all died in faith, not having received the promises,
but having seen them afar off,
were assured of them, embraced them,
and confessed that they were strangers and pilgrims on the earth.

The Epistle to the Hebrews
xi.13